THE LOVE SISTERS

A COMPILATION

CHRISTINA C. JONES

WARM HUES CREATIVE

Copyright © 2019 by Christina C. Jones

All rights reserved.

No part of this book may be reproduced in any form or by any electronic or mechanical means, including information storage and retrieval systems, without written permission from the author, except for the use of brief quotations in a book review.

I THINK I MIGHT LOVE YOU

ONE
JACLYN

"Wrong bitch. Wrong bitch, ayyy. Wrong bitch, yeah you got the wrong bitch."

I mouthed along to the music blasting in my ears as I made my way down the hall, with my suitcase rolling behind me. At the door, I twerked a little as I dug through my purse for my overcrowded key ring, sifting through those that went to places that didn't exist anymore, or I refused to step foot in, or where I was no longer welcome, to get to the one I needed. Inside the apartment, I lost the little bit of manners I'd been employing in my three-quarters tipsy state to rap along with Vanity at the top of my voice.

"*Wrong bitch, boy you got the wrong bitch! You ain't slick, boy you did the wrong shit! New niggas, same tricks. Ain't shit, but he want you on his dick! Yeah right, nigga, I'm the wrong chick!*"

I felt that shit.

I felt that shit *deep*.

Stupid ass feelings were to blame for this whole night, actually. I was always *feeling* something.

Ugh.

I let those *feelings* – and my tipsiness – drive me to the freezer, muttering along with *Wrong Bitch* as I checked inside, on the off chance I'd find ice cream that wasn't freezer burned or expired.

Bingo.

I frowned at the "gluten-free, dairy-free, low-sugar, nut-allergy-safe" pint, wondering how the hell that could possibly all work together and why anyone would want it to. I took it from the freezer anyway, then went in search of a spoon. Once I found one, I happily dug in, pleasantly surprised by the taste and texture for it to be a commercial brand.

Ice cream in one hand, spoon in the other, I bopped around the kitchen in semi-darkness as *Wrong Bitch* started up again – I had it on repeat. I hummed along, not a care in the world, until I turned around.

I was *not* alone in the apartment.

The overhead light came on, illuminating the kitchen. My mouth dropped open as I looked into the sleepy, squinted eyes of some light-skinned dude with a fuckboy haircut.

A *naked* light-skinned dude with a fuckboy haircut.

"*Who the hell are you?*" he asked, hardly audible over the music in my ears.

"*You think this shit a game, huh? You think it's funny? Hands up nigga, come up off some money!*" Vanity crooned, way too hype for me to *not* be affected by the *fuck-somebody-up* energy she was putting off. That, paired with too much to drink, sprinkled with the natural fear of a naked ass – albeit kinda fine – stranger, fueled what I did next.

I dropped the ice cream and punched him.

Right in the face.

And then, on pure reflex, I drove my knee into his kibbles and bits.

Then, obviously, I ran.

I got my ass away from him, as fast as I could, not realizing until I closed the door behind me I'd run the wrong way.

I was in the bedroom, *further* into the apartment.

"*Come on, Jac!*" I scolded myself, out loud.

This was definitely the most white girl in a scary movie shit I'd ever done.

"*Hey!*" I heard NakedDude bellow, in a deep enough tenor it shook me a little. I locked the door, then dragged the nightstand beside the bed in front of it before I moved into the closet to pull my cell phone from the pocket of the jacket I was still wearing.

I'd dialed the nine and the one before I glanced down, noticing something that made me not press the last number.

Men's shoes.

What the hell were men's shoes doing on the floor of my sister's closet?

That question made me clear the number from my phone as my mind raced to fill in the apparent blank of what in the world was going on. I didn't get much time to think about it though – a sudden pounding on the door made that all but impossible.

"*Wrong bitch, yeah you got the wrong bitch!*"

I snatched the earbuds from my ears, as Dicky McStrangerballs yelled, "*Aye, you got about ten seconds to bring your ass out of there!*"

Yeah.

Mistakes were made.

My fingers moved fast over my screen, dialing Jemma's number as ol' boy pounded on the door. I paced the tiny space of the closet, silently praying that wherever the hell she was, my sister would answer the phone.

"*Bitch pick up the phooooone,*" I whined, panicking when she hadn't answered after the third ring.

"Wow, Jaclyn," she grumbled into the phone, sounding half-asleep. "Why I gotta be a bitch at six in the morning?"

"*Why is there a stranger in your apartment with his dick out!?*" rushed from my lips as I stepped out of the closet to look around the room. The bed was a mess of sheets, Jemma's perfumes were gone from their usual place on the dresser, and her costume jewelry rack had been replaced by a whole display of hats.

Hats that matched the shoes.

"What?" she asked, losing a little of the sleepiness in her voice. "My apartment... are you talking about Kadan?"

"Who now?"

"My *tenant*, Jac. I sublet my apartment since I'm never there more than a week. *Remember?*"

"Obviously *not*," I countered, cringing as he beat at the door.

"*Aye – I'm calling the cops on your ass in three, two—*"

"Okay!" I shouted at him. "Okay, just gimme a second, damn!"

"You're way too indignant to be on the verge of an assault charge," he called, making me roll my eyes.

He was right, but still.

"Jac, what the hell is going on?!" Jemma squawked before I pulled the phone from my ear, tucking it against my shoulder to move the nightstand from the door. I took my time unlocking and opening it, not at all looking forward to what was waiting on the other side.

Kadan – apparently – was standing there, still naked, looking angry as hell. Like *real* mad.

Big mad.

There was already a purple bruise marbling around his eye, ugly and mottled, messing up an otherwise handsome face. I couldn't help my gaze from drifting down, to his dick – slightly darker than the rest of him, but not purple, at least.

Right?

"What the *fuck* is wrong with you?" he growled, taking a step toward me.

I grinned as I stepped back, holding up my phone to show him Jemma's name on the screen as her voice screeched unintelligibly through the phone's speaker. "One day you're gonna laugh at this," I chuckled, nervously.

He didn't crack a smile. "Not today."

"No," I shook my head. "Nah, not today. Not today at all. We should talk about getting you a discount on next month's rent, huh?"

"We should talk about you getting the hell out of my apartment!" he shot back, making me flinch.

"You ain't gotta use all that bass though, why are you tripping like this?"

"If you don't get your ass—" he muttered, grabbing me by the arm to pull me out of the room, and urge me back toward the kitchen.

"This is *not* necessary," I told him as I snatched away, dropping my phone in the process. I bent to pick it up, ending up with another eyeful of dick as I straightened, but quickly looked away. "It was a mix-up!"

His eyes narrowed, making that bruise look even uglier. "If I'd punched *you*, how would you be reacting right now?"

Ugh.

"Fine. Point taken. But I'm sorry, okay? Seriously. I'm Jemma's sister, and I have a key. I didn't know—"

"Yeah, yeah, get your shit and go."

He pointed toward the cactus-colored, rolling carryon parked next to the kitchen counter. When I didn't move – out of sheer stubbornness – he moved to get it for me, prompting me into action before he tossed it out a window or something.

"It's been *very* unpleasant to meet you," I grumbled as I grabbed the handle of my bag. "And I *won't* be looking into that rent discount."

"Look into not letting the door hit you on the way out, how about that?"

My mouth dropped. "*Rude!*"

The look he gave me after that was a clear indication he'd reached the end of his inexplicable patience with me. I rushed to the door with him right on my heels, and once I was on the other side, I turned to say one last thing.

I was met with a slammed door in my face.

"*Asshole!*" I shouted at the closed door.

"Ya mama!" he yelled back, making my eyes spring wide. The only thing that kept me from knocking on the door again was the

7

ringing of my cell, which a quick glance told me was Jemma calling back.

"What?!" I answered, with unfounded attitude as I scowled at her door one more time before I started down the hall.

"Girl, *simmer*," Jemma insisted, still only sounding half-awake. "What the hell is going on? What the hell was all that commotion, and why is my tenant calling me?"

"To tattle," I whined, pushing a handful of locs over my shoulder. "I may or may not have punched him in the eye. And kneed him in the nuts."

Damn.

No wonder he was mad.

"Jac, what the *hell*?"

"*You* told me I could use that key whenever I needed to! I didn't think I needed to call you, because I knew *you* weren't there. You're in Liberia or something."

"Ethiopia," she corrected. "And I definitely mentioned renting my place out."

"Probably to Joia – not to me."

"*Jac.*"

"*Jem,*" I shot back, not appreciating her scolding tone. "Whatever happened, I didn't know anybody was there, and I needed a place to crash for the night."

Ugh.

I climbed onto the elevator with an awful taste in my mouth from too much to drink, and a throbbing head from too much drama.

"A place to crash why?" she asked. "You have a whole ass apartment with your boyfriend."

A deep sigh left my throat as I closed my eyes, and the elevator started moving. "*Ex*-boyfriend."

"*What?*" she exclaimed, exactly the reaction I had not been looking forward to.

I shrugged. "I dumped his ass, after he left me for his *wife*."

"*Excuse me?*"

"Nope. You heard right," I assured, squinting against the bright light in the lobby. "I thought his ass was traveling for work – turns out I'm his second family."

Jemma sucked her teeth. "Jac, stop lying."

"Hand to God, big sister," I declared, looking up one side of the street, then the other, trying to get my bearings. "She knew about me, sort of. Didn't know we were living together until she got his credit card statements, or something, hell, I don't know. She was fine knowing he was fucking someone else, but I guess a full-blown relationship was too much. Her ass *called me*."

Jemma let out a long sigh before she spoke again. "I'm sorry that happened to you boo."

I shrugged. "Oh well. One fuckboy don't stop *this* show. I'm gonna see if I can impose on Joia long enough to sleep and get cleaned up. And then go apartment hunting, I guess."

"I'm sure she won't mind," Jem yawned, and I had to press my lips together to keep from mimicking it. "You have a key to her place too, don't you?"

"Yes, but I think I've learned my lesson about not calling first. I'd rather not run into another naked stranger."

"Wait, *naked*?" Jemma gasped. "You didn't say anything about – *ooooh*, you *did*! You said his dick was out, didn't you?"

"I did."

"So…?"

I frowned. "So, *what*?"

"So how was it, duh! Long, short, skinny, thick… details, bitch!"

"I was too busy trying not to get murdered to be concerned about his dick!"

"Jac…"

"Okay so it was a good six, but it was soft, so we could be dealing with a grower – a passing grade either way, especially when accounting for girth, which appeared to be substantial. Not too much hair, not too little either. Slightly darker than his body. Even coloring. Not ashy. No odor."

"That's important!" Jemma chimed.

"*Very,*" I agreed. "Overall, a strong showing at this year's, *I Wasn't Even Trying To See It, But There It Was,* Dicklympics."

Jemma broke down laughing, but quickly stopped. "Oop. That's him calling me again now."

I rolled my eyes. "Don't give him a rent discount."

"Didn't you punch him in the eye and knee his balls? Girl I love you, but I can't be getting sued fooling with you!"

"He was *mean!*"

"You assaulted him!" Jemma shot back, dramatic if you asked me, but I guess she had a point.

"*Fiiiine,*" I groaned. "I'll cover whatever you have to give him."

"Okay now tell me something I *didn't* know."

"Get off the phone and talk to your tenant."

"Bye!"

I hung up the phone and let out a sigh before I immediately moved to dial our middle sister, Joia. I gave her a bare-bones explanation of what I needed, getting approval to spend the night at her place.

I blew out a sigh, and switched apps to order a ride.

I hadn't completed the transaction yet when a police car pulled up to the curb, and two officers jumped out. My eyes went wide as they came straight to me, hands on their weapons.

"Are you Jaclyn Love?" one asked, shifting my wide-eyed gaze to a frown.

"Who's asking?"

The who *hadn't* asked smirked. "Ms. Love, we need you to come with us – we got a report of vandalism, threats of violence, and destruction of property from a Victor Isaacs?"

"Oh no, you've got the wrong person," I said immediately, shaking my head. "Anyway, how did you find me?"

"According to Mr. Isaacs, you screamed …" the officer pulled a tablet from somewhere, holding it up to see the screen. "I quote – I'd rather be a hobo bitch than look at your bitch ass face one more minute. You are hiding a child! Fuck you. I'm going to my sister's, but I'll be back for your ass, bitch."

My head tipped to the side. "Who said that? *I* said that?!"

"Yes ma'am, you did. He gave us the address."

"Okay, fine. I said that, but I was mad. Everybody says things when they're mad. You're here to arrest me about that?"

The officer without the tablet shook his head. "No ma'am. We're here to arrest you for the brick through the window of his Mercedes, the slashed tires, and the spray paint."

"Well that's ridiculous, I didn't—"

"So this isn't you, earlier tonight?" the officer with the tablet asked, holding it up to show me a video playing on the screen.

Surveillance, from the parking garage.

With audio.

The tires were already flat, and the brick was already through the window. But there I was, locs swinging, rapping *Wrong Bitch* at the top of my lungs while I spray-painted those same words on the hood of Victor's precious black Mercedes.

My other hand held a bottle of vodka.

I closed my eyes, stashing my cell phone in my pocket before I held my hands up in front of me, hoping at least for a peaceful ride to the station.

They got the right bitch today.

TWO
JACLYN

Four hundred hours of community service.

Four *hundred* hours of community service.

That was the price to be paid for my drunken shenanigans with Victor's car.

Carrie Underwood and Jazmine Sullivan had me out here bad.

While I couldn't say damaging his property had been worth it – I still felt like shit afterward, and now I was paying for it – I definitely found myself grateful for *this* punishment, cause it could've been worse.

It could've been a *lot* worse.

As harsh as it sounded, four hundred hours of community service sounded a helluva lot better than jail time, and certainly worked better for my life.

Something I should've considered before my anger and alcohol consumption got the best of me. I was already scarcely holding my shit together, between being a full-time student *and* running The Dreamery – the tiny ice cream franchise that paid my bills, at only twenty-four years old. I didn't have time for four hundred hours of community service.

But I was going to have to find it.

It hadn't taken much to find a new place of my own. Blakewood was built specifically around the local university, so there was always space somewhere. According to the history, the school was founded by Blackwood natives, looking to escape the big city. Thousands of miles West, they found the perfect space – naming it *Blakewood*, a portmanteau of the largest investor's name and the city they'd left, but still wanted to honor. Of course it started small, no accreditation, but a hundred years later, Blakewood was a force.

It was also home.

My new place was small, but it was *mine*, and I was in no big hurry for a change in status – not this time. I was tired of *trying* to get my life together, and ready to just *do it*. No relationship drama distracting me, no man taking up my limited time – just me, focusing on *me*.

The apartment had come furnished – something I'd gladly paid a premium for, to avoid the hassle and immediate expense of having to buy everything myself. All I'd had to bring were my personal belongings, plugging them into ready-made comfort, which was relieving.

I settled onto the couch, laptop in hand, to do a little research. The judge had given me a specific list of places where I could fulfill my service hours, and I was *not* trying to end up raking leaves at the park, or picking up trash off the side of the road.

I'd already done both of those.

A strange sound outside the window behind me pulled my attention away from the laptop. It had been pouring rain for hours while I did my homework, so I hadn't thought much of anything coming from out there, knowing how storms amplified everything. But now that my attention wasn't quite as focused, I heard it again.

A mournful, plaintive whine… the kind that came from a cat.

Instantly, my nose wrinkled.

There was only room for *one* pussy around here.

I rummaged through the kitchen drawers to find a flashlight, then went back to the window. The building had fire escapes, which gave me protection from the rain as I opened the window and peered out, looking around for what I assumed would be a neighbor's cat, so I could shoo it away.

What if it runs in through the open window though?

That thought made me narrow my eyes, suspicious of MysteryCat as the beam of my flashlight landed on fur. It was tucked into a corner nearly out of sight, and I realized my concern was unfounded. That cat wasn't "running" anywhere, not with that big ass patch of missing fur, and bleeding gash.

"*Dammit,*" I muttered, pushing out a sigh.

I didn't have time for this.

Tucking my head back inside the window, I closed and locked it, and put the flashlight away. I moved back to the couch, where my cell phone was, to look up my options for having dinner brought to me so I could eat while I decided which punishment I would endure. Did I have food in my fridge?

Yes.

Did I *want* that?

No.

But what about the cat, Jaclyn?

... what about it?

I was nobody's animal person, and hadn't told her ass to climb up to *my* window.

Homegirl had to figure her own shit out.

With that said, those sad ass *meows* seemed to grow louder, and louder, and *louder,* the same weird shit, over and over.

"Girl will you shut up?!" I yelled at the window, then turned back to my phone, scrolling through my list of options.

MysteryCat did not, in fact, shut up, which prompted me to let out yet another sigh.

Fine.

Maybe I could give her something to eat, at least. She couldn't keep up all that hollering with food in her mouth.

I THINK I MIGHT LOVE YOU

Annoyed as hell about it, I trudged to the kitchen, looking through the cabinets until I found a bowl. Opening the fridge, I glanced at the few items I'd grabbed at the grocery store, and determined the pre-cooked chicken was the best option from my meager groceries.

I put a few pieces in the bowl – then stopped to check the internet to make sure cats could even eat chicken – then went back to the window, stepping out onto the fire escape this time. I slid the bowl to her, close enough she wouldn't have to move too much to get to it. That heifer took one sniff, looked at me, then put her head down without even touching it.

I sucked my teeth. "Okay, I *know* your ass isn't being picky?" I pushed the bowl closer, prompting her to lift her head for another long *"bitch, can't you tell I don't want this??"* stare.

"Well, *fine*! Ungrateful ass," I snapped, leaving the bowl as I moved to go back inside.

Then she wanted to start that *"meow"* -ing again, making it clear she had no plans of letting me have any peace tonight.

"What more do you want from me?" I whined, pouting as I climbed back into my apartment. I picked up my phone for a new search on my internet browser.

Blakewood veterinarians

I frowned at all the cutesy ass names that came up first, scrolling right past all of those to get to *Blakewood Animal Clinic*, which was the only one still open anyway. A quick glance at their website showed enough melanin from the various images on the home screen that I was comfortable giving them my business.

I went back to the kitchen, searching under the sink for a pair of rubber gloves.

"*Yass*," I mumbled to myself, doing a shimmy when I discovered a pair of rubber dish gloves under there, which I opened and put on before I straightened again. Looking around, I regretted asking the movers to take all the extra boxes with them – even *one* would be helpful now. Pursing my lips, I turned to the cabinets again, doing another triumphant dance when I spotted a big plastic mixing bowl – part of the "furnished" apartment – that looked cheap enough I wouldn't mind replacing it.

Do I need a spatula too?

Maybe not.

Probably not.

After testing the thickness of the gloves, in case *MysteryCat* decided to try to scratch or bite, I took the bowl back out onto the fire escape with me, and did my best to gently transfer her into the bowl. Once she was in there, she seemed so *small*. Much smaller than I'd expected. Feeling bad for the abundance of skin and fur – and lack of thickness – I saw, I put the chicken in the bowl with her after a few seconds of thought.

Maybe she'd get hungry on the way.

I brought the bowl inside, leaving it on my counter while I put on shoes and a jacket, and found an umbrella. The clinic was only a block away, so I didn't bother using my rideshare app, choosing instead to walk.

Blakewood Animal Clinic was by no means a fancy establishment, if the outside was any indication. The sign was broken – but clean – and the only outside décor was hand-drawn paws and claws and other animal-related signs and symbols, done in dry-erase marker on the inside of the windows.

The waiting room was empty when I stepped in, but the chime over the door must have alerted someone to my presence. A handsome Asian man with tatted arms came from the back with a puppy wearing a cone around its' neck in his arms, followed closely by a black woman with a clipboard and a smile.

"Can we help you?" she asked, her expression changing as her eyes landed on the bowl in my hands.

"Uh, yeah," I told her, holding it out. "I found this cat on my fire escape. I think it... I don't know. Got attacked by a dog or something. Maybe."

"Aww, poor thing," the man said, and ol' girl about swooned out of her scrubs grinning at him as he stepped forward to peek into the bowl. "Char will get you taken care of," he told me, then turned to her. "I'm going to get this guy tucked away for the night, and I'll let Dr. Davenport know we have a new patient."

"Thanks Kenzo," she gushed, watching him as he walked away.

I didn't blame her either.

He had ass in those scrubs.

Once he was through that door, I cleared my throat, pulling her attention back to me.

"*Sorry*," she breathed, her light brown skin flushing as she hurried to the reception desk.

"Oh girl, you're good. I get it. He fine. You hittin' that?" I asked, knowing it was bold as hell, but I was curious. My question only made her blush harder as she shook her head.

"No. I *wish*," she whispered, damn near to herself, after glancing over her shoulder to make sure he wasn't there. "Um, okay, let's get some information down about your injured pet."

"Oh no, she's not my pet," I corrected, wanting to make that shit *clear*. "I was just minding my business, trying to work, and this thing started making all kinda noise on my fire escape. All I want is quiet."

The girl – *Char* – looked horrified, eyes wide, lips parted. "Oh. Um, okay. So I'm guessing there's no name?"

"I'm not even trying to take this thing home," I admitted. "I thought I saw you guys had animal shelter affiliation or something?"

"We *do*, but—"

"Okay so yeah, I wanna do that. Sew her up or whatever, and then take her off my hands. I don't have time to play nurse."

"Char?" a voice – a *different* voice – called, from around the corner where Kenzo had disappeared. It seemed to be getting closer – and more familiar – as he continued speaking. "Ken said we had a pa —ah, *hell*."

Ah hell, indeed.

If I was "Dr. Davenport", I wouldn't want to see me either.

He stopped on the other side of the desk, looking better than he had any business looking in bright blue scrubs. There was a surgical mask hooked over his ears, but pushed down under his chin in a way that made it cup his beard, something that had, undoubtedly, made more than one child giggle today.

Hell.

It had *me* feeling giggly too, or at least it would've, if it wasn't for the faint remnants of purple mottled bruises surrounding his eye, from where I'd punched him two weeks ago.

"What is this?" he asked. "You back to finish the job?"

I smirked. "That's funny, but I can assure you – I had *no* idea you'd be here. I don't even know you."

"Really?" he asked, eyebrow lifted. "I'd say you're quite familiar."

Something about those words was like flipping on a magnetized field. Instantly, my gaze dropped to his groin area, and… sweatpants are cool and all, but have you ever seen a dick print in scrubs? A thinner, stiffer fabric meant a more pronounced… contour.

"I don't recall," I lied right to his face, pressing my lips together and crossing my arms, daring him to offer a comeback in front of his coworker, who was looking back and forth between us.

"*Ohh!*" Char exclaimed, snapping her fingers. "Is this the homeless woman you found in your apartment?! The one who punched you in the eye?!'

I gasped. "*I have a home!*"

"Could've fooled me," Kadan replied, in the smug tone of a man who *knew* he'd scored a point in what was now, apparently, a back and forth.

My mouth opened, intent on offering a witty response, but all I could stammer was, "I was having a bad night, for your information." I hiked my nose up in the air, gesturing toward the cat, who was currently looking at all of us like we were crazy. "Now if you're done – here is this animal. Heal it, or whatever. You can send the bill to my *home*."

Kadan frowned. "Why is it in a mixing bowl with… is that *chicken?* What is wrong with you, woman?"

"*I thought she might get hungry!*"

"Or *you* were hungry."

My eyes narrowed. "I don't eat pussy, I am *strictly* dickly, excuse you."

"That puts a lot in perspective."

"Nigga can you just fix the goddamn cat?! Please?!" I snapped, propping a hand on my hip. "I have *other* shit to do."

Kadan – and Char, for that matter – frowned. "I'm sure your suffering pet has a name you could call her by, instead of *goddamn cat*."

"She is *not* my pet, first of all, and I don't even know if she is actually a she. It showed up on my fire escape, crying like Whitley Gilbert. *Dwayyyne. Dwayyyyne.* That's what the shit sounds like!"

With a deep sigh, Kadan lifted the bowl in one arm, using his free hand to run over the cat's head, soothing her. "What do you *think* happened?"

I shrugged. "I have no idea, but my best guess is she got attacked by a dog or something. I don't know."

"Okay. I'm going to take her in the back and get her checked out. Wait here."

"Okay but like I wasn't even trying to bring her back with me!" I yelled at his back, as he completely ignored me. I growled my frustration, then turned back to where Char was waiting, thinly-veiled amusement on her face.

"Will that be cash, check or credit today?"

THREE
KADAN

So... I couldn't even front on Jaclyn.

Ol' girl was fine.

Like *extra* fine.

Risk it all fine.

Problem was, she was a lunatic, evidenced by her busting me in my shit in my own house, getting arrested on the street after – which I saw through the window after I looked out to make sure Jemma's assurance she'd left the building wasn't a lie – and now, her ass bringing an injured cat in a bowl of chicken in here.

But Kadan, ain't that the type of shenanigans you're a sucker for? <- the question I could count on from anybody who knew me, especially if they laid eyes on Jaclyn. The locs, the deep brown skin, the lips, the *thighs*, goddamn. Her whole erratic thicksnack situation was *exactly* my type.

Like... *exactly* my type.

Exactly.

It was also the type I was supposed to be off of, because I was getting too old for that volatile shit. Sure, plenty of people were happy to live with the stress of great sex and high drama well past their early thirties – my father was one. But one of the last things he said to me was, "High-quality pussy ain't never done nothing to nobody. Look at me! I keep myself a steady supply of women that might stab your ass. Just don't do nothing to get stabbed and don't worry about it. Unpredictable pussy ain't gone kill you, don't be scared now!"

He died of a heart attack two days later, at sixty-three.

Mid-coitus.

So.

Yeah.

Was *not* trying to go out like that.

So I sewed up the cat – the injured one, that Jac brought in.

I agreed with her assessment that she – the cat – had likely had a bad run-in with a dog. Luckily, it wasn't too serious of an injury – I sedated her, washed the wound, and stitched her closed, then put together the cocktail of painkillers and antibiotics Jaclyn would need to make sure the cat stayed comfortable and uninfected.

If she was even still here.

I'd caught her comments about not planning to keep the cat, but had ignored them, in hopes she'd have a change of heart. She could've not bothered with the cat at all, but the fact she'd taken the time to get it here to the clinic before we closed... I had a feeling we could change her mind.

I put the cat in a *proper* carrier, and grabbed food from our stock as well, carrying it all up to the waiting room. Char and Kenzo were hanging close as hell in the tiny corner of the front desk that was hidden from customers by the wall – just talking, as far as I could tell, but they parted at the sound of my footsteps.

Like they were fooling anybody.

"She still here?" I asked, holding up the cat carrier in one hand, and the bag of supplies in the other.

Flustered, Char nodded. "Uh, yeah, but she fell asleep like twenty minutes ago."

"Probably exhausted from a long day of giving people hell," I muttered as I rounded the corner, stepping out into the waiting room.

Just as Char said, Jaclyn was fast asleep, her legs stretched across several chairs and her head resting against the wall. With her eyes closed, lips slightly parted, locs falling over her face, glasses cocked crookedly against her nose, she almost looked *sweet*.

Good thing I knew better.

"*Ms. Love*," I called, tapping the chair she was sitting in with my foot to get her attention. Her eyes popped open with a sharp intake of breath, and instinct warned me to get back – *right* on time.

Still – mostly – asleep, Jaclyn popped up from her chair swinging, prompting a collective chorus of *"Whoa!"* from me, Kenzo, and Char.

The sound of our voices seemed to pull Jaclyn further into reality, but just a little. Her face pulled into a squint as she looked around, confused, then moved to push her glasses into the right place.

"You can put those fists away, McNabb," I teased her, earning an even deeper scowl than she was already wearing. "You've got other things to occupy your hands." I held the carrier and the bag of supplies out to her, and she reluctantly accepted.

"How am I supposed to defend myself, if both hands are full?"

"Just swing what's in your hand…"

"*Oh*." She glanced thoughtfully down at the cat carrier. "I guess this thing *is* pretty heavy duty. I could knock a motherfucker out."

"I was talking about what you had in the *other* hand, but go off I guess," I told her, less confident about the safety of the cat if her first thought was to swing *that* at somebody.

"So what's wrong with her? What is all this stuff in the bag, and how much *more* is it costing me?"

I shook my head. "Costs you nothing. You pay for the visit, and we provide everything else, unless your pet needed major care. This girl got lucky – and she is, indeed, female."

"Good for her – still not my pet," Jaclyn corrected me. "What all am I supposed to be doing for her?"

"Just give her the meds, don't let her jump around, and don't let her chew at her stitches. I put a collar on her, which should discourage the chewing, but still keep an eye out. And make sure the incision doesn't start looking bad – leaking, swelling, any of that."

When I finished that short spiel, Jaclyn was looking at me with wide eyes, trying to absorb everything I'd said. But then, she shook her head.

"Listen – I run a business, and I'm trying to finish a degree, and I have a new responsibility that popped up, that's going to require even more of me. I don't have time to take care of this cat."

I shrugged. "Everybody's busy Jaclyn. I promise you, it sounds like more than it is – it'll only take a few minutes out of your day."

"*Minutes I don't have*," she muttered under her breath, rolling her eyes before she brought her attention back to my face. "Fine. I'll give it a shot because I feel bad for Miss Thing, but do *not* be surprised if I come back in a few days to drop this carrier at the desk and walk right on outta here."

"I think you and your new pet are going to get along fine Ms. Love," I encouraged. "I even stuck a litter box and stuff in that bag for you, to put you on a path to success."

She narrowed her eyes. "I want you to know I recognize a setup when I see it. I wanna remind you, I know where you live."

"Ain't no set up, woman," I shot back, alarmed. "I'm trying to help you."

"If you were trying to help *me*, I wouldn't be taking this cat home, bruh." She pushed out a sigh. "We done here?"

"We are."

"Good."

With that, she turned and walked out the clinic door, leaving me quite confident if one of her hands had been free, I would've gotten flipped off. Char and Kenzo had been hiding out once Jaclyn woke up swinging, but now they both stepped into the waiting room to join me.

"I like her," Char hummed, turning to grin at me and Kenzo.

"*You?*" I asked, surprised. "Sweet, pleasant Char, like *her?*"

Crossing her arms, she nodded. "Yep. Because I am over thirty, and tired of my go-to adjectives being 'sweet and pleasant' like I'm a cupcake."

"But you *are* like a cupcake," Kenzo told her, words that inexplicably made her blush, considering she'd *just* presented the same descriptor as a negative. "Everybody likes cupcakes."

Those words took her smile down a few notches.

"Not everybody," she countered, a sudden hint of sadness coloring her tone. "Anyway, I'm going to head out. It's been a *long* day."

I cringed. "Yeah, sorry about that Char. I've tried to tell the city we need *more* help here."

Kenzo chuckled, clapping me on the shoulder. "They exhausted the budget bringing *you* in, man. Can't afford more help unless they change the payment structure, and you know that's not happening."

Definitely wasn't happening.

"You were a necessary addition though," Char chimed in, ready to make sure there were no bruised feelings. "The caseload was so heavy before you came we were having to turn away everything except the most serious cases, and Kenzo was so busy I don't think he even knew my name."

Ken frowned. "I knew your name."

"But you were calling me *desk girl,*" she countered.

"Not like, *desk girl,*" he argued. "Like, *Desk Girl!* Like a superhero, cause you were keeping everything in order, saving the day..."

Char's eyebrows went up. "*Oh.* Oh. I never thought about it like that. But I'm a *woman*. Not a girl. Goodnight guys," she said, pushing through the door that led to the back, and disappearing.

As soon as she was out of earshot, I put on my stern face and turned to Kenzo. "When are you going to stop playing and ask her out?"

He smirked. "When am I supposed to do that? You always have her working the desk."

"Oh *I* do," I laughed. "You know we're rarely here past nine pm. Plenty of time for a date."

Ken shook his head. "Good girl like that expects dinner at seven, home by ten, panties intact. *Not* my type of date."

"So you're going to keep flirting instead of doing anything about it because you think she's not gonna let you hit on the first date?" I asked.

"Nope – I'm going to keep flirting and not doing anything about it because I know damn well she's not in the market for what I can offer. A girl like that wants the house, the kids, the *ring*."

"She already told you about that *girl* shit," I laughed. "You keep saying what *a girl like that* wants, what she expects, but have you bothered to ask the *woman*, Char, what it is she wants?"

"I *know* women," Ken assured me. "Trust me, I've got this."

I chuckled. "Aiight man – you think you got it, so I'ma let you have it… as long as you're not playing with her emotions."

"Fair enough," Kenzo agreed, returning the gesture when I held my fist out to him.

Twenty minutes later, we'd closed up for the night and all gone our separate ways, with me heading back to the apartment I was subletting from Jaclyn's sister, Jemma. I'd been grateful for the place – it was nice as hell, and a decent distance from where the college kids seemed to congregate, and mostly outside of their price range, so I didn't find myself living among a bunch of young adults.

For one, I didn't have the patience, and secondly, I couldn't handle the noise, or the big crowds of people that seemed to be a native part of living too near a college. I'd spent enough time in my 20s around strange people and excess noise – and not the innocent kind I was avoiding now. As an army veteran, I'd seen *combat*, and I wasn't trying to be near anything that even vaguely reminded me of that.

Hell, when I discharged, I didn't even want to take my skills as a trained medic into the real world with me – at least, not to work on people. Instead, I took that passion with me to veterinary school, then came back to the town where I'd grown up to put it all to use.

Fuck those college kids though.

It hadn't been surprising at all to learn Jaclyn was one of them. She didn't look particularly young –was a grown ass woman – but she rankled my nerves in the same way. She *was* young enough that the business owner thing threw me, but for all I knew, her "business" could be selling pictures of her feet on the internet or something.

I could look into it, if I felt inclined.

And honestly speaking, part of me did feel inclined, but I had zero intention of listening to *that* shit, because I knew how it would go. I'd look her up to find out more, and knowing more would make me want to know *even more*, and before I knew it, I'd be balls deep in Jaclyn Love with no idea how to pull myself out, and I didn't get the impression she was the kind of woman who'd help.

Not that she'd be stuck on me.

In fact, I highly doubted she would, which made the whole idea even more attractive – and made it even more important to stay away from. When I was younger, I'd followed my father's advice religiously – he was the *man*, and I looked up to him. He was a proud proponent of hoeing, so that's what I did, and I wouldn't even try to pretend I hadn't enjoyed it. The sex, the liquor, the drama... the shit had been fun.

Until that lifestyle showed what it cost.

Last year, when I lost him, I'd vowed right there at the funeral – while the woman who gave him the heart attack physically fought the woman he was "officially" dating – that I wasn't going to do it anymore. While the family was busy breaking them up, I was busy going over a game plan in my mind – how to *not* be like my old man.

In many ways, my father was a great person – he'd just set the worst possible example of a healthy love life, even in his relationship with my mother. There were plenty of ways to honor him, but following in those particular footsteps wasn't it.

I was *not* about to end up in an early grave like him.

As far as I was concerned, a woman like Jaclyn Love may as well have been holding a shovel, ready and willing to dig.

FOUR
JACLYN

"Girl you know I'm wanted in Canada, get that camera off me!" I fussed from behind the counter at *Dreamery* at Joia, who laughed, because she thought I was playing.

I had an unhealthy obsession with Drake a few years back, don't judge me.

Actually… hell, *I* judge me for that, so whatever.

"I have a *big* following at Blakewood," Jo reminded me, *not* lowering camera – her cell phone. In fact, she framed the two of us on the screen, making duck lips at herself as cartoonized flower crowns appeared on our heads. "If I tell them to come eat at *Dreamery*, they're coming."

"Fuck those kids," I countered, flashing a smile at her screen so she would take the picture and leave me alone. "I had to close down for two days and miss classes to restock because their hungry asses ate me out of everything in here."

Joia looked up from examining our ussie to frown. "That's not a good thing?"

"Maybe on the surface, but *Dreamery* isn't big enough to handle influencer-sponsored crowd sizes. I only have four employees, and hell, just the five of us is damn near half-capacity for this space."

"Sounds like you need a bigger space," Joia mused. "Maybe closer to campus."

"I'm perfectly happy where I am. Now, if you're not going to actually help, could you at least be quiet? I was supposed to pick where I served this community service days ago, and I just realized these spots are limited."

Finally, she put the phone down, giving me her full attention. "Sorry. We cute though."

"Duh."

"Anyway, so... limited? Meaning?"

"Meaning, there are other people who have community service to do too, and the list the judge gave me – I meant to research everywhere, and then pick a place, but then I got sidetracked."

"With Miss Thing," Joia correctly assumed, her lips curving into a smile. "I still cannot believe your ass is a cat lady now."

I raised a finger. "You mean *for* now. She can kick it with me until she's healed or whatever but then she gotta go."

"Jac, you bought that cat a bougie ass collar with her name embroidered on the bow."

I shrugged. "And? Can't I help another bitch feel good about herself after she been through something traumatic?"

"I'm *not* about to deal with you Jac," she laughed. "You know that cat ain't going nowhere."

"What I *know* is your ass keeps distracting me," I countered. "I'm out of time to research, so I've been calling each one as I have time, and their volunteer positions are filled."

Joia's eyebrow went up. "Volunteer? Girl your ass is a *criminal*."

"A criminal *mastermind* hoe, get it right," I laughed. "Although this was *not* my finest work."

"Understatement. How are you *dealing*, anyway?" Jo asked. "Like, I know you're the baby thug of the family and all, but seriously, this has to be rough. You were already crazy busy, and now an ugly breakup, getting arrested, *community service*. How are you not curled up in a ball somewhere right now?"

I blew out a sigh and shook my head. "I don't have time to break down, as much as I might want to. This is my last semester of school, and if I mess it up, that's time and money down the drain. So I am stuffing all that emotional shit in a teensy tiny box to be packed away and opened later, at some undisclosed time. Or never. Never works."

"That sounds *super* healthy," Joia drawled, twisting her lips at me. "You need to talk to somebody. You can't neglect your mental health."

I scoffed. "I'm *not*. I read a whole article about it. An article that said pets were great for mental health."

"So you admit the cat is your pet now?"

"*Don't* put words in my mouth," I told her. "And *stop* distracting me. I can't find my list, and I *need* to do this."

"It's under your laptop."

I frowned. "What?"

"The paper you're looking for," Joia explained. "You can't see it from where you are, but it's right there under your laptop. That's why you can't find it."

I dropped my gaze to where my laptop was open on the counter in front of me, and used one hand to lift it up. Sure enough, the list I needed was underneath. I held it up, and Joia reached over the counter to take it from me.

"I knew you said you had community service but *four hundred* hours of it? Harsh."

"Nah," I shook my head. "I would've gotten jail time if Vic hadn't dropped the charges. The community service is purely punitive, cause the judge is tired of me. *Jaclyn Love, you been in and out of here too much over the last ten years. I don't wanna see you again!*" I mimicked.

Her eyes went wide. "Wow, it's that same lady from juvie court?!"

"*Mmmhmm*. And I am not trying to find out what happens if I don't get one of these 'volunteer' spaces. Read the next name to me so I can look up their number."

Joia sucked in a breath. "Uh, you know there's only one more name on this list you haven't already crossed off, right?"

I froze, my fingers poised over my keyboard. "Wait, *seriously?*"

"Yeah. *Blakewood Animal Clinic.*"

My fingers automatically pecked at the keys, typing it in. It wasn't until I hit the *enter* key that those words sank in, and a picture of the clinic façade filled my computer screen.

"Oh you gotta be fuckin' kidding me."

∽

Work for Kadan Davenport, or go to jail?
Go to jail, or work for Kadan Davenport?

Shit.

I didn't like the sound of *either* of those options, but only one of them was an option at all. Even though I knew I was pushing it by not rushing to get that volunteer position before someone else snatched it up, I couldn't bring myself to move any faster than a slow trudge down the street.

I did *not* wanna do this shit.

I lingered at the front door as long as I could without looking like a creep, then pulled the door open. Like the last time I was here, Char was at the front desk, in scrubs covered in smiling gray kittens today.

She looked adorable.

"Jaclyn!" she gushed. "How are you? Everything okay with... did you name her yet?"

I glanced around the waiting room, trying not to let my disgust show on my face as I took in these strangers and these animals and their ailments.

Swallowing the nervous lump in my throat, I nodded as I made my way to the counter. "Yes, actually. *Miss Thing.* She's doing well."

"That's great to hear! But if that's the case, how can I help you?"

I cleared my throat, leaning in so I could talk to her in a lowered tone. "Well, I have um... some community service hours I need to—"

"*Oh thank God,*" Char blurted, her fluffy natural hair bouncing around her shoulders as she clapped her hands together. "You want to do it here?"

My lip curled. "Well, that's not *exactly*... I mean yes. *Yes.* Please tell me that's still an option?"

"Of course it's an option! Or I'll make them make it an option. Come on back, I'll get Kadan!"

She motioned for me to come around the corner, and I grudgingly followed her directive, trailing her to what appeared to be a breakroom. She sat me down at a table, still bubbling with excitement as she disappeared, presumably to find Kadan.

I was bubbling too.

Well... my guts were.

It didn't take long before I felt Kadan's presence in the doorway, making my stomach twerk even harder. Reluctantly, I dragged my gaze to where he was standing, his wide frame taking up the whole entry.

Arms crossed.

Smirking.

Handsome as shit.

Bastard.

"Why is it *not* remotely surprising to me that you have to do community service?" he asked, his biceps flexing against the arms of his scrubs as he shifted. "Got something to do with the police picking you up outside my building that night?"

I sucked my teeth. "That's none of your business."

"It is though, since I'm the one with the authority to sign your paperwork," he countered, finding more smugness from somewhere. "What did you do? Let me guess – assault and battery."

"No," I rolled my eyes. "It was just a little body work on my ex's car. Much less than he deserved, actually. He got off easy."

Kadan scoffed. "What, he hurt your feelings? Caught him texting his side chick?"

"Side *wife*. And kids," I corrected.

"Oh. Damn."

"Yeah. So about that volunteer position?"

He nodded, stepping into the breakroom to lean against the counter that housed the microwave and coffee maker. It had been about a week since my first visit here, and his bruise was mostly gone now.

"Yeah, about that," he said, stroking a hand over his beard. "Be real with me – why here? This your last resort or something?"

"Hell yes, that's the *only* reason I'm here," I admitted. "You think I *wanted* to see your ass again? No offense."

Kadan chuckled. "Oh, trust me – that disdain you feel is mutual. But we could use the help around here. Char is overworked, and needs the relief at the front desk, so I'm not going to turn you down."

My eyes widened. "So I can have the volunteer position?"

"As long as you keep your ass away from me as much as possible, fine. How many hours?"

"I can manage ten to fourteen hours a week," I said immediately, knowing it off top since I'd already spent time working out possible schedules in my head, before I even knew where I'd be.

He nodded. "Cool, but I meant in total – meaning, how many hours do you have to give?"

"Oh. Four hundred."

Immediately, Kadan's eyebrows mashed together in a frown. "*Four hundred*? What the hell did you do to that man's car?!"

"It's not that much, not when you think about it…"

"Four hundred hours is fifty full work days!"

I shrugged. "What can I say, I'm kind of a big deal around the courthouse."

"You're serious right now?" Kadan asked, eyes wide, and I couldn't do anything except nod.

"I got in trouble as a teenager," I explained. "And then more trouble. And then a little more. And a few more times, but I've put all that behind me, and I'm an upstanding citizen now."

He let out this laugh that was somewhere between a scoff and a snort. "Oh yeah, I can see your growth between now and when you assaulted me in the middle of the night."

"I'm *sorry* about your eye, okay?" I told him, more concerned now with getting my paperwork signed to confirm my position and cover my ass. I pulled the folder I'd brought with me from my bag, rifling through to find the initial form I needed filled out. "And your dick too. It seems to be healing nicely – your eye, not your dick. I can't see your dick. I don't *want* to see your dick."

He frowned. "What's wrong with my dick?"

"Nothing's wrong with your dick, it's a nice dick," I said, still searching for the form. "A blue-ribbon dick, if you will."

"Blue-ribbon?"

I sighed. "Yes, like prize-winning. Keep up, damn."

"What am I keeping up with?" he asked, brows furrowed in confusion. "Was there a competition?"

"The Dicklympics, Kadan, *duh*."

"The *what?!*"

I looked up from what I was doing, form in hand as I did a quick mental replay of the last minute or so of conversation.

"Never mind. I've said too much."

He shook his head, approaching the table where I was sitting. "Nah, you haven't said *nearly* enough," he countered.

"Here's what I need you to sign," I said, intent on shifting the conversation away from my ridiculous musings and back to the matter at hand. "Oh, I've got a pen for you too."

"I've got my own pen," he said, pulling one from the pocket of his scrubs.

It was covered with puppy face emojis.

Cute.

"Where am I supposed to sign?" he asked, leaning over the table, so close I could smell the antibacterial soap on him, and that was the moment I *knew* I was on some bullshit, cause...

He kinda smelled good to me.

"Uh, right here," I pointed, trying my best not to inhale as I watched him read the text that was there before simply signing his name to it.

The way he was bent over the table had his ass sitting *just* right in those scrubs. The hand that wasn't holding the pen was pressed against the table, his bicep flexing under his weight. I didn't look away as his head turned in my direction, that vaguely-present bruise around his eye giving him a little ruggedness as he looked at me, running his tongue over perfect lips before he smirked.

In different circumstances, I'd give him *all* the pussy.

Like... all of it.

So much pussy.

"I guess I don't have to ask about a background check, huh? I already know your ass is a criminal," he laughed, reminding me of what the circumstances were. "You just like to tear shit up, right? Not steal? You're not gonna be swiping credit cards, are you?"

"Ha-ha," I said, drily, as I took the signed form from his hands. I stood as I returned it to the folder, and he straightened up. "I'm not a scammer."

"Tell me anything, Ms. Love."

I huffed. "It's the truth! I don't *steal*."

"Good. *Buy* scrubs to wear while you're at the front desk, before you come back. Report to Char, and she'll show you the ropes," Kadan told me, then turned to walk off.

"Wait!" I called after him. "That's just it? That's all?"

He turned back to me, eyebrow raised. "Did you expect a welcome party or something?"

"*No.* I just... thank you, is all."

He nodded. "You're welcome. Don't make me regret it... *more*," he added, with another smirk as he walked off.

Which, I got where he was coming from, but could a bitch get credit for changing her ways?

... from a few weeks ago...?

With a heavy sigh, I returned the folder to my bag, happy I'd at least accomplished *that*. Now, I had to get back to *Dreamery* to help with the last nightly rush and close up, finish up my homework, tend to Miss Thing, wash my ass, eat some kind of dinner, and *maybe* get a few hours of sleep before my first class in the morning.

But at least the form was signed.

And only four hundred more hours of Kadan Davenport to go.

FIVE

KADAN

"Ahhhh!" I growled in some kid's face as I smacked his shot out of range of the basketball hoop he was aiming for. Of course, "kid" was a relative term, one I bestowed on anyone who seemed younger than twenty-five, which he did. He was technically an adult, but as the confidence he'd worn when he first took the shot melted into dismay at the realization I'd gotten that shit outta here, he looked like a kid ready to run home crying to his mama.

I *loved* that shit.

He was still standing there, mouth open, shocked he had *not* sunk the winning shot when I clapped him on his shoulder for one last taunt, just because he and his equally young teammate had been so confident in winning our two-on-two battle.

I looked him right in his eyes, then looked to his teammate, making sure they were both paying attention before I spoke.

"Guys," I started, my expression solemn. "I gotta say... wow, you suck. Better luck next time."

Behind me, my own partner, Jason, busted out laughing, and I joined, neither of us giving a shit about the wounded frustration on those kids' faces as they skulked off. Before the game, and through the whole first half, we'd been fifty different kinds of "old niggas at the gym", and the BC powder, IcyHot, and even PTSD jokes had been flying left and right. And this was *after* we'd had to convince them to even play against us – they had this massively incorrect idea that playing against Jay wouldn't be fair, because of his prosthetic.

They thought it was a disadvantage.

We'd enjoyed the hell out of proving them wrong.

"I would've tried to put money on it if I'd known we were gonna do 'em like that," Jay laughed, as we headed to the community center locker room. We met up here at least once a week, as part of a local veterans' group. We'd known of each other vaguely as kids, by virtue of growing up in the same town, going to the same schools. Jay was a couple of years younger than me, but I graduated the same year as one of his brothers, Justin.

"Easy money," I agreed. "Youngins never learn."

Jay and I were only in our early thirties, but to these – goddamn – college kids, that was old. They thought their twenty-year-old knees were superior, and hell, maybe they were. But the *fact* was that Jay and I – along with a few other guys our age sometimes – regularly beat the brakes off these young cats on the court.

At his locker, Jay pulled out his phone, chuckling at something on the screen. "Ay, didn't you tell me before you were trying to find ice cream you could have without fucking your stomach up?"

"I remember my stomach being fucked up and almost clearing out the whole gym behind an ice cream cone, yeah," I laughed, pulling my own bag out.

"Pretty sure they had to fumigate this place behind your funky ass," he jeered from across the aisle. "You need to see somebody about that, it ain't normal."

"You gonna tell me why you brought this up, or roast me?"

He laughed. "Both. My old lady is on it with the pregnancy cravings, wants me to grab her some ice cream from this place down the street. My cousin owns it – the *Dreamery*."

"I've heard of that," I told him. "With the gourmet flavors and shit."

"Yeah. She's got something for any food sensitivity. I was gonna see if you wanted to roll down here with me."

I frowned. "Nigga are you asking me on an ice cream date?"

He sucked his teeth. "Is this the thanks I get for trying to put you on something new? Just trying to keep you from polluting the city, bruh."

"Wow, this might be the most considerate thing you've ever done – my draws thank you," I chuckled, hooking the strap of my gym bag over my shoulder.

Jay closed his locker. "You rolling or not?"

"Yeah, I'm in," I said. "Your treat, right?" I asked, following him out.

"Why the hell would you think that?"

"You asked me on the date, you pay."

He sucked his teeth. "You not even my type."

"I'm light-skinned with a beard, I'm *everybody's* type."

∼

I, admittedly, had a bit of a sweet tooth, so I was a little excited at the prospect of finding gourmet-quality ice cream I could enjoy without my stomach bouncing right to left to do the shoulder lean.

It was a pretty ass day outside too – sun shining, birds chirping, all that. I'd gotten in some good cardio on the court, had made those dudes feel bad about themselves – it was a *great* day.

And then I walked into *Dreamery*.

There she was behind the counter, her locs tucked away underneath a vibrantly printed headwrap that popped against her deep brown skin. Big flat wooden disc earrings hung from her ears, swinging as she turned to greet her customers – us. Her fuchsia-painted lips curved into a big, pretty ass smile – maybe my first time seeing that, and *damn*.

She looked like the afrocentric answer to everything that ailed me, especially as my eyes traveled lower, taking in the way she filled out the simple dress she was wearing.

"*Jay*," she greeted, still wearing the big smile I now understood was for him. "I already have Reese's pint of honey lavender swirl packed up and ready." Her gaze skirted past him, landing on me, and that smile fizzled as her nose curled, just a little. "*You*."

Jay's eyebrows shot up as he glanced back, looking between me and her. "Y'all know each other?"

"Oh that's right," I said, stepping forward. "You've been away from the gym the last few weeks – this woman broke into my apartment in the middle of the night and hit me in the eye."

"And the dick!" she chimed. "Don't forget I hit you in the dick too. And I did not *break in*." She shifted her attention to Jason. "He's subletting from Jemma, and I didn't know. I tried to go spend the night there after things blew up with Victor, and here he comes. *In the damn way*."

Jay held up his hands. "Wait a minute, the night things blew up with Victor... you mean the night I came to bail you out? That *same* night?"

"It wasn't on purpose," she whined, taking on a tone – and pouting expression – I'd never seen from her, and never would've expected.

He chuckled. "Yeah, I would guess not, but you didn't mention any of that part at all."

She shrugged. "By the time you got me out, I was exhausted," she explained. "That was a rough night."

"That's a fuckin' understatement," Jay laughed.

I took another step into the shop, which was empty except for us at this time of day. "Why do I feel like I'm missing an important, but necessary bit of context here?"

"Why do *I* feel like that applies to most parts of your life?" Jaclyn replied, smirking as she crossed her arms.

I shook my head. "Yo, you've got a *lot* of animosity to be the one that gave *me* a black eye because of your own mistake."

"You told people I was homeless, accused me of trying to eat a live animal, and called me a criminal."

"Two of those things are true though!" I countered, while Jay laughed in the background.

"Man," He chimed in. "All that happened in one night?"

Jaclyn huffed. "*No.* Over like the last few weeks. I found an injured cat on my fire escape, took it to the closest animal clinic and there his ass was again. *In the way.*"

"The same cat you've got walking around with that big ass obnoxious bow on?" Jay asked, and my eyes went wide.

"You put a *bow* on her?"

Ignoring me, Jaclyn focused on Jay. "When the hell did you see that?"

"One of Joia's vlogs. Reese plays them on the big screen."

"I'm gonna whoop her ass, I told her not to be putting me in her videos!"

Jason smirked. "*You* aren't there. *Miss Thing* is though."

"You named her *Miss Thing*? Where the hell did you get *that* from?"

This time, she acknowledged me. "I named her after Whitley from— never mind. It's not your business *anyway*. Why are you even here?"

"I brought him here," Jay cut in, "thinking I was getting you a new customer, but I see I came to get a show instead. This is entertaining as hell."

Jaclyn sucked her teeth. "I'on know why. Take this nigga on somewhere."

"You should be a whole lot nicer to me, considering I'm going to be your boss ten to fourteen hours a week," I reminded her, approaching the counter.

She pulled that pretty ass face of hers into a scowl, her eyes flashing with annoyance behind her black framed glasses. "Ten to fourteen hours of *hell*," she corrected. "And it hasn't started yet, so I'll talk to you however I want."

"Wait," Jason interjected. "What's this part about?"

"Oh I can answer this one," I said. "This woman came to me begging for a volunteer position where she can work out *four hundred* hours of community service, and I was kind enough to say *yes*. To her criminal ass."

Jason choked. "*Four hundred*. Damn, Jac, they got you like that?!"

Her expression grim, Jaclyn nodded. "Yeah, they got me like that. But this is the *last* time I get in trouble."

"You said that the *last* time you got in trouble," Jay told her, bringing that pout back to her face. "Nah, put your lip up, cousin," he laughed, turning that pout to a smile.

There's the context I was looking for.

"I'm serious this time," she said, still smiling, but with a certain seriousness to her voice. "I've got too much riding on all this to mess it up any more than I already have. I've gotta make Aunt Priscilla proud."

"Don't start no shit now," Jay told her, but gave her a nod, exchanging some type of secret cousin code, or something, I guessed.

"*Fiiine*," she agreed. "Let me grab Reese's order so you can go on about your day. And take this person with you."

Again, Jay shook his head, chuckling. "Man... you know me and Reese used to go at it like that."

Jaclyn stopped moving, her brows pulling together into a deep crease as she frowned. "Go at it like *what*?"

"Like *y'all*," Jay countered, very matter-of-fact. "A whole lotta back and forth, fussing and shit, when really..."

"Nah," I spoke up. "Nah. No. Nope. None of that."

"Whatever you say man, just calling it like I see it."

Jaclyn cleared her throat. "Yeah, now *see* your way outta here."

"Hold up," Jay said. "We can't order too?"

"Tell me what you want and then get the hell outta here you are stressing me out," Jaclyn answered him, eyes narrowed, the words spilling out so fast there was no space between them. "Well, I already know you want butter pecan like your mama," she told Jay, the smile returning to her face. "What about you?"

My gaze moved to the lines of ice cream under the glass, in frosted containers, as she moved to fix Jay's order. "Jay said you have dairy free options – which ones are those?"

"They're the ones that say '*dairy free*' on that little tag that names the flavor," she answered, in an overly sweet tone that clearly told me I was being mocked.

I really hadn't seen that until she said something though, my bad.

"Okay, I'll do the pistachio vanilla crunch. In the dairy free option."

"The full milk option?" she asked, smirking as she handed Jay his ice cream, then picked up another cup to start mine. "Add whipped cream on top?"

"Very funny," I said, as she lowered a fresh scoop toward the appropriate canister. "Actually, hold on… do I want the salted caramel instead? Or the apple pie?"

Her eyebrows went up. "I don't know, *do* you?"

"Yeah… do the salted caramel. Wait! Nah… yeah… the salted caramel. Actually…"

"You've got like two seconds before I—"

"I'll do the pistachio. Yeah. Definitely the pistachio."

She fixed her gaze on me. "You *sure*?"

"Yes."

She hesitated for a moment, then went ahead and scooped, fixing my order before I could change my mind again, and handing it to me.

"What I owe you cousin?" Jay asked, and Jaclyn flashed him another smile.

"After you got me out of the pokey at four in the morning? Please. I can't take your money Jay."

He raised an eyebrow. "Aiight now, I don't turn down free shit."

"Our parents raised us better than to do that," Jaclyn laughed, picking up the pint of ice cream for Reese to hand to Jay. "Tell my Reesie I'm coming to see her this weekend."

"Will do," Jay nodded, turning to leave, with me right behind him.

"Um, *excuse me*," Jaclyn's voice rang out, stopping us in our tracks to turn back in her direction. "I said I couldn't take *his* money. I ain't said nothing about *yours*."

Jason burst into a cackle as he headed out the door and on about his day, leaving me to deal with his evil ass cousin. She was utterly pleased with herself as she rang me up, and I happily paid, because I knew something she didn't.

Today was the day for the weekly deep cleaning of the cages at the clinic. *Somebody* was going to have to get down and scrub all kinds of bodily fluids and hair from the floors, and we had a brand-new volunteer starting in just a few hours.

This was going to be *great*.

Jaclyn handed me my receipt with a flourish, and in return, I gave her a big smile.

"Ms. Love... I'll see you later this evening."

～

Something wasn't right.

So *not* right I couldn't even properly enjoy the vengeance aspect of making Jaclyn clean those cages – though her gagging and complaining were vaguely satisfying, from what I *could* hear.

When my stomach wasn't krumping.

It only seemed to get worse and worse as I worked through the days' patients, struggling to keep my composure. I was busy trying to remember if I'd accidentally asked for cheese or something on my sandwich at lunch, when something else occurred to me.

The ice cream shop.

"Oh she's *for real* petty," I muttered to myself, holding my stomach as it complained yet again, about what I now suspected was an abundance of unauthorized dairy consumption. Well... there wasn't shit to suspect. These bubbling guts were familiar as hell.

And there was no doubt in my mind she'd done that shit on purpose.

This was too far.

You don't get a nigga back like *that*.

Once the last patient had left for the day, I went up to the front desk, catching Jaclyn there alone. Char had been excited about how easily Jaclyn picked up the front desk procedures – probably because she was a business owner herself – and had been glad for the chance to leave earlier than usual, knowing Jaclyn had the basics under control.

I was glad too.

I didn't need any collateral damage from what was about to happen.

"You ain't right, you know that?" I asked, crossing my arms as I posted up in the entryway that led to the desk.

Jaclyn looked up from what she was doing to narrow her eyes at me. "What are you talking about?"

"I feel like you know."

"I feel like this is a stupid conversation. I'm about to go home after I finish the paperwork for the new dog that came in today, but I need you to sign off on my hours, before you forget."

I smiled. "Oh, so you have a few more minutes to be here at the desk then, huh?"

Her eyebrow lifted. "Um... yeah?"

"Perfect."

Still smiling, I turned right there in the door and farted, long and hard and loud, letting out all the gas I'd been struggling to hold for the last hour while my stomach danced the macarena.

"*Oh My God!*" Jaclyn shrieked, rolling backward as far as she could in the office chair. "What the *fuck*, Kadan?!"

I shrugged, wrinkling my nose. "If I have to suffer, so do you – you're the one that did this shit to me. Damn, that's *bad* too."

Across the small space, Jaclyn gagged, pulling her shirt up over her nose. "What the hell do you mean I did this to you?!" she asked, her voice muffled by the fabric covering her mouth.

"Don't try to play dumb – oh, here we go again," I grunted, letting loose when the urge hit me again.

"I cannot. I *cannoooottt*," Jaclyn shrieked, standing up to pace around as she coughed. "Move, let me out of here!"

"Oh we ain't going nowhere sweetheart – this is what happens when a customer asks you for dairy free, but you let petty win. Damn – here comes another one, you might wanna take cover."

"You think *I* did this?" she asked, between dry heaves, as she leaned over the desk into the waiting area, trying to gasp for fresh air. "Why would I?!"

"The same reason your ass has done *anything*," I countered. "And I don't think, I know. I should sue your ass for poisoning me."

"Okay hold up!" she urged, holding up her hands as I farted, yet again. "Oh my *God*, that sounded so wet, *ugggh*."

I frowned a little. "Yeah, I got a lil concerned at the end of that one, but it does me so much good to know you're smelling this too."

"I would *not* have given you the wrong ice cream on purpose!" she defended, still coughing and trying to wave away the rotten smell. "If anything, your indecisive ass confused me!"

"Oh so it's *my* fault?!" I asked. "Aiight." Her eyes went wide as I stalked toward her, turning right in her direction to let out yet another round of gas as she tried to get away, out the door.

But this was *easily* the worst one.

I blocked the door as she coughed and gagged, complaining of feeling light-headed.

"Oh my *God*, did something die in you?!" she whined, collapsing into her seat when I wouldn't let her out the door.

"Yeah. *Joy.* Because you tricked me."

"I did *not* trick you."

"So you say."

"Because that's what happened!" she insisted, coughing again as she slumped in the chair, defeated.

Mission accomplished.

She flinched as I approached the desk, but I moved past her, grabbing a pen to sign my initials on the schedule she needed for her community service.

"It was great working with you today Ms. Love," I told her, words she met with rolled eyes. "Flip the lock on your way out."

SIX

JACLYN

"So you becoming one of them lesbians now?"

"Donny! I told your ass not to say that!"

"I'm a grown ass man, Josephine, I done seen too much to not say what I got to say while I can still say it. You not about to silence me, woman!"

"It's offensive, fool!"

"I ain't said nothing was wrong with being a lesbian, I just asked if she was one! Now if *you* think lesbian is an insult, that sounds like a personal problem to me. Check your implicit biases, Josephine."

"You keep ya ass off the social medias, how about that?"

"So I won't be able to tell you how problematical you are? I see right through ya damn agenda woman."

"I got ya damn agenda Donny, kiss my *problematic* ass."

"Put it up here, I will, don't you test me girl."

What the hell is happening right now? I thought, raising an eyebrow at my cell phone screen as my parents continued their back and forth, both knowing damn well they'd be all over each other as soon as this video call ended.

Miss Thing sauntered up to me on the couch, stretching her furry orange and white body before she made the quick leap onto the seat beside me to peer into the camera too.

"*See there?!*" my father bellowed, his eyes lighting up like he'd answered some impossible question. "She got the cat all on the furniture – tell me the truth Jac, you let the cat kiss you in the mouth?"

I frowned. "What the he—*no*," I insisted, as she climbed into my lap, nuzzling her head under my chin like she was trying to make a point. "Nothing about the cat goes near my mouth."

"*That's what she said,*" my father giggled, earning twin groans from me and my mother. "I thought only lesbians got cats instead of getting a man, ain't it?"

I sucked my teeth. "Daddy, you gonna act like you don't know how the *last* man I had turned out?"

"You didn't pick right."

"Wow, that's the version of this we're going with?"

"Is it a lie, Jaclyn?" He asked, eyes glittering with victory. "I'm not the one who moved in with a man with a wife and kids and dog and mortgage, so you've gotta help me out here, do I have it wrong?"

"I didn't know about *any* of that!"

My mother peered into the camera, brows drawn together in confusion. "Do you think that's a good defense? Cause it makes you sound…"

"Dumm-duh-duh-duh-dummm," my father filled in for her, cracking up at his own joke.

"Well this has been a wonderful use of my time." I quipped, and of course they laughed at that too.

"Awww, look at her face Donny I think we hurt her feelings. We hurt your feelings sweet pea?" My mother asked, concerned.

"No," I answered her, shaking my head. None of us would've survived growing up in a house with Donald and Josephine Love without a healthy sense of sarcasm and reasonably thick skin. Between the two of them, they had jokes for everything, and there wasn't much of anything considered off-limits. "But I do have to go. This degree isn't going to earn itself, and I have work to do."

"So the graduation is on again?"

I frowned. "The graduation was *always* on. When was the graduation not on?"

"When your cousin had to go get you out of that jail for messing up that boy's car," My dad answered, wagging a finger at me. "How many times have I told you to do your drinking at home?"

"And how many times have *I* told you to always check for a camera?!" My mother added, shaking her head in disappointment. "You gotta be careful honey, you know that judge don't like you, and you *always* get her. I think she *chooses* your cases. I think she has it out for my baby. Next time, I'm gonna talk to her."

I wanted to scream, but I held it in. "There won't *be* a next time Mama," I assured her. Assured myself. "I'm done with that life. I just want to get my degree and make good ice cream."

"Yeah," My father nodded. "That judge is one fine piece of woman. Don't you worry about it Josephine, I'll have a word with her."

"So you weren't listening to me at all, huh? Cool, cool, cool," I said, at the same time my mother threatened to go upside his head.

Ten minutes later, I'd managed to get them off the phone, but my focus was shot. I leaned back into my couch cushions, only intending to rest my tired eyes for a few moments. That "few moments" flew by though, and the next thing I knew, it was dark in the apartment when I opened my eyes.

Shit.

I scrambled for my cell phone, trying to see the time. I had too much on my plate to waste hours sleeping during the day, but luckily nothing at *Dreamery* seemed to have burned down, and I hadn't had any time scheduled at the clinic today.

The only thing I'd lost was valuable schoolwork hours.

I pulled myself up from the couch to get some lights on. Late or not, the work still had to be done if I wanted to have my name called with the other non-traditional students at the graduation service.

I refilled my tumbler of water at the fridge, then headed back to my computer.

That was when I saw Miss Thing in a heap on the floor.

While she was prone to curl up and take a nap anywhere she felt like, I instantly knew something more was wrong. Her eyes were half closed, her leg in a weird position, and I don't know how, but I just felt it... she couldn't move.

"No, no no no no, nooo, *Miss Thing*," I whispered, running a hand over her head. "You're not about to do this to me honey." When I touched her, she lifted her head a little in response, letting out the weakest *meow* I'd ever heard. It made my stomach twist inside out.

I grabbed my phone to call the clinic, groaning when I realized it was already past closing. Miss Thing let out another of those pitiful sounds, making it supremely easy for me to decide my next step.

I texted Kadan.

After a few seconds of thought, I decided on...

"Hey nigga."

It didn't take long at all for him to text back.

"The fuck you want? – Dicky McStrangerballs"

I rolled my eyes, glancing at Miss Thing before I typed out a reply.

"Something is wrong with Miss Thing. She's not really moving, but she looks like she's in pain or something."

"What happened? – Dicky McStrangerballs,"

"She was like this when I woke up, so… I don't know?"

"Of course you don't. – Dicky McStrangerballs,"

"Kill the shade and just tell me what to do. Don't you care about animals?"

"I do care about animals, which is why I'm not

telling YOU a thing. I know how you roll. What's your address? – Dicky McStrangerballs,"

Instead of giving in to asking him what the hell kinda rolling he thought I did, I texted him the address, letting my concern for the cat overrule my attitude. He texted that he was on his way a few moments later, and that was the first time I felt like I could breathe since I saw her on the floor.

*Bitch you **are** turning into a cat lady, wow.*

I sat there with Miss Thing until Kadan's knock sounded at the door. I wanted to take my time, and make him wait, but the cat looked so pitiful I put the petty aside to let him in.

I *realllly* wasn't expecting him to look so good.

I'd seen Kadan naked, I'd seen him dressed for work, I'd seen him after the gym. What I *hadn't* seen was this... *Netflix and Chill* Kadan, in a black tee and gray sweats and a hat pulled low over his eyes.

Dick Appointment Kadan.

At least, that's what it would've seemed like if it weren't for the medical bag in his hand.

"Where's my patient?" he asked, an additional reminder of why he was actually there that spurred me to step aside so he could come through the door.

"She's over on the floor in front of the couch," I told him, closing and locking the door as he headed in that direction. I followed, but hung back, trying to give him room to do what he needed to do, but he looked up at me like I was crazy as he knelt on the floor.

"You gonna just stand there and watch, or help me?"

My eyes went wide. "Um... help, I guess, but I have no idea what I'm supposed to do."

"Just hold her," he said. "And keep her calm."

I lowered myself to the floor and gently pulled Miss Thing into my lap. I watched, awed, as Kadan carefully examined her while speaking soft, comforting words. It was sweet the way he handled her, patiently, even when she tried to nip and scratch at him when he made it to her right hind paw.

"What the hell are you feeding her?" he asked, sitting back when he was done.

"Not that stuff you gave me. I feed her Arcana," I told him, proud of myself for having researched and found the best food.

He raised an eyebrow at me as he ran a soothing hand over Miss Thing's head. "I should have been clearer. *How much* are you feeding her is the better question. She's gained a *lot* of weight since I saw her last month."

"Happy weight," I defended, pulling her close to my chest. "Of course she gained weight, she's getting steady meals now!"

Kadan shook his head. "Too many meals. She's got a sprain, Jaclyn. Probably from moving awkwardly with a sudden increase in weight. She's used to being light on her feet, and thinks she can still move like that, but she can't. *Especially* coupled with the injury she already had."

I sucked my teeth. "It sounds to me like you have an issue with a woman with meat on her bones."

"Not at all," Kadan laughed. "I'm in full support of a healthy weight, but this is too fast of a pace. She needs to be getting more exercise – once the sprain heals – and a consistent diet, on a schedule – she shouldn't be allowed to constantly graze from a bowl that stays full all day."

I opened my mouth to deny I was letting that happen, but he looked pointedly at the – full – food bowl next to the kitchen.

"Fine," I groused. "I guess *you* don't believe thick thighs save lives either, huh?"

"Not for cats," he chuckled. "For now, she needs to rest. She likely fell, and it dazed her a bit, but she'll be fine. I'm almost positive it is just the sprain, but if she hasn't improved in a few days we can bring her in for an x-ray. Okay?"

I nodded. "Yeah. Okay."

He took Miss Thing from my arms, depositing her in the cat bed near the window. I watched as he gathered up the few things he'd taken from his medical bag and put them away, then followed him to the kitchen to wash his hands.

"Thanks for coming to check on her for me. I didn't realize a vet really *would* make an after-hours house call for free."

"Free?" he raised an eyebrow as he soaped his arms up to his elbows. "This shit wasn't free, just like that ice cream. I have every intention of taking your money."

I scoffed. "Seriously? All you did was poke her a lil bit and call her fat!"

"I diagnosed the problem." He smirked as he started rinsing away the soap, then moved aside so I could wash my hands too. "If it makes you feel better, you can give her an ice pack, but most cats won't let it stay in place anyway."

"Thanks for that," I told him, hoping he picked up on my sarcasm as I handed him a few paper towels. "Now get out."

"Damn, I don't get a tour or anything? I can't go lock myself in *your* bedroom like you did in my spot?"

"It was a misunderstanding," I defended, drying my hands. "Are we still focused on that?"

He shrugged. "Considering I was the one who left the misunderstanding with a black eye, I think we can focus on it as long as I want to."

"You *farted* on me," I countered. "Surely that's restitution enough."

"Nah, not when you're the one who gave me dairy."

"I *told you* that was a mistake! Your indecisive ass confused me!"

Kadan's eyebrow went up. "Is that how you'd defend yourself in court after giving the wrong customer peanuts? You were just *confused*?"

"So you're going to sue me now?" I asked. "That's the scenario we're working with here?"

"Nah," he shook his head. "That's not the plan."

"But there *is* a plan." My eyes narrowed at him, annoyed by his calm demeanor and handsome face. "Tell me what it is. Tell me *now*."

"I never said there was a plan."

"But clarifying that something *isn't* 'the plan' leaves a clear implication that there *is* a plan."

"I didn't say that though."

I groaned. "But you implied it!"

"Did I imply it, or did you assume? You know what they say about assuming, right?" he teased, his face pulled into an impossibly sexy, impossibly frustrating smirk.

Ughhh.

"You know I'm not scared to fight you, right?"

He laughed, and shook his head. "Yeah, actually. I do."

"Then stop playing with me!"

"Ain't nobody playing with you," he laughed harder. "Your ass is paranoid because you know you're wrong."

"I haven't done anything!"

"Your criminal record would beg to differ."

For some reason, that shit knocked the air out of my lungs.

Logically, I knew he didn't mean any harm, we were just going back and forth. But the truth was… it was embarrassing. As much as I loved myself, I wasn't even remotely proud about my past, or the fact it was documented in detail for everyone to see how much of a fuckup I was. I wanted to put it behind me. Was *trying* to put it behind me.

It felt really, really, *not* good to be reminded of it.

"Hey…"

Kadan's voice was different now, with none of the amusement from a moment ago. Quickly, I fixed my face, not wanting the hurt to show, but it was too late.

"My bad," he said, taking a step toward me. "I didn't mean to take it too far."

I shook my head. "It's fine. It's whatever," I said, even though it wasn't. I couldn't be mad though, because I'd earned my record – none of it was a lie. I *wasn't* mad.

I was disappointed in myself.

"Thank you for coming to check on Miss Thing," I said, trying to send the message it was time for him to go. "I'll make sure she rests up."

He didn't move though.

"Wow," he spoke instead. "You're for real sensitive about that, aren't you? Why?"

I frowned. "Why the hell do you care?"

"Is there something wrong with giving a shit about other people?"

"No," I answered. "But there's something *weird* about it. You don't even like me."

"I never said that, but you punched me in the eye. And kneed me in the dick."

"So we're back on that again?"

He shrugged. "It's a hard thing to forget."

"Okay so what do I have to do to get us past this, huh? Are you like a toddler or something, before you can move on, you need me to kiss it and make it better?"

His face twisted in surprise. "You offering? Cause *hell yeah*."

"I was talking about your *face*, fool!" I laughed, pushing him away as he walked up on me. "I don't want your lil raggedy dick near my mouth!"

He let out a bark of laughter. "Little? *Raggedy?*" he put a hand to his chest. "*I* recall you saying it was an award-winning dick. Gold medal dick at the *Dicklympics*."

I held up a hand. "What I *actually* said was 'blue-ribbon', please get it right."

"Gold medal, blue-ribbon, same difference. Either way, you said it then, so don't be fronting on my mans now."

"Ain't nobody fronting on you, Kadan," I laughed. "The truth of the matter is, I don't have complete information to grade your dick *anyway*."

His facial expression changed, focused. "Okay, you have my attention. What else you need?"

I crossed my arms, meeting his gaze. "Well, among my girls and I, there are three parts to the score. The look of the dick, the performance of the dick, and the *trouble* factor."

"What's the trouble factor?"

I grinned. "Whether the look and performance are worth the trouble of dealing with the person the dick is attached to."

"What's my trouble factor?" he asked, smirking.

I smirked right back at him. "I'm not fucking you, so I wouldn't know."

"But if you *were*, what would it be?"

"It's not something I can guess, dude. I don't know you like that – don't know about your unstable exes or whoever you're dealing with now, have no idea what kinda stamina you have, or what your stroke is like. Hell, I don't even have enough data for a full visual report, because you weren't hard. I don't *really* know what you're working with on any level."

Kadan scoffed. "So you spark my interest then leave me hanging. That's cold."

"Sorry Dr. Davenport, but unless you're trying to submit the incomplete data, I got nothing for you."

His eyebrows lifted, and he pulled his lip between his teeth. "So submitting the missing data *is* an option?"

I raised my shoulders, just slightly. "I *am* always interested in qualitative research. For the good of humanity, you know?"

"Absolutely," he nodded, closing the distance between us again. He put his hands on the counter on either side of me, boxing me in. "Who am I to get in the way of your pursuit of the greater good?"

I grinned as I tipped my head back, looking into his face. His eyes were shadowed with lust, enough to make my thighs clench. "Are we doing this?"

He leaned in, bringing his face toward mine. "You tell me…"

"Nah," I said. "*You* tell *me*," I countered, slipping my hands between us, into the waistband of his sweats. I cupped him through the soft fabric of his boxers, grinning in his face as he grew harder – and bigger – in my hand.

"*Hell yes,*" he growled, prompting me to let out a squeal as he grabbed and picked me up. I wasn't anybody's definition of dainty, but he hooked my legs around his waist with ease, then looked me right in the face and said, "Point me to your bedroom."

So of course, I did.

"Wait, hold up!" I said, stiff-arming him once he'd dropped me onto the bed and attempted to climb on top of me. "This is *purely* for research, right? You're not going to mess around and get attached?"

He shrugged. "I won't if you won't," he answered, then pulled off his shirt and hat, tossing both aside before he went for the hem of my oversized *Blakewood* tee. I let him strip me down to nothing, and then while he was getting rid of the rest of *his* clothes, rummaged around in my nightstand for condoms.

Couldn't conduct an experiment without the proper precautions.

After donning the condom, Kadan spread my legs wide, positioning himself between them before he sank in. I gripped handfuls of my sheets as he lowered his chest to my breasts, and his mouth to mine.

I hadn't expected kissing to be a part of the plan.

But as soon as his lips touched mine, I was glad for them. They were as perfectly kissable as I'd expected, and he was good at it. *Really* good.

A low moan escaped my throat as he stroked me deep, matching the movement with his tongue in my mouth. One of his hands tangled in my locs, the other kept a handful of my ass in his grip as he moved, creating a steady pace of sweet friction.

I hooked my arms around his neck, rolling my hips with his, matching his pace as he stroked. And we kissed.

Deeper.

Faster.

Harder.

Those kisses came to an end as he sat back to hook my knees over his arms, spreading me open wide to go *even* deeper, *even* harder. My hands went to my breasts, cupping and squeezing my sensitive flesh as orgasmic pressure built in my core. His hands moved to my ankles, holding my feet high in the air as he plunged into me.

Deeper.

Faster.

Harder.

Until I came unglued, with a loud, keening cry I didn't care if my neighbors heard.

They'd deal.

Kadan didn't stop, still chasing his nut even as I came down from mine. He kept stroking, kept pounding, kept the waves of orgasm on a steady reverb through my legs as he kept moving, until he suddenly stopped, mouth wide open.

"*Ahhh shit!*" he yelled – *screamed* –loud as shit, as he collapsed to his elbows on top of me. I turned away, pressing my lips together as a laughed bubbled up from my stomach.

Jac… do not laugh in this dude's face.

"Goddamnit. *Goddamnit*," he groaned, in a strained voice that brought tears to my eyes. "Jaclyn please…*the cat…*"

I knew my pussy was good, but how in the world was I ever going to look him in the eyes again, knowing *this* was how he acted when he got some?

"*The cat… Jac… please…*," he begged, looking me right in the face, with glossy eyes.

"Damn," I blurted, before I could help myself. "Is it *that* good to you?"

"What? *No!*" he hissed, through gritted teeth. "The *cat*, Jaclyn. Miss Thing!"

I frowned. "*What?!*"

"She…" he blew out a deep, shaky breath. "She… she has… her claws in my ass."

As if she'd been waiting on her cue, Miss Thing hissed, announcing her presence in the room.

Well she'd already announced herself to Kadan, but I guess now it was time to let *me* know too.

Now that I understood why he was holding himself like a statue, I maneuvered from underneath him to see what the hell was going on. I flipped on the overhead fixture to give better light than what was coming from the lamp, and sure enough Miss Thing had latched herself to Kadan's ass.

I couldn't help it.

I laughed.

"*Can you get the cat off me!?*" he screeched, his voice in such a higher pitch than normal it made me laugh even harder between trying to soothe Miss Thing enough to carefully unhook her claws from Kadan's flesh.

"You know she did this to you cause you called her fat, right?" I asked, still struggling to keep myself together as I successfully removed her from his ass. It was a good thing he hadn't tried to snatch her off – he only had the holes from where she pushed her claw in now, but any sudden attempt to remove her would have made it much, much worse.

"She did this because you were moaning and hollering like I was killing you," he countered, out of breath, as he collapsed fully onto the bed. "*Fuck.*"

I kept right on chuckling as I deposited Miss Thing back in her designated spot, gave her a treat, then headed back to my bedroom, closing the door after myself this time.

"You know this shit ain't funny right?!" Kadan complained as I stepped into my bathroom to wash my hands.

"The hell it aint!" I called back. Once my hands were clean, I grabbed my first aid kit and went back to the doorway, holding it up. "You look like you could use some *ass*-sistance," I teased, drawing his gaze to where I was standing.

"Ms. Love, can you please quit playing and get your fine ass over

I THINK I MIGHT LOVE YOU

here and patch me up?" he asked, his eyes doing an appreciate sweep over my nude body.

I smirked. "Oh I'm *fine* now?"

"*Been* fine. Now please? I'm bleeding out."

"You are *not* bleeding out," I laughed, when I got back to him to look at those tiny pinpricks again.

Okay, they were a little bigger than pinpricks, but still.

"How are you a whole doctor – albeit an animal doctor – acting like a whole baby over this?" I asked, kinda enjoying the view as I used alcohol pads to clean his wounds. His ass was nice and muscled, probably why Miss Thing's attack hurt so bad, not enough soft fat to cushion the blow.

"Tease me all you want, that shit felt like taking shrapnel to the ass. That sprain must not be hurting her *too* badly."

I laughed. "You wanna tell me how you know what shrapnel feels like?"

"Cause I've felt shrapnel," he quipped back. "You see the tattoos, right?"

I had, but hadn't *really* looked at them. Now I did, noting here and there that the ink mimicked some I'd seen on Jay, who was also a veteran.

"*Oh*. Wow..." I mused, tracing one on his back I recognized as a medical symbol. "That's where you got involved in medicine I guess?"

"Yep. Worked my way up to medic, then got the hell outta there cause I was tired of seeing people die. Not that seeing animals die is a piece of cake, but..."

"Hits different. Yeah, I would imagine so."

I finished bandaging both his ass cheeks, then patted him to signal that I was done. He grinned at me as he turned over.

"Yeah. That's one way to put it."

For a moment, we were both quiet, taking in and admiring the other person's nudity. He was still wearing that condom – empty, since we'd gotten interrupted – and rock hard, sticking straight up.

"I hope you're not in *too* much pain," I told him. "I'm sorry Miss Thing got protective."

He chuckled, tucking his hands behind his head – getting comfy as hell in my bed. "No you're not. Your ass was laughing."

"I'm sorry, I thought that was… I thought that was just how you sounded and acted when you came, and I'm sorry, that shit was ridiculous. No lie, I was going to roast the fuck outta you with my sisters."

"Cold world," he laughed. "Cat messed up my score."

I giggled. "No, you did good. You presented well."

"Nah, it's tainted."

My gaze shifted from his teasing eyes to his hard dick, practically begging for my attention. When I met his eyes again, it was clear he was thinking the same thing I was.

"We could always run the experiment again…" I suggested, disposing of the packaging I'd used, then utilizing a fresh wipe for my hands. "In the interest of fairness, you know?"

His eyebrows went up. "Well I'm at a disadvantage now, with the injury… unless you'd be willing to provide some sort of accommodation?" he asked, as I climbed over him.

Once I'd gotten myself perfectly in line, I looked at him with a smile.

"Oh, don't you worry about that. I've got a *long* list of alternative research methods we can work through." I sank onto him, pulling a groan from both our lips. "Let's get started."

SEVEN

KADAN

So obviously I messed up.

Bad.

And the thing was, I couldn't even blame my inability to stay *away* from Jaclyn Love – due to her volunteering at the clinic – on my inability to stay *out* of her. Nah, I walked into that with my eyes *wide* open. I saw *everything*.

Which, of course, presented a new problem.

How to keep myself from going back for more?

It was one thing when all I had against me was my imagination – the fantasy of what she looked like underneath her clothes. But now that I was intimately familiar with that soft skin, those ample curves, plush thighs, pillowy breasts, tight pu...

Damn.

She got your ass bad.

So bad I was sitting in my place on my night off, beer in hand, wings on the coffee table, NBA on the tv, but I wasn't paying attention to any of that shit.

My mind was on Jaclyn.

I'd invited her over.

Obviously, she'd said no because she wasn't here, but it had taken a lot for me to push through and even ask, mainly because my ass knew better. I didn't *need* her over here, didn't *need* her scent permeating my space, didn't *need* to get drawn further into *her*. But even with all that in mind, the rejection still stung like a bitch.

"Ms. Love... I'm sure you already know this, but thorough research involves conducting your tests more than once. Varied times, varied conditions, varied settings, all that, you know?" I was nervous enough that my palms were sweating, which was... what the fuck?

Jaclyn turned from her post at the desk with that dazzling smile, clear amusement in her eyes. "As much as I appreciate a good ongoing scenario, I unfortunately have to decline. I am insanely busy, and I kinda want to graduate in a few weeks like I'm supposed to, so I kinda have to be on sabbatical. If you catch my drift?"

Immediately, I nodded. "Absolutely. Totally get it."

"Sorry," she said, like she meant it. "You're a gold medalist though, I'm sure you can find another research partner. Easily."

She was right.

I could.

But I didn't *want* a different "research partner."

See?

See?

One night of pussy, a week ago, and she had me in my feelings.

The ringing of my cell phone snatched me from my pity party as I reached to grab it from the table. The name on the screen brought an instant smile to my face.

"Aunt Cali," I greeted, picking up the remote to crank the volume on the TV down. "What can I do for my favorite Auntie today?"

On the other end of the line, she snickered. "Boy, I'm your *only* Auntie."

"That doesn't mean you're not my favorite."

"How could I *not* be?"

"If I didn't even like you."

That made her laugh again. "I'm a lovable person Kadan, everyone likes me."

"I can think of a large group of people who'd disagree," I countered back.

"And that's why they're where they are and I'm where I am," she said, with the signature sass that always amused the hell out of me. "Now stop getting me riled up so I can tell you this."

"Tell me what?"

"Guess who I ran into a few minutes ago?" she asked, sounding damn near giddy.

That meant it was one of my old teachers, an old classmate, or one of my old girlfriends that she managed to like.

"Uhh... Mr. Jenkins?" I said, pulling a name out of my ass, cause there were too many possibilities for me to *actually* guess.

"No! Deidre Daniels!"

Oh.

Oh.

No.

"Oh, is *that* right?" I asked, trying my best not to give even the tiniest inflection to suggest that was news I wanted to hear. Deidre Daniels didn't fall into any of the categories I'd mentioned before – she occupied the most exclusive group of all.

Women my Aunt Calista wanted me to make her pseudo-daughter-in-law.

"Yessss," Aunt Cali gushed. "And she was looking gorgeous as always. I know you remember her, don't you?"

Yes.

Yes, of course I remembered DeeDee with the double-ds.

Dee-Dee was fine as hell.

She was also *exactly* like my aunt, which was fine... for my aunt. The fancy parties and proper etiquette and high-society Black shit, that was all well and good, if that was what you were into. Deidre and Aunt Cali were *very* into it.

I was not.

Aunt Cali thought I'd never given Deidre a fair chance, but that wasn't it. Deidre and I had gotten down a bit as teenagers, before I went off to the service, and I even took a second dip when I came back. For a whole entire week, I subjected myself to her constant critique of everything from my haircut to my tats to my posture to my language to my choices at dinner to the clinic I wanted to work at. Everything was "shocking" or "disgusting" or "improper" or "ghetto", by which her ass meant "too Black."

I chose the most shocking, disgusting, improper, "ghetto" words I could string together to break *that* shit off.

I didn't need that energy.

And the thing was, I was sure she felt the same about me, but she idolized Aunt Cali, who saw *none* of those supposed flaws Deidre spent her time picking apart. Surely she saw them in others, but I was her only nephew, the treasured son of her "troubled" baby sister who was God knows where.

Between the two of them – Deidre and Aunt Calista – I was sure they thought I could be molded into their narrow definition of "Black Excellence", with a little refinement to my demeanor and appearance and job, but I was good.

I was already excellent as fuck if you asked me, but somehow no one ever did.

Damn shame.

"We should all get together for dinner soon," Aunt Cali suggested, bringing my attention away from my own musings and back to the phone. "Do some reconnecting."

Here we go.

"You know I don't get along with Deidre like that, so I can't imagine it would be a good time for anybody involved," I said, trying to put at least a *little* sugar on the fact that I couldn't stand Deidre.

Aunt Cali sighed. "You were practically still children the last time you even spoke. Surely you get along now, as adults?"

"I've interacted with her as an adult. It wasn't fun. I'll pass. But you should go, Auntie. Have a good time. And don't tell me *anything* about it."

"Kadan!" she scolded, with a huff. "I think you should reconsider. Deidre is a lovely young woman, who I'm sure would make a lovely life partner."

"For another nigga, sure."

"Language!"

Fucccck why did I answer this phone?

"Kadan Davenport, I am getting older," she started, and I closed my eyes, knowing where this was about to go. "I have done the best I could by you, in the absence of my sister, and now your father. Made sure you had a support system when you came back from that God-awful desert, ensured your education without any debt... you give me one *good* reason you can't indulge me in a single meal."

Shit.

Shit, shit, shit.

I just don't fucking want to wasn't going to fly, even though it was the truth.

Fine.

"I don't think my girlfriend would like it that much," I lied, using the first thing that came to mind. In my experience, if a woman wouldn't accept any other "no" for an answer, they'd at least hesitate a bit over another woman's "property".

Or so I hoped.

"*Girlfriend?!*" Aunt Cali exclaimed, and I instantly realized my mistake. I was already kicking myself, even before the, "Oh my word, when did you get a girlfriend, when were you going to tell me, who are her people, I have to meet her!" left her mouth.

That's what you get for lying.

"It's still early," I claimed, trying to backtrack. "We're not quite at *meet the family* seriousness yet, but I don't want to make her uncomfortable, knowing what your intention is for getting me and Deidre together."

Aunt Cali sighed. "Of course, I understand. You're trying to neutralize your father's negative influence by not allowing the philandering nature you inherited from him to rule you."

"Chill, Auntie," I warned. Not that she wasn't justified in her disdain for my father – his hoe antics couldn't have been particularly healthy for my mother's mental state, and as judgmental as Aunt Cali was, she was protective of her sister.

That was still my father though.

"Is that not what you're saying, Kadan? If it isn't, please explain it to me."

"I want as little drama as possible. How's that?" I asked. "Nothing to do with my father, everything to do with *me*."

"Fair enough. I want to meet this young lady. How does she feel about your work? Does she understand the altruistic appeal of it?"

"She doesn't care how much money I make," I replied, since that's what she was *really* asking. That wasn't technically a lie I guessed, since any woman I gave that title *wouldn't* be pressed about my job title.

"I didn't say anything about *money*," Aunt Cali whined, feigning offense. She may not have used that word, no, but that was the underlying question. "Does she like animals? Visit the clinic?"

"Sometimes."

"Hm," she replied, in a way that made me shake my head. Not even a whole word, just a loaded sound of disapproval from deep in her throat – the obvious implication being that an *acceptable* woman for me wouldn't deign to visit a community-sponsored animal clinic.

Or be okay with me working there in the first place.

"Kadan, you understand that I only want the absolute *best* for you, right?" she asked, like she knew she was pushing it too far. "I know you think I'm stuffy, and boring, but the truth is that your uncle and I live a good life – I want that for you as well. You're about to be thirty-five. It's *time* for you to settle with a good woman, from a good family, and—"

"I don't think we have the same definition of *good*, Aunt Cali," I interrupted her. "But I *do* believe you mean well. You just have to understand that I'm going to choose who I choose. *If* I choose."

"Now see, you're trying to give me a heart attack now."

I chuckled. "Nah, never that. Just trying to prepare you."

"Well, will you at least be bringing her as a date to the alumni ball?"

Shit.

"I will ask her. That's all I can offer for now."

"Mmmhmmm. Well you let her know I'm looking forward to meeting her."

"Of course Auntie. Consider it done."

She spent the rest of the call inundating me with details about luncheons and alumni meetings and a bunch of other boring shit I didn't have the heart to tell her I didn't care about. But, to her credit, she was beating me down with too much information for my thoughts to return to Jaclyn... at least until we hung up the phone.

Inexplicably, I found myself wondering if Jaclyn's parents were on her ass about "settling down" – if that's why she was working so hard to finish school before summer. She was only in her mid-twenties, but I knew how the shit went for women – that was around the time they started getting the "husband and babies" pressure.

But she didn't strike me as the type to care about all that.

Actually she struck me as the type to outright reject it.

I wasn't supposed to be letting her strike me as *anything* though.

I turned off the TV and pulled myself up from the couch, intent on clearing my thoughts. A shower, then bed, then sleep, where hopefully I wouldn't encounter Jaclyn.

Or hell, Deidre.

Or hell... *both*.

I shuddered, then unlocked my cell phone to enter a search term I knew was ridiculous, but I'd take whatever advice I could get on getting my ass to sleep without dreaming.

F*uck.*
Fuuuuuck fuck fuck fuck.
I was sitting in my office at the clinic when the sound of a car drew my attention to the window. It was lucky – lucky as *hell* – that history had made me more aware of my surroundings than I might normally have been, because otherwise I might *not* have noticed my Aunt Cali stepping carefully out of her Mercedes in the parking lot of the animal clinic, stopping to check her red-bottoms before she started moving with purpose toward the building.

Hence, all those *fucks* from earlier.

I moved as fast as I could, dashing to the front desk, where Jaclyn was filing paperwork for new patients since the waiting room was quiet today.

"Hey!" I called, startling her so badly that I was met with raised fists as she turned in her chair.

"*What?!*" she snapped, pressing a hand to her chest when she realized it was me.

"I need a favor – can't explain a lot, but I need you to pretend to be my girlfriend right quick, so my Aunt doesn't try to marry me off into some Black Stepford shit."

Jaclyn's pretty face pulled into a frown. "Aren't you grown? Like grown as hell?"

"Your parents don't ever get in your shit like you're still a teenager?" I countered, peering toward the doors where Aunt Cali would be appearing any second.

"Well yeah, I guess," she admitted. "Whatever. What's in it for me?"

"I'll sign off on a weeks' worth of your volunteer hours, while you're studying, or running your business, or whatever."

Her eyebrow lifted as she smirked. "That's a crime."

"Something you're *very* familiar with," I reminded her. "We got a deal or not?"

She put her finger to her chin, looking up to the ceiling as she pretended to consider it.

While I watched Aunt Cali approach the front door.

"*Jaclyn.*"

"Fine," she chirped, wearing a big smile.

"Good, cause she's here right now," I hissed, wrapping an arm around her waist as I pretended not to see Aunt Cali coming through the door. She felt comfortable as hell against my body, at least until she glanced into the waiting room. Then, her body stiffened as she turned to look at me, eyes wide.

"*That's your auntie?!*" she half-mouthed, half-whispered. When I nodded, her eyes got even bigger. "*Bruh, trust me, this ain't the lie you wanna tell!*"

"*We have a deal!*" I shot back, then looked past her, to where Aunt Cali was standing, a pair of designer sunglasses dangling from her fingers. "*Auntie,*" I greeted. "What are you doing here?"

She didn't even hear me.

Or if she did, she didn't react – she was too focused on Jaclyn, who turned to fully face her. "*Hey Auntie,*" she quipped, putting on a big, obviously fake smile that made my Aunt's nostrils flare.

"You know this person, Kadan?" Aunt Cali asked, her jaw tight as her attention shifted to me. I knew she was going to disapprove of any girl I put in front of her that wasn't already pre-approved, but *damn*. Neon pink scrubs aside, Jaclyn "looked" the part. She was pretty as hell, well groomed, all that. My best guess was that Aunt Cali had come here *hoping* to run into my "girlfriend", and was already prepared to be an asshole to her.

The problem with that though… Jaclyn would give that asshole energy right back.

"Of course I know her," I answered, even though my gut was telling me I should choose a different course of action. That could've also been the cheese on my breakfast sandwich this morning though. "This is the woman I was telling you about a few days ago, remember?"

That constipated look on my Aunt's face deepened. "No. I don't."

"Quit it Auntie – this is Jaclyn Love. Jaclyn, this is my Aunt Calista."

Aunt Cali's nostrils flared as her eyes flashed toward Jaclyn. "Oh, Ms. Love is *quite* familiar with me. Aren't you, sweetheart?"

Beside me, Jaclyn sighed. "Hey Judge Freeman."

"Hay is for horses, young lady," Aunt Cali snapped, her tone and expression as stern as if she was on the bench, not in the waiting room at an animal clinic.

"*Hello*, Judge Freeman," Jaclyn corrected herself. "Is there something I can do for you?"

"There most certainly is not," my aunt answered.

Jaclyn's eyes went to Aunt Cali's head. "You sure? We're good with pets."

Oh, shit.

"Is this some sort of joke to you? Some twisted retribution for your sentence? You've decided to corrupt my nephew?" Aunt Calista asked, her light brown skin darkening to a fairly distinct red tint.

"*She's the one who gave you that harsh ass sentence?!*" I hissed in Jaclyn's ear.

"*I told your ass this wasn't it. Her name was on the paper you signed!*"

"*I didn't actually read that shit!*"

"Ahem!" Aunt Cali cleared her throat, bringing our attention back to her as she looked back and forth between us. "I'm waiting on an answer."

"No," Jaclyn said. "No one is trying to corrupt Kadan – I didn't even know he was your nephew. But I wouldn't be here if it wasn't for you, so thank you for putting me in his path."

My aunt made that same disgusted sound she'd made on the phone the other day, then looked to me. "Is *this* who you're bringing to the alumni ball? With her *record*? You do know she has a *record*, right?"

I THINK I MIGHT LOVE YOU

"I prefer to focus on the fact that she's a successful business owner, and right on the verge of a college degree," I answered. "And of course, the fact that she's gorgeous," I added, throwing syrup on it to pull my aunt's focus to Jaclyn's positive qualities, since she was apparently familiar with the other ones.

Jaclyn turned to me with a smile. "I am, huh?" she asked, pursing her lips before she lifted them, obviously prompting me for a kiss, which of course I gave.

And lingered on.

And enjoyed a little too much.

"*Well*," Aunt Cali huffed, planting her sunglasses back on her face like she was trying to block us out. "I came here to ask you to join me for lunch, Kadan, but it seems I've lost my appetite."

"Good luck with that," Jaclyn said, before I could respond with something less antagonistic.

Aunt Cali's eyes narrowed, and she shook her head. "Kadan... we'll talk."

And then she was gone.

"That did not go like I expected it to," I said, watching Aunt Cali as she stomped off.

"Yeah," Jaclyn said, unthreading herself from my arms. "You did not think that shit through. At all."

"I didn't. *Fuck*."

Jaclyn leaned against the front desk, arms crossed. "Yeah. *Fuck* is right. I tried to warn you when I saw her. If you'd given me a *real* heads up, I could've told you that lady cannot stand me, and now she's going to work *harder* to get you with some *Talented Tenth Barbie* bitch. Your bad."

"Do you *have* to rub it in like this?" I asked, tossing up my hands.

She laughed. "No, of course I don't *have* to, but did you think I would pass up the chance? You're still gonna sign off on my volunteer hours, right?"

"You're coming to this alumni ball, right?"

Jaclyn sucked her teeth. "Uhh, that was *not* part of the deal."

73

"It is now – I know I'll get left alone if you're on my arm, seeing how she feels about you. Hell, she might even uninvite me."

"*That's* fucked up," Jaclyn snapped. "But it's also my kinda shenanigans, so whatever. I'm in. You're paying for everything though – dress, makeup, shoes…"

"Cool," I agreed.

"And three weeks off, not two."

"*Fine*," I agreed, extending my hand. "We got a deal?"

Jaclyn smiled, accepting my hand. "Yep. We got a deal."

EIGHT

JACLYN

"Hey!" I hissed into the phone. "If you have a friend who needs a job, bring them with you."

Emmi laughed as she agreed and ended the phone call, but I was deadass serious.

It was an emergency.

"Sorry about that delay," I told the next customer in the long ass line I had Joia to thank – curse out – for. She'd dropped another one of those mentions on her social media, which had people flooding to *Dreamery*, making it a much busier day than it usually would be. Which, normally, would be fine.

Not *today* though.

Today, I was paying for my hiring of a group of friends – one was pregnant, and had gone into premature labor today. It was her day off anyway though!

But.

The boyfriend/baby's father was *not* off today.

Neither was the best friend.

Guess where *none of them* were today?

At *Dreamery*.

Not that I could blame them. If the mother of my child or best friend went into labor too early, I'd be right there at the hospital too, fuck that ice cream! However, me understanding why they weren't here didn't put me in any less of a shitty predicament, when I only *had* one other employee.

Maybe I shouldn't have asked her to bring a friend, seeing how this went.

In any case, while I waited for Emmi – and a friend if I were lucky... maybe... - to arrive, it was just me, handling a growing horde of customers. Fortunately, Dreamery was adorable with it's all white and chrome interior, so plenty of people were distracting themselves with selfies and other flicks.

Which hopefully wouldn't bring in too many more people.

I had a Critical Leadership paper to finish.

I had to focus on the task in front of me though, serving the line of people at the counter properly, and with a smile. Scoop, smile, checkout, smile, send them on their way, smile. Over, and over, and over.

Until I caught sight of a familiar face in the crowd.

Ah shit.

The last thing I had time for right now was going back and forth with Kadan Davenport, but there he was anyway, a cocky smirk on his face as he sauntered past the line.

"*What the hell are you doing?*" I hissed at him as he came behind the counter, right up to me.

"You look like you could use help," he said, just loud enough for me to hear it. "So, tell me what I'm doing."

I narrowed my eyes. "You're helping me?"

"Why is that so surprising?"

"Why *wouldn't* it be?"

"Your customers are waiting," he reminded me, forcing me back to the reality of my situation. Emmi wasn't here yet, and that line was getting longer.

"Fine," I told him. "Scrub your hands, put on a hairnet and apron, and put on gloves."

Not even ten minutes later, I felt decidedly less frazzled, with Kadan at my side scooping up ice cream. He was a little slow, because he didn't know the layouts like I did, but he still kept the line moving – and did a nice amount of upselling too. We fell into a rhythm, and by the time Emmi arrived it was a lot less chaotic than it had been when I called her, frantic.

And she *did* bring a friend.

She took over while I gave her friend a quick lesson on serving the ice cream, and signed a little paperwork. At first, I thought Kadan had disappeared on me once my reinforcements arrived, but a scan of the shop showed me he'd stepped out to clear the tables and floor of discarded cups and napkins, and chat with my customers a bit.

How is everything about this man a turn-on?

Seriously.

Who the hell looks good in a hairnet and apron?

Kadan Davenport, that's who.

He was lowkey – highkey – sexy as usual, in sweats and a tee shirt under the apron. He was wearing that hat again too, and his silly ass had pulled the hairnet over it.

Still fine as hell.

I'd called to leave a message with Char that I wouldn't make it to the clinic today, because of the fiasco with the shop. I didn't think Kadan was even on staff for the day, but I was sure the message had gotten back to him. He'd probably stopped in to make sure I wasn't lying.

Maybe that was why he was helping.

He felt bad for assuming I was making it up.

Ha.

I knew *that* shit wasn't true.

Whatever his reasoning, he hung around until things slowed down, then followed me to my office. I peeled off my apron and headscarf, letting my locs fall free around my shoulders as he helped himself to my desk chair.

"Okay – you ready to explain what the hell you're doing here?" I asked, perching myself on the edge of the desk, facing him.

He shrugged, reclining back in my chair. "Just being a good Samaritan."

"Bullshit."

"Damn," he chuckled. "It's like that? That's what you think, that I'm not capable of being helpful out of the goodness of my heart?"

I raised an eyebrow. "I find it hella suspicious."

"Ms. Love, we work together, I'm subletting from your sister, you and I have been intimate, you're doing me the favor with my Aunt... I think we're at a place now where it shouldn't strike you as particularly odd that I'd come to your assistance when needed," Kadan reasoned.

"Still. Let's not forget all the shit that isn't so warm and fuzzy between us."

He scoffed. "Oh trust, I haven't. I still have nightmares about what that whole milk ice cream did to me."

"Yeah. Me too," I told him, shuddering over the thought. "Which is why I'm not sure I trust this whole *helpful* act."

A smirk spread over his lips. "Aiight real talk, Char said you'd called about not being able to come in cause you were slammed. So I came to be obnoxious. I was bored, nothing better to do, so why not go be a pain in Jaclyn's ass?"

"Like a child with a crush who doesn't know how to act?"

He shrugged. "Possibly. But once I got here, and I saw that you were *for real* slammed... was I supposed to just sit back and watch?"

"You don't work here, so why not?"

"I... I don't know. Maybe it's a military thing. Sometimes, the shit that needed to be done wasn't my job, but the shit still needed to get done. So you get it done."

He was looking at me.

Not flirtatiously, not really, just *looking*.

Focused.

I cleared my throat, and looked away. "That's right," I nodded. "You were in the army. I bet you were like a *hoe* hoe. There's no way you weren't."

"Oh I was," he laughed. "Everybody is though."

"So the stereotype is true? Everybody fucking everybody?"

He nodded. "With a few, and I do mean *few* exceptions, hell yes."

"Figures," I giggled. "So tell me something... you're an army veteran, subletting an apartment, working at a community pet clinic. You're tattooed, you curse, you hoop with Jason. How the *hell* did Judge Calista Freeman end up with *you* as a nephew?"

Kadan tossed his head back, Adam's apple bobbing as he laughed. "I'm sure she asks herself that same question on a daily basis."

"So you don't code switch for Auntie?" I asked, and he shook his head.

"Not at all, and she can't stand it, but I am who I am, and she's gonna love me anyway. Just like she is who she is, and I love her anyway. Even if I don't like her that much sometimes."

My eyebrows lifted. "Such as when?"

"Such as when she called me to complain about you," he teased, sitting up to scoot the chair closer. "Kadan Michael Davenport, do you know that woman has a *record*?! Fighting, vandalism, public intoxication, harassment, public nuisance, disturbing the peace, *more fighting!*"

I frowned. "She went through all my lil business, huh?"

"She didn't tell me *shit* I didn't already expect," Kadan laughed. "*But*, she was wrong for trying to put you out there like that, and I told her so. It wasn't cool."

"Wow, thank you for defending my honor, fake bae."

"I got you babe," he said, playfully grabbing me around the calf, and squeezing.

I was glad for my wardrobe choice of a cute spring wrap dress, even though my comfy Vans weren't the sexiest pairing with it.

My legs were freshly shaved though, at least.

"So is Judge Freeman your dad's sister, or your mom's?" I asked, shifting in my seated position on the desk.

"My mother's. My father – God rest his soul – was… let's say a rolling stone. You know, wherever—"

"He laid his hat was his home, I've got you," I nodded. "So your hoe-ness was inherited?"

"My mother and aunt like to think so," he good-naturedly agreed. "Aunt Cali couldn't stand him, but my mother loved his dirty draws, even though he wasn't good to her. Or *for* her. Sometimes I guess that's just the way shit goes though."

I sighed. "Yeah, unfortunately so."

"Unfortunate is the right word. I haven't seen her since his funeral. Barely talked to her either. Something about me reminding her too much of him or something. Some bullshit."

There was silence between us after he said that, while I tried to gauge the proper response. He wasn't giving the impression that this was a happy story by any means, but he also didn't seem particularly broken up about it.

Like he was numb to it.

"That's fucked up," was the response I settled on, and he nodded.

"Yeah. It is. Can't let the bullshit weigh you down though. What about you? You got mommy issues too?"

I shook my head. "Believe it or not… no. My parents are amazing, which I don't know… kinda makes me feel guilty?"

Kadan's brow wrinkled in confusion. "Why the *hell* would you feel bad about having great parents?"

"I don't feel bad about having great parents, I feel bad about my great parents having… me." My eyes went wide. "Wow, that sounds dramatic as fuck."

"It does," Kadan agreed. "I need you to explain that shit."

"Well, I can, because I've thought about it a lot. I think about it *all the time*," I admitted.

Why?

Who knows?

"It's like... my sisters, right? Jemma went to culinary school, travels the globe, knows foreign ambassadors and shit, never got in any trouble. Joia does her influencer thing, got her degree straightaway – again, never got in trouble. But then there's me. The fuckup. Constantly suspended in high school, had to do summer school, got kicked out of college the first go-round. I've had a record for the same length of time I've had a driver's license, but I'm not damaged. I'm not acting out. I'm not working through deep hidden trauma. I just am who I am, and that person is comfortable in handcuffs. Known on a first-name basis at the courthouse. It's *embarrassing*. Not for me though – for *them*."

Kadan stared at me for a moment, lips parted, then shook his head. "Nah, you're tripping," he said, brushing my words off. "I bet they don't even see it like that."

"Oh they definitely don't," I agreed. "But it doesn't change the fact that *I* see it. And the thing is, as much as I don't want to be *that* girl – don't want to ruin my life before I've even gotten started – *that* girl is just... who I am."

"Is it though?" Kadan scoffed.

I twisted my lips. "Man, you think I'm joking, but I'm dead ass serious. In high school – somebody messed with me, I was kicking ass. When I *left* high school, if somebody messed with me, I was kicking ass. *Now*, if somebody messes with me, I'm kicking ass. I ain't new to this, I'm true to this."

Kadan laughed. "I'm saying though – nobody can be mad about you defending yourself."

"That's not usually how the court sees it. Even if you weren't the one who started the shit, if you throw the first blow..."

"Well, *yeah*," Kadan chuckled. "I guess I'm trying to say that I get where you're coming from. Nobody wants to be messed with."

"And I got messed with *plenty*," I admitted. "*Flap Jacs*. That's what those little shitty ass kids used to call me, cause I was fat, right? I don't give a shit now, but back then, with my tall, slim, pretty older sisters? *Whooo*, it hurt like crazy. So I had to set a precedent. You fuck with *Flap Jacs*, oh we gone make pancakes, bitch, we gone smack, flip, and flatten," I said, laughing. "So shit, maybe I *was* dealing with some damage. But I never bothered anybody – I just wanted to be left alone. The rest of that stuff... got a little too drunk out with friends. Punched a dude in the face for calling one of my sister's out of her name. Ruined a motherfucker's car when I found out about his other family..."

"You've got hella stories, don't you?" he asked, and I nodded.

"Yep. I've had a colorful life, and now... I don't know. I'm just ready to settle into one specific palette. A *calm* palette."

"*Really?*" he asked, brows lifted. "I can't imagine that. At all. And not that it's up to me, but I can't understand why you want that?"

"You're right – it's *not* up to you."

I didn't want my private thoughts and desires challenged – I wanted him to shut up. And he did, but he didn't leave – he sat there staring at me, with this knowing smirk that made me want to squirm.

"What's so confusing about me wanting something different for my life?" I asked, letting curiosity get the best of me. "Why is not wanting to go to jail something to question?"

"That's not the questionable part," he answered immediately, like he'd just been waiting on me. "Limiting your colors. *That's* the part I don't get. That kaleidoscope is what makes you *Jaclyn*. It's what I was supposed to be keeping my ass away from."

"Wait a minute – *excuse me?*" I said, hooking my foot around the arm of the chair to roll him directly in front of me. "You're supposed to be keeping your ass away from me? Cause Auntie said so?"

He chuckled. "Nah, cause *I* said so."

"Why?"

"Because I have a definite type. Which hasn't been healthy for me in the past."

I planted my hands on either side of me on the desk, and leaned forward. "And what type is that?"

"Pretty ass thick women with bold personalities and attitude problems."

I narrowed my eyes, thinking about it for a second before I nodded. "That's an accurate description of me, I'll accept it. *After* you tell me about the big fine who hurt you and made you decide the rest of us were trouble."

"It wasn't like that," he laughed. "More like lack of self-control. Superior officers. Professors. Wives. Court reporters. Whatever. If I met her and I wanted her and she wanted me it was a done deal, consequences be damned. All the drama that came with it was part of the package."

"Ooooh. You weren't calculating trouble factors," I mused.

"I certainly wasn't. Got in some *shit* too. I've got fun memories and all, but that lifestyle of fucking whoever you want, whenever you want... some people can do that for the rest of their lives, but personally, I just want to be solid. No police at the door, no grade tampering, no threatening to put you on toilet duty, no suspicious cars following you home—"

"Oh, *damn*," I laughed. "You were like for real about the drama?!"

"Uh, *yeah*." He shook his head. "You have to remember, Jaclyn – I'm 34. I've been around longer than you. Time to get further around the block. Make mistakes of my own."

"Right, time to decide you wanted to be *solid*. But when I said I wanted to change *myyy* ways..."

He scoffed. "Nah, it's not the same thing though. You want to be a better person, make better decisions, by all means, do that. But from the outside looking in, and admittedly not having known you long... I think you've already done the work with that shit. Before this thing with your ex, when was the last time you'd been in trouble?"

"Years. My Aunt – Jason's mom... when she died, she left money for all the kids. Like a *chunk* of money. Mine was in a trust, since I wasn't twenty-five yet, but my parents could access it for me. I'd already fucked over college the first time, and I had no idea what I was going to do with my life. So I traveled a bit, went to see Blackwood. There was a *Dreamery* there. The owner happened to be on site, so I spent time talking with her, and by the time I got back to *Blakewood*, plans were already in motion to open a fourth *Dreamery* location. This one."

Kadan smiled. "So you just bought an ice cream franchise?"

"Yep," I nodded, returning his smile. "My Aunt Priscilla was like a second mom, and I wanted to do something that would make her proud. I decided right then that the fighting and all that shit... it *had* to be over. I had to grow up. I wanted to be successful with my business, and finish school, and have a family. I wanted to be solid too. And then Victor happened."

I pushed out a deep sigh, dropping my gaze to the floral swirls of the fabric across my lap.

"As much as I hate to defend your actions that night," Kadan started, drawing my gaze to his face. "Since they *did* result in me having a black eye... you can't let that make you feel like you're going backward. Should you have fucked up his car? Of course not. But that was some heavy shit – you *lived* with that dude, and to find out what he had going on behind your back... shit, I would've snapped too. You had a moment, for sure, but that moment doesn't negate the years you spent rebuilding your life."

I scoffed. "Then why does it feel like it?"

"Because you have your past – something that embarrasses you – smacking you in the face right now. The car thing wasn't an isolated event because of your past, so your punishment for it was heightened. It's affecting you every single day. A constant reminder. And it's messed up, but it is what it is. But it's also why I feel like there's not shit for you to change, not in the immediate. You already did the changing, it's just this messed up situation has your mistakes under a spotlight right now. Your colors are fine though. Fuck a monochromatic."

That pulled a smile back to my face. "You're only saying that because I'm a 'pretty ass, thick woman, with a bold personality and an attitude problem.'"

"And I love that shit, so maybe you're right," he admitted, laughing. "But, I'm also a big proponent of being who the hell you are. Alcohol abuse and violence aren't personality traits – I had to learn that from experience myself. So yeah, that shit can be dropped, but everything else? People can embrace you, or they can move on."

"Listen to your "Kadan, Fix My Life" face ass," I giggled, then giggled louder when he grabbed my legs again, pulling them apart to roll between them.

"That your way of telling me you think I'm wise?" he asked, letting my feet rest in the space on either side of his hips, and propping his elbows on my knees.

Completely casual.

Like this was a thing we did.

Like this was our thing.

"With your face this close to my pussy, I'll call you anything you want me to call you," I said, hiking an eyebrow at him.

Those words made him smirk, and he lifted his hands to my thighs, pushing the fabric of my dress up. "Is that an invitation?"

"One where you might want to consider the fact that this cookie has been baking *all day* before you accept it."

His face balled in confusion for a second before understanding relaxed his features, and he laughed. Instead of backing off, he reached under my dress, hooking the side of my panties as he met my gaze. "Lift up."

I did.

Without a single second of hesitation.

With my hands gripping the lip of the desk, and my feet still planted in the chair with him, I pushed myself up, letting him slide my panties down over my hips.

"You just wear shit like this on a regular Tuesday, huh?" he asked, smirking as he pulled the pretty purple underwear down my legs and over my feet.

I shrugged, way more aware than usual of the rise and fall of my chest as he raised my feet, planting them on the arms of the chair before he rolled in ever closer.

"Pretty underwear makes me feel good."

Kadan pulled the brim of his hat around to the back of his head, then lowered his mouth to kiss the inside of my knee. "Nothing wrong with it. I was just asking."

"So," I breathed, gripping the edge of the desk even harder as those kisses drifted toward the insides of my thighs. "Can I *just ask* why you turned your hat around? You trying to look cool or something?"

He stopped what he was doing to hook my thighs over his arms, spreading me so wide that my dressed hiked all the way up to my hips, leaving me open and exposed. Kadan made this ultra-satisfied sound in his throat, then met my eyes with a grin.

"I want to know how you taste. I turned my hat around cause I don't need anything getting in the way."

I didn't have time to respond before his mouth was on me.

Holy.

Shit.

My hands went immediately to his head, snatching the hat off so I could sink my fingers into the soft coils of his hair, holding his head in the right place.

Exactly the right place.

A deep shudder rushed from my lungs as his tongue lapped against me, sucking and pulling and prodding, coercing my body into producing fluids that were making it harder and harder to keep still on that desk.

"Oh *God*," I groaned, clenching my eyes tight as I tried my best to steady my ragged breathing. His fingers dug deep into the soft flesh of my thighs as he covered my clit with his mouth, torturing me with a delicious alternation between licking and sucking that made it hard to do anything except *feel*.

And *goddamn* did I feel good.

The rough, hot rasp of Kadan's skilled tongue was downright decadent, and I didn't bother trying to control myself from shamelessly rocking my hips into his face as he pressed deeper. My mouth fell open as exultations poured from my lips, and I'd never been more grateful for my employees' insistence on having the music in the shop up so loud.

It was drowning me out.

I *needed* drowning out, because Kadan's face between my legs was a *revelation*, and I wanted him to know it. After I came, with one hand gripping the desk, the other gripping a handful of his hair, he came up to do some necessary breathing of his own.

He grinned at me as he panted, his face and beard covered in the glistening evidence of what we'd just done. For a moment – *just* a teeny tiny moment – I understood why a woman might get on her knees and propose to a man.

I kiiinda wanted to lock that tongue down.

His gaze drifted up, to my head, and his smile grew even broader as he stood between my legs. "I like this energy," he declared, tugging down the brim of the hat – *his* hat – that I didn't even remotely recall placing on my head.

I couldn't formulate a response before he occupied my mouth with his. His tongue against my lips requested an invitation that I granted, greedily accepting him as he dipped into my mouth.

There was *nothing* timid about this kiss, this was the kiss of a man who knew exactly what he was doing, and exactly how I felt about what he was doing. How I felt was that he could do anything he wanted, including strip me out of my dress on top of my desk as if *Dreamery* weren't still open and conducting business hours.

As if I weren't supposed to be writing a paper.

My fingers were otherwise engaged though, with tugging off Kadan's shirt, then going for his sweats and boxers.

"Please tell me you have protection," I begged against his lips, breaking from kissing just long enough to make sure we could take this further than hunching.

I wasn't *above* hunching, and would hump this man to completion if I had to, but I *wanted* penetration.

Well.

At this point, *needed*.

"Wallet is in my pocket," he said, then resumed devouring my mouth while I dug the wallet out and fished out the condom.

Now I could do the big – *heh* – reveal on his dick, happy to see it was as perfect as it had been the other times I encountered it. I didn't waste any time getting it on him, and he didn't waste any time burying himself in me, then ridding me of my bra.

Never had I ever let a man strip me ass-naked in my office, let alone pull his dick out, but here we were, and I was *in love* with every second of it. That night at my house, I'd realized Kadan wasn't the type that just wanted to put his dick in you – he wanted to *consume* you, and I was willing to let him.

Give me all the slow strokes and hip action and long lusty looks, I silently urged as he stroked me like I was the girlfriend he'd claimed me to be – at least in front of his aunt. I hooked my legs around his waist, opening myself up more and simultaneously keeping him close as his hands cupped and squeezed my breasts, teased my nipples.

He dropped his mouth to my neck, sucking and biting as his hips moved to meet mine. My eyelids fluttered open, and I met someone's gaze.

My own.

Through the mirror on the wall.

I pushed out a relieved sigh that Kadan was too focused to even notice. He was too busy doing something with his tongue and teeth that felt amazing, but would undoubtedly leave a mark.

It was fine.

I took in my reflection – haphazard locs under his hat, glasses askew, glowing with sweat, mouth hanging open in pleasure while I got fucked in my office.

Completely unexpected.

And.... Totally fine.

Totally perfect, actually.

So of course someone knocked on the door.

"Go away!" I called, not even caring that I sounded like what was happening.

I *needed* the relief of the stress from today – hell, from the last few months-- and I had every intention of taking every piece of it.

Every stroke.

NINE
KADAN

"Wake up, punk."

Okay.

So.

Maybe what *actually* came out of Miss Thing's mouth was "*meow*", but I'd spent enough time around animals to gauge what that shit really meant. Waking up to a cat on my chest – an *actual* cat, not the cutesy nickname of what I'd have gladly welcomed first thing in the morning – was a clear intimidation tactic, and I was no fool. So while Miss Thing still had her claws put away, I gently removed her to the floor, then pulled myself up.

Jaclyn wasn't in the bed.

It only took a quick peek into her main living space to find her though, passed out at her kitchen counter with her laptop still open. There was a message up on her screen that made me approach, peering at the words - a confirmation message that she'd properly submitted whatever the assignment had been. Presumably right before she passed out.

I couldn't help myself from grinning over how peaceful she looked, glasses still on, full lips slightly parted, locs hanging halfway over her face. She was in just a tee shirt, most likely with nothing underneath, considering the circumstances behind me being here at all – a middle of the night text demanding I come through as her personal stress relief.

A text I'd eagerly answered because that was where I wanted to be anyway.

Fuck the games.

I was too old for it.

A quick glance at the time told me it was just past five in the morning – good timing for me to head back to my own place and get ready for the day before I headed to the clinic. From our conversation last night, I knew Jaclyn didn't have anywhere to be until a ten o'clock class. I didn't want to wake her.

But *I* had to leave, which meant it was necessary. I tried to do it as gently as I could, but she still popped awake like something was on fire, eyes wide as she took in her surroundings.

"What time is it?" she asked, groggy, as she straightened up, fixing her glasses on her face to check her computer.

"Like five-twenty," I told her. "You should go get in the bed."

"I need to check my answers first. I don't even remember submitting this." She stifled a yawn, then squinted at the computer.

I grabbed her hand. "You know that'll still be there after you get a couple more hours of sleep, right? You're obviously exhausted."

She shook her head. "I'm good, seriously," she insisted. "I have to check this, and then I have paperwork and stuff for *Dreamery* that I have to do before class. And then I have a shift at the clinic this afternoon."

"Not today. Tonight is the ball... remember? Today is the first of your two weeks off."

"*Three* weeks off," she corrected, with a raised finger. "Don't play with me."

I grinned. "Just making sure you're actually awake. You *do* know what day it is, right?"

"It's Friday," she said, rolling her eyes. "I got my afternoons mixed up. I'm a busy woman, remember?"

"Yeah, I do, which is why I want you to understand – you don't *have* to do this. If you'd rather catch up on sleep, or work…"

She scoffed. "And deny the public a chance to see me in my fly ass dress? Are you crazy?"

"I'm just saying…"

"Uh-huh. *Just* keep that nonsense to yourself, and make sure you're here to pick me up on time. You *are* still picking me up, right?"

"Of course," I agreed. "For now though, I gotta throw my clothes on and get out of here so I can get to the clinic."

"Ah. So *that's* why you woke me up," she correctly deduced, and I nodded, moving back toward her room, where I'd left my clothes.

Despite her protests when I suggested it, Jaclyn followed me to the bedroom, climbing into the bed to snuggle under the covers and watch me get dressed.

"How did we end up here?" she asked, half-muffled by the pillow she'd partially buried her face in. "You've really got your pale ass in my apartment, wow."

"Why I gotta be pale?" I chuckled, pulling my boxers on. "I got a lil melanin too, chill."

She laughed. "Yes, Kadan, you do, but your *actual* ass is hella pale."

"*Oh*. I don't think I've ever noticed."

"Why would you?" she asked, propping up on her elbow as I tugged my tee shirt over my head. "I only noticed because I was specifically looking… trying to figure out your appeal."

I stopped with my pants in hand, frowning. "Ain't shit to figure out shorty, I'm a handsome motherfucker and you know it."

"*Wow*," she laughed. "I wasn't suggesting otherwise, conceited much?"

"Nah, just a big fan of myself."

"I can *tell*," she assured me, in a dry tone. "You're an incredible example of Black male physicality, Kadan with the gold medal dick."

I grinned. "I'm ignoring your sarcasm cause your words are absolutely spot on. Thank you for noticing."

"Can you stop derailing my point?"

"You had one of those?"

I ducked the pillow she launched in my direction, then laughed as I pulled my pants back on.

"*Anyway*," she said. "I still want to know how the hell we got here, to DOD."

I raised an eyebrow. "DOD?" I asked, dropping into the chair in the corner to don my shoes.

"Dick-on-Demand. NetDicks. Dickazon Prime," she explained, with a distinct air of "*Duh*."

I shook my head. "Your mind..."

"Is amazing, I know," she said, beaming at me from her perch in the middle of the bed.

"That ain't the word I was looking for, but we'll go with that," I chuckled. "But to answer your question, in my humble opinion, we got here by being adults. We each have something the other wants, we admitted it, and now we both benefit. What's the problem?"

She shrugged. "I guess there isn't one. I guess."

"You guess?"

"It's not weird to you? That black eye I gave you was only like a month and a half ago. Yet, we've fucked several times, and I'm going to pretend to be your girlfriend at an alumni event tonight."

"And?"

"*And* we don't even really know each other," she argued. "What if somebody asks questions – how long we've been together, all that?"

"We tell the truth – well kinda. We met when I sublet your sister's apartment, kept running into each other, decided to see where it might go. That's barely a lie."

Hell it wasn't a lie at all.

But if I said *that*, she might freak out more than she was now.

"What if they ask *other* questions?"

"Anything more than that isn't their business, is it?"

93

She sighed, then flopped back into her remaining pillows. "I guess not, but still... it's hitting me right now how we've blurred these lines, and it's kinda fucking with me a little."

"What lines?" I asked. "I don't remember any lines."

Jaclyn sucked her teeth. "Dude, I distinctly asked you, before we messed around that first time, if you were gonna get attached."

"So that's what you think?" I looked up from lacing my sneakers. "You think I've gotten attached?"

She sat up again, looking fine as hell with her locs all pushed to one side, wearing a smug grin. "Are you gonna tell me you haven't?"

"Are *you*?" I countered right back. "Cause I remember when you asked me that, I said I wouldn't if you didn't, and I'm *nothing* if not a man of my word."

"You can't even keep your word to yourself, Kadan! You told yourself to stay away from me, remember? And yet, here you are."

That smirk stayed on her face as I stood, walking up to the bed. "Yeah," I admitted. "Here I am." I leaned in, kissing her forehead. "But only because you asked for me, babe." I stepped back as the smugness melted from her face, and her eyes went wide.

I shot her a wink.

"See you tonight."

~

"You look like you've got something heavy on the dome."

I looked up from scrubbing my hands to find Kenzo in the doorway.

"Usual shit man," I told him as I grabbed paper towels to dry off. "You finished with the Harris family hamster?"

Kenzo cringed, shaking his head. "Man... the hamster finished with me, if you get my drift."

My eyes went wide. "Bruhhh. Unicorn Nuggets went on to glory?"

"It was a ten-year-old hamster – hell yeah it went on to glory. Did you see how that littlest one was handling him? I would've died too, if my folks were letting a three-year-old dress me in doll clothes for YouTube. Had that hamster in a halter dress and boots when they brought it in!"

I cackled. "You're a fool, man."

"I'm serious!"

"Stop *lying*," I shook my head, still laughing.

"I'm *not*. Look," he insisted, pulling out his phone. Sure enough, somehow the Harris' three-year-old daughter, Holly, had gotten the hamster into a zebra-striped halter dress and boots – one hot pink, one lime.

Unicorn Nuggets had experienced a hard life.

"Why did they let her do that to him?" I asked, handing the phone back. "I knew they called and said he was looking bad, but they didn't say *shit* about him coming in dressed like he was fresh off the corner."

Kenzo shrugged. "I don't know man, but the older daughter was steaming mad when I came out to let them know. Smacked her sister right in the head. Everybody screaming."

I shook my head. "I have never been so glad to be on neuter duty," I told him. "Better *you* have to deal with that bullshit than me."

"That's jacked up," Kenzo laughed. "But, speaking of bullshit, check this out – Char went out on a date."

I raised my eyebrows, waiting to hear the bullshit. When he didn't say anything else though, I frowned.

"What's wrong with that? She's attractive, smart, funny… why are you surprised?"

Kenzo groaned as he leaned against the shelf that housed the gloves and other sterilized gear. "I don't know… I guess I thought she would…"

"Wait on you?" I asked, and got a nice shock when his dumb ass said-

"Yeah, a little."

"*No*," I insisted. "*No. Naaah*," I added, for emphasis. "That shit is over and done, these women aren't hanging around waiting on your ass to figure out if you want them anymore. I *told* you to go ahead and make that move, don't be salty now."

"Nah, I'm high-sodium as hell right now," Kenzo countered. "I was just waiting on the perfect time. This feels like a betrayal."

"You've gotta be kidding me," a female voice sounded, and both of our eyes went wide as Char stepped in through the open door, arms crossed. Her eyes were full of fire, but lucky for me, she pointed that anger straight at Kenzo.

I took a couple of steps back, and subtly pulled my phone out.

"You weren't waiting for the perfect time, Kenzo, you were putting me on hold. Cause you thought I'd wait while you played around, but guess what – *I won't*."

"I wasn't *playing*," Ken argued. "Seriously, I just... I didn't want to take it there until I was sure."

"So you expected me to sit around and twiddle my thumbs? I've done everything short of directly handing you my panties, and you *always* play it off. So, yeah, I'm going to date. A lot. And I'm going to stop thinking about *you*."

Kenzo grabbed Char by the arm as she turned to leave, stopping her. "Hold up – you're saying I don't even have a *chance* now?"

"Why should you?"

"Because of this."

Hell, *my* eyes went wide when he grabbed her by the face to kiss her – and not a peck, either. Homeboy went *all the way* in, and I was trapped in the corner, afraid to interrupt their moment.

When they pulled away from each other, Char squared her shoulders, and cleared her throat.

"Fine," she told him. "One date. And you'd *better* make it count."

With that, she walked off, with Ken right behind her, neither of them looking back to where I was. Grinning, I shook my head and stopped the video, sending it to Jaclyn along with the words, **"Your influence."**

For as long as I'd known Char, I'd *never* known her to be bold like that.

Jaclyn had been in her ear.

I was still chuckling about that whole thing by the time I made it back to my office to go through my paperwork for the day. I'd spent the whole morning preventing unwanted reproduction, and now I had to do the other part, so that we weren't putting too much on Char. Since I was taking away her help for three weeks due to my deal with Jaclyn, it was only right that I took as much as I could off her plate.

"You didn't have to be so quick to tell on me, you know."

An immediate grin came to my face as Char stepped into the office, arms crossed.

"I'm guessing that means Jaclyn hit you up," I said, and she nodded. "I wasn't telling on you though – I was bragging. Proud of you for putting Kenzo's ass on the spot."

Char couldn't help the smile that spread over her face as she stepped in and closed the door – probably so *we* couldn't be snooped on the way she had on my conversation with Ken.

"I've known you a long time, Kadan... we're friends, right?"

I raised an eyebrow. "As far as I know, yeah... why?"

"I want you to tell me the truth about Ken."

"The truth? I'm not su—*oh*. You want to know what his trouble factor is like."

Char frowned. "Trouble factor?"

I've been around Jaclyn way too much...

"Whether or not he's gonna mess around. Break your heart."

"Oh. *Yes*."

I nodded, sitting back in my desk chair. "Char, I can't give you a definite answer one way or another on something like that – I don't have that kind of knowledge. But I know Ken to be a stand-up guy, and I believe that he cares for you a lot – enough that he was hesitant to involve himself with you, for fear of hurting you."

"Isn't that a *bad* sign though?"

I shook my head. "Nah. What's concerning is when a man *isn't* concerned that he might mess up."

"I guess that's true," Char nodded. "I just... I don't want it to be awkward around here, if it doesn't work out. I love my job, and I don't want anything to mess that up."

I scoffed. "Y'all already swapped spit though, so..."

"*Kadan.*"

"What?" I laughed. "I'm just saying... if it doesn't work out, and it *is* awkward, it'll pass, and we'll be a family again. If I can get past the awkwardness of working with Ms. Love after she socked me in the eye, I feel like we can all get past most things."

Char smirked. "There's a good chance sleeping together makes getting through the awkwardness a much smoother transition."

My eyes went wide. "She told you we were sleeping together?"

"She didn't have to – it's *so* obvious when y'all are in a room together, and why else would you be giving her time off from volunteering?"

"The kindness of my heart?"

"Oh *please.*" Char rolled her eyes. "I kinda knew it was coming from the night she walked in with that cat. Your whole demeanor changed."

"She had a cat in a bowl of chicken," I defended – a defense that made her laugh.

"Sure, you can say it was that, or you can admit that you were interested. And you can admit that you're full-blown smitten now."

I couldn't deny that.

So I didn't try.

"Fine. Maybe I am. Jaclyn is intelligent, fine as hell, successful, vivacious, funny... she's an easy woman to admire."

Char smiled as she walked back to the door, pulling it open. "I agree."

"You agree with what?" Kenzo asked, wearing a goofy ass grin as he approached the open doorway.

"That Jaclyn is a great match for him."

I THINK I MIGHT LOVE YOU

"Oh absolutely," Ken agreed, nodding. "Shouldn't you be heading out soon to get ready – I thought you were taking her to that alumni ball thing tonight, that's why you wanted the early shift today?"

"Yes." I sat up, propping my elbows on my desk as Char turned with wide eyes. "I was wrapping up some work before I left."

"You got a tux for this, right?" Char asked. "And a limo?"

I frowned. "Uh... nah. I got the Charger detailed though."

Kenzo chuckled as Char's mouth dropped open. "You're taking her to a *ball* in a *Charger*?"

"What, it's a nice ass car!" I called to Char's retreating back as she walked off, mumbling about my *typical army fuckboy vehicle* choice.

She wasn't wrong, but still.

It *was* a nice ass car.

And it *was* freshly detailed.

"You feel me, don't you Ken?" I asked, and he held up his hands.

"I *just* got in good with her – you're on your own, man. But good luck tonight."

He walked off too, leaving me wondering what the hell the problem was – not that I had much time to think about it. I had plenty to do, including a fresh haircut and getting my tux from the cleaners', as well as a stop at the flower shop.

I was going to make the best I could out of this night.

∼

"G aaahdamn." was my immediate reaction when Jaclyn opened the door.

Really, it was the only appropriate response to seeing her in a sleeveless dress that fit like a glove from her breasts down to her hips, then flared into a full skirt down to the floor. Her locs were pinned up in an intricate style, her perfect lips painted deep red. She'd even switched glasses, from her usual trendy black ones to a frameless style that allowed you to see more of her gorgeous face.

99

"*Kadan stop it!*" she half-screamed, half-giggled, as I swept her up into my arms and kicked her door closed behind us. "You're gonna mess up my makeup," she whined – then moaned – as my lips met her collarbone.

"I guess you'll just have to do it again," I growled into her neck as I carried her into the bedroom, dropping her onto the bed before I pounced on top of her.

"Kadan, *wait*."

"*Whooooo!*"

"*Right in front of my salad?*"

"*Took forty-minutes to connect this call, they aint even gone make it to that ball.*"

"*Bow-chicka-wow-wow!*"

"*He's got a nice wide back, don't he?*"

"*Josephine, stop looking at that boy! Boy get your ass off my daughter!*"

I went tense for a second before I scrambled off of Jaclyn, looking around for the source of the other voices in the room.

"*Oh my God,*" Jaclyn grumbled as she sat up. "Kadan… meet my *entire* family."

She lifted a finger, and my gaze followed where she was pointing to land on her laptop, where she was apparently connected to a video call with several other people. I recognized Jemma, and assumed the other young woman must be their middle sister, Joia. In a different screen was an older couple – a scowling man I assumed was her father, and a smiling woman who looked too much like Jaclyn to not be her mother.

"*Hiiii Kadan!*" the women chimed, and I scrubbed a hand over the freshly faded side of my head.

"Uh… hey ladies," I greeted, with a little wave.

"Okay, that's enough of this," Jaclyn insisted, rushing toward the laptop. "You've seen the dress and everything, which cost me near an hour, and now, I gotta go."

I THINK I MIGHT LOVE YOU

"*Don't forget the toweeelllll,*" one of her sisters called out as Jaclyn slammed the top closed on the laptop.

"Well. That was *lovely*," Jaclyn said, pulling in then pushing out a deep breath through her nose.

"My bad," I told her, stepping closer so I could grab her hand. "You just look so good, I couldn't help myself."

"I *do* look good, don't I?"

"Beyond." I leaned down to press a kiss just below her ear, respecting her wish to not have her makeup disturbed. "Let's go ahead and get out of here – sooner we show our faces, the sooner we can leave and I can mess this up without you getting mad at me. Deal?"

She smiled. "Deal. The car is waiting downstairs?"

"Um... *my* car is waiting downstairs."

That beautiful smile melted off her face.

"Nigga. I *know* you aren't taking me to the ball in that Charger."

Um.

Okay.

Maybe I should've thought it through a little more.

Because I didn't, I didn't have any choice other than to take the good-natured roasting that filled the whole trip there in stride. It had us both in a great mood by the time we arrived on campus and pulled up to the valet, joining the line of BSU graduates young and old and in-between as everyone filtered into the event space.

For a good minute, we were having a nice time – Jaclyn and I both ran into professors we'd had and enjoyed, along with some classmates. It was fun catching up with everybody, and my mood was shifting from "get this shit over with" to "damn, I'm glad we came".

And then, Aunt Cali walked up, with Deidre on her arm.

Visually, I could never, *ever* front on Deidre – she was fine as hell. It was too bad that fineness came with the wrong kind of drama.

"Kadan, I see you made it," Aunt Cali greeted me, with a smile and her standard kiss on the cheek. Her gaze flitted to Jaclyn, long enough for her displeasure to be clear before she smiled again, and turned to Deidre. "Of course you remember the lovely DeeDee," she said, prompting Deidre to pull me into a hug that was too tight and lingered too long – I practically had to pry her ass off me.

"Of course," I agreed, frowning as I straightened my jacket. "And I know *you* remember *Jaclyn*," I said, putting an arm around her waist to pull her into my side. "My beautiful date."

Aunt Cali hiked her chin. "Right. I scarcely recognized you outside the courtroom, dear."

"*Oh*," Deidre exclaimed, in that fake-ass chipper voice of hers that grated my nerves. She reserved it for public use. "Is *this* the delinquent you told me about?"

Beside me, Jaclyn stiffened. "*Bitch*. I'm only letting Judge Freeman's fermented ass slide because I don't want to give her a stroke, but *you...*"

I squeezed her, bending to whisper for only her to hear, "*Chill, please.*"

She blew out a sigh. "You just be glad I'm committed to not catching another charge."

"How horribly *rude*," Aunt Cali declared, as if she wasn't the one who started the shit – a fact I was about to bring up when she grabbed Deidre to walk away. "I see someone I need to speak to." She had to have known I wasn't about to let that shit go, from the way she rushed off with Deidre in tow.

"I'm sorry about that," I told Jac, shaking my head as they left.

She shrugged. "Not your fault she's an asshole. I just want her to stay the hell away from me. The Wrights are over there though," Jac added, pointing in the direction opposite of where my Aunt and Deidre had gone. "Let's go say hi."

We did more than say hi.

We ended up spending the next half hour posted up with them, and I was glad for it. That run-in could have ruined the night, but the Wrights were Jaclyn's family. If she couldn't be comfortable around anybody else, she could be comfortable around them.

Unfortunately, we couldn't keep them to ourselves.

Most of the Wrights were considered distinguished Blakewood alums themselves, so there were others in the room who wanted face time with them. It wasn't until we were away from that bubble of familiarity that we both realized the same messed up thing.

"Kadan am I imagining shit, or does it seem like there's a lot of people looking at me?"

She *wasn't* imagining it.

All it took was a glance to where my Aunt Calista and Deidre were standing off to the side wearing smug grins and sipping champagne to confirm it.

"*Hell nah*," I heard Jaclyn mumble, and before I could stop her, she was off, walking right up to where they were standing. "What the *hell* is your problem?" she demanded, just as I joined her side.

"Do you see?" Aunt Cali asked, addressing me as if Jac wasn't even there. "All these important people around, and yet she has no problem *attempting* to make a scene."

Beside her, Deidre huffed. "You can bring a ratchet to culture, but you can't make her think."

"Oh I *think* plenty, *bitch. Thinking* about it is the only thing keeping me off your ass right now," Jaclyn snapped, as I hooked her again, hoping that if she *did* decide to swing on Deidre, I could intervene.

"She doesn't belong here," Aunt Cali sang, pulling an even deeper frown to my face.

"Auntie, cut the bullshit, okay?" I responded, at the same time Jaclyn spoke up for herself too.

"I belong here as much as anybody else – I'm a Blakewood student too, soon to be alumni, *and* I own a successful business in this community. My sisters went here, my parents went here, my cousins went here. My *ancestors* went here, maybe even further back than you, and I bet they would be completely disgusted with you treating people like you're better than they are."

"We just call like we see it," Deidre sneered.

"Man shut your ass up," I snapped, hauling Jaclyn backward

when I felt her pulling against my hold around her waist. "You're always up my Auntie's ass trying to be her clone – take a breather."

Deidre reeled back like I'd smacked her, but my concern for Jac weighed a helluva lot more than that girl's hurt feelings.

"Hey," I said, keeping my voice low for just her, since a bit of a crowd had gathered. "Seriously, you gotta chill."

Jaclyn's eyes were already glossy, but they narrowed at my words, and she shoved out of my hold. "Right. Let me go do that. I need to use the restroom," she declared, holding her head high as she moved off in the opposite direction.

As soon as she was gone, I turned right to my Aunt Calista, who was comforting Deidre as if their asses weren't the ones in the wrong.

"What the *fuck* is wrong with y'all?" I asked, not giving a damn who overheard me.

Aunt Cali's eyes went wide as hell, traveling around the crowd before they came back to me, full of anger. "How *dare* you speak to me this way, and in front of people?!"

"How dare you speak to *her* that way?" I growled right back. "You can dish bullshit, but you can't take it?"

"You will *respect* me, young man!"

"You don't know shit about respect," I countered. "If you did, you wouldn't have pulled whatever you pulled that had people looking upside Jaclyn's head like she was about to draw a weapon."

Aunt Cali huffed. "Are we *that* certain she won't?!"

"You know that's bullshit. You *know* that's bullshit," I repeated, shaking my head. "And I would think you, of all people, would understand giving a young woman a chance to grow from her mistakes, but I see you're selective with your memory."

"I have no idea what you're talking about."

My face screwed into a scowl. "I'm talking about your *sister*. Carmen. My *mother*! Remember her?!" I asked. "The drug dealing, the prostitution, my father having to take custody? You managed to clean her up, get her record cleared, and now you don't remember none of that, huh?"

I THINK I MIGHT LOVE YOU

"This is *not* the place—"

"You *made it the place*," I interrupted. "What, you scared for all your lil' bougie fake friends to know you had crime in your own family? That you threw your power around so—"

Aunt Cali stepped toward me, nostrils flared. "Kadan Michael Davenport, that is *enough*," she hissed.

I laughed at that shit though. "Is it?! You're embarrassed? You shamed, Auntie? But you didn't have any issue putting Jaclyn's business out in front of these people. No problem making *her* feel bad, huh?"

"*She is not good enough for you.*"

"Because she messed up in the past? So we gonna act like you didn't pull strings for me to go to the military instead of my rightful punishment for that drunk and disorderly and assault charge?"

"*Kadan...*" She was for real pleading with me now, and even Deidre was looking at her sideways, cause that was something she didn't know – something *nobody* knew, because my Aunt had done a good ass job of burying it, just like the shit with my mother.

Burying the shit didn't undo it though.

"Just... *stop.*" I shrugged. "Just stop it, aiight? I *love you* Aunt Cali, but this is not okay, and it won't ever be okay. I like Jaclyn, full stop, and I don't give a shit what you think about her, because I am a grown ass man. I was trying to preserve your feelings, trying to put a little sugar on this, but I see that was a mistake, so let me say it like this – stay outta my personal life. I've got it."

I didn't wait for her to respond before I turned away, scanning the crowd for Jaclyn. When I didn't see her, I headed to where I knew the bathrooms were, and waited. After several minutes passed, I stopped someone coming out to ask about her, but they swore she wasn't in there – even went back in to check for me. That led me outside, thinking she'd gone to get some air, but even then, I couldn't find her.

"You looking for somebody?" the dude at the valet stand asked. Recognizing him from when we first arrived, I nodded.

"Yeah, you remember the woman I came in with?"

A smirk spread over his face. "Mmmhmmm, I sure do. That woman was *fine*."

"Yeah, I know – have you seen her?"

"Mmmhmmm, I sure have."

"Okay, *where*," I prompted, when he didn't immediately answer.

"She ordered a ride on the cell phone," he told me, shaking his head. "Looked *real* upset. I'm telling you, you better take care of a woman that looks like that, or somebody else will."

"Thank you," was my dry response, and I slipped him a few bills from my pocket too.

Fuck.

I raked a hand through my thick hair, thinking back through the night to figure out what *I* had done to piss her off enough for her to leave without saying anything.

Hell.

Maybe that didn't even matter. She was only here to pretend for me anyway, so maybe she'd had her fill with the bullshit with my Aunt.

I was ready to dip too, so I couldn't even blame her.

I pulled out my phone to see if she'd sent a text, but there was nothing there from her. I shot her one of my own, asking her to let me know once she'd made it home safely before I went back to the valet to request my car.

Briefly, I thought about stopping by her place, but after the shit with my Aunt… she probably needed space to breathe. Reluctantly, I set my course for my apartment, hoping to get a text back from her by the time I made it there.

If not… space be damned.

I'd see her tomorrow.

TEN
JACLYN

"Why are men?"

I posed that question to my sisters and then took another long drink of wine, straight from the bottle.

"Why are men... what, Jac?" Jemma asked. She was coming in from a night out herself, and I'd caught Joia up doing her meal prep for the following week.

"Yeah," Joia chimed. "Your drunk ass didn't finish the question."

"I'm not drunk, and I *did* finish the question. *Why are men?* Dassit. That's the question. Just why at all?"

Jemma sighed. "Girl, why *indeed*. Remember the guy I was telling you about from the other day?"

"The 'transcendent' dick you told us about in vivid detail?" Joia giggled. "How could we possibly forget? Actually - never mind, I did forget. Tell it again."

"Well, I would if I wasn't feeling some kinda way about his ass dropping off the map without bothering to say goodbye! I woke up and his ass was gone. And I'm in Havana, so it's not like I might even run into him again. He's not from here either."

Joia sucked her teeth. "Sounds like a perfect affair. Assuming of course that he didn't take - or leave anything you can't get rid of - when he went."

"Oh that's not an issue. Can't be a hoe in every international country code without precautions."

"Don't tell me you caught feelings for this one?" I interjected.

"For him? No. For his sex?... Maybe."

That set off a round of laughter between the three of us, because we'd all been there.

Unfortunately.

"Well, at least you've got good memories from your latest '*Why are men?*' encounter," Joia spoke up. "I, on the other hand, have Theodore Graham in my inbox talking about a collab. Nigga, collab my cheeks and kiss. Ugh!"

Under my breath, I snickered, and from the silence on the phone line, I had every reason to suspect that Jemma was doing the same. Teddy was one of Joia's peers in the small circle of popular social media influencers in the growing Blakewood population. While Joia was more focused on women's health, beauty, fitness, and the like, Teddy was all about laughs, haircuts and sneakers, with sports commentary thrown in.

Oh, and he was Joia's first love.

And first heartbreak.

She couldn't stand his ass.

"It ain't funny!" Joia declared, correctly surmising that we were laughing. "He gets on my nerves."

Jemma chuckled. "I think you're still holding on to residual feelings for Teddy Grahams."

"Tuh. The cereal *only*. Which he ruined for me, by the way!"

I scoffed. "Oh please, Miss Fit Bitch," I laughed. "Your ass wouldn't be caught dead with a box of cereal anyway."

"Don't be making sense in my face Jaclyn!" she countered, struggling to keep herself from laughing too, cause she knew it was true. "Speaking of fitness, you should bring your ass back to the gym with me. There's a new boxing instructor," she sang.

"You mean, to replace the one Jaclyn ran off?" Jemma asked.

"*He told me to give it everything I had!*" I defended myself. "Not my fault he got his ass kicked. And Joia was the one who vlogged it."

"My bad."

We all broke into laughter about *that* shit too.

"Okay sis," Jemma spoke. "You've told us all about Kadan's bitch Aunt, and raggedy Deidre, who I think I might know, but that's a different conversation. When are you going to tell us what *Kadan* did?"

Joia scoffed. "Not until she figures that part out herself."

"Oh shut up," I said, even though she was right. I knew how I felt, I just hadn't yet figured out how to verbalize aloud to explain to my sisters.

I just wished he'd been different.

Not that he *owed* me different, when the only reason I was even at the ball with him was to make excuses for his aunt. A woman who had no issue telling me to my face that she didn't think I was good enough for Kadan.

Which... no lie, those words hit different in the face of the fact that he and I were sleeping together... nothing more.

Hell, maybe *Kadan* didn't think I was good enough for him – all that *"calm down"* energy he had for *me* while those other bitches were the ones creating the problem...

I shouldn't have been surprised.

"Jac, listen – fuck them, if they can't see how *incredibly* dope you are, okay?" Joia said. "A hater bitch ain't *never* stopped the *Love* story, and we're not about to let it now. You're fine as hell, you own a business, and you'll officially have a degree in a few weeks. You *are* still doing that, right?"

I sucked my teeth. "Don't even play with me. My graduation application was in by the deadline, my regalia is ordered, my advisor is on board, approved everything... I'm definitely walking across the stage, but whether or not I actually *get* the degree... that relies on me not dropping the ball right here at the end."

"Which has to be a difficult balance," Jemma mused. "You have a *lot* going on. Especially with the addition of this community service mess."

"Yeah," I huffed. "I was busy enough without it, and now…I've barely felt like I had time to breathe."

"But it'll be over soon. You basically just have finals, right?"

"Yes. Papers on papers. All the papers. Details this week," I said, closing my eyes. I didn't want to think about that.

"Well, we're here if you need us, Jac, you know that," Joia said.

Jemma agreed. "Whatever you need us to do."

"Just have your asses in the stands to watch me come across that stage."

That wasn't in question anyway, and they made sure I knew that before we got off the phone. I knocked back the rest of my wine and tossed my cell onto my bedside table, fully ready to pass out asleep until I heard the distinct rapping of a fist at my front door.

It was *way* too late for unannounced visitors, but tipsy curiosity wouldn't allow me to simply ignore it. I fought my way out of bed and trudged to the door, rolling my eyes when I saw who was on the other side of the peephole.

"What do you want?" I called through the closed door.

"To make sure you're okay – you're not answering your phone, or replying to texts," Kadan answered. The sound of his voice – even muffled – cut right through my annoyance with him to latch onto the natural horniness that plagued me every time I drank.

Shit.

"That's because I blocked your number!"

"*Blocked?*" Kadan called back, confused. "What the hell did I do?"

Before I could stop myself, or had any sort of plan, I'd unlocked the door and snatched it open. "*Nothing.* That's what! While those two bitches humiliated me, all your puppy-healing ass did was tell *me* to chill!"

He frowned. "I was trying to *help* you," he argued. "You're the one who was talking about wanting to change – not fighting and shit anymore, which is what they were trying to goad you into. So you'd get in trouble again, which is what you didn't want."

"Why didn't you tell *them* to chill?"

His hands went up. "I could've sworn I did, multiple times, before you walked off, and I *definitely* got in their asses about it after, but Jac... they weren't my concern at the moment. *You* were. I wanted to make sure *you* were good. But obviously I fucked that up, so tell me what you'd like me to do next time something like that happens."

I blinked. "Next time?"

"Yes. Not that we'd *want* something like that to happen again, but shit... just in case. Tell me how to make sure you feel taken care of."

For several seconds I stared at him, lips parted, trying to make sense of what the hell was happening, but... shit, I couldn't. I shook my head. "I can't deal with this right now."

I turned to walk away from the door like this wasn't *my* apartment, and Kadan followed me inside, closing it behind him.

"Can't deal with what right now?" he asked, so... *God*, so endearingly confused that it pissed me off – and turned me on – at the same damn time. "And why are you still in your dress?"

Shit.

Because my tipsy ass can't undo the hook wasn't an answer I was about to give him, not in this state, so I focused on the other, more loaded, question.

"I cannot deal with you coming in here with this... I don't know, concerned boyfriend act. This whole little stupid fake bae shit is over, Kadan – and was a massive fail by the way. Judge Freeman is *never* going to let you rest. She's not going to let *me* rest either. So thanks for that."

That goofy bewilderment melted from Kadan's face, replacing itself with frustrated resolve. "My Aunt isn't going to do shit to you – trust me on that. She knows she took this shit too far, and I've got the voicemail theatrics to prove it."

"Is that supposed to make me feel better?"

He shook his head. "*Better?* No, probably not. But her fucking with you can be one less concern on your mind."

"Noted," I shrugged. "Now what?"

"Now," he started, stalking toward me so fast that my brain had barely registered his approach before he was behind me, unhooking my dress, which had started to painfully dig into my flesh. "We talk about this '*whole lil stupid fake bae shit.*' He smirked as he stepped back around in front of me, even though there was only a little space between me and the couch. "And I point out that I *never* called you that, and the only time I faked a thing was the day I asked you to do it."

I narrowed my eyes. "Okay, and what is that supposed to mean?"

"What do you mean, *what does it mean?* It *means* I'm not faking this shit, Jaclyn."

"Okay, and what is *that* supposed to mean?"

Kadan chuckled as he perched on the arm of the couch, pulling me between his legs. "It means that every time I've called you babe, every time I've kissed you, every time I've sought you out, or came sprinting because you summoned me… it's only been because I *wanted* to, not to put on a show."

I blinked, hard.

"Okay and what is that supposed to *mean?*"

Again, he laughed. "It means at some point, without either of us realizing it, I decided you were mine, for real. And I have every intention of acting accordingly." He reached up, cupping my face in his hand to draw me closer. Our lips were almost touching when he tensed, and pulled back. "Wait you *blocked* me?"

"Hm?"

"Seriously?"

The exasperated expression on his face instantly put me on defense.

"Yeah, *seriously*," I said, propping a hand on my hip. "As far as *I* could tell, it seemed like you were more on their side than mine, and I thought you thought you were too good for me. Or something."

I THINK I MIGHT LOVE YOU

He blew out a sigh. "What have I ever done to make you think I thought you weren't good enough for me?"

"Well we can start with the criminal record jokes," I snapped.

"And we can end with those too, because it was that – *jokes*. Do you seriously think I'm judging you *for real* about that shit? Jac, if it wasn't for me knowing somebody who knows somebody, *I'd* have a record too."

My eyebrows shot up. "I didn't know."

"No, you didn't. But the more important point is, I know it's a sensitive topic for you now, so I won't make those jokes. Because we communicated about it. You talked, and explained an issue, giving me a chance to rectify that issue before you *blocked* me."

"Why do you keep *saying that?!*"

He scoffed. "Why did you *do* it?!"

"Because you hurt my feelings!"

"With *jokes*? Jaclyn, you have roasted me about pretty much every facet of my life, and you can't take *jokes*?"

I crossed my arms. "You know what? Fuck this, if you're going to be mean," I said, turning to walk away.

Kadan didn't let me get far, grabbing my elbow to bring me right back between his legs. "Bring your ass back here, ain't nobody being mean to you. We're *gonna* talk about this shit, and get past it, because this is... this is *nothing*, aiight? I am sorry, truly, for making you feel unworthy, because it's the furthest thing from what I believe. From the moment I met you, I *knew* you were somebody I'd get wrapped up in, and here we are."

"Which is *where*, Kadan?"

"With me sitting in front of you putting all my shit on the line right now, *Jaclyn*," he countered. "I *want you*, and I don't know how to be any more transparent about it. I *like you*. I like your energy, I like your sense of humor, I like your brain, I like your face, I like your booty," he said, grabbing it for emphasis and making me laugh. "I like you," he repeated. "And I'm aged out of playing games when it comes to that. So yeah, that's where we are. We're at *Jaclyn has to make a decision*."

I blew out a sigh, and shook my head. "What if I can't make a decision? What am I supposed to do with *any* of this? I got my heart *shattered* like six weeks ago, or something, and I haven't even begun to process it because I haven't *had time*. Because I have too much to do to grieve a relationship. Can you even imagine? I haven't let myself think about it, because I don't have time to be a mess behind a breakup. I had to find a new place, and take care of a cat, and keep up my grades, and run a business, and repay my debt to society, and *now* you want me to make a decision because *you like me*. Well guess what, Dr. Doolittle - *I don't have the bandwidth!*"

I tried my best to snatch away, but he wouldn't let me – instead, he stood, wrapping his arms tight around my shoulders. That was all it took for the tears to come, and I couldn't do anything but melt into his hold, accepting the comfort he was offering.

Comfort I was grateful he was willing to give, because *seriously Jac?! WHAT THE FUCK?*

I had no idea where any of that had come from. Which I guess was a sign my subconscious suppression of everything Victor related had worked beautifully. I *hadn't* given myself any time to process that breakup, and now here I was a short time later with a different man – a *better* man – wanting me.

Wanting more than I could fathom having to give right now.

"I'm sorry," he muttered into my hair, kissing the top of my head. "You're right. I didn't realize."

I shook my head, peeling myself back enough to look up and meet his gaze. "It's not your fault. You just happened to be here when it all came out."

He raised his hands to my face, using his thumbs to wipe the moisture from my cheeks. "Doesn't mean I can't be sorry for adding to the stress of it all."

"You've actually been a good stress relief these last few weeks. I appreciate it."

I THINK I MIGHT LOVE YOU

"Glad I could be of service to you." He pushed out a sigh, and took a step back from me. "I think it would be good if we *didn't* do that though."

"... what?"

"I'm saying, maybe we shouldn't see each other for a bit? You know? Give you time to finish school, get yourself settled. And we won't see you at the clinic until *after* you graduate."

My chest tightened, and fresh tears pricked at my eyes. "You're mad at me."

"*No*," he answered, shaking his head. "No, Jaclyn. Not at all."

"Then why are you doing this? Why are you saying this?"

"You think I *want* this?"

I shrugged. "Maybe so! If it's not what you want, why would you do it?"

"Because it's what *you* need," he countered. "What I heard from you is that you're stressed and overstimulated with everything t going on. That you need peace. That you need *time*. So that's what I'm trying to give you!"

"Okay so why can't we do what we've *been* doing?" I asked, trying not to sound as desperate as I felt.

Kadan shook his head, giving me a smile. "Because I want more than what we've been doing. If you don't, that's fine, we can go on about our lives. But if you're telling me you need time and space to make a decision, then let's do that. Let's do it the right way."

"This doesn't feel like the right way," I admitted. "It doesn't feel good, at all."

"It rarely does."

Finally, he approached me again, taking my face in his hands. This time he didn't pull back, instead granting me a kiss filled with a sweet sort of intensity I could hardly handle without bursting into tears again.

"Stop acting like I'm breaking up with you," he whispered against my lips. "I'm giving you a break from *me*."

"Shut up," I whispered back. "You're not making it better."

"Sorry." He kissed my forehead, and let me go. "It's a few weeks. A few weeks, and then we'll see what happens."

I knew what was going to happen.

He was going to walk out of here, and we'd never find our way back to the moment of possibility, where there might have been something between us. I wanted to take it all back, wanted to not have drunk that whole bottle of wine, wanted to not have left the ball alone, whatever it would have taken for this night to not have ended this way.

But I couldn't take it back.

I'd told my truth, and he'd told his, and I *couldn't* take any of it back, even though this shit hurt.

It hurt bad, actually, because I...

Shit.

I liked him too

A lot.

But I would be lying if I took back anything I said, and even though I knew what it meant... I had to let him walk out my front door.

a few weeks later -

"Jaclyn Love."

Whew.

I'd never, *ever* been so glad to hear my name called.

Not, *Jaclyn Love, you're under arrest*, or *Jaclyn Love, you're sentenced to*, or *Jaclyn Love, get your ass*... none of that. Just my name, paired together with the degree I'd earned, spoken aloud.

I promised myself I wouldn't cry about it, but I broke that promise as soon as I heard the seemingly thunderous reaction of my family as BSU's president placed the symbolic diploma in my hand, and moved my tassel from one side to the other. I couldn't help myself – I burst into tears, because this shit had been a long time coming, and had taken *so* much out of me.

But I'd made it.

My huge family group descended on me as soon as the ceremony was over, making me smile for what felt like hundreds of pictures, but I didn't mind, at all. It was amazing to have them all there for me – my parents, Joia, Jemma and the Wrights too – Jason, Reese, Justin, Toni, Joseph, Devyn, Imara and my Uncle Joe, and all the kids. Even Kenzo showed up, with Char on his arm, and several of my people from *Dreamery*.

Everybody.

It felt really, *really* good.

With the exception of this one face I hoped to see, but obviously... didn't.

I shouldn't have been surprised – with Kenzo and Char at the ceremony, *somebody* had to be there for the animals of Blakewood, but I couldn't pretend it didn't sting. I was careful not to bring him up – not to Kenzo or Char, or to Jason – and they didn't bring him up either.

I *wanted* to ask though.

Badly.

But I refused to be pressed about him if he wasn't pressed about me.

He sent flowers though, remember?

Yeah.

Okay, fine.

So, he sent the most gorgeous, huge bouquet of congratulatory roses the day before the graduation ceremony, along with a small lemongrass plant for Miss Thing. I *had* been happy about it, and fully expected to see him there with everybody else to celebrate.

The wrong expectation, apparently.

This was a happy day though, my celebration. So instead of focusing on Kadan, I focused on *that*, letting my family take those endless pictures and *genuinely* smiling big as hell in each one. Once the pictures were done, I was whisked off to a surprise party that really was a surprise, where I ate, and danced, and drank, and laughed, and happy cried, and danced and ate and drank more, all to my heart's content.

It had been a long ass time since I felt so light.

I was still tipsy and happy and full in more than one way when I stepped off the elevator in my building. I'd thought long and hard about staying over with my sisters and cousins for a massive grownup sleepover, but all I really wanted to do was sleep in my own bed without an alarm the next day.

And check on *Miss Thing*, of course.

When I rounded the corner to my apartment, my steps slowed, taking in the sight of Kadan, sitting across from my door. He scrambled to his feet when he noticed me.

"What are you doing here?" I asked, convincing my legs to start moving again.

He smiled his smile – that goofy smile I adored – as he raked his fingers through his hair. "I was waiting on you at the 'doe... wow, that sounded so much less corny in my he—"

I didn't give him a chance to finish whatever the hell he was saying – I dove at him, crushing my mouth to his to start making up for the weeks of kissing we hadn't done. He immediately snaked his arms around my waist, hauling me into him to take over, which I didn't mind in the least.

I was just glad he was there.

Glad he was just as pressed as I was.

"You weren't at the ceremony," I blurted, as soon as we came up for air.

"Because I didn't want to make *your* day about me," he shot back, just as quickly. "But then I couldn't fuckin' stay away. I hit up Jason and asked him to let me know when you were on the way home."

I raised my eyebrows. "*I* didn't even know I was leaving until like ten minutes ago. And *you* live about ten minutes from here too."

"Oh, I never told you, did I? My middle name is Usain."

"Is *not*," I laughed. "But I guess this means you still like me?"

"Did you think I would stop?"

"Duh."

"*No*," he chuckled. "Now I said I would wait until you were finished with school – you've graduated. You're all glowing, and happy and shit, you're feeling good... don't break my heart, Ms. Love."

"Like you broke mine?"

His eyes went wide. "Don't tell me that... that fucked with me. A lot."

"Same here," I nodded. "But I'll admit, I *did* need time. More than I knew. But I came to a conclusion I need you to not freak out about, or give more weight than you should."

"Okay, hit me," he said, looking me right in the eyes, ready for whatever I had to say. More ready to hear it than I was to say it, even though I'd been sitting with it long enough.

I pushed out a sigh.

"I think I might... love you," I admitted. "Just a little though. Like, right at the beginning, you know? And I know it's stupid soon to say something like that, but it's just the truth. So if me being a weirdo and saying that isn't too much of a turnoff, then—"

"Stop it," he interrupted, scooping me into his arms again. "I had a little realization myself, when I was doing everything I could to respect your space these last few weeks."

"And what realization was th—oh. *Duh.*"

"Yeah," he laughed. "I think I might love you too."

∼

the end.

I THINK I MIGHT NEED YOU

ONE

Joia.

"*I ain't gotta copy off of no chick*
 If you listen to me, you already know this,
Van only got time for her own shit
I know you mad about it hoe but don't trip
You only pressed cause you don't get what I get
But come here baby let me drop some knowledge
Your track record can't touch what I did,
And you'll never be hot like me, bitch."

"Joia, I know you're going through it right now, but I need you to play another song, or I'm about to bounce," Jaclyn insisted, throwing the comb she'd been using to help me remove my braids down on the table. "Nobody *really* thinks you copied that lil wack ass girl, except the people who *want* to have a problem with you anyway. Hell, I'm the one who gave you the idea for that video anyway."

I rolled my eyes at her assertion – I'd decided to do a time-lapse video after seeing a random one of a plant reacting to being watered.

It had come up on my timeline while I was scrolling social media. Jaclyn had been with me while I mused out loud about what I could do, and her exact words had been:

"Your ass don't do nothin' but work out and meal prep and play in makeup anyway, so it may as well be that."

And so, I *had* filmed myself putting together my meals for the week – along with the other people I did them for – and then sped it all up to just a few minutes of video, set to music from a friend of mine who was an up and coming artist. People *loved* the video, to the point that it ended up trending – and then here came some random ass girl accusing me of copying her concept.

I'd never seen even a *second* of her videos before.

So, yeah... Vanity was really talking to me with *Don't Trip*.

I'd been pissed off for almost two weeks.

"I get what you're saying, but... she came for my integrity with that shit! Hopped in my inbox talking about *I know you saw my video Joia!* She –"

"Called you by your fucking name, like you even fuck with her like that to be addressing you that way and assuming you saw her shit," Jac finished for me. "Yeah, I know. I've heard this spiel like twelve times. We get it, you're pissed."

I *was* pissed.

I was so, *so* pissed.

"But, you also did nothing wrong, and homegirl needs to focus on her audience instead of trying to police your shit – as if *all* of you fit motherfuckers on the internet don't meal plan in the same damn containers, with the same damn terminology, with the same lil nasty ass chicken and broccoli."

I narrowed my eyes. "Excuse me?"

"Fine." She sucked her teeth. "So your food isn't nasty, but all the other shit is true. She was bugging, and so are you – let's move on. This braid takedown is the shit you *should* be filming."

I laughed. "Oh girl I am, you don't see the camera setup over there?" I pointed, and Jac flipped me off once she confirmed what I was saying. "I may be pissed, but…"

"A hater won't ever stop the *Love* show," she finished for me again. Indeed.

I'd luckily already filmed other content that had been published since the controversy with the meal prepping video, but hadn't been able to get out of my own head enough to do anything else since. I'd come to a conclusion, however, that I couldn't let that drama hold me back – especially when I knew I hadn't done anything wrong. I'd planned to do several of these timelapse videos, each one focused on a different aspect of my life, while still being related to the usual content of my super-popular social media accounts.

So I was *going* to do my damn videos.

A hater won't *ever* stop the *Love* show.

I kept working and so did my younger sister, Jaclyn. Now that she was freshly graduated from college and had a little extra time on her hands, I hadn't hesitated to recruit her help taking down the braids that had secured my natural hair underneath my sew-in weave.

"You're lucky I love you, Jo," she whined. "My hands hurt – you should just get it loc'd, like mine," she said, securing a handful of my massive hair with a ponytail holder. There were only a few braids left to undo.

I frowned at her, and shook my head. "You know I have commitment issues," I reminded her, as my phone chimed. I grabbed it from the table and held it up after reading the notification across the front of the screen. "It's Jem. Her plane just landed."

"She wants us to pick her up?"

I nodded, sticking the metal end of my comb into another braid. "Yeah, so we gotta get a move on – I'll just toss my hair into a ponytail when we finish, then we can head out."

So that's what we did.

We, meaning *me*, because we were at my apartment, and would be returning there – Jemma was coming off yet another trip, this time to Argentina, and was only here for a few days. Her book launch was this coming weekend, at *Tones&Tomes,* a local bookstore we all frequented. From there, she was off on tour around the world, promoting her book about solo travel and cooking and... hoeing.

Her words, not mine.

In any case, it didn't take us long to scoop her up and bring her back to my apartment, where she was staying for the duration of her trip. It *also* didn't take her and Jac long to decide they wanted to eat junk food and drink – and it didn't take much convincing to get them to agree to do it all on my live stream, for an episode of *Live with the Love Sisters.* Something we didn't get to do very often, since these days we were rarely in the same place at the same time.

"So what are we talking about today guys?" I asked, once I'd gotten the camera set up, and started the live stream. Already, the number of people who were watching live was climbing past a hundred.

"I don't know about y'all, but I'm trying to hear about whoever Jem met in Argentina. I know she got her a fine one," Jaclyn said, settling into her seat at the table, where my phone was set up to include all three of us in the frame. She took a sip from her lemonade and watermelon vodka combo. "Spill it bitch. With all the details, come on."

"*Oooh,*" I mused, nodding. "That's where Steph Foster's fine ass – no disrespect intended to his beautiful wife – is from. He got a look-alike back home?"

Jemma shook her head, sending her braids gliding across the back of her shoulders as she grinned. "*Nope,*" she said, sipping from her drink – the same thing Jac was drinking. "If these people wanna hear about *my* hoe-tivities, they gotta read my book."

"Yes," I laughed. "How Jemma Got her Back Cracked, out in three days at *all* major retailers."

"Oh *shit,* that's good!" Jemma giggled. "How come you didn't give me that when I was asking y'all for name suggestions?!"

"Sis, I been working on that for like a month, I'm not the funny one in this trio," I reminded her. "That's your baby sister over there."

"My bad," Jac shrugged, topping off her drink from the bottles on the table. "You know I was busy trying to graduate, I didn't have any extra brainpower. Your title is good as it is though, you did well."

"Yeah," I agreed, smiling at Jemma. "I'd want to read it even if I didn't know you."

Speak, Play, Grub was described as *"a Black woman's guide to culture and cuisine, language and leisure, introspection and intimacy around the world"*. I couldn't think of a better way to describe the many, *many* stories she'd relayed to Jaclyn and me in the years since she'd randomly quit her job and decided to explore the world.

I made sure to name drop the book by the *real* title, then got up to grab a bottle of water while Jemma answered the questions people were asking about it in the live stream. When I sat back down, Jac nudged me.

"The people want to know why you're drinking water while we're over here getting lit," she said, taking a very pointed sip from her drink as I unscrewed the top on my bottle.

I shook my head. "Too much sugar for me – I've already got this little pudge that won't go away."

Jemma and Jaclyn *both* nearly choked on their drinks.

"A pudge *where*, Jo?!" Jemma exclaimed, laughing.

I sucked my teeth and stood, pointing to what as – to me at least – a distinct rounding of my belly.

Jac and Jem exchanged a look, then laughed again.

"Lawd, here you go – girl that's just a little gas," Jaclyn chuckled. "Lift your shirt."

I frowned. "Why?"

"Just do it," she insisted, so I did.

"Seee!" she exclaimed. "Girl, you've got a damned sixteen-pack of abs talking about a *pudge*."

"*There's a pudge*," I maintained, laughing with them now. Maybe I *was* being ridiculous. But still. "My leggings are fitting tighter, and my hoe clothes don't look like they used to," I told them, sitting down. "No matter how clean I eat, no matter how many damn crunches I do – it will not go away!"

"Okay... maybe you're pregnant," Jemma offered, making me sputter and choke over my mouthful of water as I shook my head.

"No. *Nah.* Nope. *Negative.*"

Jaclyn laughed. "You don't sound sure at all, could you think a little harder?"

"I haven't even... been engaging in the activity necessary for conception," I said. "So, *hell nawl*," I added again, then looked into the camera. "Do y'all see how they do me? It's cause I'm the middle child, I know it is."

"*Mmmmhmmm*," Jemma snickered. "I'm just saying, I feel like you're brushing the pregnancy option off a little too easily, when it would explain what you're talking about. And you're talking about *too much sugar* in the alcohol." She sucked her teeth. "Shit seems mighty convenient to me, Jaclyn."

Jaclyn wagged a finger in the air. "You know what – she did have a *stomach bug* a few weeks ago. I think Jo-Jo is gonna be a mommy."

"*Oh my God*," I laughed. "The *stomach bug* – which *was* a stomach bug was *months* ago. I am *not* pregnant, stop playing with me!"

"Prove it," Jac dared, lips pursed as she stared me down.

I threw my hands up. "How the *fuck* am I supposed to prove I'm not pregnant right now?!"

Jemma's eyes went wide, and she jumped up from the table. "Oh I got you boo," she said, going for her purse. When she came up with an unused pregnancy test, still in the little foil packaging, me and Jaclyn both tipped our heads to the side.

"Okay, why is *your* ass walking around with a pregnancy test at the ready?" I asked, and Jemma shook her head.

"Uh-uh. Worry about yourself. Go take this."

"I don't have to pee."

I THINK I MIGHT NEED YOU

Jaclyn sucked her teeth. "As much water as you drink, *Miss Fit Bitch*, I *know* you stay drug test ready. Girl go take that damn test."

I blew out a stream of air through my nose and then stood up, snatching the test from Jemma as I stomped off to the bathroom, already knowing what the damn thing was going to say. Still, this was good ass content – nearly two thousand people were watching the live stream when I walked away.

Knowing my sisters would keep the audience entertained, I peed on the damn stick to prove them wrong, then put the protective cap over the end before I slid it back into the little packet it came in. I washed my hands, then brought it back to the table with me smug as hell to hand to Jemma.

"As you requested," I quipped, returning to my seat.

"I knew you had to pee," Jaclyn laughed. "How long we gotta wait? It's two minutes, right?"

Jemma nodded. "Probably just one, cause of the time it took her to get back. I bet it's twins," she said, grinning at me. "I mean looking at how you're carrying."

"Oh, fuck you," I giggled. "You know, I wonder if my abs are overtrained..."

Jac shrugged. "Or you could just be constipated. You always *have* been full of shit, you know."

"I really cannot stand *either* one of you," I said, rolling my eyes as Jemma held up the pregnancy packet with a grin, wiggling it in her fingers.

"*Showtiiiime*," she sang, sticking her tongue out at me as she pulled the test from the packet. I expected her to play it up since we were live, teasing me about what was surely a negative test.

Instead, her eyes bulged wide, then shot up to me, then to Jaclyn, before she handed the strip of plastic to her.

Neither said anything.

"Okay," I laughed, shaking my head. "This is some Oscar-worthy acting, but come on. Stop playing." I reached across the table, pulling the test from Jaclyn's hand to show the camera the "*negative*" sign.

129

Only... there wasn't a *negative* sign.

It was a plus sign.

"*Holy shiiiit*," I whispered, dropping it on the table like it had suddenly grown hot in my hands. Somehow, that seemed to spur my sisters into action, while I sat there frozen.

Jemma grabbed the test, while Jaclyn grabbed my phone, smiling into the camera.

"Thank you for tuning in to *Live with the Love Sisters* – the first episode of our scripted series, all scenes dramatized for your enjoyment. Good night."

She shut off the phone and looked at me, eyes wide.

We were all wide-eyed as fuck, together.

Jemma was the first to break the silence, giving me an awkward smile as she held out the test.

"Umm... told you so?"

TWO

Joia.

"To' up, from the flo' up?
  Nah fuck that, it's time for the glow up.
Don't need no consensus, don't need no permission
They can watch us grow up
You wanna be that bitch?
Well okay bitch it's time to show up.
We ain't tuckin' our tails no more
Oh nah baby, we about to blow up."

Vanity's pseudo-female-empowerment anthem blasted in my ears as my feet pounded the treadmill at full speed – one last sprint, one last push to completely wring me of energy after the heavy lifting I'd done at the gym today.

Not that it was going to make any type of difference.

Not when I was growing a baby.

I... still wasn't even sure how that shit happened.

I mean, I knew how it happened, but I didn't know *how* it happened. I'd been single for damn near six months at this point, and my sexual encounters since then were basically non-existent. Last I checked, you couldn't get pregnant from heavy-petting, and even *that* disaster of a date had been a few months back.

I was happily focused on my career, working on opportunities that would stretch beyond social media. I had my sisters, I had friends, I had a little box in my bedside drawer that could more than deliver on any of my sexual needs.

I wasn't thinking about a *man*.

And I damn sure wasn't thinking about a *baby*.

Did you get drunk and have a fling or something? Sleepride the dick? Immaculate conception?

Shit.

I finished my cooldown and climbed off the treadmill, trudging all the way to the showers. Even in this private gym, it felt like everybody was looking at me – some of them *definitely* were, because even though it was a thriving college town, Blakewood could still feel small.

Especially with all my business in the streets.

On the internet, I could easily pretend it never happened, ignoring any comments or questions about it. Of course, that wasn't stopping anyone from asking, but the last thing I had any capacity for right now was strangers invading this aspect of my life.

As if that live stream hadn't invited them *right* in.

I really could kick my own ass for that.

I never – *never* – would have taken that test so cavalierly, and definitely not live with thousands of viewers, if I'd considered pregnancy as even a loose option. And I knew it wasn't a false positive, because Jaclyn and Jemma had gone out to get more tests, which I'd promptly taken, hoping for a different result.

They all said the same damn thing.

My parents were finally getting their damn grandbaby.

I THINK I MIGHT NEED YOU

After my shower, I dressed in sweats and a hat, hiding the bulk of my face behind oversized sunglasses. Seemingly overnight, I'd developed a whole host of new symptoms related to my... condition.

My breasts and back were aching, I was over the top exhausted, and all I wanted to do was eat my way through one of the two gallons tubs at *Dreamery*.

Of course, that could've all just been my obsessive research talking.

It had started with me making sure it was okay for me to go to the gym – I *needed* that outlet for all this mess, or it would drive me crazy. I'd quickly gotten a "yes" about that, but of course I hadn't stopped there. Once I started, I ended up awake until three in the morning, reading horror stories about women who hadn't known they were pregnant until the baby was *literally* coming out.

So... when I thought about, I'd gotten lucky, I guess.

I was halfway across the parking lot, on my way to be obsessively early for my prenatal appointment at University Medical Center. My cousin, Joseph Wright, was chief resident there, but I was more concerned with getting to his wife, Devyn. Nothing against Joey, but having my male cousin examining my pussy wasn't *quite* something I wanted to do, but I was more than comfortable with Dev.

I would *not* be live-streaming the appointment this time.

"Yo, Joia!"

The sudden sound of my name nearly made me jump out of my skin, and I glanced around the parking lot, heart racing. Alarm was *quickly* replaced with annoyance when my eyes landed on the source of that unnecessary loudness.

Theodore Graham.

Damn him for looking as good as he did.

I'd read something about baby hormones making you crazy horny, so I attributed my suddenly hard nipples to that, and *not* an overwhelming attraction to all six feet, ten inches, two-hundred-eighty pounds of Teddy. Although, that *had* always been part of what drew me to him, even back in college, where we'd first met. He was a big, sprawling sort of man, the kind that was distinctly... climbable.

And boy did I want to plant my pussy *right* at the top of that tree.

He was wearing a frown as he strolled toward me, dressed like an ad for a summer issue men's magazine. I'd never admit to him – hell it hurt to admit it to myself – but he looked damn good too, in his casual loafers and floral print shorts, with the matching button-up undone enough to show his chest. The mint green base of the fabric popped against his dark-brown-sugar skin, making it glow.

He looked *goodt*.

Yeah, with the "t" on the end.

Real goodt.

"Joia, I really can't believe you – I thought we were better than this, baby."

He stopped in front of me, smelling like cedar and linen.

Shit.

"What the hell are you talking about?" I asked him, crossing my arms to hide my nipples, which were so hard they were showing through my damn sweatshirt.

He pursed his lips. "Don't play that shit with me girl, you let another nigga get you pregnant, like *I* wasn't supposed to be the one to ruin your Summer. That's cold as hell, Jo."

"I will fucking *kill you*," I threatened, as a grin spread across his face. "You're *not* funny!"

Teddy clapped a hand to his chest like I'd wounded him. "Why you gotta take it there?"

"Why *you* gotta take it there?!" I countered. "This shit isn't funny."

"My bad, baby. Tell me what you need."

"I *need* you to stop calling me baby. We broke up *eight* years ago. I'm not your baby."

"But you're about to *have* a baby," he explained. "I'm just feeling a little sentimental, that's all. I ain't even know you were fucking with anybody like that."

Because I wasn't.

"Why does it matter to you anyway?" I asked.

"Cause I was getting ready to make my move and get your fine ass back, girl," he declared, narrowing his eyes at me.

"What makes you *ever* think I would want you back like that? Do you not remember why we broke up? It only takes me *once* to get disrespected, and guess what – you had your chance."

He sucked his teeth. "Man you always bringing up the past, like a nigga ain't changed between now and then."

"I don't know what you've done between now and then, other than be a goddamned fool on the internet. If you say you've grown up, good for you. But a *relationship* between you and me? That was never going to happen, baby or not," I explained, which was honestly more than he deserved.

I'd *loved* Teddy.

Loved the hell out of him.

Yes, we'd been young, but we'd also been cute as hell together, me as a cheerleader and him a rising star on the football team. We were *that* couple.

Or so I thought.

Until I found out he'd been telling his homeboys and teammates I was *not* his girl.

I was just somebody he was smashing.

I may have been in love, but he didn't give a shit about me – not enough to claim or respect me.

And now he wanted to act like I was the lost love of his life?

Nigga *please*.

"Daaaamn?" he grunted. "That's really how you feel?"

I looked up into his handsome face like I was squinting into the sun – those pretty eyes and pretty white teeth, that lush beard and full lips... I'd get burned if I looked too long.

"Yeah, Teddy – that's how I feel. I don't want to collab, I don't want to date, and I don't even want to be friends, honestly. We can be cordial when we see each other, but that's it. I wish you the best though, seriously. But I have an appointment to get to," I told him, swallowing hard after my somewhat harsh words.

I *wanted* to be past this shit with him, but his tendency to *not* give me any space if we were near each other made it hard. Maybe time would've made my heart grow fonder if there'd been a little absence, but it seemed like he was *always* there.

We were even peers online.

We'd agreed not to make our status as exes a thing online, but we hadn't kept it secret either. Because of that, people regularly asked about Teddy and me being a "thing" – a small annoyance that added to the bigger ones.

Like him asking to collab with me.

Because of our shared interests in fitness and nutrition, there was honestly some overlap between our audiences. But other than that, I was hair and beauty, while he was sports commentary and comedy sketches.

We were as far apart as we could be.

There was no reason for us to make things more than what they were.

"An appointment for the baby?" he asked, and I nodded. "Cool. Well... I know you think I'm not shit and all that, but... good luck with all that, aiight? I think you'll be great as a mother."

I smiled. "Thanks, Teddy."

I turned and made my way to the car, blowing out a deep breath once I was tucked into the driver's seat. I buckled my seatbelt and pulled out, heading for the hospital as Teddy's last words replayed in my head.

Making me panic.

I'd barely accepted the fact that I was pregnant... I hadn't even factored in the obvious endpoint, if everything went like it was supposed to.

I was going to have to *mother* this thing.

Shit.

I THINK I MIGHT NEED YOU

"Wow. Wow. *Wow.*"

"Yeah."

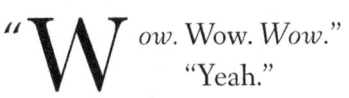

"*Wow.*"

"Mmmmhmmm."

"It's like... a whole ass baby."

"Yep."

"Like a for real baby, not...a blob. Or like, the little jellybean with feet thing. That's... a baby."

"Yes, Joia. It's a baby."

I turned my gaze from the – utterly *fucking* ridiculous – image on the ultrasound screen to Devyn, who was pressing the imaging wand to my still mostly-flat belly. When she realized I was looking at her, she looked at me, and we looked at each other, like Diddy and that nigga with funny hair from that meme.

I was waiting for her to tell me somebody was playing a *really* intricate joke on me.

Had to be.

"*How?*" I asked, finally, when she just kept staring at me with that same blank ass look, giving me nothing. "This is stupid. Right? This is stupid. *How* did this happen?"

Finally, she snickered. "Well, sometimes when a man and woman—"

"I know *how* I got pregnant, Devyn, I'm saying there is a full-blown fetus on that screen!"

She nodded. "Yeah. Yeah, there is. It's right there. I see it. Judging from these measurements your baby is right in line with about eighteen weeks."

My eyes bulged. "*Eighteen?!* Isn't that halfway through the fucking pregnancy?!"

"Yes. Yes, it is."

"How are you so calm right now?" I asked, pushing the wand

away from my belly to clear the image from the screen, and stop the steady throb of uterus music from the speaker.

Devyn's eyebrows lifted. "Cause *I'm* not the one having a damn baby. Got enough of those already."

"*Devyn!*"

"*Joia*," she shot back, immediately, laughing. "Listen, it's not uncommon for women to not know they're pregnant until fairly late. You've been my patient long enough that I know your cycles tend to be irregular, and you told me a little bit ago that you'd had light bleeding every month, even though you're obviously pregnant – that's not uncommon either. I remember you having the "stomach flu" a couple of months ago. That was probably morning sickness – lots of very lucky women don't suffer from it very long. You've never been pregnant before, and you're incredibly fit – that's why it took a while for you to start showing at all. *None* of this is surprising to me."

"Well that's great for you, but *I'm* about to start screaming," I told her.

She laughed as she grabbed my hand and squeezed. "Please do not start screaming in this room," she asked. "I understand it's overwhelming, but I hope *you* understand… you're going to be perfectly fine. The baby looks great, you look great, your bloodwork was great. And you have a family who is going to look out for you at *every* step, okay?"

I pushed out a deep sigh. "Um… okay. Okay," I repeated, shaking my head. I could say it all I wanted, but the truth of the matter was that the shit didn't *feel* okay.

It felt… nonsensical.

"You have to start taking prenatal vitamins, *today*," Devyn told me, getting back to business. "We may be starting late, but we need to get you on track with all of that. I'm assuming no drugs, right?"

I nodded, blankly. "Uh… right. Just my usual protein supplements and vitamins… but I've eaten brie, and I've drank in the last… shit, *five* months. Five fucking months. I'm *five* months

I THINK I MIGHT NEED YOU

pregnant. I've been in a hot tub, and I... hell, I went zip-lining two months ago! And, and... hookah! I've been at—"

"*Joia!*" Devyn insisted, squeezing my hands again. "Calm down, okay? You should cut those things out now, but please hear me when I say that your baby looks perfectly fine."

"But you don't *know*, right?" I countered, my heart racing as I looked her in the eyes. "There's all kinds of stuff that you don't know until the baby is born, and I've... probably already poisoned it, and ruined its' life, and—"

"You *cannot* think like that," she interrupted, her tone soothing. "The baby looks fine, like I said. In two weeks, we'll bring you back in for the "big" scan, okay? And if you're really concerned, amniocentesis is an option, but it's risky, and I do not think it's necessary. We'll test everything that we can without doing anything too invasive, and if there *is* something wrong, there are so many amazing surgeries and treatments and therapies and *whatever else* your baby might need. We've got you."

I pushed out a deep breath, trying to calm myself down before I nodded. "Okay. *Okay.* I hear you," I said, nodding again.

"Good," Devyn smiled. "Now... have you told the father yet?"

"What?"

She raised an eyebrow. "The *father*, Joia. Does the father know you're pregnant?"

A lump caught in my throat as my brain rolled back nineteen or twenty weeks, the time I would've had to conceive – right around the beginning of the year.

Maybe New Years?

Or maybe New Year's Eve...

Shit.

Shiiiit.

I remembered the party.

I remembered the drinks.

I remembered wanting to end the old year with a bang.

I remembered starting the new year *getting* banged.

"*Fuuuuck*," I groaned, covering my face with my hands as everything came in startling clear for me.

"Oooh," Devyn hissed. "That bad, huh?"

I pushed out a sigh, shaking my head as I dropped my hands to meet her gaze. "You have *no* idea."

THREE

TEDDY

"Wow, nigga, she really got you in your feelings, huh?" my cousin jeered over my shoulder. He was obviously talking about Joia's face on my cell phone screen, and I didn't even bother hiding the shit either.

She *did* have me in my damn feelings.

So much so that I wasn't paying any attention to the oversized computer screen in front of me, where we were supposed to be editing our latest skit. That shit was due to go live tomorrow, but I was much more concerned with what Joia had going on.

Damn.

She really about to have that nigga's baby.

Even after we broke up, I'd always kinda kept an eye on her – mostly because I couldn't believe how fucking stupid I was, letting her get away.

Well... *pushing* her away.

Top three mistakes in my *entire* life.

Cause now, I had to watch her get older and finer, and watch other niggas get the experiences with her that should've been mine. There had been this one moment where I thought I maybe had a chance, but then... next thing I knew, her ex was back in her face, dancing in her videos and shit.

And now she was about to give him a kid.

Damn.

I really lost the love of my life to *Happy Feet*.

That shit was hard to swallow.

I looked up at the computer screen just in time to see myself giving the camera a disturbing small smile, just before I turned and shot a basketball from all the way across the court. It had taken a bunch of repeats to get that shit right, but we eventually did, editing in a bunch of extra shit the ball did at the rim before finally going through the hoop for the game-winning shot we were parodying.

I couldn't tell if the shit wasn't funny or I just wasn't in a laughing mood.

"Looks good to me man," I told Len, so he could finish the editing without me holding us back. I got up to leave the "editing suite" – the second bedroom in my apartment – so I could grab something to eat.

I was still staring into my fridge when Len joined me in the kitchen.

"I could've told you ain't shit in here," he said, loud as fuck for no reason as he settled at the counter with his laptop. "I'm about to order some wings."

"*Bet*," I nodded, grabbing a beer instead, and handing him one too. I was quiet as I cracked it open, draining half of it in one gulp.

Len shook his head, lips pressed into a straight line as he looked at me. "You, my friend, are pitiful."

"The fuck you talking about?" I asked, leaning into the counter behind me.

"You walking around here sad as fuck over Joia instead of... just fucking getting her back."

I scoffed. "She's pregnant, bruh. You know she's about to get back with that nigga, that's how it goes."

"You talking about Dalton?" Len sucked his teeth. "You really admitting you don't have more juice than *that* nigga? That's sad."

"It ain't about *juice*," I said. "I *know* Jo – she's gonna try to make a family with him."

Len shook his head. "I'm telling you, *nah*. Dalton's wack ass played her to the left in that interview like they were just fucking. Sound familiar?"

I gave him a gas face behind that shit. Me and Len were family – had been tight since the playpen and stayed that way through college, so he knew *exactly* how the shit with me and Joia went down.

"Yeah, it's familiar – if I did basically the same shit, why would she deal with me if she won't deal with him?"

"Cause it's still fresh with him," Len explained. "We were kids back then man – we're coming up on thirty in a year or two. I bet if you dig down, she's not even really mad about that shit like that anymore."

I shrugged. "Even so, it doesn't change the fact that she's having his kid. What I look like trying to push my way into that situation?"

"You look like Russell Wilson swooping in to be a family man," Len laughed. "What your wack ass wants to be anyway. Just don't let her name that baby Dalton, please."

I chuckled. "You wild for that shit Len," I told him, shaking my head.

According to him, this was simple math, but from my purview… it was anything but.

Just yesterday, in the gym parking lot, she'd made it clear she didn't want shit to do with me, so the idea of pushing myself between her and the father of her child? The chances of that going in a way that was even remotely favorable for me were shaky.

Real shaky.

"All you gotta do is get the public on your side – you should make a video about her. *Yeah*, that's it right there."

My head popped up, tuning in to Len's words. "*What?*" I asked, frowning. "Man, *hell* nah. *Hellll* nah. Joia would hate that shit."

"But her fans would eat it up," Len insisted. "I'm telling you – you look like a superhero swooping in to save her and the baby from a fuckboy like Dalton. Your followers go up, *her* followers go up, everybody gets invested in seeing y'all become a happy family and shit. Then all you gotta do is sit back, watch her come around. Next thing you know, y'all got a joint brand, sponsored by Nabisco and shit. You see it."

"*Nigga,*" I groaned, wrinkling my nose. "You realize you're suggesting I use the internet into manipulating her into fucking with me?"

He gave me finger guns. "So you feel me. Let's get it. What's step one?"

"Step one is you *never* saying this shit out loud again," I laughed. "You're the *last* person I would ever take advice from on anything to do with women."

He frowned. "I get all kinda pussy my friend, you could stand to learn a thing or two from me."

"Didn't you have to take like two weeks' worth of antibiotics to get rid of—"

"*Whooooaa!*" he interrupted, shaking his head. "That's a low blow!"

I laughed. "Nah, what it is, is the truth. I don't need you to teach me *shit* about women."

"Aiight man, you got it," he told me, in a tone that clearly indicated he didn't think I did.

There was a difference between me and Len though – he thought it was only right to plow through the growing list of women that social media notoriety had put in our sphere of influence. I wouldn't front like I hadn't enjoyed the attention too, but I was a lot more reserved – a lot more *careful* – than Len was.

Hell, I was surprised no one had popped up yet with *his* baby.

I couldn't front – part of me wondered if my hesitation to dive face deep into that pool of women and get a comfortable backstroke going was because of Joia's constant presence in my peripheral. If we were just regular exes it would be easy to move on, but the overlap in our careers, in a city the size of Blakewood, made it impossible to really forget each other, like exes usually would.

Her ass was always *there*.

Randomly in the grocery store, or not so randomly at an influencer event, even on trips for certain brands. I couldn't get on social media without seeing her face – amplified by the fact that I'd chosen to follow her, but still.

I hadn't even called the agent I'd been put in touch with by Justin Wright.

The Justin Wright.

Because he was her cousin – a tidbit I hadn't realized until later. When she and I were together, he hadn't yet become *the* Justin Wright, so I didn't know him. And we never did make it to the point of introducing families, so there was no reason for him to know me.

He was already a big deal by time she and I reconnected on social media. When I saw him, months back, around Christmas, I wasn't even thinking. Well, I *was* thinking – about myself, and what he could maybe do for me. I didn't want to act a fool on the internet forever – it was fun, and I made decent money, but I was trying to get into something with some staying power.

So I talked to him, briefly.

He gave me the card.

I walked away.

And then remembered the video Joia had posted from Thanksgiving dinner with her family. Her *whole* family.

The Wrights included.

So that was the end of *that*.

I couldn't have her - or anybody else for that matter – thinking I was using her as a come-up.

That wouldn't fly.

While Len ordered up the wings and shit, my mind was

somewhere else – several places at once, to be honest. I forced myself to push Joia out of it, focusing instead on what I *should* be a lot more pressed about.

My *job*.

"Ay, when was the deadline for that *WAWG Fresh* pitch contest?" I asked Len. "Still not for another few weeks, right?"

Len looked up from his laptop and nodded. "Yeah... you thinking about it again? I thought you were off that?"

I shrugged. "Shit... maybe not."

It definitely wasn't an opportunity to brush off. WAWG – We All We Got – was a huge Black media company, featuring a full-blown television network. They'd just introduced a web presence, *Fresh*, and they were looking for talent. Writers, singers, artists, you name it – they were looking for everything. Part of that search was a pitch contest for streaming content and web series.

Well... contest wasn't quite the right way to frame it, since they'd made it clear they weren't choosing just one thing. There was plenty of room at the table... if only I could decide what the fuck to bring.

I got big laughs and viral shares for the parodies and shit online, but opening it up to a wider audience was a whole different beast. Trying to decide on one specific lane to brand myself in felt like trying to choose a favorite child... or at least, what I assumed it was like.

No way to choose a favorite without upsetting the rest of the crew.

"Aiight," Len said, giving me his full attention. "Let's pin that shit down, bruh. What you got for 'em? You on your Bernie Mac shit or your Billy Blanks shit? Stephen A Smith or Wayne Brady. What you got?"

"I got *nothing*," I told him, truthfully. "I get a decent response for everything I put up, so how the fuck am I supposed to choose?"

Len nodded. "Okay, okay, I feel you. So... let me pitch something to you."

My eyebrows went up. "Okay..."

"Picture it," Len grinned, his eyes glazing over. "Me and you, road-tripping, seeing everything this beautiful country has to offer. Mountains, lakes, trees, desert... and ass."

"Ass?"

"*Ass*," he repeated, rubbing his hands together. "We ask the people to tell us the best strip club in every state, we hit 'em up, judge for ourselves. I even have a name for it already – *Hoes Across America*. Tell me that shit ain't an instant classic."

I shook my head, chuckling. "You gotta get somebody else for that," I told him. "*But*... I'm not opposed to your dumbass being on screen with me for this. Hell, we can get the whole family involved – the Grahams are some entertaining motherfuckers."

"That we are," Len grinned. "Come with it though, what you got?"

"Graham Table Talk. We sit around, shoot the shit, eat smores and shit."

"Nah."

"American Ninja Graham – I'll wax the whole family on some gladiator shit."

He shook his head. "Man ain't nobody climbing no rock walls and shit. Gimme something else."

"The Nigga – like the bachelor, but all the men in the family compete to figure which one of us is *that* nigga. Spoiler alert – it's me."

"Definitely not you, but we can write that shit down. What else?"

"Dancing with the Grah – nah, nevermind. I can't sink to that nigga Dalton's level. The Graham Race – my parents would be all over some global scavenger hunt shit. Graham Factor. Make everybody eat your sister's potato salad," I laughed, thinking about how hard Lachelle had gotten roasted about it at Easter.

"You trying to give me nightmares nigga?" Len asked, frowning as he put his hand to his stomach. "I was sick for a week behind that shit, and you know Chelle *still* swears "our palettes just aren't refined enough"?"

I busted out laughing. "Nah, our goddamn *intestines* weren't refined enough. That was some Becky-ass potato salad, cuz. Chelle gotta keep her ass off Pinterest and get in the family recipes."

"She wants to try again for the fourth of July."

I scoffed, shaking my head. "Hell nah – my independent ass won't be in the blast radius this time."

Len chuckled. "She's using Big G's recipe supposedly. No telling how it's gonna actually go though."

"You know what – *that* shit might be worth putting on camera. *The Graham Cookout Cookoff*. Challenges with our family recipes from our ancestors and shit."

"Ain't no way you're serious," Len scoffed. "Nixon would bring his ass over from *The Heights* and wash *all* of us in the kitchen."

I shook my head. "Nah, him and Charlie too busy being Hollywood and raising all those damn kids. They don't even cook like that anymore. Out of practice."

Len sat back, a dreamy look on his face. "*Mm.* Charlie's fine ass..."

"She's family, nigga!"

He sucked his teeth. "By marriage, not blood, which means she's fair game for my admiration."

"That's mad incest-y Len, but I'ma let you rock," I told him, frowning. "Anyway – you writing this shit down?"

"Hell nah, it's all wack," he countered.

"It's not *all* wack, and it's called brainstorming, fool. I'm trying to put us on."

Len waved that off. "Man, you know the Grahams ain't gone act right. Unless you're trying to make it a cage fighting thing."

I tipped my head to the side. "Hmm. GGH – Grahams Got Hands. I'm kinda into that shit. And my moms still owes yours an ass whooping over Uncle June, so shit... we can probably make it happen."

"You know my mama got fibromyalgia dude, that ain't funny," Len replied, giving me a sour face.

I THINK I MIGHT NEED YOU

I nodded, solemn. "You right, my bad. Mama and Aunt *Shelby* should box."

Len's eyes lit up. "Yeah, there you go. *That's* the match."

My mom and her sister Shelby had been feuding since before I was born, and when they got in the same room, it was straight comedy. Jokes, fists, wigs – anything was liable to start flying, and it was the highlight of family events for me and my cousins.

It really didn't belong on the screen though.

"I'm overthinking this shit, right?" I asked Len, and he nodded.

"Yep," he agreed. "And you a funny dude Teddy, but when you get in your head... critical wack."

I sat back in my chair with a sigh. "Damn."

"You've got too much on your mind," Len guessed – correctly. "This shit ain't due for weeks, so don't sweat it. If something comes to you, it comes, and if not, this wasn't the opportunity for you. We gone eat these wings, pop some brews, and I'ma whoop ya ass in 2K."

"Hashtag, self-care."

"So you *feel* me," he exclaimed.

"Yeah," I nodded. "Let's get this shit going."

FOUR

Joia

Who the fuck doesn't know they're five months pregnant? *How?*
How?
How?

That question had been playing in my head, on a nearly constant loop, since my appointment with Devyn. In those two days, everything seemed to have amplified again. Or... maybe I was just paying attention now, whereas before, when pregnancy hadn't even been a possibility, I easily wrote off every twinge, every ache, every little change to my body.

Now, I was obsessively hyper-aware of it all.

Fresh from the shower, I stared at my body in the mirror, no longer confused about my growing breasts and midsection. I shook my head, thinking of the months I'd spent kicking my ass in the gym and fervently avoiding sugar to combat those very changes.

My *Ms. Fit Bitch* nickname had been well-earned, and it was one

I was proud of. Nevermind the fact that I'd *started* working out to get a little of what my sisters had naturally. Jaclyn had been blessed with the body type the internet referred to as *Big Fine* – healthy servings of beautiful curves. Jemma was naturally slim, with more than her fair share of ass and hips, and perfect c-cup breasts that looked good in everything. She traveled the world eating all manner of carbs and spending *no* time in the gym, and yet... she looked like she did.

If I didn't have my ass in the squat rack multiple times a week, I wasn't *Ms. Fit Bitch*.

I was *Ms. Flat Back*.

With a lack of tits to match.

But I'd come to love it.

Even with my complaints and comparisons, I'd built a body that I loved, doing something I loved, and it was hard to accept what felt like a ridiculously sudden change to that. I'd worked my ass off for abs, and seemingly overnight, they were fading.

Maybe this was the type of thing that, if I'd known sooner, I could've prepared for.

I closed my eyes, scolding myself *again*, because seriously... *What the fuck, Joia?!*

I'd pushed it out of my head before, but the night of that party was so, *so* clear now. I'd looked good as hell in my little metallic mini dress and sky-high heels, not caring that I was towering over a decent portion of the crowd.

I was having a great time – exactly like you were supposed to in Vegas. *Bet on Black* was an organization started by the Drake family, with a focus on supporting and amplifying Black talent in a wide range of categories. I'd been excited as hell to get the invitation to their annual New Years' Eve party, knowing the exposure for my brand it entailed.

And it didn't hurt that they covered the travel expenses.

It was a party full of Black people all dressed up in shiny things – probably my favorite kind of party. Lots of familiar faces from the big screen, the small screen, the internet, the radio, and a lot of new people to meet too. Great music, good food, plentiful liquor. It was exactly what I needed coming off a fresh breakup.

I wasn't thinking about Dalton's ass *at all*.

I was laughing, talking, drinking, dancing, *no tears left to cry* and all that jazz.

But then, of course, because anything else would've been too good to be true... there *he* was.

"Dalton – what the hell are you doing here?" I asked, scrambling to cover myself with the oversized tee I'd laid out on my bed before my shower. I'd opened my eyes now, and was back in my room, just me and what apparently had decided *not* to stay in Vegas.

And goddamn *Dalton*.

My question seemed to pull him out of whatever trance my naked frame had put him in – he blinked, and held up his key ring.

"We broke up. Why exactly do you still have a key to my place?" I asked, not bothering to suppress my scowl as I moved to my dresser to retrieve a pair of panties. "And again, what are you doing here?"

He squinted at me – always with the stereotypical light-skinned shit, ugh. "You're not answering your phone, or returning messages."

"I don't have any missed calls or messages from you Dalton, because I blocked you on all possible mediums when we broke up. You don't exist to me anymore."

He frowned. "You don't think that's harsh?"

"You told *Sugar & Spice* magazine that you and I "weren't even like that" and "were just having fun", while also implying that my career wasn't good enough for you. And oh yeah – whatever bitch that was you described as your *dream girl*? Definitely didn't sound like me."

Dalton sucked his teeth, moving toward me as I pulled on a pair of jeans. "The chick doing the interview asked my preference, that's all," he offered as a rebuttal, like that made the shit *any* better.

"Yeah... and it sounds like you don't *prefer* me, so I did us both a fucking favor."

I let out a sigh of relief as the jeans easily buttoned over my stomach. I was using every bit of stretch they had, but still.

A win was a win.

"That's your problem – you always tripping over what shit looks like, instead of what it is. We were good until I *said* some shit on an interview, trying to keep my female fans happy. That makes sense to you?"

I rolled my eyes. "Dude – I'm not about to rehash this with you. I felt disrespected, plain and simple, so I bounced. *Six months ago.* Give me my key, and get the fuck on. We don't have shit to talk about."

"You're *pregnant*, Joia," he said, his tone switching from annoyed to stern. "We actually have plenty to talk about when you're having *my* baby."

"*I love* how you assume it's yours," I shot back, propping my hands on my hips. "Do I *look* six months pregnant to you?" I asked, knowing I barely looked *any* months pregnant, let alone what most people would think of as six.

He scoffed. "Stop fucking around, you know *damn* well I've been in that pussy since we broke up. You weren't fronting two months ago, or the time—"

"I didn't fuck you two months ago," I interrupted, with a fresh scowl. I *had* been guilty of doubling back to him in weakness, but it certainly hadn't been two months ago, or even close.

Dalton's lips pursed. "Joia... come on, we're the only ones here. You ain't gotta front."

"Nobody's *fronting*. I haven't even *seen you* since we ran into each other at the BSU Valentine's Day mixer thing. And I didn't fuck you *then* either," I told him.

His gaze went to the ceiling, eyes narrowing as he thought about it. "Damn... you know what..."

"No, and I don't want to," I told him, closing the distance between us to pull his key ring from his hand. I knew exactly which one it was, still on the black ring I'd given it to him on, so I had my key off before he could protest. "Get the hell out of my apartment, Dalton," I said, tossing the rest of his keys back to him. "I'm still processing this news myself – I am *not* about to discuss it you, on any level, and you can't make me."

He stared at me for a few moments and I stared right back, honestly prepared to kick his ass if he didn't leave. Dalton and I were the same height, damn near the same weight, and I knew for a fact I was more of a beast in the gym than he was.

I liked my odds, honestly.

"We *will* talk about this shit *soon* Joia – you really don't have an option," he warned, as he turned to leave.

"Yeah, kiss my ass," I called after him, then followed behind to make sure he'd actually left before I locked the door.

Shit.

I had enough to worry about without him popping up unannounced. I could only deal with one mistake at a time, and he was furthest from my priorities, especially when I didn't need his trifling ass involved in any aspect of this pregnancy.

He wanted to downplay what he'd done, but as far as our relationship went, it had been an extinction level event for me.

Growing up in the Love household meant knowing how to take a joke, knowing how to roast back, knowing not to take yourself or others *too* seriously. Room for flexibility and all that. It also meant watching my mother and father – and my uncle and aunt – love each other fiercely, without ambiguity. I wanted the same thing for me.

Both of my parents drilled into us to never let anybody make us feel unworthy, or unwanted, in *any* capacity. On a job, in a friendship, in a relationship – there was always room to walk away.

So I did.

I was willing to argue and make up. Willing to apologize when I was wrong, to forgive if needed. Willing to put in work when it wasn't always pretty – those things had been modeled for me.

I was *not* willing to be denied.

Instant fucking deal breaker.

What Dalton *didn't* want to acknowledge is that we were the *height* of serious with each other when he gave that interview, just after Thanksgiving. He ate with my family, played with my little cousins, drank with my father. We were looking for a place together.

I *loved* him.

I was good with not mentioning him in my videos, or posting selfies and shit – I didn't want the internet in my business that much *anyway*. I was fine with him dodging questions about who he was dating, or being vague. I wasn't stupid, I knew it was part of the business. Sure, he was a professional dancer and choreographer, and got paid good money from big stars to amplify their stage. But his *fame* came from the internet – videos of him dancing went viral, women lusted over him, paid to attend his pop-up classes, and all that. There was value in him appearing to be attainable.

And that was *fine*.

But then that interview came.

And instead of simply dodging the question about me, he rolled his eyes. *Adamantly* denied being involved with me, in a manner that made it seem like it was ridiculous that he'd choose me. He went on a tangent about the internet making stuff up – and turning "anybody" into a faux celebrity they could link with a *real* one.

It was clear which of us he thought belonged in each role.

Honestly, I was done there, but then the kicker came – this *stupid* fucking game they always played at the end, where the guest built their "dream girl/guy".

Petite. Quiet. Curvy. Nympho. Caramel Skin. Homebody. No Weave.

It was like he was *trying* to describe the polar opposite of me.

And he expected me to... take it?

Wrong bitch.

I heard my cell phone chiming from my room and rushed to check the screen, answering immediately when I saw that it was Jemma.

"I know I'm running behind," I told her before she could start on me. "I'm on my way, I swear, I just got interrupted. Dalton popped up out of nowhere."

On the other end of the line, Jemma sucked her teeth. "*Ugh*. I'm assuming he wanted to talk about the baby? He *is* planning to step up, right?"

"Not ready to discuss, Jem," I reminded her. I loved my sisters, loved my parents, and I knew they had questions, knew they wanted to support me, but like I'd told Dalton – I needed a minute to process the shit myself, without any input other than the doctor.

I still didn't even fully believe this mess was happening.

So before I heard what *everybody else* thought I should do, or should've done, or wanted... I needed to figure it out on my own.

"Oh *fine*," Jemma sighed. "Anyway – I was actually *hoping* you were still home. I need you to bring me a different pair of shoes – the ones I wore for the party are killing me."

I chuckled. "Ah, perils of a bad bitch. You have another pair in your luggage that would work, or you need me to bring a pair of mine?"

"Do you even really need to ask?"

"Nah." I thought back to what she was wearing as I moved to my closet and looked around. "Nude sandals with a chunky heel work? Three inches?"

"Sounds perfect. Thanks little sisterrrrr," she sang.

"You're welcome. I just have to finish getting dressed and do my face, then I'll be heading to the bookstore. Do you need anything else? A coffee? Gum? A bowl of weed?"

She laughed. "All of the above honestly, but I'll settle for just the shoes. And your face in the place. *Hurry*."

"I'm coming," I promised before we exchanged goodbyes and hung up. Jemma's book had launched today, and she was already freaking out about her climbing Amazon sales rank and the preliminary reviews. As far as I knew, the reception so far had been positive. I hadn't expected anything else though – Jemma's social media presence was nothing to sneeze at. She was popular, and well-liked.

And honestly, the book was good as hell.

She had *nothing* to worry about.

I took off the tee-shirt I'd donned because of Dalton's presence, replacing it with a bra to support my aching breasts – a brand new purchase, since I'd finally given up on trying to make the other ones fit. This one was a pretty, delicate thing made of ultra-soft lace that I topped with a sheer button-up. With my high-waisted jeans, and the hem of the shirt hitting me at the hips, you couldn't even tell I was pregnant.

Other than my swollen face.

Jaclyn swore I was imagining it, but *I* could swear I was filling up like a balloon. So I took the little extra time to do some contouring on my face, giving some definition where there was none anymore, and taking my hair down from my puff to let it hang around my face for even more camouflage.

Not that any of that mattered, when *everybody* knew.

All because of that stupid live stream.

The whole embarrassing thing had been downloaded and shared countless times, for everyone to see. And the thing was, they didn't even know yet just *how* mortifying it actually was.

But they'd know in about four months when I popped up with a baby.

Hell, before then, when my midsection morphed into a watermelon.

I pushed out a sigh, and left the mirror alone, focusing on getting myself out the door, with the shoes Jemma had requested. As much as I wanted to just crawl in bed, there was something much more pressing on my agenda.

Supporting my sister.

FIVE

Teddy

"Ay, ay, ay – make sure you get the sandals in there boy," I shouted to Len, posing in front of the grill with the long-handled fork in one hand, spatula in the other.

My mother shook her head as she walked past us, peeling the protective film off a brand-new bottle of bubble solution for the group of kids running around the yard. "Theo, you see what you've started?"

She wasn't talking to me – she was talking to my father, who'd come to join me on camera as Len streamed live from my phone. His hands were full, hefting a huge container of seasoned ribs he was getting ready to put on the big grill in the backyard, in preparation for something my mother's church was hosting the next day.

He'd just bestowed me with a privilege I'd been waiting on my whole life.

"Aiight, stop playing and come on son," he called, turning his attention back to his duties as grill master. "Time to put the ribs on."

I grinned right into the camera, cocky as fuck as I nodded. "For those of you who may not understand the gravity of this moment, let me break it down for you – being the one to put ribs on the grill isn't something to take lightly. It's an art to this shit, and I been observing my whole damn life – never got to touch the ribs. I had to put in the time, you know? Mastering the perfect seasoning rub, the perfect sauce. Taste testing. Studying cook times and heat zones and grease splatter, all that. Dedicated myself to the swine, you heard?"

I switched hands, using one to hold up my shirt so the live viewers could see the words across my stomach. "Y'all see this shit? This is dedication – *Rib Life*."

"Lil' boy you'd better not have tattooed *Rib Life* across yo' stomach!" Mama hollered from across the yard.

"I didn't choose the *Rib Life*, the *Rib Life* chose me!" I answered her, wagging my tongue at the camera since the shit was obviously done in washable marker. "I got the Jesus sandals. I got the crew socks. I got the fork *and* the spatula. I got the muhfuckin' *tongs* over there, just waiting on me, I'ma flip the *shit* outta these ribs."

My dad laughed. "*You gone do what now?!*"

"*I said*, I'ma flip the *shit* outta these ribs," I replied, easily going along with his call-and-response. "But I gotta put 'em on first, so come on, let's do it. Len, make sure you get in here real good, make sure you pick up this sizzle."

"Oh we ready, we ready for it, come on," Len encouraged, walking with me to join my father at the grill.

My father had already put the ribs down on the outdoor counter, and now he held up his hands, stepping between me and the grill. "Hold up there young buck. You need one more thing."

"Oh *God*," my mom muttered as she passed us again, going back inside. "A house full of fools."

"Before you touch this grill," he continued, like she hadn't said anything. "I bestow onto you... the hat."

"*Ohhhh shit*," Len exclaimed, as my father removed his hat – a faded red BMW – Black man working – hat I'd given him two decades ago as a birthday gift, purchased with money I'd earned trimming hedges around the neighborhood. It was tattered and stained with God knows what from the *everywhere* he'd worn it. Fishing trips, hiking, water parks, cruises. You name it, that hat had been there, and hadn't been washed the whole time.

I was excited as a mothafucka for him to put in on me though. *Backward.*

"Yo. Yo," I said, nodding at the camera as I choked up a bit. "This is... man... y'all, look at my motherfuckin' *drip* right now!" I roared at the camera, hitting them with a little spin so they could take it all in. "Y'all can't take it – I *know* you can't take it. This is high-quality Black dad swag, uncut, premium, *you see it.*"

"They gotta inject this shit straight into the veins, yo," Len agreed, gassing me as my father cracked up, and my mother watched from the screen door into the kitchen, straight-faced.

"Are you fools gonna put that food on the grill or not?" she asked, sounding annoyed at my antics, but she would be the first person to hit the "like" button whenever I posted a clip from this.

"Anything for you, Mama. *Anything* for Selenas!"

"*Anything for Selenas!*" Len repeated, prompting her to roll her eyes.

"Don't be calling me by my first name, y'all ain't too old for me to make you go get a switch!" she warned, pointing between us. "Even you, Theo."

My father grinned. "I'll go get it right now, long as it goes both wa—"

"*Naaaaah!*" I yelled, waving my hands. "Ma'am, sir, this is a Wendy's!"

"I'm too young for this kind of content," Len chimed in. "There are laws against this."

"There's gone be some laws against your *butt* if those ribs aren't ready by tomorrow," Mama said, giving us the stink eye again.

"That don't even make sense, Mama. Why you always saying stuff like that?"

"I'ma make sense upside your head if you keep questioning me."

I looked straight into the camera. "*See?*"

She was serious though.

And it was getting later in the day, damn near sundown – we *did* need to get these ribs on.

"Listen to that – y'all hear that fuckin' *sizzle?*" I asked the live audience as I carefully lined up slab after slab on my dad's big custom grill. "*Grah-ams baby back riiiiibs,*" I sang as I finished, admiring my work. "Aiight y'all, let me drop some knowledge on you. If we were talking wine, I'd be your *sommelier,* but we ain't that fancy 'round here, so this is from Theodore Graham Jr, your official *Grill-melier.* Barbecue ain't just about the taste, aiight? It's the taste, the tenderness, the texture, the *aroma.* Y'all smell that right now? Nah, you don't, but it's fuckin' delightful, trust me."

On the other side of the phone, I watched Len glance at his watch, and then his eyes went wide. A moment later, he was giving me the "wrap it up" signal.

Damn, what time is it now?

I couldn't check my own watch, but I went ahead with what he was prompting me to do.

"Aiight y'all, it's been real. Ribs are on, and now they need their privacy and all that, so we gone let them do what they do behind closed doors and I'll make sure to update y'all with the finished product. Later."

I gave the camera a one-handed salute as I held my shirt up again, and a few seconds later Len lowered the camera, giving me a thumbs up to let me know I was no longer live.

As soon as I was clear, I looked at my watch, immediately understanding why he'd reacted like he did to the time.

I was off schedule.

I'd come over here to check in with my parents and do the grill thing with my father – the live stream was impromptu. I hadn't, however, intended to stay as long as I did. Not when I'd been contacted and recruited by Toni Wright as "press" for Jemma Love's book launch.

Tonight.

"We gotta head out," Len said, returning my phone, and I nodded.

"Already on it," I answered back, extending a hand to my father to say goodbye.

"Come by in the morning to get a picture of these ribs – and pick you up one of these pretty young church girls," he suggested, accepting my hand. Before I could say anything, he used his free hand to retrieve his hat from my head. "*What?*" he asked, in response to my open mouth. "I know your ass didn't think I was *giving* you my hat."

"But the... you *bestowed* it!"

"I be-*loaned* it," he chuckled. "I was helping you put a lil bit of... what you call it? *Drip* on your show."

"I see you Uncle Theo," Len laughed, dapping him up. "We might have to get you in on this a little more often, I like the improv."

"You young niggas ain't the only ones know what's going on," my father quipped, turning to go inside. "Ask about me."

Len and I shared a laughed about *that* shit, then went inside to say goodbye to my mother. A few minutes later, we were headed out – I was dropping him at his own place, then heading to mine to try to make something happen in the... *forty-five* minutes I had before this book launch party started.

Before I was back in the same space with Joia again.

With her fine ass.

All the Love sisters were fine, but Joia was a special kind of beautiful – though I could be biased. That pretty ass copper skin, those cheekbones, those lips, long ass toned legs, all that hair, and those deep brown eyes that could get a nigga lost.

Hell... we'd been broken up for years and I was *still* mesmerized.

With Len in the car, my thoughts couldn't drift too far, not with his constant stream of commentary and questions. Once I'd dropped him off though, I was free to let my thoughts wander... straight back to Joia, of course.

In fact, the more I thought about it, the more Len's dumb ass advice from the other day seemed... less dumb. Yeah, Joia might be inclined to make a family with Dalton's ass because of the baby, just because it seemed like the simple, best option.

So... maybe I should give her a better one.

SIX

Joia

He smelled like ribs.
    Not the wack, chain restaurant stuff either. His aroma was smoky, mouthwatering... real ribs. Even over the smell of books and magazines and champagne, his scent prevailed.

Just a whiff at first.

Calling me.

I turned around and there he was, hugging Jemma, his cell phone camera pointed at both of them as he rattled off details about the book, telling people where to purchase, what it was about, all that.

It was great promo, honestly – so good that I wasn't even mad about him being there. Toni had pulled me aside to warn me about it, but Jemma had already broken the news that morning.

"Protecting my energy", she'd called it.

I appreciated both of them for looking out for me like that, while also not letting the personal shit interfere with good marketing decisions. It would be different if it were Dalton, where the offense was much deeper, and still relatively fresh. Sure, I'd told Teddy I didn't want much to do with him behind our breakup, but honestly... *honestly*... I was pretty over it.

I wasn't bothered by his presence.

At least, not in the sense of being angered by it. I was *plenty* bothered – nobody else seemed to notice that he was carrying the scent of a Summer cookout, but I sure did, and it was making me hungry as hell. And looking at him was making me *horny* as hell.

He'd always been handsome, and every detail of his face was well-imprinted in my mind. Still, for some reason, his smile was doing extra things to me tonight – his lips, those beautiful teeth, the way his eyes damn near disappeared, getting lost in his cheeks. It wasn't just the mechanics of it either – when Teddy smiled, it made you want to smile too, which could be dangerous.

That smile, that charm... it was how he'd gotten me in the first place.

I really didn't need to get snared again.

"JoJo," someone behind me sang, and I turned just in time to catch a glimpse of Reese's face before she pulled me into a hug. I returned the gesture easily, rocking with her back and forth, and grinning when we finally parted. "So... are you feeling okay?"

I nodded, already knowing what she was asking. Reese was one of my biggest fans – and another of my cousins, since she'd married Jason Wright. This was my first time seeing her in person since accidentally announcing my pregnancy.

"I do feel okay," I told her. "Just processing." I stepped in, bending a little to tell her what no one besides Devyn knew as of yet. "I'm already eighteen weeks in."

Her eyes bugged wide as she turned to meet my gaze. "Are you serious?!" When I nodded, she touched her own belly – *much* more pronounced than mine. "Joia, that's only like two months behind me!"

"Yeah. *Yeah*." I blew out a breath. "It's... a lot to manage, mentally."

She nodded. "Uh, *yeah*. The emotions that come with pregnancy are tough enough on their own, but to find out so suddenly, when you're *this* far along... girl..."

"So you feel me then."

Reese laughed. "Uh, yeah. I do. Have you told the father yet?"

"No."

Her eyebrows went up. "Are you... going to?"

"Yes. *Yes*, of course," I insisted. "I'm just not ready to have that conversation with him yet. He can be a lot, and..."

"This is *already* a lot," Reese finished for me, nodding. "You have time, so don't sweat it... if you can help it. Your biggest concern right now is your health. Physically and mentally. Take care of yourself, Joia."

I nodded. "I'm trying. I promise."

Reese kissed beside my cheek – to not get lipstick on me – and then moved on, leaving me to think about what she'd said. She was seven or eight months along now, and she and Jason were *so* cute together. So happy and in love and *thrilled* to be having a baby, especially after their tragic loss of a pregnancy a while ago.

They'd wanted this.

Prayed for this.

And here I was halfway through it by accident, kicking myself about it.

Shit.

It wasn't that I didn't want children – I *did*. I'd thought about – dreamt about it – with every boyfriend I ever had, and a few I hadn't. I just never pictured it happening... like this.

"Can we get everybody's attention," Toni said over the mic, bringing a bit of order to the crowded venue. "Thank you all so, *so* much for being here, to support Jemma and her new book. I know we're having a good time partying, but it's time to sign some names, and before that, Jemma would like to say a few words. Jemma?"

I watched, proud as hell, as Jemma approached the center of the room to take the mic from Toni. Happiness was just *radiating* off of her, and when she started speaking, you could hear it all in her voice.

"So I'm going to try not to cry," she started, fanning her face with her hand. "But y'all already know the deal, so I'm just gonna cry and talk, how about that?"

I made sure she was centered in the viewfinder as I pointed my cell phone at her, streaming her speech to my audience. As she spoke, I glanced around the crowd to pinpoint our family – every face I found was beaming with pride.

She'd *done* it.

Something she'd talked about for so long, and finally accomplished, along with everything else. This was working out to be a big year for the Love sisters – Jaclyn graduating from college, Jemma with her book release.

And... me with a baby.

I sucked in a deep breath, fighting back the urge for tears. My reasons were myriad – a mix of pride in my sisters, shared emotion with Jemma who was full blown crying now, and... something else.

Something not-so-pretty.

I was supposed to be pitching an idea to *WAWG Fresh,* which could be a huge opportunity for my career. My sisters and I had been planning a joint trip together, to Bali, at the end of Summer. It was occurring to me now that the trip wouldn't be happening anymore – not with me at least.

All my little goals, all my plans for the rest of the year... rendered useless.

Pointless.

Gone.

As soon as Jemma finished her speech, I made sure I was one of the first people surrounding her for hugs – which meant I could also be one of the first to sneak away. I *hated* feeling like this, like I couldn't even keep it together long enough to focus on Jem and her big moment, but I... I just needed a fucking break.

So I took it.

I made my way through the store, taking refuge in the quiet and solace of... the children's section. I folded all five feet, nine inches of me down into one of the tiny chairs and stretched out my legs, closing my eyes as I pushed out a deep breath.

And another.

And another.

Until finally, the urge to cry had passed.

For now.

"You practicing already?"

My eyes popped open at the sound of Teddy's voice. I looked up to find him standing in the entrance of the children's section, looking like a wet dream.

Or maybe just mine.

"Practicing what?" I asked, averting my gaze. Teddy had never been afraid of color against his deep brown skin, and tonight was no different – he was in a smoky-purple tracksuit made of sweatshirt material that clung to his strong biceps and stronger thighs and... *goddamn* he looked good.

You're not supposed to like him, Joia, remember?

"The mommy thing," he explained. "Since you're in the kids' section?"

"Oh!" I shook my head. "No, I'm just... taking a moment."

He scraped his teeth over his lip as he gave me a slow nod. "Aiight. You need anything, or you good?"

I took a chance on looking up, meeting his eyes. "Seriously? Why are you being all... cool? I know you're here for Jemma, but that doesn't mean you have to be nice to me."

"You're the one who doesn't like *me*, Jo. It was never the other way around."

"I don't *dislike* you," I told him, even though I'd definitely just scolded myself about this exact thing less than thirty seconds ago. I *wanted* to dislike Teddy, and for years, it had been very easy to stay in that mode. With me, there were only three shades to the way I engaged people – black, white, gray. I didn't fuck with you, I fucked with you, or I was *extremely* neutral.

As an ex, Teddy had been on my *"IDFWU"* list since that fateful day on the yard.

But with so much else on my mind now, I... hell.

I couldn't find it in myself to keep acting on the *"active hostility"* part of my grudge.

Teddy's reaction to my claim of *not* disliking him was a cringe of active disbelief, which I couldn't blame him for, considering our last interaction, in the gym parking lot.

And the one before that, just a few weeks ago, when I'd cursed him out for daring to ask me if I wanted to collaborate on a fitness video tag together.

I could see now where I'd maybe overdone it a little.

"You might be the first woman to ever be *nicer* once the pregnancy jumps off. Baby got your emotions hitting a little different, huh?" he asked, grinning.

Before I could tell him just how much he was pushing it, my stomach spoke up, growling loud as hell to complain about my current lack of dinner.

Teddy's face pulled into an amused frown. "Damn. You want me to go grab you something?"

"From the catered stuff?" I wrinkled my nose thinking about the way my body had instantly revolted against the table of food as soon as I ventured too close, and shook my head. "Nah. The smells were making me gag."

He shrugged. "Okay." Instead of walking away, he came in closer, taking a seat across from me at the table – with his large body, it was even more ridiculous than me folding myself into one of the chairs. "So what do you want instead?"

As soon as I inhaled, I caught another whiff on the BBQ scent clinging to him, and moaned out loud before I could help it.

"Damn," he said, a smirk spreading over his soft brown lips. "If

I'd known a new cologne was all it would take to get you to make that sound, I would've pulled this shit out long ago."

"No it's not your cologne," I told him, shaking my head. "It's something else. Like...charcoal and heaven or something."

"First of all, charcoal and heaven is real specific," he said, laughing. "Second, I took a shower, so how are you even still smelling all of that?"

I shrugged. "I guess it's the pregnancy thing. Got my senses all discombobulated and heightened like I'm fucking Spider-Man or something."

"Well, pregnancy *is* a very superhero type of process, right? Something grows inside of you for nine months, you push it out through your pussy, and... *bam. Waah, waaah, somebody put a titty in my mouth!* You gone tell me that's *not* some superhero origin story shit?"

I laughed. "That's definitely a way to think about it, but I can't say that's the specific angle that was on my mind. Really wasn't thinking about it like that."

"You have to start thinking about it though," he said. "You're not going to have forever before its time to give up your titties, Jo. How long *do* you have, actually?"

I sighed, shaking my head. "I really don't want to talk about that, actually. I'd much rather talk about where you've been that has you smelling like hickory-smoked deliciousness. That's what I'm trying to hear about."

"Nah," Teddy grinned. "You don't know nothing about this. And you don't want to know nothing about this. You're not ready for it. You can't handle it."

"Okay, so see *now*, I'm especially intrigued because you're talking about I can't handle it, but I'm gonna show you that I can handle it, if you stop playing, and put me in a position *to* handle it," I responded, suppressing a grin. We used to have a *lot* of fun with this silly ass cyclic conversation style, back when I was sneaking him into my dorm past curfew to cut up with friends.

He sucked in a slow breath through his teeth. "You think you can handle it? Like *for real?*"

"I know I can handle it! *What?*"

"Okay, okay, aiight," he nodded. "I want you to know, I wouldn't do this for just anybody. But. I'ma put you on. I'ma put you in touch with what's got me smelling like I'm smelling. Come on. Let's go."

So... I went.

Was I hungry?

Hell yes.

Was the smell of BBQ really enough to make me get in the vehicle with Teddy to head to some unknown place?

... also hell yes, apparently.

I didn't even have to think about it very hard.

Jemma was more than occupied with fans and friends and family, so the likelihood she'd miss me was low, especially with the party heading into hour three. As far as I was concerned, I was free to chase down the scent that had my mouth watering.

Is this really who I've become?

Not even a week ago I was telling Teddy how I wanted nothing to do with him. Now, I was climbing my pregnant, hungry ass into the passenger seat of his truck – an oversized, chromed-out blue monstrosity that was scarily identical to what he'd described to me as his dream vehicle back when we were dating in college.

I couldn't believe I remember that.

Honestly though... there was a lot I remembered about Teddy, including the fact that he was always going out of his way to get me anything I wanted or even needed. I was pretty sure *that* made finding out he hadn't been claiming me as his girl hurt even more.

How was it that when he was in my face, he was the sweetest, most attentive guy in the world, but when I wasn't around, he could act like I meant nothing to him?

When it happened, part of me wanted to overlook it. But then I remembered the advice that my mother had given me and my sisters

171

back when Jemma first started dating, two years before I could even think about it, and Jac wasn't even a teenager.

"Whatever you overlook now, you'll be overlooking for the rest of your relationship. Maybe for the rest of your life. If it doesn't feel right, don't you dare let that nigga slide, or he'll treat you like his own personal waterpark."

So I hadn't let it slide.

Not then, and not anytime after that.

I didn't pay much attention to the music that Teddy started in the truck, opting instead to focus on him – taking him in, in a way I hadn't in so, so long.

The serenity on his face as he leaned back in the soft leather of his seats, completely relaxed as he navigated traffic. The slight flex in his bicep, highlighted by the delicious fit of that sweatshirt as he easily piloted every turn. The soft cursing he did under his breath when one of the other drivers made a stupid decision, the mean-mugging he did when he passed them up, practically daring something to pop off.

Wow bitch are you really getting turned on by your ex-boyfriend driving?

Are you serious right now?

I looked away from him.

I *had to*, before my hard nipples and damp panties drove me crazy.

My eyes narrowed as I took in our surroundings, noticing that we weren't remotely close to any of the commercial areas in Blakewood, and were instead cruising through a tree-lined, residential neighborhood.

"Uh... where exactly are you taking me?" I asked, peering out the window as he pulled into one of the driveways.

He smirked. "You said you wanted the BBQ, so... here we are."

He turned the truck off and climbed out, coming around to my side to open the door for me. As soon as I stepped out, with his hand at my back, the smell of lingering charcoal hit me.

I THINK I MIGHT NEED YOU

I looked up, meeting his gaze. "This isn't... you didn't bring me to your house, did you?"

"Nah, not *my* house," he said, even though I watched him choose a key from the ring in his pocket and push it into the spot on the door. Strangely, I didn't feel nervous at all following him into the house once it was unlocked.

Well... I didn't until he yelled, "*Mama! You still up?*"

My eyes almost bugged out of my head as I gripped his arm. "*Mama?!*" I whisper-yelled. "*Seriously?!* You really brought me to your mother's house?!"

He shrugged as he pulled me further into a home that looked like something straight from a home-décor magazine, except with definite black touches. Instead of figurines or dishes, the glass-doors cabinets held copies of *Jet* magazine and vinyls from Stax records, and Malcolm X, Martin, Coretta, Michelle, Barack, Beyoncé and Serena Williams had places of honor on the wall of framed pictures, mixed in with everyone else like they were family.

I didn't get a chance to look as hard as I wanted, due to footsteps on the stairs.

"Lil' boy I done told you about coming in my house hollering like you don't have any – sense," a woman yelled, and I turned to see animal-printed house-shoes and pedicured toes on the way down the staircase. "I'ma knock you upside the—oh! *Oh*. Well... hello."

There was an instant shift as Teddy's mother made it to the last steps from the bottom – far enough down to see me standing there with him.

"Um... hi," I said, stepping forward, with my hand extended, because I didn't know what the hell else to do. She was a beautiful woman, with Teddy's deep brown skin and apparently his smile, which she aimed back and forth between me and him.

"Who is *this*, son?" she asked, ignoring my hand to pull me into a hug.

Damn, does everybody in this family smell good, I wondered, trying not to be a weirdo by inhaling, but she smelled like sweet potatoes and macaroni and cheese in the *best* damn way. In any case, she hugged like my own mother, who gave amazing hugs, so I melted right into it and hugged her back.

"Mama, this is Joia Love, another influencer here in Blakewood," Teddy explained. "And... we dated for a while back in college before I messed it up."

Me *and* his mama looked upside his head like he was crazy.

Why would he say that to her?

"Why would you mess up with this pretty brown girl Theodore, I could have some grandbabies by now!"

Mentally, I shot daggers at him, hoping he wouldn't feel the need to tell her I was pregnant – I'd survived one mama-powered interrogation from my own – I wasn't sure I'd make it through another.

"Chill, mama," he said instead, brushing it off. He did give me this annoying-ass smirk before he turned and started walking to another area of the house though, and of course I followed. "Joia's sister had a book launch party tonight, but the food was wack. I told her I could take her somewhere with some top-tier grub." He stopped walking, turning to his mother with mischief in his eyes. "I mean... unless you don't really have any extras like that."

His mother's head reeled back like he'd slapped her. "Excuse me? Boy I know you must be playing." She hooked an arm through mine. "You hungry, baby? Teddy and his daddy put some meat on the grill, and then I've got some yams, greens, cucumber salad, baked beans, potato salad, macaroni and cheese, some black-eyed peas, corn on the cob, some green tomatoes, squash casserole, a pound cake, a pecan pie, a cheesecake, you tell me what you need baby and I'll make you a plate, okay?"

What I... what did I need?

Tell her what I needed?

I... I needed... *all of it.*

My eyes welled with tears at the thought of that plate, and I blinked hard, trying to keep them at bay, because that was... that was... *crazy*, right? I loved good food as much as the next girl, but I'd never been *emotional* about it.

Until today, apparently.

When I couldn't bring myself to speak for fear of bursting into happy tears, Teddy grinned from me to his mother. And then, as if he was reading my mind, he opened his mouth to say what I couldn't.

"She'll take a little of everything."

SEVEN

Teddy

"Ohhhh, you got you a bad one there don't you boy," my father jeered, slapping me on the shoulder as he reached past me to grab a pair of tongs.

Joia was just on the other side of the patio doors, eating in the kitchen while I helped Pops take the rest of the meat off the grill. I wasn't afraid to leave her with my mother – wasn't afraid of the conversation that might happen. My mother wanted grandkids too bad to say anything too embarrassing, for fear of scaring Joia off. I didn't bring women home, so I already knew what was brewing in my mother's head – hell, it was the same thing I was hoping for, honestly. And from her facial expressions, I figured Joia wouldn't say too much either, even if my mother asks her to elaborate on that whole breakup situation I mentioned.

She didn't want to talk about it, and didn't want to encourage anything.

I definitely should *not* have mentioned that Joia and I used to date, but what was done was done now. All I could do was react to the situation as it was. And as it was, I had a feeling that showing Joia some of the best parts of me - by which I meant my parents - would only endear her to me even more.

A plate of my mother's good ass food could endear anyone.

"*Had* a bad one," I corrected my father, shaking my head.

I couldn't blame Joia for still being salty about the way things ended between us.

I was stupid.

I was stupid as hell.

But I was also *young* as hell when that shit went bad. That *had* to account for something when it came time for her to consider making us a thing again. And I *definitely* planned on making her consider it.

Bringing her to my parents' house was a good first step.

"How did you mess that up?" my father asked, turning to me as he closed the grates on the grill to put the fire out.

"The usual stupidity," I told him, truthfully.

There was no point in fronting about it to my father.

"Must not have been too bad, if she let you bring her out here," he said, giving me an encouraging nod. "Any woman let you bring her to your mama's house, that means you still got a chance with her."

"Well, in fairness, she didn't exactly know I was bringing her here. So I don't know how well that applies."

"She knew you weren't taking her to the burger joint up the street," my father laughed. "And she didn't go running in the other direction when your mama came downstairs in those slippers either."

I chuckled. "Yeah, I guess that's a pretty fair point. But I'm saying – I'm just going to take it easy. Take it slow. Not read too much into anything, you know? I messed up with her, so I know that's going to take some time to get back. To get her to trust me again, after what I did."

The amusement on my father's face turned to disapproval. "You weren't out there sticking your dick where it didn't belong were you? I know I taught you better than *that*."

I shook my head. "Nah, wasn't that. I may have... misrepresented the relationship. Made it seem like less than it actually was."

"Ah," my father nodded. "Trying to keep your ad in the paper after it was already answered, huh?"

"*What*," I asked. "What does that even mean?"

My father chuckled. "Oh you know what it means. Too much juice in your cup. You thought you was cool enough to have your cake and eat it too. But that girl in there wasn't like one of the ones you were trying to impress, was she? Found out you weren't doing right and dropped you, didn't she?"

I frowned. "How did you know that?"

"Experience, son. Almost lost your mama the same way. Luckily for me- and you too, or you wouldn't be here - I had enough cool factor to get her back."

"Cool factor?" I chuckled. "You mean *swag*."

"Whatever y'all calling it these days, I had it," my father boasted. "And I had enough of it to get *my* lady back. The question is, do you?"

"Oh I've *got* the swag old man, don't worry about that. It's just..." I shook my head. "It's a little more complicated than that with Joia."

Pops whistled, shaking his head. "Complicated sounds like there's another nigga in the picture," he correctly guessed.

If only you knew.

"That's what I thought," he said. "You want to roll up on him? We can grab Len, grab your Uncle Bobby, and we can go. You know I'm *always* ready."

"Nah, slow down Pops, that's not necessary," I laughed. "No need to roll up on anybody."

"Okay so then what is your plan? Just being handsome ain't enough to get the girl no more. You gotta do a lil more than that these days, and you already ain't got no real job."

"I *have* a job," I defended myself. "But honestly... I don't really have a plan. I just know I want her. All I really can do is be myself and show her that's valuable."

I THINK I MIGHT NEED YOU

My father nodded. "Sounds like a good plan to me, son. Now go on in there and *be valuable*," he teased. "I got the rest of this."

Obviously, I took another few minutes to help him finish getting the ribs off, and stowed in the huge aluminum pans set up for that purpose. When he switched to cleaning his tools and stuff though, I did go, hoping that my previous assumption about how my mother and Joia would get along was correct, and I wasn't walking into anything crazy.

Joia looked up with a smile when I came through the doors that led to the back patio, pausing with another forkful of food halfway up to her mouth.

"Yo," she said. "This *food*. Your mother put her foot in this. Don't tell my Mama I said that though."

My mother and I both laughed.

"Don't worry baby, it's our little secret," my mom said, beaming with pride as she got up from the table. "It was nice to meet you Joia, with your pretty brown self." She turned to me with much less honey than she was throwing Joia's way. "Teddy don't you leave this house without cleaning up these dishes you hear me?"

I sighed. "Yes ma'am."

She gave me the *I'm not playing with you boy* look, then shot Joia one last winning smile before she turned to exit the kitchen, leaving me and Joia alone.

"Tell me something," Joia spoke. "How do you think your mom would feel about me taking like… a lot of that cheesecake home with me tonight?"

"My mother loves when people love her food, so I think she would be *very* flattered by that," I told her, grinning. "And she'd probably make me go pull a switch from outside if I let you leave without it. I'll get you a dish to take it home in."

"Thank you," she nodded. "This is all so amazing." She went quiet for a moment, then looked at me again with a little smile. "Thank you for bringing me here. I needed this."

I shrugged. "No problem. Whatever you need, I got you."

For some reason, those words I'd intended as reassuring made the smile melt from her face, and she let out a little sigh. "Why?"

"Why not?"

She huffed. "Seriously, Teddy. Why are you being so nice to me?"

I thought about it for a second, then opted for what my parents had always insisted was the best policy. "Honestly... I'm trying to get back on your good side, Joia. There's no reason after eight years that we shouldn't be able to be cool." The look on her face made me quickly correct myself. "I mean, at least I don't... think so. I know we broke up because I was stupid but... I was a kid. We were kids, Joia."

She put her fork down and looked at me. "Yeah Teddy. We *were* kids, that's true, but... that feels like a cop-out. *You* messed us up, when it could have been *so* different. Why?"

I blew out a deep exhale through my nose. "I know you probably want some deep reason, some good explanation, but honestly... it just is what it is. Very simple. *I fucked up.* And I own that. But that's all it is. I was just stupid."

Joia pushed out a deep sigh and shook her head. "Yeah. I'm ready to go home if that's okay."

Shit.

"Yeah of course," I told her, knowing there wasn't anything I could say right now to make it right.

Not *right* now.

Fixing what was broken between us was going to take action, not words.

"Let me hit these dishes real quick, and get this cheesecake for you. And then we'll go."

EIGHT

Joia.

You messed us up, when it could have been so different.

The ride back to my apartment was quiet as hell.

I had no idea what Teddy was thinking about, but *my* thoughts were consumed with that little statement, wondering if *that* was the root of my prolonged anger against him.

I believed him when he said he was just being stupid – it made sense. We were eighteen, nineteen years old. It was prime time for dumb shit, that was just how it went. But... I couldn't help thinking about what could've been.

We could be a decade into this thing by now.

The house, the kids, the YouTube channel featuring our cute ass Black family and pretty praline babies. Maybe a big ass fluffy dog. I hadn't met Teddy's parents before, but now that I had, I knew that I probably would've loved them as in-laws. And my parents would *love* Teddy.

But... it hadn't happened like that.

Because he was stupid.

Emphasis on *was*, since I was fully willing to believe he'd matured – more than just physically – into a grown man. But that didn't change the fact that back when we were together, I'd – perhaps naively – thought we had a future together, that didn't pan out. And us not being together had led to other experiences – like *Dalton*. Which had led to the position I was in now.

Very pregnant, in much less than ideal circumstances.

When it could've been so different.

It… probably wasn't fair to put that on him. Nothing that had occurred in *my* life since he and I broke up was his fault – I was responsible for my own decisions, and honestly, I'd done some stupid stuff too. With a child on the way, it really felt silly to even be dwelling on this, and holding grudges. *Especially* when I knew what kinda village raising this child was going to take. I needed all the allies I could get.

Except Dalton.

Fuck Dalton.

I pushed out a sigh and closed my eyes, trying to clear any shred of negative thoughts from my mind. It must have worked a little *too* well though, because the next time I opened my eyes, we were in my building's parking lot.

"Wake up baby," Teddy said, reaching across me to unclip my seatbelt. We were parked, and he was already on my side of the truck to help me out.

"Sorry," I told him, shaking my head as I accepted his hand to get down from the truck. "I guess I didn't realize how tired I was."

He smiled as he closed the passenger door. "Long day?"

"You could say that. Filmed a few brand videos, did some editing, took some promo shots. Read a bunch of pregnancy stuff, then it was time to get ready for Jemma's party, and Dalton came by."

Teddy grunted. *"That motherfucker."*

"Trust me, I feel the same way," I laughed. "But I got rid of him, finished getting ready for the party, *went* to the party, then... got whisked away."

He grinned at me as he pulled the front door to the building open, after I'd used my keycard to disengage the lock. "I like that phrasing, *whisked away*. Makes me sound like your knight in shining armor."

"Well..." I raised an eyebrow at him. "Isn't that what you call yourself trying to suddenly be?"

"Just making sure you noticed," he quipped, pressing the call button for the elevator.

I smirked. "Uh, yeah, I noticed. But I hope I don't get whiplash from this drastic change. You weren't trying to be in my face like this before."

"You weren't having a baby before."

My cheeks grew hot as he stared at me, waiting for a response. But luckily, the elevator arrived, providing an escape.

A *momentary* escape, since he followed me into the elevator.

I pressed the button for my floor and kept my eyes straight ahead, trying to pretend I didn't feel Teddy staring at me. Once we arrived, I hurried off, anxious to get out of the enclosed space.

"I'm not trying to freak you out," he called after me. My footsteps stilled, and I waited for him to catch up. He rounded in front of me, taking me by the elbows. "I just..." he shook his head. "I don't want you thinking Dalton is your only option."

I frowned. "*What?*"

"With the baby," he explained, bringing a lump to my throat. "That nigga can go on about his business, dance off the side of a building for all *I* give a fuck. You don't need him. I got you."

A smile crept onto my lips as I met Teddy's gaze – there was *so much* sincerity in his eyes. "That's really how you feel?" I asked.

He nodded. "*Hell* yes. No doubt."

"Okay Teddy." I returned his nod and looked away, trying not to give away too much of what I was feeling. "I'll keep that in mind."

"Hey, that's all I can hope for. For now," Teddy said as we

finished making our way to my front door... which there really hadn't been a need for him to walk me to.

I turned to him at the door, giving him the eye, waiting for him to say something. When he didn't, I spoke up myself. "Why did you walk me all the way here?"

"Honestly?" he glanced up and down the hall, then moved in a little closer, tipping his head to the side. "I was hoping the vibe would turn in my favor just enough that I would get a chance to kiss you."

My head reeled back. "Kiss me!?" I shook my head. "Teddy... We got along with each other for a few hours, and you're already trying to make your way around the bases? You don't think that's moving kind of fast?"

He shrugged. "Nah. As a matter of fact, I feel like it's kind of slow," he admitted. "I'm looking at you right now like, *damn you really let eight years pass without trying to make that happen again? Nigga you stupid, you better get on that.*"

I smiled. "Yeah... it doesn't exactly work like that."

"Why not?"

"Because it just *doesn't*."

"But it could," he insisted. "The way I see it, you and I are a done deal. Meant to be. This time apart was a setback. I want you; you want me... let's make it happen, you know?"

"No, I *don't* know," I laughed. "You don't get to just decide that I —*mmm*."

Apparently, he *did* get to decide that we were starting something up again.

At least, that was the impression that I got from him grabbing either side of my face and luring his mouth to mine, pressing a kiss on me that took my breath away. I surprised myself by not pulling back - I gave right into it, melting against his body as his tongue lapped against mine.

It felt natural.

It felt *familiar*.

Instantly, my body recognized and responded to the familiarity of

Teddy's tongue in my mouth. My nipples were hard, panties wet all over again as he massaged his tongue with mine, pulling back to take little nibbles against my bottom lip, soothing them with his tongue before he dove in again.

A little gasp escaped my throat as he backed me into the wall in the hallway, his large body swamping mine as he devoured me with that kiss. His big hands went to my waist, gripping and pulling me against him, the impression of his hard dick against my stomach leaving no room for me to wonder exactly how he was feeling.

It was just my luck that the feeling was mutual.

I'd been feeling it before we left Jemma's party. Hell, from the moment I laid eyes on him in that *damn* purple. At this point, I wasn't sure if I could blame it on the pregnancy hormones. That extreme horniness that I'd heard about, it didn't seem like that usually kicked in until the *third* trimester.

I hadn't quite reached that milestone yet.

Nah, this was all Teddy and his fineness.

All *me*.

All my suppressed attraction to him, all my suppressed feelings for him, all my suppressed memories of how good we were together flooded back as he kissed me like I already belonged to him again. And I really couldn't front…I wasn't about to be the one to correct it.

Not when I was fully ready and fully willing to let him do a lot more than *kiss* me.

"I need to get my keys out," I told him, my hands shaking as I fumbled with my bag.

His eyes were low and shadowed, filled with lust as he stepped back, giving me some space. "Is that an invitation inside?"

"Do you really need to ask."

Teddy blew out a sigh, shaking his head as he scrubbed his fingers through his thick hair. "Honestly, yeah I do. As much as I'm on my *fuck Dalton this, fuck Dalton that*, I really need you to be sure that you want to do what I think you're saying we're about to do. Niggas get real protective about the mother of their children, and I just want to make sure that I'm not creating a problem for you."

I shook my head as my fingers closed around my keys. "Trust me. This isn't going to be a problem at all."

Those words seem to be enough for him.

Any hesitation he had quickly melted away as he approached me again, grabbing me by the waist to plant another one of those deep, slow, panty-wetting kisses on me. He pulled back just enough that his lips brushed mine as he spoke.

"Open the goddamn door then, Joia."

I really didn't have to be told twice.

He was on me as soon as the door closed behind us, barely giving me time to lock it before he had me pushed against the wall again.

I gasped as he hefted me up, hiking my legs around his waist as he kissed me. I barely had time to breathe, time to think, before his hands were underneath my shirt, underneath my bra, cupping my throbbing breasts. The pads of his fingers skimmed across my sensitive nipples making my back arch away from the wall from just that simple simulation.

It had been *so* long since I'd been touched by anybody else, it damn near seemed like just that was enough to make me come.

But of course, that wasn't all he had for me.

"*Holy shit*," I breathed, as he dropped his mouth to my neck, sucking and biting that sensitive area. Somehow, he remembered exactly the right spot, exactly the right pressure, exactly how much to give me - benefits of having been the one to discover that spot in the first place. I whimpered as he bit down harder, and chuckled against my skin.

He knew *exactly* what he was doing to me.

Just like that plate of his mother's food, I didn't know how much I needed this until it was happening. My hands dug into the soft coils of his short, faded fro, gripping to guide his head lower as he easily undid the buttons of my shirt. He pulled me forward off the wall, using one strong arm under my ass to hold me up. He used the other to pull my shirt off and toss it away. Seconds later, he'd unclipped my bra and tossed it away with the shirt, leaving my ultra-sensitive nipples exposed to him.

"These are definitely not what I remember," he teased.

I wanted to scold him for his playful mocking about my swollen breasts, but before I could, he closed his mouth over one of my nipples, sucking and biting until a high, keening moan left my throat. I gripped his hair even harder as he went on like that. Torturing me with pleasure until my nipples were even harder than before - stiff, sensitive peaks that he teased with his thumb, teased with his tongue, teased with his whole mouth, covering me and sucking hard.

I couldn't stay still.

Couldn't stop *squirming*.

And the fact that he hadn't pressed me against the wall again, instead using pure strength to keep me up... for some reason, that turned me on even more.

Teddy's size had always been part of his appeal, but we were grown now. Back then, as kids, we both had limited sexual experience. Now, I knew exactly what the benefits of his size could be, and I fully intended on taking advantage of every single one.

Visions of vertical fucking danced in my head.

"Bedroom," I said. One simple command that Teddy immediately responded to, his mouth full of my breast as he nodded and turned to head in that direction. With Dalton, I never would have been in his arms like this, first of all. He would have acted like it was the biggest burden in the world, carrying me to my bed to engage in sex. "*I can't risk injuring anything,*" he would have whined. True enough, I was a tall girl, with plenty of muscle on me. But I wasn't heavy like that for him to be concerned. His ass was just a fucking baby.

With Teddy... it was no problem.

He didn't hesitate at all to take me to my room, eager to get to the treasure that waited for him there. At first, he accidentally turned into my guest bedroom, but it only took a quick moment of redirection to get him to the right place. Once we were there... it was on.

He laid me across the bed, pulling my shoes off first and then heading for the button and zipper on my jeans. He deftly undid them, then slid the jeans down my legs and tossed them away, just like he'd done with my shirt and bra.

But then he stopped.

Staring.

Staring, at my stomach.

"Wow," he murmured. "You're like... for real having a baby," he mused, reaching to touch my stomach. I expected to recoil at his touch, expected it to feel foreign and unnatural and uncomfortable.

Instead, it felt a little *too* comfortable.

So, I redirected his attention.

I grabbed the back of his hand, pushing it up past my belly, up towards my breasts, prompting him into action – to lower himself on top of me.

"Wait," I laughed. "Am I going to be the only one naked here?"

Teddy chuckled too, shaking his head. "Nah. There's just something else I gotta tend to real quick first."

I quickly found out what that *something* was.

He kissed his way back down my body, not lingering at my belly, which I'd hoped that he wouldn't. No, he went straight for my panties, pulling them down my thighs and tossing them in the same general direction as my jeans before he spread my legs apart and dove straight between them, headfirst.

"*Holy shit,*" rushed from my lips, again, as his mouth made contact with my sensitive flesh. Not that Teddy had ever been afraid of, or stingy about having his head between my legs, but the years had certainly imparted some fresh wisdom, because I didn't remember it being like *this*. In next to no time, he had me gripping my light comforter tight, back arching away from the bed as I hollered.

His strong fingers gripped my thighs, keeping my legs pulled apart, keeping me open for him as he devoured me, his tongue licking and lapping, playing and teasing and *taunting* me with every swipe. He put his whole face into it, not grudging or prude at all - he was *all* the way into it, sucking and licking me clean like I was a plate with the last piece of pecan pie.

My head fell back, mouth open, panting and whimpering as his tongue moved, offering a steady onslaught until the pressure in my core built, and built, and built, past the point of keeping it contained.

I couldn't do anything except cum all over his face.

I was still panting when he moved back, lip between his teeth, as he looked at me -he was obviously *very* pleased with his performance.

Hell, so was I.

I sat up on my elbows to finish catching my breath as he stepped back from the bed to get undressed.

"Wait, hold up," he said, holding a finger up to me as he pulled his cell phone from his pocket, while he used his free hand to wipe some of my juices from his beard. I frowned as I watched him, wondering what was going on. I hoped like hell he wasn't about to return a text, or respond to any type of social media notification while I was laying there, spread eagle across my bed, completely naked, waiting for him.

I rolled my eyes when Ginuwine's "Pony" started up, blaring from the speakers of his phone.

"Teddy," I said. "I know for a *fact* that you are not about to..."

Oh.

Yes, he was.

And... I couldn't lie to myself – Teddy looked pretty damn good hiking up the front of his sweatshirt to show me his solid midsection as he ground his hips to the music.

"*Whooo!*" I yelled at him, clapping as he pulled the sweatshirt the rest of the way off, winding it over his head like a helicopter. His expression was completely serious as the chorus started, and he let the sweatshirt go, sending it flying in my direction to smack me across the face.

"You are *such* a goddamn fool," I laughed, as he turned around and started rocking his ass at me.

And *what an ass* it was.

Teddy had *cake* in the best possible way, and he knew how to move it. Despite my general disdain for male strippers as a profession and community, I was enjoying the hell out of Teddy's performance - especially once he toed his way out of his shoes and then got rid of those sweatpants and boxers to get fully naked.

A *glorious* sight.

There was just something about a big, wide, motherfucker who looked like he could build me a house that just… turned me on. And Teddy had *exactly* that type of vibe. He'd lost the softness his body held back when I remembered it from before. His consistency in the gym had replaced it with solid grown man weight that looked good as hell on him.

That I couldn't wait to have against me again.

And his dick - my *God had I shrunk it in my memory since I was mad at him?* Cause I definitely didn't remember it being like *that*, but I was ready for it now. I lifted a hand, making a hooking motion at him with my finger. He obliged, climbing back on top of me on the bed.

"Yeah, you liked that shit, huh," he nodded, cocky as hell as he pushed me back.

"I really can't stand you for the fact that you did it, but… I actually *did*," I admitted.

He grinned and lowered his mouth to mine, kissing me again as he reached a hand between us to spread my legs apart.

"Hold up," he said, meeting my gaze. "Protection?"

I let out a laugh. "Kinda already knocked up," I reminded him. "And if I was concerned about anything else, I wouldn't be having sex with you at all."

He nodded "Okay, so we're on the same page. Last chance to back out… you sure you want to do this?" he asked, his voice suddenly all husky and sexy and filled with lust, just like his eyes.

I THINK I MIGHT NEED YOU

"Teddy," I whispered, planting my hands on either side of his ass. "Stop playing with me." I squeezed.

Then he buried himself in me.

We both let out a low, guttural, *"Fuuuuck,"* at the same time.

Logically, I understood that Teddy was hung like a horse - I'd literally *just* seen it.

But still, somehow, I hadn't expected the way he stretched me to feel quite so good, hadn't expected his length to fill me so deeply. Hadn't expected it to feel like *exactly* what I had been missing - exactly what I had *needed* for so damn long.

I dug my nails into his firm ass cheeks as he started moving, building up a rhythm that had me whimpering in no time. It was beyond good - it was perfection. The kind of perfection that came from a man who knew your body, knew exactly what angles to come at you from, knew exactly what spot to hit, knew exactly how deep he had to go to get you right where he wanted you to be.

And where he wanted you to be, was deep in the throes of pleasure.

"You feel so fucking good," he growled at me, his gaze locked with mine until he decided he had a better use for his mouth. He brought his lips back to my neck, back to that sweet spot that only he seemed to know about, sucking and biting me there as he stroked me deep and hard.

Yes.

Hell yes.

Just like that, I thought, but didn't verbalize.

I didn't have to.

Teddy knew exactly what he was doing - giving me the best dick I'd had in a long, long time. My body was screaming with pleasure, and so was my mouth - unable to hold back anything I was feeling about what he was giving to me.

And he was giving it all.

He hooked my legs around his midsection as he buried himself deeper, drove harder, stroked me faster, and faster, and faster, until my thighs were shaking around his waist.

Yes.

Hell yes.

I could feel the flexion, feel the tightening of the muscles in his ass that let me know he was getting near his own orgasm, but I knew Teddy well enough to know - he wouldn't take his before he'd given mine.

He pulled out of me, and I wanted to complain about the sudden emptiness from the absence of his dick between my legs, but I didn't have time before his mouth was on me again. Sucking and licking with a vengeance. He covered me with his whole mouth, slurping and licking as he buried his face deeper, and deeper, until I was right at that peak.

And then he buried his dick in me again.

Deeper this time, somehow.

Faster, longer, more intense strokes that had me gripping his ass, gripping the sheets, gripping my breasts, gripping my hair, looking for anything to hold onto, anything to keep me tethered to reality, since he was clearly trying to drive me out of it.

Trying to drive me out of my mind.

And then it hit me.

Like a sonic-fucking-boom, setting off static in my ears, making my vision blurry, making it hard to breathe, hard to think, hard to do anything except *feel* the pleasure of him buried deep inside me.

My pussy was still throbbing, body still contracting, trying to pull him deeper, trying to get more of him, when he came with the growl of his own. I wrapped my arms around his shoulders, holding onto him tight as my body milked his release from him, taking it all in.

"*Holy shit,*" I whispered again.

"Yeah," Teddy grunted in my ear, as he fell to the bed beside me.

He hooked this arm across my chest to pull me in closer to him, and I didn't have any complaints about that at all. Instead of wondering how I could convince him to leave, I settled into his body, enjoying the feeling of his heat and the scent of his cologne.

And the lingering scent of that damn charcoal.

This whole thing was the ribs' fault to be honest.

As much as I hated to admit it, being in this bed with Teddy… just felt right.

Which kind of made me mad all over again.

Because this whole thing could have been *so* different.

NINE

JOIA.

"Somebody got some dick last night, somebody like some dick last night."

I was pulled from good, deep sleep to find Jemma in my face, wearing a bigger grin than she had last night for her party. I groaned, then rolled over, not quite yet interested in what she was saying to me, but she grabbed my shoulder, pulling me back in her direction.

"No ma'am," she said. "We're going to talk about this. I've let your ass sleep in all late. It's already ten in the morning now, and it's time to talk about it."

"Talk about *what*, Jemma? Wait. Did you say it was ten in the morning?"

"Yeah. I guess good dick will do that for you - have you all discombobulated, not even knowing what time it is."

"Could you stop?" I asked. "Where are you even getting this information from?"

She smirked. "Oh my information is from the very reliable source of my own eyes. When I brought your car back – thanks for letting me use it yesterday by the way - to your building at about 2:00 this morning... I saw somebody sneaking out of here. I mean, as if he could sneak, like nobody was gonna see his big ass wearing all that purple."

Internally, I groaned.

"Ohhh, what is his *name*," Jemma continued. "Oh yeah - Theodore Graham is his name. Yeah. Him. I saw him sneaking out to the parking lot. And then I get up here and *what's* all up and through the atmosphere? Certainly *not* the Holy Spirit."

"Jemma, I have no idea what you're talking about."

She rolled her eyes. "Oh, Joia. I know you're on your extra sensitive, secret squirrel shit because of the pregnancy. But let's *not* pretend like I don't know you very *very* well. I saw you sneak out of the party with Teddy. What else would you have been doing other than riding that man like the big ass thoroughbred he is?"

"For your information, he took me to his mother's house to eat. Since all you had was that nasty food at your party," I jabbed, desperate to re-route the conversation.

"Oh girl *please*," Jemma laughed, not taking the bait. "Sure maybe he did take you to his mother's house to eat. But when he brought you back *here*? I guarantee there was something else on the menu. Pregnant coochie."

"*Jemma,* please!"

"Ain't nobody lying on you! But as I said, I know you extra sensitive these days."

"I just would like to not have assumptions made about me."

"It's not an assumption," she corrected, flipping her hair over her shoulder. "It's an educated guess. Based on finding the bra you were wearing last night in the living room. Or are you suddenly not a neat freak anymore either?"

Shit.

No more denying it now.

"Okay fine, so I got some. What's wrong with that?"

She shook her head. "Absolutely nothing. I'm hoping it lightens your ass up some."

"Are you saying I've been uptight?"

"Do you think you haven't?" Jaclyn asked as she breezed through the door of my bedroom too, stopping beside Jemma.

Great.

"So the whole family is available for my sleep in of shame?"

"The only person shaming you is *you*." Jaclyn said.

"Right," Jemma agreed. "Teddy is fine as hell, and I thoroughly support you getting that old thang back."

"That shit is definitely going on their wedding program," Jac laughed. "Please join us for a beautiful ceremony as we celebrate Joia Love and Theodore Graham getting that old thang back."

"I hate y'all so much."

"No you don't," Jemma laughed. "You know you love us. Now get up so you can get ready. Mommy is cooking today, and she wants us all over there."

"No can do," I said, sitting up in bed. "I've got to get to the gym first. And then I'll get ready and come by. But I can't miss a day."

Jac. "Girl, you're only *barely* showing. You still hold your *Miss Fit Bitch* title. Give that baby some breathing room."

"It's not about that," I snapped. "I don't care about a damn title. I just need some normalcy. *Something* in my life that can stay like it's been, and my gym schedule seems to be one of the few things I can control. So it is what it is."

Jac and Jem exchanged a look, and then Jac sat down at the end of the bed.

"Jo, you know we're just messing with you, right?" she asked. "You *have* been off since finding out that you were pregnant, understandably. I can't even say that I get it, because I don't. I can't imagine what you're going through... how scared you must be, how confused you must be. But seriously... you know we got you, right?"

I pushed out a deep sigh. "Yes, I do. Devyn says the baby is perfectly fine. I know I have you guys as support. I know that when it really comes down to it, everything is going to be fine. But it's like...*still*. I just feel numb or something. Like I barely believe it's happening."

"Probably because you haven't talked to anybody about it," Jemma said, joining me and Jac on the bed. "You can't just wear this burden by yourself. I know how your mind works. You *need* to talk to somebody about it."

I nodded. "I know, I just... I haven't talked to the father yet. And I don't feel like it's right to talk about it with anybody else, when I haven't talked to him yet."

"Okay, so when are you going to talk to him?" Jacqueline asked.

"I don't know. I feel like I need to have my thoughts together before I have this conversation with him, because I have no idea how it's going to go. I have no idea how he's going to react. I have no idea if we're going to be able to get along for any type of co-parenting setup. It's all just confusing."

"You do see how circular that is," Jemma asked. "You want to talk to him about it, before you can talk to anyone else to put your thoughts together. But you don't want to talk to anyone else to help put your thoughts together, until you talk to him. You're going to drive yourself nuts Jo."

"I know," I whined. "But I really do not know what to do."

"I can tell you what to do," Jac said. "First, you go to the gym and sweat it out. Then you shower that off of you, and come to the house and let Mommy and Daddy get on your nerves. Then, when you've got yourself a full stomach, and you've worked off your stress at the gym, and you come back home and get yourself some wine... well, wait, no wine. Hell, kombucha or whatever it is you drink to relax. And you call him. You talk to him. You *tell* him. And you get this off of your chest, so you can move on without the stress. So you can focus on being a mommy."

I blew out a heavy sigh, and let myself fall back onto the bed, staring up at the ceiling. "Yeah. You're right. I can't just keep pretending this isn't happening."

"Nope," Jemma said, patting me on the thigh. "You sure can't. So come on, get up. Let's get you off to the gym."

~

"Joia! Joia! Wait up!"

Reluctantly, I slowed my steps.

There was no part of me that wanted to actually wait up, after the way I'd just worn myself out in the gym. I was already regretting my decision not to use a rideshare to get there in the first place. I'd driven, which meant I had to drive back.

This was the shit nobody told you about making financially responsible decisions.

I didn't recognize the voice that had called out to me, which meant it was more than likely a social media follower. As soon as I turned around, that suspicion was confirmed, as a trio of young women walked up to me beaming, cell phones already out.

"Hi guys," I said, pulling up as much cheerfulness as I could, even though I was exhausted, and all I wanted to do was get home and take the shower I'd opted not to take there at the gym. I was hot, my clothes were sweaty, and my breakfast had worn off about halfway through the workout.

I really wasn't in a mood to be "on brand", but that didn't matter.

People like these - who liked me, who watched my videos, who clicked my links, who hit the subscribe button on my channel, they were the ones who basically paid my bills, by giving me an engaged audience.

If they wanted Joia Love, they were gonna get her.

"I told you it was her," one of them said, as they stopped in front of me.

One of the other girls shrugged it off. "Oh my God, you're *so* pretty in person. You're not even wearing any makeup right now, are you?"

I shook my head. "No, thank you!" I said. "That's really sweet of

I THINK I MIGHT NEED YOU

you to say, and I appreciate it, because I *certainly* don't feel that pretty right now."

We all shared the laugh about that.

"We saw you working out, but didn't want to interrupt," the one who hasn't said anything yet spoke up. "It seemed like you were going really hard to be pregnant."

Seriously?

"Well, since I was already super active before, my doctor suggests that it's not something I should change. The best thing I can do for the baby and for my body, is to keep my same activity level, without overdoing it."

"Yeah, I just don't understand why you would want to take a risk like that. It just seems so much safer to take a break."

Girl, if you don't get the fuck out of my face..."

I forced that smile to remain on my face. "I totally appreciate your concern, but I think I'm just going to follow the advice of my doctor, and trust that she wouldn't steer me wrong."

"Ashley, could you not?" The girl who'd initially call out my name scolded her friend. "You don't remember she did a video with her doctor right before Christmas? I'm sure she knows what she's doing."

I was getting ready to thank *this* girl for her wise counsel to her friend, but then she reached out a hand, aiming it directly for my stomach - which was currently obscured under my flowy workout tank. Instantly, I jumped back, avoiding her touch.

"Whoa," I said. "I would really prefer that we *didn't* do that," I told her, making sure to keep my tone light, even though I couldn't believe her nerve.

She wrinkled her nose. "*Oh.* Sorry. I was just trying to see if you had a baby bump yet. You haven't mentioned it at all on your channel, or on Instagram or anything. I mean... we want to know what's going on. How far along are you? How are you feeling? Who's the father?"

I shook my head, still keeping that smile on my face even though it was about as far opposite of how I felt as you could get. "I totally understand the curiosity guys, but I really would prefer to keep those things private for now. As soon as I'm comfortable, I'll do an update or something," I promised.

The pregnancy expert, Ashley, frowned. "That's funny. You took a pregnancy test on a live stream and found out you were having a kid in front of everybody. *Now* you want to be private? Girl, bye."

I, quite literally, had to bite my tongue to keep the *fuck you* from rolling off.

"Okay, that's my time," I said instead, turning to walk to my car. "You ladies have a wonderful rest of your day, okay?"

I *had* to get out of there before I said something ugly.

Not out of character.

Just ugly.

"These influencer bitches are always so rude," one of them said as I walked off.

My fists clenched, and instant heat rose to my face, but I forced myself to keep walking instead of turning around to address that comment. Ten times out of nine, it would end up all across social media, and of course I would be presented as the one in the wrong, as the aggressor.

It wasn't even worth the frustration.

As much as I loved my career, loved working for myself, loved being able to create, loved being able to relate and talk to people, and suggest things that I knew worked, etc, this was the worst thing about it. Every time I was out in public, I had to be on guard instead of being able to just live my life like a regular person.

Most people were respectful enough to engage you like you were human, just like them. Those were the people that kept me going, and kept me doing this. There had been times where something that I suggested completely changed someone's life for the better. There were times when a passing mention of, *"hey make sure you study today"*, or *"make sure you drink plenty of water"* etc, was just the push someone needed to make better choices for the day. Or times when seeing me plan my meals got someone to plan theirs. Or seeing me doing my workout at the gym inspired someone to put their own plan into action.

Or even something as simple as the live stream, which I rarely did with any sort of rhyme or reason or script or plan, just spending that time with the people who followed me, talking to them and engaging... it mattered a lot to them, and it mattered a lot to me.

But then people like *this*, who treated you like you were their own personal entertainment, or some puppet for them to pull strings as they wished. I couldn't wait to see how this interaction with going to be spun into something *I* had done wrong.

I didn't have to wait long.

I was barely out of the shower before my phone was going crazy with notifications, and as expected, the commentary was ridiculous. Of course there was no video evidence of the interaction, because the video wouldn't have supported those women's claim that I was rude and aggressive with them, that I'd smack that girl's hand away from my belly, or that I'd snapped at *anyone,* after giving me "useful" advice for my pregnancy.

I always knew something was off about her.

You can tell she doesn't even want to be pregnant. She's probably trying to kill that baby at the gym. Can't tell me any different.

These influencer chicks always think they're more important than they are.

Nobody cares about her ass being pregnant. She's not talking about it because she wants people to ask. Wack ass bitch.

It went on and on like that, and those were just the ones people actually *tagged* me in, bold as hell from the other side of a computer screen. Against my better judgment, I composed a message of my own, and hit send.

"Had no idea that stepping away from a complete stranger trying to touch my stomach, or assuring someone that I was under guidance from a medical

professional, could be construed as rude or aggressive. But here we are. #NoteTaken."

I knew better than to hit send.

I *knew* better than to hit send.

But I couldn't help it.

This mess was ridiculous.

And no sooner than I sent it, was there a new flurry of information of commentary going around, based on my singular message in my own defense.

These influencers get on here and get so bold with the ranting.

She ought to be ashamed of herself for even commenting on it, encouraging people to bully those girls - don't you have something better to do? RAISE YOUR BABY, BITCH.

You know she sits around searching her name, don't you? She should know better with a follower count like that, not to even comment on it, because you know her fans are going to go after those girls now. This is another form of bullying if you ask me.

Wait.

So... people could lie on me and say whatever they wanted to say, and that part was totally fine. But when I spoke up or defended myself, suddenly *I* was the bully in the situation? *I* was the one in the wrong?

Yeah.

Time for me to get off social media now.

I muted my notifications from all social media apps, across the board. I put the phone down and got up, focusing instead on getting dressed to go spend time with my family.

It was a *much* better use of my time.

∼

"Well, would you at least tell me *when* I'm going to be a grandma," Mama demanded more than asked of me from across the table.

So much for a better use of my time.

The whole time I'd been at their house, I'd been fielding questions, even after I made it clear I didn't want to answer. But they were my parents, and if they want to ask me questions while I was in their house, they could ask me questions while I was in their house.

But there were certain things that I just honestly wasn't ready to answer, and wouldn't.

Especially considering that I was almost thirty, did not live with them, and paid my own bills.

At this point though... I was just tired.

"In about 4 months if all goes well," I said, then put another forkful of food in my mouth.

That little admission set off a bomb blast of quiet around the table, and then an aftershock of what I can only describe as chaos.

"Four months, meaning you're five months pregnant right now?!"

"Wait a minute if you're five months now, that means..."

"Yep, that baby was conceived around New Years."

"And for New Years, Joia was in Vegas!"

"Welp," my father spoke up, chuckling his ass off. "You did Vegas all wrong, didn't you? What happened in Vegas followed you home!"

"Go ahead and get all your laughing in," I said shaking my head as I forked another mouthful of my mother's bomb ass chicken and dumplings. "You were going to find out soon enough anyway."

"Yeah, when you had this baby two or three months earlier than any of us were expecting!" Mama exclaimed. "You don't even have a baby bump or anything yet!"

"That's because she has abs," Jaclyn said, laughing. "They're holding back the floodgates right now."

"She's actually right," I admitted. "Basically, my steadily swelling uterus is going to *rip* my abdominal muscles apart in about a month or so, tops, to accommodate the baby. So that is going to be an absolute *blast* to rehab. Just so much fun."

"Awww, JoJo!" Jemma said, reaching over to rub my back. "You'll still be fine. We'll still call you Miss Fit Bitch right up to delivery when you're all swollen and gross, okay?"

I rolled my eyes and laughed about that. "Thank you, so much. I appreciate it."

"Well, it has been real as always, my beautiful family," Jemma said, "but your girl has a flight to catch."

"Where you off to this time baby?" my father asked.

"Just New York," Jemma answered. "Moving on with book tour dates."

"What happened to the trip you were supposed to be taking with your sisters?" Mama asked.

Once again, the table went quiet, as everybody turned to look at me.

"Well, we didn't think that Joia would really be up for the travel this summer, so we figured we'd postpone it for now," Jemma said, with a glance at Jaclyn.

"Yeah," Jac agreed, nodding. "We'd rather wait than do it without her. You guys are going to babysit for her while we go live it up after she drops this baby, right?"

"Hell yes," my mother said. "Joia, you don't ever hesitate to bring my grandbaby to me, you hear me?"

I laughed." Of course, Mama. I already know."

"Jac is dropping me off for my flight this time," Jemma said. "You coming with?" she asked me.

I shook my head. "No, not this time. I'm pretty tired. Probably going to head home and get some rest. I really, *really* need to get some work done tomorrow."

"But we're ignoring that bullshit on social media, right?" Jac asked. "Cause I'm really ready to get tagged in. Hell... ready to find those bitches to be honest, but I'm being cool."

"Yes, please be cool, and stay out of trouble so you can enjoy your degree and your new man," I urged, laughing. "I'm going to ignore it all, I swear."

Since Jemma and Jaclyn were leaving, the next few minutes were

I THINK I MIGHT NEED YOU

absorbed with goodbyes. We were used to seeing Jem off for her travels at this point and so it wasn't necessarily a big deal, but just in case, we always made sure to love on her before she caught a new flight. Once they were gone, my father made his way to his den for his usual *fall asleep in front of WAWG sports* session.

Which left my mother and me alone to clear the table, put away the extra food, and do all the dishes. But I didn't mind.

For a while, we were quietly working, which I knew meant something was brewing. Quiet was not particularly high on my mother's long list of virtues.

It took a while, but as we were drying the last of the dishes, after a little bit of small talk here and there, she finally turned to me, dish towel in hand and tears in her eyes.

"You don't seem excited about this baby, Joia," she said, meeting my gaze.

I opened my mouth to respond to that, but she held up in hand, shushing me.

"I understand it's a lot to take in unexpectedly," she said. "I understand it even more now that you finally told us how far along you are. I am *not* scolding you about this, Jo. I know you're probably scared, and confused, and frustrated right now, and those feelings are overwhelming your room for anything else. I *know* you're going to *love* this baby. I know your excitement will come. But in the meantime, I just want you to know..." She reached out to grab my hands, squeezing them between hers as a broad smile spread over her face. "*I'm* excited. My *first* grandbaby! You have no idea how happy I am about this."

I smiled back. "I'm not going to lie to you Mama... I really want to say, that makes one of us. But I *can't* say that, because I'm really not sure *how* I feel. I don't necessarily hate the idea of being pregnant, and you know I've always wanted kids. I've always wanted a family. I just really did not imagine it happening like this."

My mother nodded. "Of course you didn't. But this is how it happened. You've got to come to terms with that, sweetheart."

"Yeah," I agreed. "I know. And I will."

"Oh I know you will," my mother said in her usual wise owl tone, turning back to the last of the wet dishes. "So, Vegas, huh?"

"No, I am not pregnant by some stranger that I met in Vegas."

"I didn't think you were," she said. "That would be way too simple for you."

"You know... you might be right. If it was someone I barely knew, it honestly might make this easier. It would eliminate a good 50% of the concerns on my mind."

"Uh-huh. Cuz now you got to make it work with...?" My mother let that trail off, obviously waiting for me to fill in the blank, but I shook my head.

"I haven't talked to him yet. So I really don't want to put it out there."

"Can you at least tell me if he's willing to step up and do the right thing?"

I nodded. "Yeah. I am pretty sure he is going to make his presence *very* apparent, whether I want him to or not."

My mother shrugged. "Well in that case, the only thing left is for you to have that conversation."

"Yes, I know. I talked about it this morning with Jem and Jac," I told her.

"Okay, so when are you going to do it?" she asked, putting her towel down and giving me her full attention as she looked me right in the eyes.

I let out a sigh. "Tonight. I'm going to make that call."

∽

I *did* make a call, but it definitely wasn't about the baby. The call I made was to get Teddy back to my apartment - back into my bed.

So, the time I was supposed to be spending having a heart-to-heart with the father of my child, was actually spent attempting to ride my college boyfriend off into the sunset.

"Damn," he breathed grabbing my hips to slow me down. "Did you drink a red bull before I stopped by or something?"

"No," I laughed, anchoring my feet on either side of his powerful thighs, and digging my toes into the mattress. I used my hands against his chest for balance as I rode him harder. "Are you complaining?" I asked, halfway breathless.

He shook his head. "*Hell no.*"

"Good. Shut up then."

He did.

Well, mostly.

From there, he had nothing but grunts, groans, and moans of pleasure and encouragement as I bounced on him, working my hips in circles, giving it all I had, until we were both wrung out and empty.

I spread myself out on the bed beside him, panting and staring up at the ceiling until my body had finally calmed.

"So is this our new dynamic now?" Teddy asked, turning on his side to look at me. "Exes with benefits?"

Shaking my head, I kept my gaze pointed upward instead of looking at him. This really hadn't been in my plans for the day, but as the day wore on, the need for release had only grown stronger. The idea of doing it myself, while convenient and drama-free, just didn't seem quite as appetizing as it had before Jemma's party.

My eyelids slammed open wide as the weirdest sensation crept across my belly. I looked down, thinking that maybe Teddy was caressing my stomach, but his hand wasn't even close to me. Not to mention, this didn't feel like something happening on the outside of my skin.

This was happening inside me.

Like something in there was moving around.

Like the *baby* was moving around.

"Hey, you okay?" Teddy asked, sitting up on the bed.

I shook my head, still staring at my stomach as that foreign sensation continued. "I... I think I just felt the baby move."

"Man! For the first time? Really?" Teddy asked, then he covered his face with his hands. "Ah, damn... you think it's cause of what we were doing? You think I was like... knocking it upside the head?" he asked.

I laughed at his silliness, and shrugged. "I don't know, maybe?" I thought about it for a second, pulling my lip between my teeth. "Do you want to feel it?"

"Seriously?"

I nodded, grabbing his hand and pressing it firmly to my stomach on the side that seemed to be getting the most activity. "Do you feel that?" I asked him.

He was quiet for a moment, concentrating before he shook his head. "Nah. I don't feel anything."

"It's probably too soon. Maybe once the baby is bigger, it'll be more pronounced," I guessed. "And that's when other people will be able to feel it as strong as I do."

Logically I actually *knew* that was the case, but it was still a little disappointing.

All this time - with the exception of the ultrasound of course - there hadn't been anything to really make this real. And even the ultrasound was just an image on the screen – still fairly abstract. But *feeling* it, knowing for sure that this baby was definitely there, definitely growing inside me...it was different.

I kinda wanted to share it with somebody.

"Yeah," Teddy nodded. "Maybe. Probably not right for me to experience something like that before the father does anyway, right?"

Again, I bit my lip. "Yeah... it probably *would* be a great experience for the father to be the first person other than me to feel the baby move," I agreed. "So I guess we'll just have to keep trying."

Immediately, Teddy's face pulled into a frown, but he didn't say anything. He just looked at me. "What does that even mean?" he finally asked, when I just looked at him too.

"I think... you know what it means, Teddy."

"Nah, I think you need to clarify. You can't be saying what I think you're saying, because before the other night, me and you hadn't even kicked it like that since..."

"Since Vegas."

"Yeah," he nodded. "Which was..."

"About 5 months ago, yeah."

"So you're saying..."

"Yes," I confirmed, blowing out a deep breath as I finally spoke aloud the truth I'd been wrestling with for days. "I'm saying that the baby growing inside me right now... is *your* child."

Teddy shook his head, climbing out of the bed as he scowled at me, and started grabbing his clothes. "Joia, seriously? This shit ain't funny. *At all*," he said."

I sat up, watching him. "No. It's *not* funny at all, and I'm not trying to *be* funny. I'm trying to be real with you here."

He sucked his teeth. "This is real to you?! If I hadn't been making an effort to get back in good with you, were you going to tell me? Or were you just going to let me believe the baby was Dalton's?!"

"I've *never* insinuated to anybody that this was Dalton's child, first of all. You made an assumption and ran with it – I didn't correct you because I'm still fucking freaking out about it myself. Besides that, as soon as I found out how far along I was, I knew *exactly* whose it was. And *of course* I was going to tell you, Teddy. I found out less than a week ago, and I was trying to process it all. I didn't even mean to blurt it out just now. I... thought I would prepare a speech or something."

"Were you *processing* when you let me take you to my mama's house and eat up all that food?! Or when you brought me over here, twice now, to use me for my body?!"

"Actually," I nodded, "Yeah, I was."

"*That doesn't make this not fucked up*," he bellowed, straightening to a stand once he'd finished dressing. "Man... give me my baby, I'm about to go."

He stared at me, completely serious, for several seconds.

I stared right back, before finally speaking again. "You... do realize that can't happen, right?" I asked. "Since I haven't actually *had* the baby yet."

His eyes narrowed. "I'm not dumb," he said. "I'm just practicing for when I inevitably have to argue with your ass, since I see you like keeping secrets and shit. I already *know* we ain't gone fucking get along!"

"You're acting as if I've known this whole time!"

"Maybe you have! Why the fuck should I believe that you really are just now finding out?"

I glared at him. "You don't have to believe *shit*. But it is what it is. And if *this* is how you're going to act? You can go."

"Whatever Joia," Teddy snapped, snatching up shoes and heading for the door. "You ain't gotta tell me twice."

TEN

Teddy.

What the fuck.
 I pushed myself back from my desk and leaned back in my office chair, crossing my arms. I was pissed off, nothing was helping, and I didn't even know what to do with it.

I'd already tried distracting myself.

I'd channeled my energy into a tool my therapist had given me years ago to help decompress and relieve some of the jumble that happened in our brains.

Journaling.

I wrote out everything that I felt about this bullshit with Joia.

The break-up, having to constantly see her over the years, finding out she was pregnant, trying to get back with her, and then finally, the cherry on top of the shitty ass cake, finding out that the baby was mine.

She really could have come with that shit a whole lot earlier.

Of course I'd seen it along with everyone else, when she found out about the pregnancy "by surprise". Right along with everybody else, I'd believed she had no idea - the reaction she and her sisters had to that positive test was something that just didn't seem faked.

But at the same time... the shit was so ridiculous.

How the *hell* could she not know she was halfway through a whole ass pregnancy?

I may not have been in touch with her much over the years, but I followed Joia, watched her videos sometimes, and kept up with her brand because some of it overlapped mine.

She was incredibly conscious of her body.

Self-conscious to be honest.

So I couldn't understand how she would have missed the changes in her body that would have come along with being pregnant.

But then again... pregnancy wasn't something I had experienced or even *could* experience. I didn't live in a woman's body, and more specifically, I didn't live in *her* body. So it really wasn't for me to say what she should have known or not.

Joia was a smart woman, and I couldn't imagine her going through this whole elaborate prank just for some views on a live stream video. She was serious about her brand, but she didn't put her real life out there like that, not like some others. I mean, she was her *real self*, don't get me wrong. But she didn't have the whole world in her business.

I knew that because, again, I kept up with her.

I saw when her videos posted, saw when she put up new statuses, etc. Ever since that live stream, no matter what she talked about, all the commenters wanted to know was extra-intrusive, detailed information about her pregnancy. How far along was she, how did she feel, who was the father, was it an accident, has she been assaulted, was she drunk – all asked and speculated about with various degrees of ugliness. People were taking this whole thing way left and Joia was astute enough to know the storm a stunt like this would bring.

But... it wasn't a "stunt".

I knew that.

And yet, I still felt room to be pissed about it.

Which was stupid, especially when this really worked out in my favor.

I wanted Joia back. There was no question about that. To the point I was willing to insert myself in her life enough to make myself *more* valuable than the man I initially thought was the child's father.

But *I* was the child's father.

So that should make the whole thing easy for me, right?

Here it was, right here, the family I called myself wanting. And instead of embracing it, instead of considering her feelings, instead of acting like my mama had raised me right... I got mad at her.

Stormed out.

Like *I* was the fucking baby.

I had to get my shit together.

So I did the journaling. Recorded a few videos, but very specifically nothing where I was trying to be funny, cause I just wasn't in the damn mood for it. Took my ass to the gym too, purposely lifting heavier than before, smashing through personal records.

All in pursuit of distraction.

Now, I was sore as hell physically, but mentally and emotionally, my shit wasn't any better. I'd even try to do some other work, taking out the time to write my pitch for the WAWG Fresh thing, and submitted it. Now more than ever, with a kid on the way, I *really* hoped it got accepted.

I may not know much about babies, and even less about pregnancy, but I *did* know that shit was expensive. Which meant it was time out for the bullshit. I had to get real, *real* serious out here.

At some point, I was going to have to talk to Joia and make it right.

This pregnancy really was out of nowhere for her, and when it came down to it, *she* was really the one who needed the support in this situation. And now, instead of just having to overcome some shit

I did eight years ago, I was going to have to overcome the stupid shit I did a few *days* ago.

Making my goal of getting her back – not just co-parenting, but being *with* her - that much harder.

One thing I never been scared of was a challenge though.

So whatever I had to do to make the shit right, I would.

Cause when it came down to it, just like I told her that night in the hallway of her building... Joia and I were a foregone conclusion.

It was time to bring it back to life.

∽

"So... you sure you want to do this?" Len asked, from the passenger seat of my truck.

"Hell nah, I'm not sure. But sometimes, you just gotta do what you gotta do," I answered, sharing his somber mood.

He huffed. "Man... I just... I really didn't think I'd ever see you do something *this* drastic."

"Me either."

"You don't think there's any other alternative?"

I shook my head. "Nah, man. This is how it has to be. I gotta let it go."

"You think we ought to have some type of memorial service or something? Something to commemorate the loss?"

I blew out a sigh. "I don't know man. Honestly, it's too soon for me to even think about it. Too many memories. Let's just do it."

I opened my door stepped out of the truck – which had been my baby all this time.

As a damned teenager, I'd dreamed about this truck, with these exact details. Big wheels, with chromed out rims. Chrome trim on the body, popping against the immaculate, cobalt paint. Buttery-soft leather interior, tinted windows, state-of-the-art sound system... every last detail had come from a long-standing vision of my *dream* vehicle.

I THINK I MIGHT NEED YOU

And it was *paid for*. All mine, didn't owe a single dime to anybody for it. The money I made from the *"Teddy Grahams, No Milk"* brand on social media had all gone toward procuring it, after I helped my parents with their forever house, and after I'd set aside a good amount for savings.

This truck had been my splurge.

The thing that was all for me, all about me.

Blue magic.

Now, it was time to let her go.

Reluctantly I made my way through the door of *J&P Auto Sales*, glad for the opportunity to give the same dealership who sold me the truck my business again. It was quiet inside, since it was the middle of the day, so the owner, Big Joe, found me immediately.

"Theodore Graham," he said, his hand extended as he approached me. "What can I do for you today son?" asked. "Don't tell me something wrong with that truck?"

I accepted his hand, honestly pleased by the fact that he remembered his customers so well. "Nah man," I shook my head. "It's just time for something a little more... family-friendly, I guess."

He grinned. "Oh you got yourself a lady friend, about to get married?" Joe asked.

"No, not quite on the ring," I admitted. "But I do have a baby on the way, and I don't think the truck is really car seat conducive."

Joe whistled. "No, you sure don't want a car seat denting your leather, and you'll want a lot more enclosed room. So you looking for something new, or you thinking about trading it in?"

"I don't think it's wise to pick up a new car note at this point, so probably trading it in – *if* you can give me a good price on it, and I can get something at about equal value."

It was an expensive ass truck, which made it hurt to let go. But I had already looked up what the value of it was, and knew I could get something decent in that family SUV range.

Even if the thought kinda made me sick to my stomach.

"Okay," Joe said, clapping me on the shoulder. "Let me go look at the truck, we can run some numbers, and then I'll show you what I got."

I nodded. "Sounds like a plan."

Thirty minutes later, I was sick as fuck, looking at these wack-ass family-friendly ass vehicles. Joe was giving me a great number on the trade-in, so I had no complaints about *that*, but these damn family SUVs...

I was *definitely* going to have to come out of pocket for some rims, some dope interiors, some tint on the windows, *something*.

Acadias had exactly zero swag.

Subarus were even worse.

There *was* a Benz SUV on the other side of the lot that was calling my goddamn name, but I knew better. Knew that wasn't the wisest financial decision for me right now.

Could I afford the payments on it?

Yeah, probably.

But it was time out for making vanity decisions. I'd always said that whenever I had a kid, whenever I had a family, *that* was when I would have to start being smarter.

I hadn't secured a big enough bag yet to be riding around with a car seat in a Benz.

Not when the Tahoe a few rows over looked good enough, and the price on the sticker was right up my alley.

Instead of letting it drag on, I said that was the one, and gave the go-ahead for Joe to get started with the paperwork. While we were waiting, Len showed me the video footage he'd been gathering from this whole ordeal. It certainly wasn't anything that we were going to put together for public consumption anytime soon, but I had to admit - the look on my face through most of it, like I'd lost my childhood pet or something, was pure fucking comedy.

With the right editing, it could definitely be something, and that was the type of shit I had to think about. Not just what was comfortable for now, but what could eventually become content that could provide for my kid later on.

He was still showing me footage when my phone buzzed in my pocket. I pulled it out, halfway hoping it was Joia. Three days had gone by since she dropped that bomb on me, and honestly... I didn't even know how to approach her. So I was hoping she would be the one – be the bigger person.

This wasn't that though.

My eyes damn near bugged out of my head when I saw it was an email marked urgent, from the people at WAWG Fresh.

Immediately, I tapped my screen to open the email, frantically scanning the words on the page.

Teddy, this is Carmen Waters, head content editor with WAWG Fresh.

I'm reaching out personally to let you know that we absolutely loved the pitch you sent.

It was so unique, so unlike any of the others.

So absolutely... fresh.

Your method of sending it in as if it were pulled straight from your personal journal, ranting about this very transitional point in your life... it really touched me. Really, really captured my attention.

I want to move forward with this with you as soon as possible.

With Joia's pregnancy so far along, it puts us on a pretty strict deadline, and we want to try to get in some footage during the pregnancy. It's why I'm reaching out now, instead of waiting until the pitch contest is over.

*We're very **very** excited to partner with you two to make this series. No scripting, no added drama, just you and her trying to come to the point of peaceful co-parenting, possibly getting back together, and us documenting everything along the way.*

We cannot wait to get started.

Please respond to this message as soon as possible so that we can work out the details. We'll need you and Joia to sign off, but we're ready to do this.

Let's talk numbers.

-Carmen Waters.

What?

What?

What!?

What the *hell* was she talking about, about a "unique pitch, journal entry style"?

My pitch to *Fresh* was about me and Len checking out all the wing spots in our state, and talking about sports while we did it.

It had *nothing* to do with Joia, nothing to do with the baby, nothing to do with...

Oh, shit!

I sat back in my chair, my brain working in overdrive as I ran the day I submitted that pitch through my mind. I remembered having a document for my journaling open in one tab. I was writing my pitch in another.

But my head was so messed up, overwhelmed with that little piece of breaking news from Joia...

Had I copy/pasted and hit submit on the wrong damn thing?

Actually... reading through that message again, there was no doubt about it - it was absolutely what I'd done.

But... they liked it.

And they wanted to talk *numbers*.

Numbers that could mean everything, from a huge corporation like that, when we had a baby on the way. I couldn't speak for Joia, but I could definitely use a boost in income.

"Yo, what's up with you" Len asked, finally noticing that I wasn't paying attention to his video clips anymore.

I shook my head, unable to verbalize it to him quite yet.

Not when I had a million things scurrying through my mind.

Most important being... how the hell I was going to get Joia to say *yes*.

ELEVEN

JOIA.

"You want me to say yes to *what*?"

I stepped back, glaring at Teddy and not letting him pass the threshold of my front door. His *first* mistake was showing up at my door unannounced after *three* goddamn days of virtual silence. His second mistake? Thinking I was going to agree to have a camera in my face for the rest of this pregnancy.

"Absolutely *not*," I said, as soon as he opened his mouth to actually answer the question I'd asked him. "People are already in my business enough, and you think I'm ready to *invite* them into it?"

"I get where you're coming from Joia, I swear I do," he insisted, his large body filling the door frame. "But listen... if we do this, you get to control the narrative. Remember a couple of years back, your homegirl Nubia Perry was talking about this, when she did that behind the scenes thing about her pregnancy."

"I know you think it's flattering for you to compare me to Nubia Perry, and in most other circumstances it would be. In *this* circumstance though... nigga are you out of your goddamn mind? No, never mind, I take that back. It's not a question. You *are* out of your goddamn mind. You have *lost* your goddamn mind. And when you *find* your goddamn mind, *then* you come back and talk to me."

Shout out to NeNe Leakes.

"You're tripping! This could be a good opportunity for *both* of us."

"Maybe so, but when it involves me putting myself out there even more than I am right now, I really can't say I'm interested in that."

I walked away from the door and he followed me inside, closing it behind him. "I *get* that. I know it feels intrusive. But WAWG is all about their *we all we got* shit. You know they're not really with the exploitation and stuff, know they're going to make sure you're taken care of, right?"

"I'm really not trying to depend on anybody except myself for *that*," I told him with a pointed look that he picked up on immediately.

Good.

I could understand him being upset over suddenly finding out about the baby like this. I hadn't even meant to tell him in such an abrupt, unplanned way, so I wasn't even that bothered about him being pissed off at me.

Initially.

But it had been *three* days, and as far as I was concerned, his silence has spoken volumes.

Teddy had never been a stupid guy, so of course he immediately picked up on the ugly inflection of my words. He pushed out a sigh, shoving his hands into the pockets of his jeans.

Damn him for looking good when I'm mad at him.

He'd gotten a fresh lineup since the last time I saw him, and had the nerve to come over here smelling all good, bringing up memories of our recent intimacy.

Asshole.

I wasn't going out like that today though.

My hormones may have been on ten, but my pussy was dialed down to zero.

"Listen," he said. "I understand that it wasn't cool for me to go radio silent about this. Even if I was upset – and I was - I should have reached out enough to make sure you know - I have *every* intention of doing my part with this child. *More* than my part. *All the parts.* But you have to know, you came out of left field with this."

"Oh trust me - I understand how it feels for this to hit you out of left field. But at least you don't have the swollen abdomen, gas, back pain, swollen breasts, constant hunger, insane hormone fluctuations, etc."

I really wasn't trying to be *that* pregnant girl but damn.

"We all got pain," I told him, crossing my arms.

Some of us more than others.

I really didn't give a shit about his complaints, since he wasn't the one who had to *carry* the baby. But still... there was a slump in his shoulders that spoke to his guilt about the way he'd reacted.

It kinda made me feel bad.

"Hey," I said, choosing maturity over the pettiness I wanted to give in to so, so bad. "I'm not saying that this isn't rough for you too. I know it is. And I'm sorry for the way it all came out." I shrugged. "I'm sorry it's happening at all. I'm not trying to disrupt your life, and honestly, if you don't want to do this, you do *not* have to. But I know the kind of guy you are, Teddy. Which is why I *did* tell. Or rather, why I *planned* to tell you. I don't know why I told you when I did, like I did, it just came out. And I'm sorry about that."

Teddy shook his head. "You don't have to apologize. I mean, don't get me wrong, it was pretty abrupt, especially considering what we'd been doing about ten minutes before that."

I nodded. "I can accept that."

"But I can only imagine how hard this has been for you. Physically, mentally, emotionally, all that. It has to be rough."

"Yeah," I huffed. "All sorts of things I had no idea were pregnancy symptoms are making a whole lot more sense now. Things that I had written off as nothing, I realize now were all signs that I missed. All because pregnancy was just... never a consideration in my mind. So in addition to everything else, you feel kinda... stupid, you know?"

"*You?*" Teddy asked, his face pulled into a skeptical scowl. "Stupid?" He shook his head. "Nah. Not you."

"Well, the evidence says something different, but you know what? I'm just going to take the compliment. Thank you."

"You're welcome." He stared at me for a second, and then his gaze traveled down to my clothing. It was early afternoon, and whereas I would usually be in athleisure gear, I was actually dressed today, in a comfy floral short set that concealed my little belly.

"You going somewhere?" He asked.

"Yeah," I answered. "I have the twenty-week prenatal appointment. The big one."

Devyn's initial thought had been that I was eighteen weeks pregnant, based on the quick measurement she'd taken at that first ultrasound. But going from the actual date of conception was a different story.

The baby was a measuring little on the small side, probably because I hadn't been eating in a way that supported growing a new life. I was pretty consistent with my daily multivitamin, and ate lots of leafy greens as my standard diet, which helped with making sure I'd gotten enough folic acid. Still, one of my first changes had been to start a prenatal vitamin, and to eat more, now that I knew my stubborn midsection wasn't about me not eating a clean enough diet.

Teddy took his hands from his pockets, throwing them up in the air. "Come on Joia, really? Why wouldn't you tell me about something like that?"

My eyebrows shot up. "Maybe if you hadn't spent the last few days not talking to me, I would have told you about it."

Teddy's nostrils flared as he clamped his lips together and nodded. "Okay. That was my bad, I'll eat that."

"I know you will," I said. "Cause you're right, that's *your* bad."

The defeated look on his face made me sigh. "Do you want to come with me?"

"Hell yes," he said, perking right up. "I'll drive."

I wanted to roll my eyes at his sudden enthusiasm, after not having anything to say to me for three days. But in the interest of not being petty, especially since I was about to be in the truck with him, and then stuffed into a room together for this appointment, I didn't.

Instead, I simply nodded, grabbed my keys and purse from the counter, and motioned for him to come on.

In the parking lot, I had to slow my steps because I didn't see his truck. That thing stuck out like a sore thumb, so there was no way I was simply overlooking it.

I turned to him, confused.

He grinned at me as he held up his keys, making a big deal of pressing the unlock button. I heard a vehicle chirp in tandem with that unlocking mechanism, but still, I didn't see his truck.

I watched, baffled, as he walked up to a shiny black Tahoe - a nice looking vehicle, for sure. But again... not his truck.

"What is this?" I asked, as he opened the passenger side door for me.

He didn't answer until he'd secured himself in the driver seat and turned the SUV on, sending heavenly air-conditioned waves in my direction - a needed respite from the increasingly hot pre-summer weather.

"This," he said, "Is me being real serious about this thing. Showing it to you, and showing it to myself. Did I love the truck? Yes. Did I have some great memories in that truck? Yes. Did that truck get me a lot of ass? Yes."

I rolled my eyes.

"But the important thing here," he continued, "Is that the truck wasn't really a practical vehicle for carrying a family around in."

I raised an eyebrow. "Seriously Teddy? You're already thinking about driving a *family* around?"

He shrugged. "Why not?"

"I don't know. It just seems... Abrupt."

"Well," he said, grabbing the gearshift to move. "Almost a decade ago now, I had this girlfriend who taught me a very important lesson about not half stepping. So now, when I decide I'm about something... I'm not halfway into it. There's no ambiguity. I'm all in."

I shifted my gaze away from his, already knowing what that was about.

I... was surprised to hear it.

It was one thing for him to be willing to step up and take care of the responsibility he'd assisted in creating, and quite another for him to still be pursuing me on a romantic level.

If that's what that meant.

~

"*Oh damn.* It's a for real baby, huh?"

I forced myself not to let loose a smile at Teddy's enthusiasm over the picture of our baby up on the screen.

Devyn seemed pleased too - not just that I'd brought the father along with me, but by his apparent delight, which was... infectious.

This time, the ultrasound felt a lot different.

Instead of being scared and confused, barely believing what was happening, I felt a pinch of excitement myself. This wasn't my first time seeing the baby or hearing the heartbeat, but those two things along with having felt it moving - with feeling it move right now, and watching those movements happen on the screen as well... It was just different.

I didn't feel anxious at all.

"Would you guys like to know if it's a girl or a boy?" Devyn asked, carefully charting certain measurements as she looked back and forth between us and what was happening on the screen.

"No," Teddy and I said at the same time.

This time, I did give in to the smile, because I was glad we were on the same page. "Everything else about this baby has been a surprise. May as well let that be another one."

"Yeah," Teddy said, giving me a sly grin. "I bet our fans would like that angle too... hint, hint."

I rolled my eyes about that, but now that I was seeing the baby again, hearing the healthy, steady heartbeat, now that this moment wasn't filled with tension and uncertainty... I could honestly see the benefit of contacting *WAWG Fresh* about their idea.

And... I thought about it on the drive over.

Teddy was absolutely right - it could be a great opportunity for us. And while I still wasn't so sure about putting my child up for other people's entertainment purposes, it couldn't hurt to make a little money during the pregnancy.

We would *both* need a steady income in order to take care of a child. That really wasn't up for debate. WAWG was huge – I knew they could pay us well for the show, and we could probably negotiate some type of royalties too. Not to mention what the visibility could do for both of our brands.

It would be silly not to consider it.

I wasn't signing away any type of options for extended visibility of myself or my child. The risk was, on one hand, fairly limited. But on the other hand, the risk was huge. I was putting myself out there for more abuse than I'd already experienced, and I wasn't sure I was up for it.

But... there was always love from people too.

Much, *much* more than the hate. And the more I thought about it, the less inclined I felt to turn down something that could be amazing in favor of hiding myself away because of haters.

To me, and probably to a whole lot of other people, there was value in seeing Black faces navigate something like this. Sure, the *didn't know I was pregnant for the first half of it* thing was probably uncommon, but figuring out how to get through a pregnancy and raise a child with someone you weren't necessarily with?

There was no question in my mind that there were people who could relate to *that*.

And even if it wasn't about relating, just exposing people to unconventional relationships had value as well. Not that there was anything particularly special about a heterosexual man and woman having a kid, but our dynamic was certainly not the *first comes love, then comes marriage, then come the Grahams with a baby carriage* type.

More like *first came the gin, then came the sin, now oh shit, I gotta deal with **you** again.*

"I'll be right back," Devyn said, excusing herself before either of us could question her sudden exit.

I looked up at Teddy, whose eyes were still trained on the screen. The baby wasn't live streaming anymore, but he was so enthralled by those images that it set off tightness in my chest.

In a good way.

"Hey," I said, getting his attention.

He turned to me with this wonder-filled look in his eyes that only intensified the tightness in my chest. "What's up?" he asked.

"I've been thinking about it," I said. "And... I do think the show is a wise choice for us, but only if we have a *whole lot* of creative control over it all. We both have great quality camera equipment, we both know how to edit, we have backdrops, all of that. I want them to let us do our own filming and production. We're capable of it. We can film what we want, cut it, and send it off. I'm even willing to work with a consultant, if they want that. But if we do this... it has to be our way."

Teddy bit his lip, nodding. "No complaints here. I like the way you think, baby."

"Did they give you any idea what the numbers looked like?" I asked.

Teddy grinned. "Oh yeah."

Seconds later, my eyes went wide as he rattled off a number that wasn't *huge* money, but it was definitely *good* money.

Really good money.

I THINK I MIGHT NEED YOU

Stupid to walk away from it, if they agreed to let us have creative control, good money.

Before I could respond to it, Devyn came back in, with my cousin Joseph in tow.

Joseph Wright was chief resident of the women's center at University Hospital. Devyn wasn't technically a "doctor" - she was a nurse practitioner. With that title, she could do pretty much everything any other doctor in the women's center could do – and with her advanced certifications, more than some of them - so it concerned me that she'd gone to get Dr. Wright.

"What's going on, cousin?" Joseph greeted me, walking up to wrap me in as much of a hug as he could with me in an inclined position for the ultrasound. His cheeriness made me feel a little better, but still... Something was wrong here.

"Honestly Joey, I'll be a whole lot better if you just cut right to the chase. She didn't bring you in here for nothing," I told him.

He and Devyn – his wife – exchanged a look, and then he nodded.

He didn't say anything at first, instead going to look at the ultrasound pictures with Devyn. They used her personal screen, so I couldn't see what was being pointed at, but my untrained eyes were all over the large monitor trying to spot anything that could possibly be wrong.

We'd been here for hours, taking all kinds of blood tests after I'd drunk some nasty orange concoction. Devyn had spent time pointing out all of our babies' limbs and organs, the brain, etc, gushing about how everything looked really good.

Obviously though... it didn't.

"Okay Jo," Joseph said, after he'd reviewed my ultrasound images for himself. "The good news is that the *baby* looks perfectly fine, as Nurse Wright has already explained to you. There's not anything of concern there. What might be of *slight* concern is the fact that your placenta is sitting quite low, to the point of nearly covering your cervical opening. This is something called placenta previa, which is not necessarily something to panic about. It's something for us to keep an eye on, and monitor as you get closer to delivery," he said.

But he wasn't finished.

"There is, however, something potentially a little more serious for us to keep an eye on. You see this dark area right here?" he asked, pointing at something on the screen - not the baby, but close to where he'd just pointed out the potential issue with my placenta. "We can't tell right now, but Nurse Wright is slightly concerned that this dark area is your placenta pulling away from the uterine lining. Now, that's something that usually - if it *does* happen, doesn't happen until after you've passed your 20-week mark. Usually the third trimester. It *could* be nothing. It *could* be scar tissue or just your normal landscape. Could be any number of things that are absolutely *not* harmful to you or your baby. But...we want to be cautious."

My mouth was so dry that I couldn't even verbalize any of the million questions that immediately came to my mind.

"Okay," Teddy spoke up. "Tell us what we need to do."

"Really, there's nothing to do unless we're *sure* it's a placental abruption. Which I'm not saying that I think it is, not saying that I think it isn't. I'm saying that it's a possibility. A *small* possibility. But it's too early to tell."

Teddy nodded. "I get what you're saying. You're not trying to scare us; you just want us to be aware. So what do we *do*," Teddy asked again.

"For now," Joseph said, glancing directly at me with a look that immediately let me know I wasn't about to like the next thing out of his mouth. "Semi-bed rest. That does not mean you have to lay in your bed, flat on your back all day. What it *does* mean is... Joia... cousin... I know how you like to do. I *know* how you like to move around. But... you can't be Superwoman at the gym until we know for sure that you're okay."

"So I caused this?" I asked, eyes wide. "My gym habits have done something that's going to hurt the baby?"

Immediately Devyn and Joseph both shook their heads.

"Absolutely not," Devyn answered. "You have absolutely *no* control over where the placenta attaches. And it would take a pretty intense trauma for *you* to have caused a placental abruption. A *major* hit to your stomach, like a car accident or something like that. You haven't had anything like that have you?"

"No," I shook my head." But still. This whole thing has me second-guessing every single thing I've done for the last 5 months. I'm trying to figure out everything that's happened that I forgot about. Everything I shouldn't have done. All the soft cheese I shouldn't have eaten. Just... *everything*."

"And that doesn't help you, and it doesn't help the baby," Joseph said shaking his head. He abandoned his place at the screen and came to me, grabbing me by the hand. "Joia... you are *family*. This baby? Is *family*. You trust me and Devyn to take good care of you and your baby, right?"

I blew a long stream of air out, then nodded. "Yes. I do."

"Okay then. Don't sweat this, alright? Just take two weeks off from embarrassing the muscle-heads in the weight room, and we'll take another look. You can be up and about – I don't recommend that you stop being active. Just for now, get comfortable with... power walking."

"*Power-walking?*" I groaned. "Fine. *Fine.* I'll do whatever you tell me to do, for this baby."

"And you will *both* be just fine," Devyn smiled. "All *three* of you will," she amended, a correction that put a smile on Teddy's face.

"What about sex?" Teddy asked, out of nowhere, making my eyes damn near bug out of my head.

Devyn rolled her eyes, and even Joseph gave him a bit of a side eye. "Sex is... fine. Just take it easy."

"That ain't no problem," Teddy acknowledged, shaking his head. "I was just asking."

After a little more time spent on my instructions for the next two weeks, Joseph and Devyn stepped out, leaving me to clean the ultrasound gel off my stomach and... panic.

"That girl from the gym was right," I told Teddy, letting him take over the drying of my stomach. "My obsession messed something up, and now the baby isn't going to get all the oxygen and nutrients it needs."

Teddy stopped moving to raise an eyebrow at me. "That's what you heard?"

"That's what they *said*," I insisted.

He laughed at me.

"I'ma let you have your space to freak out, but for the record – nobody said that shit to you. They said *if* it's a placental abruption, that *could* happen. And that *if* it's a placental abruption, *you* did not do anything to cause it."

I sucked my teeth. "Of course they said that, they *love* me. They don't want me to feel bad."

"So you don't love yourself then?" he asked, looking me right in the face.

"*What?*" I frowned. "What the hell are you talking about?"

He pulled my shirt back down, covering my exposed belly. "Well, your logic is that the people who love you, don't want you to feel bad. So, following that, if you love *yourself*... why are digging into this narrative that only serves to make you feel bad?"

I opened my mouth to counter that, but... there wasn't shit to say.

"Okay," I conceded. "Point taken."

"Shout out to my therapist, giving me tools to pass on and shit," Teddy said, tossing an imaginary ball into a hoop somewhere near the ceiling, and then cheering for himself.

Wow, Joia.

This is really the dude you're having a baby by.

"Come on," he said, helping me down from the table. "I know you couldn't eat before all this, so you gotta be hungry. We can grab some grub, then head to... one of our houses."

I turned to look at him before we left the room. "One of our houses to do *what?*"

"Well... we have some things to talk about, right?" he asked. "The pitch for *Fresh*, baby gear, coordinating my schedule around your appointments so I can be there. Oh, and getting this power-walking shit down – it's some old ladies down at the mall in them big white sneakers that want smoke with me. I got a partner now, we can go get that shit popping."

I laughed – something that felt really, *really* good behind the stress of finding out this potential complication with this pregnancy.

A laugh I sure as hell needed – something he'd never failed at providing.

"In all seriousness... you know the Wrights – and the Loves – aren't the only ones that have your back, right?" he asked, meeting my gaze. "You carrying a Graham baby, baby. The first *grand*baby. The Grahams got you too."

I nodded. "Yeah."

"Aiight. Let's get it then," he said, holding the door open for me to step through, putting a hand at my back to steady me.

Wow, Joia.

This is really the dude you're having a baby by.

... not bad.

TWELVE

Joia

"Hey people, so we're back with another episode of *Live with the Loves*, our scripted series," Jac said, looking directly into the camera.

No clue how *she* managed to do so with a straight face, but I laughed, and so did Jemma from her hotel room in… wherever she was currently on her book tour. We'd patched her into the chat, even though she wasn't physically here with us – I felt like I could use all the sisterly moral support I could get during my first time going live since the pregnancy test disaster.

"I appreciate your commitment to the cause, but you know you can let that go now, right?" I asked, still chuckling over her silliness. "Not going to lie though -- that was some quick thinking."

"Well *somebody* had to do something, fooling around with you. Miss *There's No Way I'm Pregnant*."

I shook my head. "I definitely didn't want to believe it."

"Well that belly of yours certainly ain't lying on you," Jemma said. "No hiding it anymore."

She was right – I'd finally really popped, and it was obvious now that the growth in my midsection had nothing to do with a sudden change in diet. I had a clear maternity situation going on.

"I'll have you know, I think I'm *quite* cute with this belly," I said, putting a hand over it.

"Oh you're definitely that," Jemma agreed. "And then we got Jaclyn over here with her freshly fucked glow going on. Y'all out here settling down and shit. Wonder which one of y'all are going to get married first..." she mused, sipping from whatever was in her glass.

"Well, I don't even have a boyfriend," I reminded her. Sure, Teddy and I had been getting along well enough over the last few weeks since I had finally revealed the truth about the pregnancy. And... we'd maybe even gotten it in a time or two. But as far as I was concerned, he and I were still working on being *friends* again.

We weren't a *couple*.

"Oh girl *please*," Jaclyn waved me off. "Maybe it's not settled yet for real for real, but everybody knows it's coming."

"Don't forget we're on live," Jemma warned Jaclyn. "We already told all Jo's business to the internet once – she might disown us if we do it again," she laughed. "Not that all this stuff is gonna be secret too much longer anyway, right?"

"Nope," I agreed. "Not at all."

Teddy and I had already submitted two episodes worth of content to *Fresh* for the upcoming show, and we'd been out and about together quite a bit. Mercifully, nobody had approached us, but I figured it was only a matter of time before everything came out - either assumptions based on seeing us out, or from the show, which had a "surprise" premiere next week.

Neither Teddy nor I had said anything publicly yet about it.

"Fine," Jac said. "I'll be cool until then. But on our next episode of *Live with the Loves*, I want you to be prepared for me to clown you about how I saw this coming. With details about exactly why and all that."

I shook my head, laughing. "I am *sure* you have plenty to say about it, and I'm ready to hear it all."

From there we moved on to other topics, going along with what people commented about in the live stream. But as soon as we were done with that, I couldn't help addressing Jac about what she said.

"Okay, so you know I'm not waiting until the next episode, right?" I asked. "I need you to tell me what you mean when you say you saw this coming."

Jac grinned. "Okay so I'll admit to not necessarily knowing it was Teddy right off the bat. When you didn't know you were pregnant, there was this immediate assumption that it must be *recent*. But I don't think you would have been as quiet about it, if it had been Dalton's."

"What makes you think that?" I asked.

"Well for one," Jemma chimed, "You never miss an opportunity to drag Dalton for one thing or another, and you *always* tell us when you backslide with him."

"Exactly," Jac nodded. "The fact that you *didn't* was a key indicator that something about this was different."

I laughed. "*A key indicator that something was different*. What is this, Love & Order or something?"

"See you playing, but I actually like that," Jac said. "*Fresh* ain't closed their little contest up yet, I will pitch that shit. *Love & Order – Fuckboy Victims Unit.*"

"God knows we've got the content between the three of us," I replied.

"A whole season's worth," Jemma added. "But back to the topic at hand – girl we're your damn sisters – we *know* you. When you came back from that Vegas trip all extra quiet on us, I knew something was up. And *then* the fact that you were suddenly *extra* anti-Teddy after not really being pressed about him for a while… Yeah something was up."

"Obviously we didn't think you were pregnant," Jac said. "And neither did you, because so much time passed before *Baby Love* made him or herself obvious, but there was an *inkling*. And then you left Jemma's party with him, and she saw him leaving here, so yeah... pretty much settled."

"But neither of you said anything."

On screen, Jemma shrugged. "You said you wanted to keep it private, so we respected it."

I sat back in my chair with a sigh – and a smile. We may get on each other's goddamned nerves sometimes, but I loved that my sisters were my *friends*, along with everything else. No matter what, they *had* me.

"Oh bitch. *Bitch. Biiiitch!*" Jaclyn squealed, scream-laughing as *Forever My Lady* started blaring from her phone. "*Holy shit,*" she – barely – breathed, clutching her stomach as she bent over, still laughing. "Joia, *girl*. Your social media notifications are about to be *tore* up," she giggled, wiping tears from her eyes.

"What?!" I asked, at the same time as Jemma. "What's going on?"

Jac waved me over as the view from Jemma's front camera shifted – she'd picked up her phone too. Before I could make it to where Jac was, Jem gasped.

"*BITCH!* No the fuck he didn't. Nooooo the fuck he *didn't*," Jemma choked out, before she started laughing too.

And now that I saw what they were looking at... I couldn't look away.

"Teddy is gonna *kill* this motherfucker," I muttered, leaning in to get a good look as Jaclyn started the video over.

A video of Dalton, with my face on his tee shirt, dancing in some dark studio to *Forever My Lady*.

"*So you're having my baby...*"

My stomach lurched as the first line of the song started up, and I shook my head. "This isn't actually happening, right?" I asked Jac, who was now crying full-blown tears of laughter.

"Read the caption, oh my *God*," she managed to get out.

I shook my head. "Nah, I'm not going to do that."

"Oh you *have* to," Jemma laughed. "It's so good. It's *so* good."

There was *no* way there was anything "good" about that caption, but I forced my eyes to the words underneath the video anyway.

"Just a sneak peek of what's to come, what I'll have to offer forever... my lady @JoiaLove."

"FOREVER," Jemma and Jac exclaimed, in unison, still cackling.

This, of course, was the *other* side of having these two as sisters.

"This is the wackest shit I have *ever* seen in my life," Jemma said. "And I've seen some *wack* shit, okay?"

"My nigga Dalton said *just a sneak peek*," Jac said, her shoulders bobbing as she kept laughing. "Whew, I would seriously feel bad for him if he weren't such a literal human turd."

I shook my head. "I feel *seriously* bad now – I haven't even thought about him, and I have him blocked everywhere. I guess this is his way of getting through to me?"

"Girl, maybe so, but whoever filmed and hyped him into doing this, they don't love this boy. There's *no* way." Jemma stopped, thought, and then laughed again. "Also fuck him though."

"You're right, but still... let me reach out to him so he can delete this. I can't even imagine what Teddy must be thinking – I need to call him too. Or better yet, just go see him. I was supposed to drop by today anyway."

"Awwww," Jac said. "Listen to you, thinking about your man – and I don't wanna hear that shit that he's not. He totally is."

I sucked my teeth. "You're one to talk, like you weren't fronting about Kadan, not even two months ago!"

"You're both whipped, smitten, whatever you want to call it," Jemma spoke up. "Whatever it is, just make sure you keep that shit over *there*."

I smirked. "Uh-huh. Keep talking, your turn is coming up. You can't let us be boo'ed up and having babies by ourselves."

"I absolutely *can*."

I THINK I MIGHT NEED YOU

Jac grinned. "Come *onnn* Jem. Gone and settle down with one of those foreign hotties and give the family some expat babies."

Jemma shook her head back and forth, with exaggerated firmness. "Not for nothing, I ain't goin', I'll be *forever* hoein'."

"*Bye*," I laughed at her lyric remix.

"Y'all read the book, I ain't playing," she insisted. "But I will gladly pet sit, babysit, brother-in-law sit, whatever you need."

"We know," Jaclyn said. "And we love you for it."

We spent a few more minutes with that back and forth, but then I had to get Jemma off the phone. I needed to call Dalton and get that over with, before I linked with Teddy to figure out how – or if at all – I needed to address him putting this video out, essentially claiming the baby I was carrying as his.

"So… question – *why* is Dalton so sure this baby is his?" Jac asked, as she packed up her things to head to Kadan's. "When was the last time…"

I pushed out a sigh. "I had to already be pregnant the last time I messed around with Dalton. Groundhog Day. Don't ask."

"I *definitely* wasn't going too," Jac laughed. "Seriously though – send that nigga a text. *"This ain't it, chief. And the baby ain't yours either."* Boom. Solved."

I raised an eyebrow. "Like it wouldn't be all over social media ten minutes later?"

"Good point," she admitted. "But still – I don't want you getting on the phone with him, stressing yourself out – cause you *know* that's what he's gonna do. And you don't need that."

I *didn't*. I'd already been cleared of the scare with the placenta, but now my blood pressure was elevated – stress was the last thing I needed.

"I can't just *not* tell this man the baby isn't his, when obviously he thinks so – you *see* this stunt he pulled, and tagged me!"

Jac pursed her lips, and nodded. "True, he does need to know. Hmm…" she thought about it for a moment, then nodded, pulling her phone out. She tapped at the screen for a bit, then held it up for me to see... the tweet she'd just sent.

"@youngjac_love – *my niece or nephew ain't Dalton's. Thanks, management, bka Jaclyn Love.*"

It was accompanied by an "*Anybody wanna fight?*" gif, and @jemmaoutchea had already retweeted it.

I opened my mouth, but Jac immediately held up a hand.

"Nope," she shook her head. "Problem solved. Bye."

She didn't wait for a response before she sauntered away, leaving me alone with my – now constantly pinging – phone. I pushed out a sigh and picked it up, and... turned all my social media notifications off.

I needed to go see my child's father.

Teddy

Piece L connects to R, and then R connects to Y and...

"Hip bone connects to the ankle bone or something, goddamn."

I put down the instructions to the crib Joia had gushed over, taking a break from putting it together. For a "small" fee, I could've simply had it delivered already assembled. But the damn thing had already cost enough, and I was a pretty handy motherfucker.

So, I figured I could do it myself and get the points for surprising her with it, *and* points for building it.

I was *real* close to pulling up the "*We Gotchu*" app instead - some Blakewood graduates had created a small jobs app, where you could commission anything from a babysitter to somebody to pick up your dry cleaning, to somebody to mow your grass.

Or... build an overly complicated crib to impress the woman who was damn near six months pregnant with your child.

I cleared a space among the mess on the floor and laid back and stretched out, not caring about the camera set up in the corner. When I thought I would be able to get this crib built with no trouble, I'd had the idea to record it for a quick time lapse we could use as B-roll footage for the *Fresh* show.

Now this shit was straight up blooper reel material.

I had no idea where my phone was, but I knew it had to still have power - it was supplying the sound pouring into my headphones. I'd set it to *Do Not Disturb* while I was working on the crib, with Joia and my mama set as the only exceptions who could get through that filter. With that in mind, I closed my eyes.

Swedish engineering was fucking exhausting.

I fell asleep wondering about the practicality of putting all this shit back in the box and finding a nice solid Nigerian company to purchase a crib from.

The next time I opened my eyes, Joia was standing over me with a grin on her face.

"Hi," she said.

"Hi," I said back.

She glanced around us, motioning at the parts to the crib before she pointed at the box. "What's all this?"

"You know *exactly* what it is, baby," I told her, grinning as I sat up.

Damn she looked good.

Her hair was out and wild, floating around her shoulders like a lion's mane. She was finally embracing her baby bump instead of hiding it, and even though it was still small, it was prominent in the bright blue maxi dress she was wearing - and so were her titties.

I forced my gaze back to her face just in time for the scolding I knew was coming.

"Well... it *looks* like you are already nesting, so much harder than I am. And, it looks like you bought the crib that was twice as much as the one we decided on together at the store. I'm assuming that's because you knew how much I loved it, which is ridiculously sweet. But it's also... not the best financial decision?"

I nodded to acknowledge her concern. "True, this one was quite a bit more expensive than the other ones we looked at. *But.* You didn't see your face," I told her. "None of those other cribs gave you that same look. So this is the crib we're getting."

She raised her eyebrows a little, probably at the authority in my voice. But she didn't challenge that. Instead she kneeled down beside me.

"Teddy... you know we need *two* cribs, right? One for your place, one for mine."

"Or," I suggested, wrapping an arm around her waist to pull her closer. "You can stop playing with me, and we can just have *our* place."

Joia shook her head. "If you think I am moving in with someone when I don't even know completely where I stand with him, you're out of your mind."

"And you're out of *your* mind if you don't know where you stand with me Joia. Ain't no ambiguity about how I'm trying to move with you."

She let out a quiet scoff. "Yeah... I got a little too comfortable with that before, and we see where that went. I know where I *seem* to stand with you. We're getting to know each other again; I feel like you're truly a friend. But you know what happened between us. Why we were apart in the first place. I'm not asking you to do anything - I think we're in a good place. I don't *need* you as a boyfriend - I need you as a partner in this, romantic or not. I could absolutely see you as more, but I'm not comfortable assuming shit. Just, honestly," she admitted.

I nodded. "Okay. I see exactly what I need to do."

I released my hold on her waist to get up, looking around among the wood pieces and instructions and packing materials and everything else from the box that the crib had been delivered in. Finally, I found my phone and picked it up.

"Oh!" Joia exclaimed. "Hold up before you look at that! There's... a video that might upset you a little. But if it helps, it's already been addressed, and the original was already deleted."

I looked up from my phone with a frown. "What video?"

I THINK I MIGHT NEED YOU

Joia cringed. "Well, it seems as if Dalton was still under the impression that the baby was possibly his. And since I wasn't talking to him, he decided to make... A grand gesture?"

Shaking my head, I unlocked my phone and headed straight to social media.

The first thing I saw, the first thing *everybody* seemed to be talking about, and tagging Joia in... was Dalton.

Dancing.

This motherfucker...

"Yo," I said, as the video started up, with the music playing in my ears. "Ol' boy stole my idea, I'm gone smack this dude next time I see him."

"Please don't," Joia giggled. "Like I said, it's already been addressed. Already been handled," she tried to assure me.

"Nah," I shook my head. "*I'm* about to handle it."

I went back over to where Joia was sitting and joined her down there on the floor. I switched my cell phone to my front facing camera and held it up, making sure that me, Joia, and the crib box and shit were *all* in the picture. With no prompting, Joia smiled into the camera and so did I, snapping the picture. I showed it to her for her approval, which she hesitantly gave. Before she could change her mind, I tapped out a caption for the picture and posted it.

When I showed her my phone again, she smiled.

"First Graham family portrait," she read aloud. "You don't think the *"Graham"* thing is presumptive?"

I shook my head. "Nah, not at all. I messed up with you before by not making my intentions and feelings clear. Won't catch me slippin' again."

I watch the emotions play over Joia's face. Watched her try her best not to break into a big smile. After a few seconds she gave up, and shook her head as she grinned.

"Well, in that case... You should probably let me help you put this crib back in the box. It'll be a lot easier to move into a new place that way."

"Man, I've been recording this for the show," I complained. "I'm very hype that you're rocking with me on the "let's shack up" thing, but… All my hard work, just going down the drain."

Joia lifted an eyebrow, looking around at my "hard work". When her gaze returned to me, she said, "That's okay. Next time… we'll do it together."

"Hell yeah," I agreed, biting my lip as I pulled her into my arms. When I looked down, she was wearing a smirk that made me ask, "What?"

Her eyes glittered with mischief. "You know I'm about to get on your damn nerves, right?"

The end.

I THINK I MIGHT WANT YOU

ONE

JEMMA

What you need a name for?
    Boy you know what I came for.
No identities needed,
Just my exact instructions heeded
Fuck me good, and then you gon' eat it.
Look me right in the eyes,
Put in work between my thighs...

"Okay now Jemma," Arizona grinned at me as the music phased out, bringing us back from a short break on the *Arnez and Arizona* show. "I know you already know what the next question is, don't you?"

I pressed my lips together to stifle my immediate smile, because yes, of course, I knew what the unspoken question was, and I already had my answer prepared for it. "Y'all know I love you, but... Jemma Love does not kiss and tell."

Arnez put down his customary teacup and leaned forward. "Oh

but you've already told it all, *except* what we all want to know – what is that nigga from chapter five's name, sis?"

I leaned back in my chair, shaking my head. "I ain't gone be able to do it," I said. "All the good parts are already there in the book, in vivid detail, like you said. His *name* is probably the least interesting thing about him."

"That dick though..." Arnez said.

"That *mouth* though," Arizona chimed, with a little shimmy.

And no lie... I felt that.

Literally.

The memory of my experience with "that nigga from chapter five" was still potent.

It was potent as *fuck*.

"I didn't call it the most transformative sexual experience of my life for nothing," I admitted. The truth was, I didn't actually *know* his name, which made it a helluva lot easier to evade the question.

Of course, they didn't need to know that though.

"Hell, *that shit* was the most "transformative sexual experience" of *my* life too sis," Arizona laughed. "I had to get a stiff drink and a fat blunt after reading that."

"Had to make *myself* a damn sandwich too," Arnez added. "Woke my man up, his old ass talking about he tired, like I ain't see him eat three chili dogs for dinner. You ain't tired, you're bloated and lethargic."

Arizona laughed. "Oh my God, you sound so mad."

"I *am* mad, honey," Arnez said, scowling. "Back to NoNameBigDick though – you hitting that again or nah?"

I shook my head. "As evidenced in the book, I just like to let the experience be that – no need to try to recreate the same magic twice. We had a great time together, one that elevated my entire trip to Cuba. I meet someone damn near everywhere I go, after I've done exploring on my own. It always heightens the whole experience."

"I got it, so it's like that Mr. Rogers thing, about finding the helpers," Arizona said. "Only instead of finding the helpers, you find the niggas."

I cocked a finger at her, nodding. "You're exactly right."

"I cannot believe you're encouraging her nonsense," Arnez laughed.

Arizona shook her head. "It's not nonsense – it's *complete* sense."

After that, the rest of the interview went on, talking about other elements of the book. This was something I *always* enjoyed, even if I did have a little bit of nerves going on at first every time. Getting to talk about my words, about my experiences traveling the world, the lessons I learned the people I met... It was what my whole "brand" was built upon.

No, there wasn't anything particularly new about being a black woman traveling the world. But that didn't make *my* voice less valuable. There was room for every single one of us. I was – at least according to myself - fun, I was cute, had my own opinions, my own experiences, all of which I'd used to develop this book which seemed to be resonating with people all over the world.

And now, I was here with Arnez and Arizona, living out a dream of being interviewed about something I had created, with a duo I watched religiously for their funny, smart content.

Writing a book was something I hadn't even been able to fathom before Toni suggested it. Her family owned Blakewood's local bookstore, and she was married into the Wright family as well.

Actually, *soon* to be married into the family. She and Justin were still in the planning process, but it was coming soon.

She smiled at me as I stepped away from the interview couch after it was over. "That wasn't so bad was it? I mean, of course I know it wasn't *bad* to you, and you were excited, but... you were a little nervous too."

"True," I agreed, "But you're right - not bad at all. They made it fun," I assured, as we headed back toward the dressing room area. "Not gonna lie, I wish there was less interest in Mr. Chapter Five, but oh well. I knew it was coming."

Toni grinned. "Good, cause I was about to say... can you blame them?"

No.

I couldn't.

It would have been silly of me not to expect readers, and interviewers, and even people who hadn't actually read the book, but were following the snippets online, to be keenly *over* interested in the tale I'd weaved between those pages. Truthfully, there was very little creative liberty taken for that chapter, unlike some of my other encounters which had required little embellishments here and there to make them book worthy.

Ol' boy from chapter five was worth a whole book on his own.

It was wearing on me more than a little that it had been months now, but I still could not get him off my mind. Sure, I remembered the men whose company I'd enjoyed through the course of my travels — when they gave me something to remember — but I wasn't usually... *enamored* with them, like I had found myself with... him.

I couldn't get him off my mind.

I thought writing about it would cure me of my lingering interest, but all it had done was keep him close to the forefront of my mind. Which was a key indicator that I needed something else to do.

Maybe *someone* else to do.

"Okay," Toni's assistant said as she bustled up to us. "You ladies have four hours to grab a bite, check out, and get to the airport to make your flight back to Blakewood."

"Yep," Toni nodded. "We *cannot* miss Big Joe's birthday cookout."

"It's at Joseph and Devyn's, right?" I asked.

"Yes," Toni confirmed. "Who are you staying with while you're in Blakewood this time?"

"I'm actually at a hotel this time," I told her. "Since I'll be hanging around for a while. Reesie is gonna pop and have this baby any moment."

"You're absolutely right," Toni agreed. "So, let's eat, then get on this plane. Wright family duty calls."

～

"Jemma Neutron," Jason greeted, as soon as I walked through the door of Big Joe's cookout. Devyn and Joseph lived in one of those idyllic family neighborhoods with the perfect grass and all that, that kinda creeped me out. But I loved *their* house, specifically, and I loved them, so I came out whenever I was invited.

And, obviously, I wouldn't miss my Uncle's birthday celebration just because it didn't seem like the dogs over here barked.

"What's up family?" I laughed at Jason, accepting his hug and then moving on to greet the rest of the family – my siblings and the Wright siblings and all the kids, and the other cousins, and... apparently a large chunk of Blakewood I didn't actually know.

"Who are all these extra people?" I asked Devyn when I found her at the buffet table that had been set up on their fully decked out back patio. There was food for *miles*.

"I think a couple of us invited extra people here and there, including Big Joe. I'm pretty sure everyone who has visited the car lot in the last two weeks got invited out to come fix a plate, and these negroes sure as hell did accept the offer."

I wrinkled my nose at her, patting her shoulder with a teasing grin. "Good thing you guys decided to get the supersize backyard, huh?" I asked.

She huffed. "Girl, if you say so. I hate I offered to host this thing once I saw how many damn people it was. I'm just ready for these damn folks to *leave*, so the crew I hired to clean all this stuff up can come in and return my house back to normal."

"Cannot say I blame you," I said. "But for what it's worth, it looks amazing out here."

"Thanks cousin," she said, kissing me on the cheek. "For what it cost, it'd *better* look good out here. When you recommended the people who did your book launch party, I forgot you were all *Big Baller Brand* now, with your best-selling novel and all that," she teased.

"Please," I waved her off, grinning. "I'm a *long* way from balling."

"If you say so," she said, looking up to gaze across the yard. There were kids all over the place, and bounce-houses and ball pits to accommodate them, in addition to the bar and pool table for the adults. "Oh," she said. "Joseph must have caught Levi at home for a change. I see he invited him over."

I followed Devyn's gaze across the yard, peering through the crowd for an unfamiliar face. I'd heard her mention the name Levi before, as one of their neighbors, but I've never met him myself. As I watched, the crowd seemed to part in the middle, and Devyn yelled out to get his attention.

"Levi," she called. "Come on up here and fix yourself a plate!"

I was still looking, expecting *"Levi"* to be one of the older men I saw sitting together in a group with Big Joe – one of the ones talking shit and drinking with him at the Spades table.

Nah.

What *actually* happened was that, a few feet away, a man's head lifted and turned in response to Devyn's insistent prompting.

But his face wasn't unfamiliar at all.

"I gotta *go*," I said, more to myself than Devyn, but before I could get anywhere, she grabbed my hand.

"Hold on," she said. "I really want you to meet him, cause I think he's single, and I *know* his ass is fine. This is the artist who did that portrait of me that's in Josie's room, remember? Joseph's Christmas gift."

Those words made my heart race even more than it already was, as "Levi" made his way to where we were standing.

Those words confirmed what I wanted to call my eyes a liar about.

It was *him*.

Mr. Chapter Five.

There he was, with that delicious butter pecan skin and rugged stubble I vividly remembered as heaven against my thighs. Chiseled jaw. Full, sensual lips, perfectly kissable, perfectly sittable. Broad shoulders and big hands.

Check, check, check, check and so on.

Yeah, it was him.

Those intense brown eyes of his narrowed with recognition as he approached, and his footsteps slowed, but just a bit. Those lips curved just the slightest bit, into a half-smile.

"Levi," Devyn greeted, warmly. "I want you to meet my cousin Jemma. You're always out jet-setting, traveling the world," she said, then gestured toward me. "That's Jemma's thing too! I bet the two of you would have a ton to talk about!" She turned fully toward me, so that Levi wouldn't see her wink at me.

She was *so* pleased with herself.

And I mean, in a typical situation like this, she should be. She was being a good cousin – a solid ass wing-woman, introducing me to a fine ass single man, knowing that fine single men were exactly my type.

What she *didn't* know was that Levi and I were already very, *very* well acquainted.

"She even wrote a book," Devyn gushed, in slow motion. Or... maybe that was just my brain's reaction to her sharing that particular tidbit. "About traveling. You should *totally* read it."

I finally seemed to remember how my mouth worked, enough to shake my head and step forward, hands up for emphasis *and* defense.

"No. Uh-uh. Nawl. Nope. Nah... Definitely, definitely should *not* do that," I insisted, hoping I didn't sound as ridiculous as I undoubtedly did. "There's like a whole chapter on menstruating in third-world countries, and I'm sure he's not interested in reading that," I said, looking Devyn right in the face, hoping she would take my hint.

"I actually love reading," he said, in that indistinguishably sexy hybrid accent that had seduced me into bed with him in the first place. His dark gaze was locked on mine, smoldering and unrelenting. "I'll definitely be checking it out. Jemma Wright?"

"No," Devyn corrected, "Jemma Love, actually. And the book is called *Speak, Play, Grub*. It's all about her travels, and the food she ate, the people she met, all that. I don't remember a whole *chapter* of period stuff, but it's enlightening, and good information for anyone. There's hot sex too."

"Oh really?" Levi asked, his eyes going a little wider.

"Devyn nodded. "Oh yeah, it's all people can talk about." She paused, with a little frown. "Wait, you're not like a prude, are you?" she asked, making Levi laugh.

"No," he chuckled, the sound forcing my thighs together in a quick squeeze to control my slutty ass hormones. "Not at all."

No, definitely not.

"Okay good. *Whew*," she said, mimicking the motion of wiping sweat from her forehead. "I was ready to brag about being a good saleswoman, unless I talked you out of the sale," she laughed.

"No," Levi assured. "I'll definitely be checking it out."

"Good stuff. Okay, well come on over here and get you something to eat, I know my husband probably snatched you off the street as you were heading inside. You fix yourself a plate okay?"

Instead of moving, his gaze lingered on me, as if he were recommitting my face to memory. Then, he dragged those perfect white teeth over his perfect, velvety smooth bottom lip. "Nice to meet you, Jemma," he said, his eyes glittering with something I couldn't recognize. "Thank you, Devyn."

Holy shit, I muttered to myself as I hurried away, before Devyn could find any new reasons to keep the conversation going. I deftly avoided any of my family members as I snuck into the house, which hadn't been made open to the nearly fifty people milling about the back yard.

Sorry.

But I needed a quiet spot to process the fact that I had just, in the most innocuous way possible, ran into a man I never expected to see again.

And it had been so... quiet.

But I knew from our two-day-two-night stand in Havana that that was part of his charm... part of his *danger*.

He was so lowkey, so unassumingly sexy, so seemingly harmless that you got sucked into his web of pleasure and forced to cum until you blacked out.

Web of pleasure, Jemma? Really?

Okay.

Maybe I'd been reading too much.

But as ridiculous as my internal phrasing was, it was no exaggeration. Those two days and two nights together with him had knocked me completely off-kilter, and then I woke up on the third and he was simply gone.

Not real anymore, but not a figment of my imagination either.

A fond memory to revisit.

A great, juicy story to tell.

Oh, and apparently... my cousin's across the street neighbor.

TWO

Levi.

A blank canvas.
Otherwise known as the bane of my whole fucking existence.

Unfortunately, I was now intimately familiar – too familiar – with the taunting off-white expanse mounted on the easel in my studio.

Creativity had evaded me for a while now.

Ever since my mother died, the usual allure of the pigments had been painfully absent, skipping over me in favor of what seemed to be... everybody else.

All my peers in my creative circle, from photographers to sculptors to recipe bloggers to spoken word artists, everyone was creating.

Everyone except me, it seemed.

It was to be expected, I guess.

I'd gone through a similar period of stagnation after the death of my father, which had hit me hard. I was close to my parents, talked to them often, no matter where in the world I was. When my father was diagnosed with cancer, I put my traveling on hold, feeling like I needed to be close.

I was right.

It took him quickly.

Soon after that, I quickly discovered that what had been pulling me home was the impending need to be available to comfort my mother – not to simply share space with my father in his last days. They'd been married 37 years, a little longer than I'd been alive. It was hard for me, sure, losing my father. My mother, on the other hand, had lost the love of her life.

So I made myself available.

Sure, I still traveled some when necessary, but often I simply took her with me. I was able to show her something new, to capitalize on my father urging her, at his deathbed, to see and do as much as she could with the rest of her life.

I did my very best to make that happen for her.

But just after Christmas, she'd been called back to her hometown because of an accident in the family. She was going home to take care of her hard-headed father, who had fallen off a ladder while doing some gutter repairs he was supposed to have left to people who *weren't* eighty-years old with arthritis. He was having a hard time getting around, with the ankle injury he suffered from the fall.

While she was there, while she was out picking up groceries and other things he needed around the house... she was hit by a drunk driver.

One of my most vivid memories of that time was of the police telling us she died on impact, and hadn't experienced much, if any, pain.

As if that made it better.

Breaking news: It didn't.

In the months that had passed since then, I hadn't been able to create anything that wasn't commissioned. Someone else telling me what the end result should look like, versus something I had to pull from the dark recesses of my own head.

There was one lone exception.

Havana.

After Havana, or more accurately, after Jemma, there had been these two weeks where things have been beautiful for me. I wasn't consumed by grief. My hands didn't feel like useless blobs of skin attached to the ends of my arms. My brain wasn't foggy.

I was able to paint.

I was able to *create*.

A portrait actually, of the woman whose company had felt like a sanctuary in the middle of an emotional storm.

Jemma.

Of course, that wasn't the name she'd given me. She'd given me Kira, an obviously fake name that she barely remembered to respond to, but that was fine. Names hadn't been very necessary for what we were doing.

Our bodies took on the bulk of communication.

I glanced at that portrait now, admiring my approximation of her glowing copper skin, big brown eyes, and that lush, perfect mouth.

Soft curves, and soft skin.

Ass.

So much ass.

But of course, that wasn't included in the portrait, just vivid in my memories of her, and the time we spent together. In the portrait her braids were wild, lips parted, eyes still flush with pleasure.

It was a fond memory of a look I'd vastly enjoyed putting on her face. An expression I'd gifted her with over, and over again. And of course, she'd gifted me with more than a few deep pleasures too.

Remarkably attractive, wickedly fun, deeply sensual, incredibly intelligent, worldly without being haughty or arrogant. She felt like a blessing.

I'd been wandering. Traveling aimlessly, with no rhyme or reason, no purpose to my life. And then, in that sweltering little bar deep in Havana, I sat down for a drink. She was the one who approached me, walking up to my table and leaning in, giving me a fantastic view of her cleavage and a big, bright smile.

"I know an American when I see one," she'd said.

And it was on from there. For two days, and two nights, no one existed but us. Sex, room service, and Cuban rum, for breakfast, lunch and dinner.

By the time we passed out of pleasure-induced exhaustion on that second night, I knew what I had to do. Knew I had to get away while I could, let it all go before I took it further than it needed to go. She was like a drug I couldn't let myself get hooked on.

So before she woke up the next day, I left.

I hadn't seen her since then.

Until yesterday, of course.

Just as fine as I remembered, in a soft yellow dress that gave her skin even more of a glow. She'd changed her hair, no longer wearing the braids from my memory. Now it was straightened, long and loose around her shoulders with golden highlights that made her look like some type of goddess of Summer.

It felt like fate.

It had to be, right?

What other explanation could there be, when at just the moment I was succumbing to my inability to create, the very woman who had proven herself as a muse stepped back into my life?

At my neighbor's cookout of all places.

I was barely ever home – especially since my mother passed, I preferred to be in unfamiliar places – home was rife with too many painful memories, usually.

It was only because of a flight that had been canceled and not rescheduled that I was even home at the time Joseph, spotted me, and insisted I come and join their festivities, or at the very least fix myself a plate.

Unfortunately, that short encounter hadn't proven enough to get my creative juices flowing again.

But there was something else that might.

I left my studio and took a shower, grabbing a bottle of whiskey and a glass of ice before I picked up my tablet and took it to my bedroom with me. I poured myself... more than a shot worth... and settled in, checking my social media notifications and doing a bit of socializing before I moved on to my true goal.

I tapped around on the screen, pulling up my e-reader app to navigate to the built-in store, with a specific agenda in mind.

To purchase Jemma's book

Speak, Play, Grub.

I smiled at the book's tagline - *a Black woman's guide to culture and cuisine, language and leisure, introspection and intimacy around the world* - and then moved forward to read her acknowledgments, the foreword by Toni Wright, who'd published the book through her *Scattered Seeds* publishing company, and then on to the first chapter.

In no time at all, I was hooked.

As a writer, Jemma's voice was exactly what I knew her to be. Fresh, humorous, with a healthy dose of sensuality that made it very easy to devour page after page. Before I knew it, I'd made it to chapter five, which had a very familiar heading.

Havana.

It was like deja vu, reading her account of the way we'd met. Of course, she started the chapter with other topics - tales of learning more about the regional dialect, immersing herself in the local culture, experiencing authentic Cuban food, all of which were fascinating subjects, sure.

But then, her storytelling arrived at me and her, and that was where things got really interesting, to me.

It was quite enthralling, reading her first impressions of me. She noticed the melancholy in my eyes, noticed my subdued emotional energy. But she saw something else too – she saw my passion for life even in grief, saw my deep yearning for creative expression, appreciated my respect for travel and international cultures.

According to her...I just had a good vibe.

And, according to her... I was incredibly sexy.

The feeling was mutual Ms. Love, I mused to myself. *The feeling was very, very mutual.*

And then, of course, there was the sex.

There was sex in some other chapters too, but she approached her retelling of our experience differently than the others. With a certain reverence and respect that permeated every word on the page. According to her, it was special.

It had shifted something for her.

She'd left our experience *changed*.

*When he touched me, there was no rush, no urgency to his movements. He knew I was his for as long as we had together in our little villa. And I most certainly was **his**, in every sense of the word.*

*I would have done anything he told me to do to him, or to myself, anything to keep the pleasure on his face while I rode his dick. He was touchy — **oh, so touchy**. His thumb rocketing against my clit, torturing me with pleasure while I rode him, hard, his other thumb shoved between my lips.*

"Suck it," he urged, the same gentle command he'd given me before, while I bruised my knees on the hard stone floor in front of him, trying my best to swallow him whole. His hands tangled in my braids, mascara ruined and running down my face, gagging as I struggled to take him down my throat, struggled to accommodate him.

*But I wanted this, wanted it **so bad**, wanted to taste and feel him, needed to feel the hot spurt of his release down the back of my tongue. Needed to swallow it, needed him to know I was serious about this shit.*

Needed him to know I was no selfish lover.

Not after I'd already cum countless times with his head between my thighs, because he couldn't seem to get enough of it. My pussy was like heavenly manna for him, necessary sustenance for every next second of his life.

After his tongue, there was his dick. Long, thick, an impossibly perfect fit, filling and stretching me, driving me head on to an orgasm that felt like an extinction-level event.

If I had a job, I'd quit.

Just so I could fuck him all day.

It was just that good.

*And he **knew** he was good, not arrogantly, just as a point of fact.*

*I let him put it anywhere he wanted, and he wanted to put it **everywhere**.*

And every time, he made me cum, made my body produce sounds and shivers and fluids at levels I had no idea were even possible.

The kind of sex that completely shifts you.

The kind where you have to come to grips with the fact that nobody else is going to do it to you like this again.

The kind where you had to just be grateful for the experience.

Plenty of people never get it.

"Well, *damn*," I muttered, leaning back against my pillows and cupping my uncomfortably engorged dick. Consuming her words had taken me right back into those moments of bliss, right back into the sights, sounds, smells, feelings.

She was right — that experience had represented a shift.

One week, two weeks, two months ago, I would have done a whole lot to find myself immersed in the experience of Jemma's pussy again.

Now, I knew I didn't have to do that much to get to her.

She was close as hell, easily within my reach, assuming, of course, that she wanted it.

Now… it was just a point of getting an answer to that question.

Does Jemma want me, like I want her?

I would get that answer soon enough.

In the meantime… I had some reading to finish.

THREE

JEMMA

"Whoa. *Whoa. This* is the nigga from chapter five?"

I pushed another spoon of honey vanilla ripple into my mouth and nodded, confirming Jac's words as we gathered around her laptop propped on the counter at Dreamery. It had taken me a few days to fess up to it, but... the proverbial cat was out of the bag now.

Joia snickered, her spoon dangling inches about her half-finished cup – inches away from her prominently rounded belly. She was coming up on seven months now, and it *showed*.

"No wonder you wrote a whole chapter about him. That is a beautiful man. Look at his mouth. Look at his *lips*. And look at his *hands*," she groaned, then sighed, then scooped up a heaping portion of ice cream and stuck it in her mouth as she leaned onto the counter with a plaintive sigh. "*God,* I need Teddy to bring his ass back to Blakewood."

It was *my* turn to laugh then. "Umm... didn't he just leave this morning?"

"*Right*," Jac teased, her face pulled into a smirk. "And you're already like, dangerously horny. Seek help."

Joia's head popped up. "I *know* you aren't talking, like you didn't almost catch a public indecency charge with Kadan like two days ago. Two apartments between you and you still wanna fuck outside. *Ya nasty.*"

"Kadan is *subletting*," Jac countered, and I frowned.

"What the *fuck* does that have to do with literally... anything?" I asked, laughing at *both* of them.

Jaclyn shrugged. "I mean... I don't have a real defense, but I had to say *something*, right?"

"Wrong," I laughed harder. "Man... I never imagined there would come a time when *both* of you were so wrapped up in dick. That's *my* role, I thought?"

Joia giggled. "Well, in our defense, I'm pretty sure we're both more wrapped up in the man attached to the dick – the dick is just a perk."

I nodded my agreement. "Speaking of dick though – and then we gotta talk about something else – y'all... what the hell do I do?"

"You go another round with him and then hop a flight to Colombia, *duh*," Jac said, moving to the computer at the counter. *Dreamery* wasn't technically open for the day yet, but we regularly worked around our schedules to get time like this with each other whenever we could.

"He's Joseph and Devyn's *neighbor*," I reminded them. "Which adds a whole other layer to this. He *literally* has an invite to the cookout."

Joia shrugged. "Okay what's the problem though? It's not like you're just *always* at their house or something, and doesn't he travel like you anyway? He's probably barely there."

I sighed. According to Devyn, she was right – Levi *was* barely even at home, but still.

"I get what you're saying," I spoke up. "But, y'all know this is not how I operate – I don't wife 'em, I one night 'em."

"You two-nighted this one," Jac reminded me.

I huffed. "Okay, fine, but my point stands. I'm not trying to get attached to anyone, so I have the experience, and once it's done, *I'm done*."

"Okay... sooo... what's the problem?" Joia asked. "If you have your "one time only" mantra that you're sticking to, what is even the point here? If you're done, you're done."

Jaclyn sucked her teeth. "She ain't done – that's what the problem is," she laughed. "Levi knocked her pussy off the hinges, and she can't let it go."

"Off the hinges?" I countered, laughing, which was really all I could do, because... well... she was right.

I was having a hard time letting go.

Since Levi, all my sexual experiences had been rather... tepid. Which was a problem for me.

"That's what I said, cause that's what I *read*," Jaclyn replied, grinning at me. "So *I* think you should take him for another ride. Have fun. Maybe make him your "in-house" dick."

"Oooh," Joia mused. "You two could meet up whenever you're in the same place, since y'all both travel. A rendezvous in Morocco, in Thailand, Antigua... wherever. How *sexy* would that be?"

I shook my head. "For someone else, *incredibly*. For *me*... I don't know. I'm not trying to be tied down like that. *Ever*."

Joia and Jaclyn exchanged a look, and then Joia went back to her ice cream, Jac back to whatever she was doing at the computer.

"*What?*" I asked, prompting both to return their gazes to me.

"Nothing," Jo insisted. "Not... *really*. It's just... do you think you're *so* anti-attachment because of Shawn?"

Shit.

Just hearing his name sucked a little of the air from my lungs.

"What the *hell* does he have to do with anything?" I asked.

Jac cleared her throat. "Um... maybe... *everything?* You were *engaged*, Jemma."

"Yeah, I know the story – I lived it," I quipped. "I had the perfect job, the perfect wrapped bob, the perfect fiancé... until I didn't. So I decided to be a hoe. *Happily*, might I add."

"Until you meet this one dude who throws you for a loop and you're scared to do him again because... you're scared of getting attached. Because of what happened with Shawn," Joia blurted out, then scooted away from me a little, her expression wary.

"Oh my God, it has *nothing* to do with Shawn," I insisted, with much less fervor than my annoyance wanted me to give those words. Because... *did it* have something to do with Shawn?

The relationship had ended six years ago, for typical reasons – he was a cheating bastard, and I was tired of ignoring the obvious. It was something I should've been able to move on from fairly easily, and I likely would've... if one of the people he was cheating with didn't have a man of her own – a particularly angry one, who'd kicked in my door and put a gun in my face looking for Shawn.

Shawn ended up getting shot... a lot.

The guy went to jail, obviously, but that was a lot to handle at twenty when your name wasn't *Jaclyn* Love. Jac probably would've pistol-whipped that man with his own gun and sent him on his way, but I, *Jemma* Love was a little fucking traumatized.

Of course I realized that was an extreme situation, and *of course* I didn't think anything even close to that was going to happen again.

But it was possible.

So between that possibility, and the usual pain of betrayal and grieving the end of a relationship, and grieving the death of someone I loved... It was so much easier to just get the only thing men had – live dick – that I couldn't find elsewhere, use it until I was done, and then be on my merry way.

So... passively, maybe it did.

And?

"The bottom line is, I do not *want* to want this man," I explained.

"So, if you two could kindly just... stop teasing me, and *help*. What do I do?"

Joia smirked. "Well... you know what Mama taught us about this, right?"

"The best way to get over a man..." Jac trailed off, knowing I could easily finish the popular statement on my own.

Get under a new one.

~

D*amn I look good.*
I grinned at my reflection in the mirror as I smoothed my dress over my hips.

I *fully* intended to follow my mother's old advice, even though I was sure she'd act scandalized if I actually talked to her about it. She already had a million things to say about the content of my book... as if I hadn't noticed her copy was particularly well worn, and full of highlights.

I loved that woman so much.

Anyway – I had a task at hand, one I was committed to carrying out. I double-checked my hair, double-checked my makeup, made sure I had condoms and wipes – hoe supplies – in my clutch with my cell and keys and mini-taser and pepper spray, then slipped my feet into my heeled sandals.

It was time to go.

I would scope out the scene at the hotel bar first, seeing if I could snag myself somebody's big brother or young uncle traveling for Blakewood's Summer Block Party festivities that were starting soon. If I didn't have any luck there, I'd go across town to *Refill*, a safe distance from the undergrads, and Logan Lewis was performing tonight.

That would definitely bring the mature crowd out.

I checked myself in the mirror just *one* more time, then forced myself to get out the damn door before I found something wrong.

I took my time down the hall, getting my mind right before I made it downstairs to the bar. This was another thing I didn't do – going on the prowl to forget someone. My usual hunting habits were strictly appetite based, but I was in emergency need of readjustment.

For my appetite and my *attitude*.

Shit.

As soon as I pushed the button for the elevator, I started second-guessing my decision to go out tonight at all.

I was all about sexual liberation – I proudly honored my body by respecting and indulging my sexuality. I really didn't give a shit what anyone else thought about it and refused to be offended by the "hoe" label.

Embraced it.

But... using sex as an avoidance tactic wasn't really... *me.*

Not in this context, at least.

Working off anger, taking a break from sadness, getting in some stress relief, fine.

Toss-up sex with a random to avoid thinking about *amazing* sex with Levi?

That shit is barely logical, Jemma.

I pushed out a deep sigh and turned around, and was already around the corner to go back to my room by the time I heard the elevator chime to signal arrival. Already, I felt better, my mind playing through the prospect of a long, hot bath in that jetted tub. Maybe some room service.

I stopped at my door, digging through my clutch for my room key as I planned a whole new course for the night in my head.

"Jemma?"

My fingers stilled at the sound of that voice, and I looked up to find Levi Anders strolling down the hall in my direction, an overnight bag – the same one he'd had in Havana – slung over one shoulder.

The breath rushed from my lungs.

"Levi... what are you doing here?"

That sexy smirk crept up on his face as he closed the distance between us, stopping just inches in front of me. "I check into a hotel for a mental break sometimes, even when I'm at home. Feels like I'm on a trip."

"Makes sense," I nodded. "Like a staycation."

"Something like that. Looks like we're neighbors here too," he said, pointing at the door a little further down the hall – the next door.

Shit.

He looked, smelled, *sounded* so good.

I had to get the hell away from him.

My fingers closed around my key card and I whipped it out, passing it in front of the sensor on the door to unlock it. I'd already pushed it open when he spoke again.

"I read your book."

I stopped, eyes closed. I didn't open them again until he was right behind me, close enough to feel the simultaneous warmth and minty coolness of his breath on my neck.

"What do you want from me?" I asked, just above a whisper, even though I already knew the answer.

His hands went to my hips, pulling me into him as he leaned in, pressing those insanely perfect lips of his against my bare shoulder.

"Everything."

I pulled away, turning in the door to face him, already out of breath. His gaze rested on my face and then traveled lower, taking me in – so intensely that I could feel everywhere it landed, and my nipples beaded in response.

I stepped aside in the open doorway, leaving room for him to get through in my unspoken invitation.

He accepted.

The door had barely swung shut behind us before he was on me, cupping my face in one hand as his mouth crashed over mine. The other hand snaked into my hair, his fingers settling into a gentle but firm grip to keep me exactly where he wanted me. I settled right into his hold, with zero hesitation, fisting handfuls of his tee shirt as his tongue lapped in my mouth.

So easily.

He fell into a seat on the chair in the corner, pulling me with him, into his lap. He tugged down the top of my dress, freeing my breasts from the confines of the fabric before covering one of my nipples with his mouth. His hands went to my ass, gripping and squeezing as he sucked my breasts, back and forth, dividing his attention between the two.

"*Fuck*, Jemma," he grunted, looking up to meet my gaze. He fisted my hair again, dragging me in for another breath-snatching kiss that didn't last nearly long enough before he pulled away. "Take this off," he demanded, referring to my dress, and I didn't hesitate.

I stumbled on my heels climbing out of his lap, but he caught me by the hips, steadying me before his fingers found my zipper and tugged it down. My dress fell away, leaving me in nothing but a pair of microscopic panties – a view Levi obviously appreciated, judging from the harsh breath he pushed out.

He leaned back in the deep confines of the chair, staring at me for a long while before he sat up, extending his arms to plant his hands on either side of my hips. "You're *perfect*," he declared in his deep rasp, as his fingers sank into my flesh.

"You *left*," I countered – a response that surprised both of us.

His eyebrows went up, and mine did too – a movement he must've taken as a challenge instead of the confusion it actually was.

"I had to," he told me, moving to the edge of the chair. The positioning put his nose right in line with my pussy, and he inhaled, deep. "Let me make it up to you."

It wasn't a question.

It was another of his imperatives, and my weak flesh and I went right along with it as he propped my foot up on the arm of the chair and slid my panties aside. Not that I *needed* any sort of apology, but I much preferred *this* use of his mouth. His hot tongue lapped at my slick, sensitive flesh, prodding and teasing and licking until there was a sticky mess between my legs he seemed intent on slurping clean.

With one hand, he gripped my ass, helping me stay upright through the onslaught of his mouth on my pussy – with the other hand, he added to the pleasure, dipping his middle finger into me for lubrication before he pushed it into my ass. His thumb went into my pussy, and he pressed in on either side of that dividing wall, stroking both places as he covered my clit with his mouth.

My pussy clenched tight as my pleasure coiled in my stomach, and the one leg that was holding me up gave out. Only his grip kept me upright as a blissful scream ripped from my throat, and my body convulsed with the spasms of a powerful orgasm as it tore through me, leaving me momentarily unable to breathe, unable to move, just... pure euphoria.

I collapsed onto the ottoman, just watching, as Levi pulled himself up from the chair.

"There are wipes in my bag," I told him. "And condoms."

Levi smirked at me as he licked his thumb, but he did use the wipes for his other finger. I was still catching my breath when he finished undressing, then moved the chair.

I was confused for a second, then realized why he'd moved it.

In front of the mirror.

I yelped in surprise as he easily snatched me up from the ottoman, carrying me to the chair with him. He sat down first, already sheathed in a condom, then pulled me in front of his open legs, so that we were both facing the mirror.

All I could see were his legs as he leaned forward, pressing his lips to my ass cheeks, following those kisses with little nibbles – soft, hard, then soft again. He brought his hands to my hips, pulling me backward... guiding me down onto his dick.

I couldn't help the whimper I let out as my pussy stretched to accommodate him, and he didn't stop until he was buried to the root. He pulled my legs apart, anchoring my thighs over his with my feet no longer touching the floor.

His hands went to my breasts, cupping and squeezing, plucking my nipples as he moved in me – not pronounced enough to be a stroke, but his length and girth caused enough friction that it was... *fuck*, it was good.

And I could see it all – his fingers tugging my nipples until it hurt so good, the sway of his balls hanging beneath us, the subtle in and out of his dick in me, the beautiful array of brown skin on brown skin. I couldn't take my eyes away from it, too enthralled by the eroticism of it all, even when his teeth sank gently into my shoulder. Even when he urged one of my hands between my legs to strum my clit, and the other to pinch my own nipples. Even when he grabbed me at the waist, pulling me off his dick, slowly, then bringing me back down hard and fast, and repeating that, over, and over, and over.

But then I *had* to look away.

Had to close my eyes because I couldn't take how good it was, but then he stopped, pushing my feet down to the floor and grabbing me by the neck in another of those firm, gentle grips.

"Open your eyes and fuck me, Jemma."

So of course, I did.

And *fuck me*, I loved what I saw.

Loved how I looked with his hand at my neck, loved the raw lust of his facial expression over my shoulder, loved his hand between my legs as I rode him with abandon, lips parted, hair wild...

Perfection.

That's what this was, and I hated it for being that, because it wasn't *supposed* to be, not with him, not *again*.

His name spilled from my lips though, over and over as he lost his resolve to let me do the work and started fucking me back, slamming his hips up to meet mine. The space between my utterances and his filled with the steady smack of skin – music to my ears. I worked my hips in circles as I bounced against him, determined to give just as good as I got until I doubled over, paralyzed by pleasure.

He hooked an arm around my waist, catching me as he crashed into me one last time and then brought me backward with him, keeping his dick buried painfully, blissfully deep as his hips pumped in response to his own orgasm. I was throbbing around him, my pussy contracting with the natural mechanism of milking his dick.

My eyes closed again as my breasts heaved and I relaxed against him, trying to catch my breath. Gently, slowly, Levi pulled out of me, catching the messy condom and easing himself from underneath me to dispose of it before it got everywhere.

When he was gone to the bathroom, I pushed out a deep sigh, trying to find balance between my self-loathing and the extreme sense of euphoria I felt. After a few moments had passed, he was back, with a soothingly warm towel that he used to clean between my legs.

And then he tossed the towel away and buried his face in my pussy again.

As I gripped the arms of the chair, I made a quick decision – the easiest decision of my life.

I was just gonna go with it.

FOUR

Levi.

I didn't leave this time.
But, the look on Jemma's face almost made me regret that decision.

I woke up in her bed at the hotel to find her sitting up, staring at me with this stricken expression like she'd seen a ghost or something.

There I was, thinking she'd be glad.

I mean, she was the one who'd made the comment.

"*You left.*"

An accusation.

The kind of thing that only a woman upset about it would've said.

I didn't want Jemma upset with me, so I stayed – simple as that. So instead of letting the moment linger into something too awkward, I sat up too. Grabbed the back of her neck to pull her into a soft kiss that finally made her blink, which was progress, I guess.

If only I could ignore the blatant panic in her eyes.

"Good morning, Jemma," I said, pulling myself from the twisted sheets to stretch. I had no idea what time it was, but the sun was up, and streaming undeterred through the sheer curtains over the windows.

The light made her glow.

Jemma's flustered gaze traveled from my face to my chest, down my bare stomach to my dick, then back up.

"Good morning, Levi," she answered, her fists bunching in the portion of the sheets she was using to cover her nude body, as if I hadn't seen and tasted every inch of her already. "Um... I... did you sleep well?"

I chuckled, propping my hands at my waist. "Yes, actually. Between that and spending the other half of the night inside you... I feel amazing."

"Don't..." she sighed, and shook her head. "Don't do that."

I shrugged. "Don't do what?"

"Stand there with your dick out talking to me like last night was some normal thing."

"I would argue that last night was the *most* normal thing," I countered, dropping my hands to amble toward her side of the bed. "Incredibly natural."

She rolled her eyes. "Seriously? That's the approach you're taking here?"

"It's not an approach, Jemma," I said, stopping in front of her. Her gaze went to my dick again before it came back to my face. "It's a truth. *My* truth."

Jemma's head tilted, and she took on a look wholly different from my favorite one, but one I enjoyed all the same – her *challenge* look: eyes narrowed, jaw tensed, eyebrows poised and ready to provide a mirror to whatever was about to cross her lips.

"What makes it the truth? Just because you *say so*?"

"Is anything else required? I said *my* truth, no?"

Again, she rolled her eyes. "Whatever. The point is – last night was not a *usual* thing, and we're not about to normalize it. *This*," – she gestured between the two of us – "is *not* about to happen."

"I'd never try to force you into anything you didn't want, love." I grinned. "But... of course, that's the problem, isn't it? You *do* want this. Or I wouldn't be here."

Her face pinched into a frown. "Excuse me?" She flipped the sheets back, baring that exquisite body of hers to me, her glowing copper skin now marred by the evidence of my appreciation for it – an appreciation I'd shown with my mouth. She smirked as my dick grew even harder than it had already been. "You were the one who wanted *everything* from me. *Remember?*"

"I most certainly do," I admitted, closing what little space there was between me and the bed. I grabbed her by the calves, pulling her body toward mine, one leg on either side me. "I don't have a problem admitting that shit either... you're occupying that particular space all on your own."

I licked my lips as Jemma's soft hand wrapped around my dick, followed in quick succession by the other.

"You're saying it's a problem for me to admit I want something?"

I grabbed her chin, lifting it up, so her lips were only barely *not* touching my dick. "Isn't it?"

Something crossed her face, shifting her expression from defiance to determination, filling her gaze with something lustfully wicked. She opened her mouth, and when she closed it again, it was with me inside. My hips bucked in reaction as she sucked, hard, her gaze locked with mine as she swallowed me all the way down to where her fingers were, and then pulled back *slow, slow, slow.*

Shit.

My hand went into her hair as she went to work, gripping a fistful as she sucked me off. Hands, tongue, teeth, throat... that fucking *eye contact* as she made the best kind of mess, gagging and humming and smiling about it all, all while my dick was buried in her throat.

I was *not* playing when I called this woman perfection.

I THINK I MIGHT WANT YOU

"Does it still seem like a problem?" she asked, finally breaking away to take a full breath, her hands still pumping as she smirked.

I shook my head. "Nah, love. Not a problem at all."

∼

I really did do more with my time than just traveling and fucking. To prove it – to myself – once I finally peeled myself away from Jemma, I went to my own room, for another shower and to get myself dressed for the day, so I could go do some work.

It helped, of course, that Jemma's cousin had gone into labor.

If it weren't for that, I could have easily – *gratefully* – been laid up with her all day, gladly recreating the time we'd spent in Havana. Because she had other things to occupy her time, I had no choice except to give my attention to my own tasks.

No lie though – it stung a little, how relieved she'd been to get that call.

I wouldn't pretend I didn't know that the issue was – Jemma wasn't the type of woman to double-back on a fling. She was the woman who said she only wanted sex and actually *meant* it, the one you wanted to pin down and couldn't.

The one who got away.

Except, apparently, it just wasn't meant for her to get away from me.

It rankled her, which in turn, rankled *me*, because… not to be arrogant, but fuck it – I knew I'd shown her a good ass time. I couldn't fathom any solid reasoning for her to be bothered by the prospect of another night.

Of course, logic wasn't necessary for these things.

She had her reasons that weren't mine and never would be, so it was probably best for me to thank my lucky stars for the opportunity, and go about my own business.

Thanks to her, I had some.

Instead of heading home, I made my way to the gallery space I'd purchased downtown – an investment that had cost a pretty penny. The plans I'd made – plans I'd hatched and refined and cultivated with the wisdom and input of my mother before her passing – were still in progress. When it was done, *The Marie Anders* center would house classrooms for all ages, studios for pottery, sculpting, painting, and photography, a gallery for those artists to showcase their work, and more.

What had started as a tribute to my father would be a tribute to both, and maybe I was imagining it, but... *damn*. The place was already crackling with creative energy. That plus the surge of inspiration I'd gotten from sharing a bed with Jemma led me straight to one of the studios that were already finished – my personal one, reserved for my use away from home.

I propped up a fresh canvas, a big one, one of the many I'd personally mounted for use in the studios. I grabbed a palette and gathered my paints, mixing and testing for the rights hues and tones, not settling for anything less than perfect.

It was what my subject deserved.

I picked up a brush and got started, in bold, broad strokes at first. To create the shapes. And then, little by little, the details layered on, turning the crude shapes I'd started with into something more substantial.

Something more... *her*.

I kept going.

Even as my shoulders, hands started aching, even past the time my alarm went off reminding me to eat, twice, I kept on, and on, until I was gazing back into the face of the very beauty I'd left this morning.

Jemma, again.

Without the braids this time, and with a different expression than the first. This time, it was that *you got me fucked up* face, the one I knew to take seriously, but still the same one that, perhaps irrationally, turned me the hell on.

"*Beautiful*," I muttered, then smiled at the canvas, wondering

I THINK I MIGHT WANT YOU

what the actual woman was doing now. More than twelve hours had passed since we parted ways – long enough that I was missing the feel of her body, missing the taste of her pussy... but, she'd assured me I wouldn't get a chance to indulge again.

It was nice running into you again.

That was people's polite way of brushing you off, the courteous dismissal of someone you never planned to see again. They were the words Jemma used as we parted – as she discharged me from her hotel room and her presence, palpably hoping that our paths never crossed again.

Only... it hadn't been *nice running into her.*

Just as she'd said in her book, it had been... perspective shifting.

Not even remotely the type of thing you just walked away from like everything was still the same – or worse: the type of thing you *forgot.*

Whether or not she wanted to admit or accept it, there was *something* between me and Jemma – some force insistent on bringing us together.

Obviously, I wasn't going to push it. I didn't believe in forcing things outside of their natural path if I could help myself.

But I certainly wasn't going to fight it.

FIVE

Jemma

"*Jem... I need a big favor.*"

I sat up in bed, groggy as hell from yet another sleepless night. It had been a week since my little tryst with Levi in my hotel, and I hadn't had a single night of peace since then.

He'd really, *really* messed my head up.

Not even a rendezvous with my trusty bedside boyfriend had been able to clear my mind, which was honestly a little bit terrifying. I *depended* on orgasms, needed them to clear my head and regulate my moods, besides the fact that they just flat-out felt good.

Had giving in to this man really messed my head up?

Anyway, back to the matter at hand.

"Devyn," I replied to the person on the other end of the call that had roused me from my sleep. "What, what is it?"

She sighed. "Well, a few little ones at the kids' daycare have a nasty bug going around. I'm trying to keep it from ending up in *my* house, and especially don't want the baby sick. Mine, or baby

I THINK I MIGHT WANT YOU

Nayara," she said, referring to the newest addition to the family, Reese and Jason's daughter. "Joey and I are both on call today, so... if you're not busy, do you think you could—"

"Yes," I answered, before she could even get the question out. "You need me to watch the kids. I will. I gotchu boo."

It wasn't that I just enjoyed children in general, but Devyn and Joseph's kids were cute as hell, and I could really, *really*, use something valuable to do. They were small - a toddler and an infant. Prime ages to be a proper handful, which was exactly what I needed.

"Yes," Devyn confirmed. "I would appreciate it *so* much if you could help."

I nodded like she could see me. "Yeah, no problem. Give me a second to get out of bed and take a quick shower and I'll be there. Thirty minutes tops."

Devyn let out a relieved sigh. "Thank you, so much!"

"Not a problem at all, cousin," I told her, then we exchanged quick goodbyes before I got off the phone.

I didn't waste time moving ahead with what I needed to do to make myself available for Devyn and Joseph's childcare. She may have called because they needed me, but I definitely needed them more.

After my shower and brushing my teeth, I dressed comfortably in shorts and a tee-shirt, and brushed my flat ironed hair into a quick ponytail. I threw on tennis shoes and grabbed my keys, purse, and cell to leave, heading for the rental I'd reserved for my extended time in Blakewood.

It was time to head back to the suburbs.

~

"Auntie Jem!" Jaden gushed, rushing up to me as soon as Devyn let me in the front door of their house. I grinned, extending my arms to him.

Technically he was my cousin, but all the Wright kids called my sisters and me aunties, and as far as I was concerned, they were my nieces and nephews.

Once I'd given him a big hug and covered his sweet, adorable face with kisses, I accepted baby Josie from Devyn's arms. "Whoa," I gushed, shifting her to my hip. "You've gotten to be a juicy, juicy girl, haven't you?" I asked, tickling and making her laugh. "Look at these cheeks, and these rolls. It should be criminal for her to be this cute Dev," I commented, covering her with kisses in the same way I did to her big brother.

Josie gave me a toothless grin as Devyn laughed and grabbed her bag. "Yeah, all fun and games until you've got a little boob monster hanging off your tit, smacking you in the face cause the milk isn't coming fast enough for her little greedy butt." Devyn stopped in front of me, pulling me into half a hug. "Thank you again for coming through."

"Not a problem at all," I told her. "Seriously. I needed some good old-fashioned auntie time with my sugar babies anyway."

Devon scoffed. "Sugar babies? Girl, more like sour patch kids."

"We're gonna have fun *all day* Auntie Jemma," Jaden said, wrapping his arms around my leg as he grinned up at me, looking just like a perfect caramel mixture of his mother and father.

"Look at this face, there's no sour there. You out here lying on my babies," I teasingly accused Devyn, shaking my head as I used my free hand to run my fingers through Jaden's short, soft coils.

Her eyebrows hiked up on her forehead, and she gave me an amused grin. "Uh-huh sure. Y'all have fun."

I watched, smiling, as Devyn said her goodbyes to her children. It was a sight I'd witnessed before, with my various nieces, nephews, and cousins, but that never made it hit me any different.

It was sweet.

Not just the love she had for her children, but the love in her eyes when she interacted with their father as well. It struck me at that moment, that of our section of our overall family unit, I was now the only one who wasn't having babies and getting partnered off.

Damn.

I wracked my brain, counting through my family one by one until I came back to the same conclusion.

…I was really the only one.

To my family's credit, no one was rushing or pressuring me to do anything.

Besides a little good-natured teasing from my sisters, I didn't have any undue influence over the course of my life. They were pretty comfortable letting me be. Any uncertainty about my singleness was my own, and it had very little, if anything, to do with any societal pressures, social media expectations, none of that.

All this time, I'd been happily single, to the point that I wondered if I would have even been happy had Sean and I ended up married.

Well…he was a cheater so probably not him, but anyone.

I loved my life as it was, loved my freedom to come and go as I pleased, loved having such control over my own time, and not having a great deal of responsibility to anyone. I didn't even have a traditional job I was beholden to, so my freedom was on ten.

I *loved* my life.

But I had to admit — just to myself, not out loud, never ever to anyone else… I was a little lonely.

And I fucking *hated* it.

The single girl, living life on her own terms, traveling the world, eating what I wanted, screwing who I wanted, moving on when I wanted, that was *me*. It was who I was.

But.

There was something missing.

Truthfully, I couldn't see myself with Devyn's life, as beautiful as I thought it was. I wasn't yearning for a husband, wasn't longing for the big house. Even having children was something that I didn't feel that strongly one way or another about. Not with us already having so many in the family, where I could get my fill of babies and toddlers and whatever other age range anyway, pretty much any time I liked.

I didn't want that for me.

I just wanted something... *else*.

Some other compliment to my life that I couldn't quite identify.

But I could go into an existential crisis another time.

For now, it was time to focus on being Auntie Jemma, and giving these kids the best babysitting of their life.

Once Devyn was out the door, I turned back to where Jaden was and matched his smile. But then his grin slipped away, replaced by an impish expression as he promptly stuck his finger up his nose.

"You ready to play, Aunt Jemma?" he asked, and if I didn't know better, I could swear he'd taken on a whole new, devilish tone of voice.

I didn't understand how *not* ready I was for Jaden until we were fully in the throes of about the tenth thing he pulled out. When Devyn left the house was spotless, but in the span of the morning there were LEGOs, there were trucks, there were trains, there were superheroes, there was a construction site, a kitchen setup, a hospital set up, there was a racetrack, there was a grocery store, and there was *slime*.

And then it all started over again.

The endless loop of *let's play!* was only interrupted by lunchtime.

Joseph had left meals already prepared and packed for both kids, since it was something he would have done anyway for them to go to daycare. As soon as I put his tray of grilled chicken, cutesy shapes of cheese, and vegetable sticks on his special tray in front of him, Jaden promptly flipped it over, turning all the food onto the floor.

"Don't want that."

My eyebrows shot up. "Okay. So... what *do* you want then," I asked him, kneeling down beside him at the table so that we were at the same level.

"*Sandwich*." he demanded. "Peanut butter and jelly."

I nodded. "Peanut butter and jelly it is," I agreed. "And while I'm fixing your sandwich, I need you to get up and clean up this food you dropped, okay?"

He gave me a big nod as if we were on the same page so I turned away, straightening to a stand so that I could get started on his alternative lunch. But then I glanced back to check on him as I gathered the ingredients, and ended up taking a carrot stick to the face.

"Ohhhh. No food fighting baby," I urged him, holding up my hands to get him to stop.

There were already toys all over the place, the last thing I needed was food too.

"But it's *fun*," he insisted, then promptly turned to where Josie was sitting up in her highchair, peacefully enjoying her bottle as she watched us. Next thing I knew, *she* was taking a carrot to the forehead too.

As expected, she immediately dropped the bottle, hands stretched out to her sides in full-blown stress mode as the wailing started.

"*No sir!*" I stressed at Jaden, whipping around to stare him down. "I know you're pushing your little boundaries since your parents aren't here to snatch you back in line, but what you may not know, is Auntie Jemma has been granted full authority over here. You get your little butt over there and clean that food up, you hear me?" I warned him. "And you'd better not throw anything else."

He stared at me for a second, mouth open, eyes full of deep betrayal like he was shocked that I'd spoken to him with any type of firmness. We'd been pretty chill all morning, because he hadn't done anything to warrant a scolding until now.

Apparently, he wasn't really into receiving admonishment from Auntie Jemma.

As I watched, his face crumpled into a heartbroken expression, and he started wailing too, damn near louder than Josie was. Still, I knew Josie's comfort was the more pressing issue.

I hurriedly removed her tray and unbuckled her from the highchair to get her up into my arms. I grabbed a bottle too, hoping that between the warm breast milk and the soothing pats I was giving to her shoulders, she'd be able to calm down.

"Jaden," I said, shifting Josie in my arms so I could wipe away the stream of tears down his cheeks. "Auntie didn't mean to hurt your feelings baby, okay?" I asked, as I continued rocking Josie, who didn't seem interested in letting up anytime soon. "But you have to do what I say okay?" I asked Jaden, and he nodded through his tears. "You can have however long you need to work your emotions out, that's fine. But while you're crying, I need to see you picking up that food. You understand?"

He nodded, and went to pick up the food, gathering up chunks of chopped grilled chicken in his little hands and returning them to the plate. Satisfied that *that* was under control, I focused my full attention on getting Josie-bug calmed back down.

A glance at the clock told me that, per the tip sheet Devyn and Joseph had left, it was almost time for Josie to go down for a nap. Which made sense, since she was acting just like I *wanted* to act when I got tired. Her plaintive sobs finally seemed to be coming down when somebody rang the doorbell, sending the loud chime echoing through the house.

Josie did *not* like that.

That set her off again, which set Jaden off too.

"Somebody's at the door!" he exclaimed, excited.

So excited that he accidentally knocked over the tray of food he was almost done retrieving from the floor, sending it all flying everywhere again. Before I could tell him it was okay, he was crying again too.

Shit.

Shiiiiit.

The doorbell rang again, with me having no intention of answering, because obviously I didn't have any free hands to open the door. And apparently, I wasn't going to have ears either, between two small children screaming their lungs out expressing their displeasure.

Whoever was at the door though - probably just the mail or some other delivery - would either have to wait or move on. I had to figure out something to get these kids calmed down, and *both* of them down for naps, so that I could have just a second of some breathing room.

I turned around, heading back to the foyer table where I'd left the list of tips the Wrights had given me. However, as soon as I stepped into the hallway, I nearly collided with a figure I was *definitely* not expecting to see there.

"*Ahhhh!*" I screamed. "What the fuck?!"

I took a couple of rapid steps backward, almost stumbling with Josie in my arms. Before I could fall, Levi reached out to grab me, holding on until I'd steadied my feet on the ground.

"What the hell are you doing here?" I hissed, trying to calm my racing heart.

He'd scared the shit out of me.

"Devyn made arrangements for me to come by today to check on the mounting of her portrait. She said she felt like it was loose," he explained. "I rang the doorbell twice, and when nobody answered, Devyn unlocked the door for me remotely. She told me to come on in."

Okay, I said to myself. *Definitely going to kill her ass.*

She was *not* slick with the setup.

The fact that both kids had suddenly grown quiet did not escape my notice. Josie was too busy staring at Levi, intrigued by a new face to look at to keep screaming, but when I looked around for Jaden, he was nowhere to be found.

Suddenly, I heard, "*What the fuck! What the fuck! What the fuck!*" being repeated at a high volume, over and over and *over*.

Shit!

A few steps toward the living room, I found Jaden jumping up and down on the couch as he repeated my unfortunately timed phrase as he jumped.

"Boy you know you're not supposed to be on that furniture," I scolded him, and he immediately jumped down with a sheepish grin. "And how about we not say that, okay? Like ever?"

"But *you* said it," he reasoned.

"Yes," I told him. "Because Auntie Jemma is a bad person."

His cute little face dropped into a scowl, and he shook his head. "You're not a bad guy," he corrected me, looking very hurt and scandalized that I would say such a thing about myself.

"Okay maybe not. But you still shouldn't say that, okay?" I asked, and he nodded, already over it as he moved on to go back to smashing trucks together.

I turned back to Levi to find him standing close – too close – behind me, wearing a big grin.

"You know that's going to be the first thing out of his mouth when his mama comes through that door right?" He quipped.

I nodded, with a deep sigh. "Yeah, I know. Of course it is."

"How have you been though?" he asked, meeting my eyes with that usual intensity of his.

I shook my head, looking away. "I've been good, I guess. Just enjoying being at home, being around my family. How about you?"

"The usual. Working on the gallery, painting where I can."

My eyebrow went up. "The gallery?"

"Yeah," he explained. "Taking over this huge empty space downtown, for a kind of... a school, I guess. My parents were both artists as well, so this is something like a tribute to them."

"Oh *wow*," I exclaimed, still bouncing Josie on my hip. "That's... *amazing*."

"I'm really hoping it will be. Honor their memories, and all that."

"I'm sure they're looking down at you with a whole lot of pride," I said. "How long has it been?"

Levi's stance shifted. "About seven years for my dad. My mom... about seven months."

My eyes went wide, and my brain immediately solved the math problem that spurred to the forefront of my mind. If it was seven months ago now, that meant that during our time together in Havana, that melancholy I felt around him was actually...

"Oh," I said. "Levi, I'm so sorry. I had no idea."

He shrugged. "You wouldn't have, since I wasn't exactly in a talking mood about it. I'm still not, actually."

"Understood," I assured him. "Definitely. We don't have to. Unless you wanted to, then yeah. But of course you don't."

Levi smiled over my not-at-all-typical-for-me awkwardness.

It was like I couldn't help myself with him.

"I appreciate that," he told me. "But I'll let you get back to the kids, and go check on this painting, okay?" He turned to head upstairs to Josie's nursery, where the painting in question was hanging.

"These aren't my kids!", I yelled after him, for some reason.

He stopped to look at me, with a grin on his face. "Yes, I know."

Heat rushed to my face as I quickly turned away, embarrassed. Of course he knew these weren't my kids – he lived across the street from the family, and had obviously been in the house.

Surely, he recognized these kids were Joseph and Devyn's.

I pushed away my unfamiliar anxiety, and went back to the kitchen where I replaced a calm Josie into her highchair. I grabbed the broom and dustpan and swept up the food that Jaden had spilled, not interested in the meltdown that might come if I tried to make him pick it all up a second time.

I washed my hands, fixed the peanut butter sandwich Jaden had requested, and then called him back into the kitchen for lunch.

Finally, there was some degree of calmness again.

"Well," Levi said from the kitchen doorway, startling me again. "I got the mounting on the painting fixed. It almost looks like somebody tried to rip one of the corners out of the wall, which... don't even understand how something like that happened."

I did.

*Oh Devyn was **plotting** plotting.*

"In any case," he said. "I did get it fixed."

"I'm sure Devyn will be very grateful," I told him, not bothering to share my theory that this was just part of her plan to get us back in the same space, not knowing that that had already happened.

"Mr. Levi," Jaden shouted. "Don't go yet! I gotta show you my painting from school!"

I glanced at him just in time to see Jaden stuffing the rest of his peanut butter sandwich into his mouth all at once before he jumped up from the table and shot towards the stairs, up towards his room.

"Stop running with your mouth full," I called after him, a request that obviously got ignored.

Levi chuckled at Jaden's excitement as Josie started getting fussy again in her chair. I swept her up into my arms just as Jaden returned, with not just a painting, but a whole binder full of art projects.

I shook my head. "Jaden, I don't think Mr. Levi has time to—"

"It's fine," Levi interrupted, with an easy smile. "I mean, it's fine with me, if it's fine with you."

Jaden very obviously didn't care if it was fine with me like Levi did, because he'd already grabbed Levi's wrist to pull him to the kitchen table, where he planted that binder and sat down, motioning for Levi to join him.

"Um... Yeah, it's fine with me. I'm going to go try to get Josie down, while you look at the book with him, okay?"

"Sounds like a plan to me," Levi said, reaching to grab Josie's little fist. "Sleep well little one," he kind of... *sang* to her, a sound that made her give him an adorable gummy grin, and made me and my pussy swoon a little.

A lot.

Okay.

Time to get away from him.

Upstairs, I changed Josie's diaper and gave her a quick wipe down before changing her into fresh pajamas. She was so exhausted from her little seven-month-old-world that her eyes were already closed before I even put her down in the crib.

Still, I hung around for a few moments just in case, making sure she was comfortable before I made any moves to leave. When I arrived back down in the kitchen, Levi was still there with Jaden, complimenting him on the variety of techniques shown in his binder of preschool art.

"Jaden," I called. "Baby it's time for you to take *your* nap too, okay?"

Jaden groaned, but he flipped his book closed and got up without too much argument. "Bye Mr. Levi," he said. "Thank you for the tips!"

"You're welcome little man," Levi responded, holding out his closed fist for Jaden to tap with his own, something that put a huge grin on Jaden's face before he took off upstairs again.

"So... you're good with kids," I commented, as Levi stood up from the table too.

He shrugged.

"Isn't everyone who only has to interact with them for a limited amount of time?"

I laughed. "No, not everyone. But I do see your point."

There was quiet between us for a moment, but then...

"Have dinner with me tonight," he said, seemingly out of nowhere. But I had a feeling that nothing was really *out of nowhere* when it came to Levi.

I shook my head. "I already have plans," I lied.

"So change them," he countered, as if it were really that simple.

I mean, it *was* that simple, since my "plans" were really with Netflix and a bottle of wine, but still.

"What makes you think you can always make demands like this with me?" I asked, crossing my arms. "I should just drop everything I have to do because you want me to?"

"No," he answered with a sexy smirk. "You should do it because *you* want to."

Uh-uh.

He got me with that logic before.

One second, I'm holding firm in my resistance, the next second, I'm happily trying to swallow his unborn children.

I was *not* going out like that again.

"I'm *not* going to be some sex on demand doll for you," I proclaimed, chin in the air.

"Good," he countered. "Because this isn't about that. That's why I asked you *to* dinner, instead of asking you to *be* dinner."

I squeezed my thighs together. "You didn't *ask*, you *told*. But fine, you got me. I'm curious. If it's not about sex, what is it about?"

"It's about the fact that since I met you, I've only been able to create with your face in mind," he said. "And the work you've inspired has been... magnificent. At a level I've never been able to reach before."

I raised my eyebrows. "Are you saying... I'm your muse?" I asked.

He smiled the smile of a man who knew he'd gotten what he wanted. "I'm saying... I'll pick you up from the hotel at eight," he said, and then he was out the door before I could offer a rebuttal.

But I'd definitely be ready at eight.

SIX

LEVI.

Exquisitely beautiful.
That was the only suitable description for the impression Jemma made on me as soon as she opened the door to her hotel room that night.

Her hair was curled into loose waves that framed her face and hung around her shoulders, sultry deep crimson coated her lips, and a deceptively simple form-fitting black dress hugged her lush curves.

I wanted to take her right there, right in the damn doorway. Kneel in front of her and push that dress up her legs, push aside whatever underwear was hiding underneath, and... worship.

Fuck those dinner reservations.

But, when I proposed this time together, back at Joseph and Devyn's, I told her this wasn't about sex.

I intended to honor that.

The deep lust she inspired aside, I really did want to get to know her beyond the connection we'd forged through sexual intimacy. I wanted to know everything there was to know, period.

I wanted *her*.

So I behaved myself.

At the restaurant, I sat across from her, barely able to stop myself from staring once the server had finally left us alone to browse the menu and enjoy our wine.

Jemma looked up from her menu, meeting my gaze with a smile. "You clean up quite well," she said, picking up her glass to take a sip. "I'm used to seeing you much more dressed down than this."

"I could say the same about you," I countered, giving her a wink that made the most adorable, embarrassed smile cross her face."

"Touché." She took another sip from her drink. "So what exactly is it that you want to know about me?" she asked.

'Whatever you want to tell," I told her, honestly. "Especially after reading your book, and taking a peek around your social media profiles, I feel like I've only brushed the surface of this... beautiful, fascinating creature named Jemma. And I really try not to be a *surface* kind of guy."

She raised an eyebrow. "So you're telling me that what happened between us in Havana... it's not something you do all the time?"

"It's not, actually. For me, you were an anomaly, especially with what I was going through at the time. I, unfortunately don't have that ability of so many, to have... passive sexual encounters."

She tossed her head back. "Is that judgment I hear in your tone?"

"No, not at all," I assured her. "More like envy. Why the *hell* would I judge you for having the very experience that I've gotten to reap the significant benefits of?"

Nobody got great at sex by accident, and nobody started out that way either. One way or another, Jemma had put time into her craft, and I wasn't mad about it.

She smiled. "Oh, you'd be surprised. You said you looked around my social media, right? So I'm sure you've seen some of the knock-down, drag-out that goes on in my comments? Everything from the

I THINK I MIGHT WANT YOU

warnings that I'm going to hell, to the assurances that I *must* have some sort of disease from fucking around the world, to the very *very* concerned men and women who are just desperate to let me know that no man in his right mind would *ever* want to settle down with a woman like me. Which is obviously the end of the world. No one will ever want to make me a wife. No one would ever want a mother, who says the things I say, someone who shares the experiences I've shared. It's all quite lovely, actually," she quipped.

I laughed and shrugged. "You're right, I definitely saw some of that. But that shit doesn't faze me, and I hope it doesn't faze *you*. People love passing judgment based on their own values, not understanding that their ugly words, that anger and negativity they get on the internet and project toward a perfectly happy stranger... that says so much more about them than it'll ever say about you."

Jemma sat back in her chair a little bit and nodded. "I must admit, it's very refreshing to hear. Honestly, it's rare to meet a man who isn't threatened by -hell, even the idea that a woman they want has been with another man."

"And what does that tell you about the way they view themselves and their peers, that they think their touch defiles a woman," I replied, picking up my own drink. "Yet, we like to consider ourselves the logical ones."

"Mmmmm," Jemma grunted, pulling her lip between her teeth. "Stop it. Before I have to cut this dinner short and take you back to my room."

I laughed and shook my head. "Nah, now. We said we'd get to know each other, so that's what I intend to do."

"Sure," she smirked. "We can roll with that...for now. So what else do you want to know?"

"Are we going to play twenty-one questions now? That's how you want to do this?"

She shrugged. "I'm just the muse, Mr. Anders. It's really your show."

"So you'd embrace that role for me?" I asked, raising an eyebrow.

"I didn't say all that," she replied. "I don't even know what it entails."

"Nothing you wouldn't enjoy. Immensely."

Across the table, her eyes narrowed, and she gave me this sexy smile that made me hard. "Oh I'm sure I would. And it would be enough if I were solely driven by my libido. Unfortunately for you... despite my obvious inability to resist your D2B-"

"D2B?"

"Dick too bomb," she explained, then quickly brushed off my interruption. "Despite my weak ass flesh... the promise of pleasure isn't enough to make me override all my personal convictions to play Girl with Pearl Butt Plug for you."

My eyes went wide. "Girl with the... *wow*," I laughed, as she shrugged.

"I'm just saying. As enjoyable as that might be, I need... more than that."

I nodded. "Okay... Tell me what you need then."

"Oooh. Give you an instruction manual to fuck me over?"

"Ah," I sighed. "There it is. The answer to the question that's been nagging the back of my mind - what exactly is Jemma running from?"

Her eyes narrowed, and I could practically hear the "who the fuck do you think I am?" running across her mind.

"What makes you think I'm running from anything?" she asked, clearly annoyed by my assumption.

I ran my fingers through the condensation on my glass. "Isn't every traveler?"

"Isn't every traveler what?"

"Running from something," I said. "Boredom. Depression. Family. Commitment. Poverty. Incarceration. Accountability. Grief. *Something*. It's *something* for every single one of us."

She cleared her throat. "Interesting theory. And you think *I'm* running from...?"

"Getting fucked over again."

Whatever her response would've been, it was interrupted by the server returning to take our orders. Once we were alone again, I met her gaze with a smile.

"You gonna tell me if I'm right or not?" I asked.

That question made her drain the rest of her drink, then clear her throat.

"Maybe?" She admitted. "I was engaged before. It ended... tragically, I guess."

"You guess?"

"I know," she said. "My fiancé was cheating, so I broke up with him. But then just a little bit after, while I was still grieving the relationship, I got a knock on my door. From the boyfriend of the woman he was cheating on me with. Actually, knock is a misnomer. He kicked my door in and put a gun in my face."

"You're serious?" I asked, frowning.

"Unfortunately, yes. He didn't hurt me or anything, but that didn't make it any less terrifying," she explained, brushing her hair away from her face.

"Yeah, I can imagine. That's fucked up."

"And that wasn't even the end of it," she went on, shaking her head. "He did catch up with my fiancé. He killed him, then killed himself. So it was just fucked up all around, and pretty traumatizing, honestly. For a while, I tried to just go back to life. I was working, and after a while I tried to date, and I just tried to be the girl I was before. But I *wasn't* the girl I'd been before. I didn't know *who* I was, I just knew I wasn't her anymore. And I knew I couldn't figure that out while I was still doing the same things I used to do. So by your logic... I ran away from the sameness, the uncertainty, the boredom. I ran away from this idea of staying in Blackwood for the rest of my life, and finding a cute little husband, and a cute little house, and having cute kids. Ran away from what was expected."

"You're still running now," I said. "That's not a critique, just an observation. There's nothing wrong with it, it's just the mode you're in right now."

Jemma leaned in, propping her elbows on the table, chin in her hands. "And what mode are you in right now? What are *you* running from?"

"Grief," I answered immediately. "Lack of creative energy. I met this amazing woman in Cuba and had the privilege of this...insanely gratifying intimate experience... I'm running from the fact that she's running from me."

"That doesn't even make sense," she accused, but was unable to suppress a smile. "In Havana, you were the one who ran from me."

"You're not going to let me forget that, are you?" I chuckled. "That's fine, I'm not afraid to admit that I ran. Yeah. You were... some kind of intoxicating, and I knew I had to get away. I'm done with that now though."

"Why?" she asked, her face a beautiful mask of curiosity that brought a hint of a smile to my face.

"Because, something about you, brings out something in me, that I feel like I cannot live without."

Jemma shook her head. "Okay, now you're just talking crazy."

"Whoa," I cautioned. "Don't take that the wrong way. I'm not saying that I think you're my soulmate or my future wife, nothing necessarily like that."

She laughed. "Nothing *necessarily*. Meaning, it's exactly like that, you just don't know or maybe we don't want to, put a name on it."

"That may be correct," I admitted. "I'm just trying to ease your mind that I'm not some stalker, that I'm not trying to put a ring on your finger tonight, not trying to take anything *there*. I'm not a man obsessed. Or shit... maybe I am. But is that really such a bad thing?"

"That's yet to be determined," she said. "While you're making yourself clear, I want to make myself clear too. There is no part of me that's interested in being tied down. In all my traveling, I have discovered that it's just not in my nature."

I nodded. "Okay, so tell me what *is* in your nature? We're back around to this again, to me asking you to tell me what it is you need. Lay out your terms, love. I'm willing to negotiate."

"You sure do know how to talk a good game, Levi Anders." Jemma settled back in her chair.

"That's the thing, Jemma, it's not game. It's just my truth."

"Oh, that again," she grinned. "Levi's truth."

I shrugged, "Yeah, here we are again. You're avoiding the question."

"I'm avoiding the question because I don't have an answer," she admitted. "Trust me, it has been a *major* point of contention between me, myself, and I, that I really don't know what it is that I want."

"But you know you want me?" I asked.

She met my gaze. "Yeah. I do."

∽

"Wow."

That one word, breathed with such awe and reverence, did more to gratify me and cement my positive feelings about this space than anything else over the last few months of watching it come together. It made me that much more confident about this place opening in just a few weeks.

I watched as Jemma stepped into the large open space after I'd unlocked the door of the *Marie Anders Center* for us. The sexy, strappy stilettos she wore accentuated her long legs as she turned, her gaze darting around the room to take it all in. This space where we were standing now would be the gallery, big and open, the first thing people saw when they walked in. The studios and classrooms were toward the back, and would be nice spaces too once they were done.

But this was the showpiece.

Floor to ceiling glass windows that extended from one end of the building to the other, specially treated so that the rays from the sun wouldn't damage any of the artwork. That would be the space for everything, room to show off work from the students and other local artists alike, to help them get the visibility they deserved.

I wanted a space that would really add to and enhance, that would invest in the community of Blackwood. The same way that the scholarships my parents founded had helped many art majors attend BSU. Those scholarships would go on through endowments, funded by investments they made before they died. Their gift would live on for years, and I would make sure that I picked up that banner before I died as well.

This was something else though.

This was something that the whole community could see and be a part of, something that wasn't exclusive to the students at BSU.

I just wanted to be as valuable as they were, give back as much as they did.

Based on Jemma's reaction, I was well on my way.

"Levi, this is amazing," she gushed. "When you mentioned a gallery space, of course I thought it was cool. But I don't I think I imagined *this*. This is huge. And it'll be open to the whole community, right?"

"Yeah," I nodded.

"I'm thinking about the jobs you're creating with this. The kids who wouldn't otherwise have an outlet that will be able to come here and express themselves through something positive."

"Yes," I smiled. "All that."

Jemma turned to me with a grin. "You're being super low key about this, like it's nothing."

"Nah," I shook my head. "Not at all. It's...everything. I'm just taking in your reaction. Letting it all marinate and sink in."

"Okay," she nodded. "Well, come on. This is all empty right now, but there must be something else in here to look at, right? Show me everything, take me on a tour. That's what got me here, after all."

That was true.

After dinner, I certainly hadn't been ready to let her go, but I was trying not to end up back in her hotel room either. Not because I didn't want her - it wasn't that at all. But I did feel like I had a point to - that sex wasn't a necessary part of our connection.

So I brought her here, to the center, with a promise that I'd give her a private tour.

"Okay, come on," I said, grabbing her by the hand and lacing my fingers through hers. She looked down at where our hands were joined together, staring at them for a second. I half expected her to pull her away, but she didn't.

"Fine," she agreed, with a smile. "Lead the way."

So I did.

I took her around the whole space, showing her the classrooms and private offices, then the kitchen and break room area. Then, we moved on to the studios, with me showing her the places that would be available for local artists to lease for short or long periods, and perhaps even do art installations and private shows.

And then we made it to mine.

As soon as Jemma stepped in, she sucked in a breath. I kept my eyes glued to her face as her gaze went to the two portraits that were now both hanging up in my private studio here at the gallery. Her steps were slow as she ventured further inside, and I closed the door behind us.

"You painted these?" she asked, not looking away from the portraits - her portraits - hanging up on the wall.

"Yes."

She let out a sigh.

A gratified one.

"Wow. I mean... of course I saw the painting you did of Devyn in the nursery, and I even saw your work at the hospital too. I mean, before I knew it was you. And work online. I knew you were good, but... *wow*."

I stepped closer to her, resting my hand on the small of her back as I leaned in, speaking into her ear.

"This is what you do for me, Jemma. This is what you bring out of me," I told her.

She looked at me over her shoulder. "That's a *lot* of pressure, you know?"

"No pressure at all," I told her, anchoring my hands at her waist as I pulled her into me. "All you got to do is keep being yourself. That's more than enough."

She turned in my arms to face me. "So what are you going to do? Are you just going to keep painting my face for the rest of your life? I mean, it *is* a pretty good face, but I don't know how good that would be for your career."

"Are you suggesting you don't think I can create anything else?"

She shrugged. "I don't know, you tell me. Pick up a brush. Get to work. Make it happen right now," she challenged, wearing a devilish smile.

"Oh damn, is that a dare," I asked.

"Only if you're up to it," she counted.

"I'm *always* up to a challenge."

I didn't waste any time getting to it, taking off the nice shirt I'd put on for dinner and even slipping off my shoes.

"Ooooh, Jemma gushed. "You getting naked to paint?" she asked.

I turned to her with a wink. "Only if you want me to."

She lifted an eyebrow, staring at me for a second before she smirked.

"Uh-huh. I do."

That wasn't a problem for me.

She watched, completely amused as I stripped all the way down to my birthday suit, then picked up an apron. Once I had it on, I turned to her with my arms out, rotating where I stood to give her a full view.

"This is a *very* good look for you," she said. "I'm very, very into this. But I still want to see you work."

I scoffed. "I keep trying to tell you, it ain't no problem."

I went over to the canvas that I already had mounted on my easel, thinking about what I would do. But then, with the chilled air of the studio against my ass, I had a different idea. I turned to where Jemma was standing, waiting.

"You get naked too."

Immediately, her face pulled into a frown and she shook her head.

"What the hell would I get naked for?" she asked. "This show is *all* you."

"Right now, yeah. But how about we make it me *and* you? Get naked," I told her again, not waiting for a response before I walked over to one of the rolls of canvas in the corner.

I unfurled it across the floor, then went over to the stack of supplies for the classrooms stocked here for temporary storage in a different corner. I grabbed several bottles of tempera paint in different colors, bringing them back to the canvas with me. I stopped to look at Jemma, who still hadn't moved.

"Do I have to take that dress off you myself?" I asked.

She stared at me for a long moment, as if she were really considering her options.

Then she moved.

I watched, enthralled, as she unzipped the side of that dress and then slid the straps off her shoulders, letting it drop to the ground. She was braless underneath, and wearing another of those tiny pairs of panties that were maybe going to be the death of me.

"Everything?" she asked, and I nodded.

"Yeah. Everything."

She took the panties and shoes off and I took the apron off and brought a bottle of red paint with me as I approached where she stood. I opened it, coating my hands with it before I reached out to her, rubbing it over her breast and shoulders.

'You want to tell me what this is about?" she asked, and I winked at her.

"Yeah. We're about to make something beautiful."

With a hand at the back of her neck I pulled her into me, covering her mouth with a bruising kiss. I pushed my tongue between her lips, tasting her, savoring every drop of the lingering taste of the wine we had with dinner. I forgot about the paint for a second, dropping it in favor of being able to get both hands on her supple, velvety skin. I lowered my hands to her ass to grip and squeeze, pulling her against my dick.

"Come on," I told her. "Let's get started."

Jemma smiled, completely game without me having to spell it out to her - an adventurous spirit that was one of the many things I enjoyed about her.

We spread the different shades of paints on different parts of our bodies, taking care to avoid the genital areas, obviously. And then I spread Jemma out on top of that canvas that I'd rolled out on the floor, pushing her legs wide. Exposing her beautifully bare pussy to me before I buried my face between her legs.

She was so fucking sweet to my taste buds.

I couldn't get enough- I'd *never* get enough.

I licked and lapped and slurped until she was squirming and shaking, leaving the imprint of her beautiful body all over that canvas as I made her come.

As a matter of fact, she was *still* shaking when I moved positions, slipping into her pussy for the first time with nothing between us. I paused for a second, still buried deep and enjoying every second of her unfiltered wetness hugging me tight as I met her gaze with an apologetic lift of my eyebrows.

I hadn't even been thinking.

I'd just needed to be inside her.

"You're in it now anyway," she said with a shrug as she tightened her pussy around me. "But you'd better fuck me *especially* good now."

Yet another thing that would *not* be a problem.

I propped her legs up on my shoulders and proceeded to stroke hard and deep, exactly the way I knew she liked it. In next to no time, she was squirming for me, again screaming my name in a way that echoed around my studio walls.

All I wanted to do was make her come.

Again, and again, and again, as our bodies mixed and blended the pigments of paint together on the canvas with every movement.

In and of herself, Jemma was a masterpiece, but this was on a whole other level. Her breasts, her stomach, her thighs, her back, her ass... everything was covered in red, yellow, orange and gold, streaked together like some kind of molten goddess.

I groaned as I drove deeper into her tight, wet heat, relishing the feeling of her body clenching around me in those involuntary spasms of pleasure.

And her *face*.

Shit.

Mouth open, head thrown back, eyelids fluttering as she gave in to the bliss of me inside her. That made it even better for me, knowing just how good it was for her too.

I could live like this.

Buried deep inside of Jemma Love, making something beautiful on this canvas.

And then her orgasm hit, with a tightening of her hips and a whole new tension in her body, her nipples beading into hard peaks beneath the paint that decorated her skin. Before it could completely wash over her, I flipped her over, grabbing her by the hips and pulling her into me as I drove into her from behind.

"Holy *shit*," she whimpered and moaned as she threw it back at me, sending paint splatters and bodily fluids flying as our bodies smacked together.

"Shit," I groaned, as the familiar sensation built in my balls. Honestly, I felt that shit all the way down to my toes, amplified by the sight of her fat ass coming back at me every time I slid into her pussy.

She turned, looking over her shoulder at me - not with cockiness, but with pure pleasure as her body shuddered with another orgasm. "Don't pull out," she begged. "I wanna feel it all."

I swear that shit made me cum even harder as I grabbed her waist, driving into her with a loud, animalistic groan. I held onto her hips, keeping her locked against me as I pumped into her, emptying everything that I'd pent up since the last time I was in her.

We fell away from each other, gasping and panting as our bodies created a whole new imprint on the canvas.

"Whew," Jemma said. "Is that the type of stuff you guys are going to be teaching in these classrooms?" she teased, and I chuckled, shaking my head.

"Nah, love. This particular lesson was just for you."

SEVEN

Jemma

I pushed out a heavy sigh as I headed down the hallway of what used to be my apartment. In some ways, it was bittersweet to be here again – every so often, I kinda missed not having a permanent place to land. But on the other hand, I knew this space was better suited for someone... not me. Which is why I was here at all, really.

I fished my keys from my purse, cursing myself in my head for leaving this task to the very last minute. What I *really* needed to be doing was getting ready to get on a plane tomorrow night, but I did still have to tend to my responsibilities.

I was more than a little exhausted after spending a rather... *creative* night in the company of Levi Anders. What was supposed to be "just dinner" had turned into me getting a private tour of his art center, which turned into me *face down, ass up,* covered in paint. A little adventure that *definitely* would've made it into my book if it had happened sooner.

Now though... I *had* to find my way to some new adventures.

It was why I'd moved my flight up, not wanting to wait the extra few days for the original flight - more time to get myself further wrapped up in Levi. As *great* as the sex was, and as captivating as Levi was, I really, *really* needed to get away, while I still had the wherewithal to do it.

First, duty called.

I needed to do my inspection of my apartment for Kadan's benefit, so we could renew his lease agreement. I was technically a landlord now, and part of that was making sure the place hadn't been turned into a meth lab or something.

Something I really could've just taken his word for, but I liked to just make sure.

Men liked to lie about shit when they didn't have to.

I unlocked the door and stepped in, immediately frowning over a familiar smell... sex in the air. I knew *plenty* about that. Only... Jac had already told me she was going to be at *Dreamery* all morning, and supposedly Kadan was at work too so...

Damn. Am I gonna have to kill this nigga today?

With my keyring pepper spray in hand, ready to season the whole room if I didn't like what I saw, I stepped around the corner into the full, open view of the apartment.

"Oh *God!*" I shouted, quickly covering my eyes to block out the sight of Jaclyn and Kadan going at it on top of my granite counters.

"What the fuck are you doing here?!" they both said, in unison.

"I'm *supposed* to be here – we *talked about this*," I exclaimed, peeking through my fingers to see Kadan moving to pull away and cover himself. But Jaclyn wrapped her legs around his legs, keeping him locked in the place.

"Uh-uh," she scolded him. "We have business to take care of!"

"Actually, *I* have business to take care of," I said, turning my back to them. "I'm here to do the inspection, at the time and date we *agreed* on. You niggas are supposed to be at work, and yet here we are with your naked asses banging in my kitchen in the middle of the day. Can we... put on clothes?"

I THINK I MIGHT WANT YOU

"No," Jac countered. "*You* can go. Come back later."

"I *can't* come back later; I have a full schedule today. Your ass knows I'm getting on a plane tomorrow."

I heard the tenor of Kadan's voice, but not his words before Jac groaned. "*Fine.*"

I stepped into the guest bathroom to give them a little privacy while they made themselves decent again - or maybe finished what they were doing for as long as it took for Kadan to come knock on the door and tell me the coast was clear.

"My bad Jemma," Kadan said. "I completely forgot that was supposed to be today."

"Can we please just pretend it didn't happen?" I asked. "Jac and I talk too much, and I already know way too much about your penis, soo..."

Kadan nodded. "Well, I read some of your book and I'm pretending *that* didn't happen so..." He extended a fist to me. "Selective memory loss?"

I tapped his fist with mine. "I don't even remember what I'm supposed to be forgetting."

"His pale, naked ass! You're welcome!" Jac yelled from across the room as Kadan and I left her to make the trip through the apartment to do the inspection.

When we were alone in the second bedroom, without Jaclyn's commentary, Kadan turned to me with a serious expression on his face.

"Hey, so now that I am starting to get more and more settled," he said, "I'm really starting to think about not renting anymore. Thinking about something more permanent."

I grinned at him. "Ooooh, are you thinking about getting a little house or something?" I asked. "Maybe so you have space for a... family?"

"Not quite yet," he laughed. "Things are going good with Jac, but you know how her last thing turned out, so really we're just trying to enjoy being together right now. And it's only been a few months."

"I understand." I told him. "So... what *are* you saying though?"

"I'm saying... that I think you should let me take over this lease for you. Like *for real*, not subletting. I want to convert it to the building's buy option."

"Ahhh," I nodded. "That's actually already what *I've* been doing. Every time you pay rent to me, it goes straight back to the balance left on this place," I explained.

Kadan sighed. "Damn. So I guess that's out then."

"No, actually," I answered. "I am *never* here, and it's actually started to become more of a hassle than anything. Back when I did it, I thought it was something that was going to be good for me. I thought I would be in Blakewood a lot more often than I actually am. It really doesn't make sense for me anymore to *own* a property, so I would be thrilled to make a shift here."

Those words brought the huge grin back to Kadan's handsome face. "Seriously?" he asked. "Because I *am* settled here, and this place is perfect for me. And... yes, potentially Jac too."

"*Seee*," I teased. "Y'all are so disgustingly sweet. Who knew the day she called me from the closet to tell me she'd busted you in your shit would turn into something?"

"Definitely not *me*," Kadan chuckled. "No lie, I thought your baby sister was off her rocker."

"I mean... she *is* off her rocker, but you love it," I said. "What has it been, like two months and you're already thinking about asking her to move in with you?"

"Wow, Jemma, it was just a thought," Kadan defended himself, and I shook my head.

"You don't have to explain it to me, I know what a gem my sister is, and I'm glad you see it too. And like you said, we remember how her last thing turned out. I let that nigga off easy because I wasn't here, and Jac had already caught that charge. But *you*," I told Kadan, as I stepped into full big sister mode. "*You*, I will take personal," I told him. "I vouched for you a little bit, I told her you were a good guy. Please don't make me regret that."

I THINK I MIGHT WANT YOU

Kadan put a hand to his chest. "You got nothing to worry about, Jemma, I promise you."

I smiled and nodded. "I believe you. And we can consider this inspection done. Everything looks good. I'll get in touch with the property manager and we can figure out what our next steps are with letting you take over."

"Sounds good to me," Kadan agreed, extending his arms, and I met him halfway for a hug before we went back out to where Jac was in the kitchen disinfecting my countertops. I spent a little time talking with them before I had to go. I had a full day of plans before I got on this plane – yes, that was part of it. But also, my heart really couldn't take how damn sweet they were together.

Just like with Joseph and Devyn, it was hard to watch them without comparing their life to my own. I wasn't one of those people who put too much stock in "relationship goals", especially not ones I saw online, where everybody was putting their best foot forward and only showing the good parts.

Of course, that was normal. Nobody - at least nobody with good sense - posted about it online every time they and their spouse got into an argument, every time their partner got on their nerves. Social media was the highlight reel.

But when I saw these beautiful relationships in such proximity to me, saw the obvious love in their eyes, saw the way they cared for and loved on each other... Those were the *real* goals. When someone could give you the space you needed because a relationship was causing extra stress, but would be right there for you when you were ready. Or like in Joia's case, a casual fling turned into a full-blown second chance with a man who would bend over backward, do anything for her and the baby their one-night stand had created.

Seeing the people in my life falling in love – *staying* in love - was fucking with my resolve not to be part of their number. So... yeah, it was definitely time for me to go. I needed a reset, bad.

"What's wrong with you?" Jac asked, catching me in the hallway where I had stopped to take a breath, and obsess about my current predicament. "Is that dried paint in your hair?" she asked, reaching to pick it out. "Oooh!" she exclaimed, rapidly putting the clues together. "You've been with Levi again, haven't you?"

"Mind your own business, baby sister," I said, waving her off.

She met that with a snicker as we headed to the elevator together. "You just saw me spread-eagled on your kitchen counter and it barely phased any of us. I don't think we have a barrier on where your business ends and mine begins," she suggested.

I laughed "You know, you may have a point there."

I considered it a blessing that Jac, Joia and I had never really gone through that phase that so many other sisters did, of not getting along. Sure, we got on each other's nerves sometimes, but I couldn't remember ever having that point where we like...weren't speaking to each other for longer than maybe a day, or anything like that.

As such, Jaclyn was right.

There was quite a blurry line between what I would and wouldn't tell my sisters. And the feeling was shared between all three of us. It's partially why Jac and I didn't really trip on Joia, weeks back when she was tight-lipped about who the father of her child was - or even the fact that she'd been with Teddy again at all. It was something she wanted to keep to herself, for whatever time she could, and we respected that.

Because... hell, we knew everything else anyway.

"I'm going to have to respectfully ask that next time you guys *don't* share that with me," I laughed as the elevator opened to let the two of us on. "I know we're close and all, but that's *real* close."

Jac laughed. "Yeah, cause I'm pretty sure whatever you and Levi were doing for you to have paint in your hair, is something I would not have wanted to walk in on."

I shook my head. "No, *you* definitely would not have wanted to be there for that. But... considering the tastes of the general public... we probably could've made good money on that."

"Oh y'all *nasty* nasty," Jaclyn accused, laughing.

"Hey," I shrugged, "I'm just trying to not have any regrets when I look back over this life, okay?"

Jac sucked her teeth. "And you don't think *not* locking Levi and his dick down is going to be something you look back on and wonder what in the world was your problem?"

"Duh. Why do you think I moved up my flight?" I asked, laughing. "Of course I wonder if it's a mistake. But making something of that is a possibility that I don't even feel equipped to process right now. So, I'm going to do what I always do."

"Go somewhere sunny and stop answering your phone?" Jaclyn asked, grinning as I answered with a nod.

"I've *always* said nobody knows me better than my sisters."

～

Levi Anders was the man of my dreams.
   Literally.

That face, that dick, that mouth, had all been making their way into my dreams, damn near every night.

Even before our little rendezvous at the gallery.

All part of what had fueled my incision to take off early. Last night had been especially vivid, leading me to wake up with wet panties and a really hard time not contacting him to get a live reenactment of the things my mind had played out during my slumber.

I hoped I wasn't making things worse.

Hoped I wasn't messing up.

That I wasn't employing an absence that would only make my pussy grow fonder.

That would *really* be messed up.

I sat back with a sigh in the airport lounge, pulling up a mindless, time-wasting game on my phone. I needed to distract my brain until it was time to get on this flight, with something other than visions and fantasies about what could never be with Levi.

Then, my phone rang.

"Jemma," my mom's voice rushed out in a panic, making me sit up straight in my chair. "Have you boarded your plane yet?" she asked.

"No, I haven't. Why? What's wrong?"

Mama sighed. "Your sister went into labor."

"*What?*" I asked. "Joia is *barely* seven months pregnant!"

"Yes," my mom agreed. "Which is exactly the problem. Dev and Joey did everything they could for them down at the hospital, but they can't stop it. The baby is coming *now*."

"Okay. Okay," I said, my hands shaking as I stood. "Okay, um... I'm leaving the airport now. I'll use the app to catch a ride. I'm on my way."

I didn't hesitate once I was off the phone with my mother to summon that ride and grab my carry-on, to get to the hospital for my sister. By the time I made it there, she was already in full-blown labor - Teddy and my mother were in the room with her.

Everyone else was out in the waiting room, including Teddy's parents. There wasn't much conversation going on, even though our two families got along well. We were worried about Joia and the baby on both sides. I took a seat between my dad and Jaclyn to do the only thing I *could* do.

Wait.

After about an hour had passed, the doors to Joia's room swung open. A whole team of people in scrubs and masks came rushing out, wheeling an incubator that undoubtedly carried my brand-new niece or nephew. They had to be heading to the NICU, to do whatever was necessary to make up for such an early delivery, and Teddy was right behind them, staying close to his baby.

My mother stepped out next, coming straight to us but addressing Teddy's parents too. "Joia is okay," she assured us. "They're getting her cleaned up, but I knew all you guys were out here waiting on an update. They're worried about the baby's lungs, but everything else looks good. They're confident he's going to be okay."

"He?" I asked, jumping up. "So it's a boy?"

My mother beamed, reaching for Teddy's mother's hand to grab and squeeze. "Yes. Theodore the third."

"Oh my goodness!" Teddy's mother sighed happily, and his father grinned. "We had no idea they were going to do that."

"You can go down to the NICU waiting area," Mama told her. "That's where Teddy will be, watching through the window as they get him settled. If it's not anything too major, which they didn't think it was. Joia insisted that he stay with the baby as much as he could, and I bet he could use some company."

They didn't waste any time – Teddy's parents went to go join him, and see if they could catch a peek of their new grandbaby. The Loves went to check on Joia first – there could only be so many people in the NICU at once anyway.

We walked in the room to find Joia looking fatigued, worried, but also deliriously happy as she spoke to Joseph. We hung back a little until they were done, and then made sure to speak to our cousin, but I was the first person at her bedside once she was free.

"Jo-jo," I gushed, leaning in to press my lips to her sweaty forehead. "Girl, you had a *baby*. Finally a boy on our side of the family."

She let out a tired laugh that really told the story about how exhausted she had to be. I'd just seen Joia earlier in the day – we'd had lunch together. She'd complained a little about feeling more tired than usual, and I'd walked her all the way up to the apartment after we were done with our sister date, just to make sure she was okay. We both thought it was just normal third-trimester fatigue, and didn't think too much more of it.

Apparently, we were wrong.

"It hurt like a bitch," Joia said, shaking her head. "We skipped the epidural because it all happened so fast. I am *never* doing this shit again."

We all laughed, and Jaclyn moved around to the other side of the bed, running her hands through Joia's wild hair to smooth it down.

"You took this one for the Love Sisters team," Jac said. "Cause this was stressful as hell for *me*, so I can't imagine how *you* must feel. Not to mention... you're the tough one. If you say this shit hurts, it *hurts*. Definitely ain't gone be no other grandbabies now."

My mother laughed. "See, I knew I shouldn't have brought them in here. You are scaring them from getting me the rest of my grandbabies, girl!"

We looked up as a Devyn came in to join our little group, coming up to the foot of Joia's bed. "Okay family, I know it's been a busy and emotional time, but we've got to let our newest mommy get some rest. We need her charged up and able to walk down to the NICU to get some skin on skin time with baby TJ as soon as possible, okay?"

"He's so tiny," Joia said, all the amusement leaving, replaced over again with worry. "But he's so beautiful. Head full of hair. We haven't gotten to hold him yet. I had to make Teddy go to make sure he's going to be okay."

"Of course he's going to be okay," Devyn assured. "Our NICU team is top notch."

"And you know Teddy is *not* going to let it be any other way," I added. "He would tear this place down for you and baby boy."

Joia nodded. "I know. I'm just... I just need this to be okay. We found a place," Joia told me. "After you dropped me off, he came by, and we looked through all our options again. We agreed on one. A place for the two - *three* of us together. A place for our family."

"And you *are* going to get to be a family, Jo," my mother assured her, the whole thing tugging at my heart in a way I hadn't anticipated and didn't welcome.

Selfishly.

Seeing Joia's concern about baby TJ, seeing that worried determination on Teddy's face as he'd raced down the hall behind the incubator... it certainly wasn't an ideal situation by any means, but still.

It was... *beautiful.*

And that beauty made it hard to not wonder if I was missing out by not wanting it for myself.

The trouble was, with the baby being here now, and especially under *these* circumstances... there was no running away from those feelings now. I couldn't up and leave with my sister and nephew in anything less than prime condition.

I had to figure out how to manage them.

EIGHT

Levi

Soon.
Just that thought put me in a better mood than I'd been in for days.

The cause of my less-than-cheery mood?

Simple.

My lack of contact with one Jemma Love.

I wasn't trying to be one of those dudes who just couldn't take the hint, so I hadn't sought her out. But I had to admit that it stung a little bit that she hadn't seen a need to employ the use of my number, which I had made sure to leave her with when we parted after our rendezvous at the center.

But I had to realize that was completely her prerogative.

Not a thing I could do about it.

Nothing, that is, except put my focus into my work. Not painting though, because the last thing I needed was to pour myself into another portrait of Jemma's face. No, I was focused now on these last few things required to get the center up and running, since the construction element of the renovation was pretty much complete.

Distraction was the name of the game.

"You said you were going to get this done, and I see you really made it happen."

I looked up from clipboard containing the final list of things we had to do to find Morgan - my homeboy and fellow artist - heading in my direction. He and I went way back, to the early days of social media, where we'd both been early adopters trying to make a name for ourselves.

I extended my hand to clap his, pulling him into a half hug. "Man, what are you doing all the way out here from Blackwood? Got the names inverted on your way home from some fancy gallery showing or something?"

Morgan chuckled, shaking his head. "Nah, bruh. I came out here to see what a real deal profess-sion-nal artist looks like in his element. You know, gotta come see what's what, gotta check things out if I'm trying to get like you."

"Fuck that – *you're* the one out here living it up. I'm trying to get like *you*, since you finally made that move on Elaine."

Morgan's eyebrows shot up. "Are you saying what I *think* you said?"

I shook my head. "If I'm honest with myself, not really. It's probably a pipe dream."

"I don't mean to be discouraging," Morgan said, "But yeah, you probably right. Your ass is the poster boy for all those solitary artist stereotypes, almost messing it up for the rest of us."

I couldn't be too offended about that, because he was right.

As much as I wanted Jemma - wanted her *bad* - the truth was that I *was* a great example of the "artist archetype". There were periods of time where all I wanted to do was be locked up somewhere in my studio for days at a time. Not beholden to anyone else, nobody waiting for me at home, nobody asking about me, questioning where I was, none of that. I just wanted to be able to be me.

Be *free*.

Too bad that didn't make me want Jemma any less.

"No offense taken," I told Morgan, shaking my head. "Mostly because you're right."

"Yeah," he said, "I know. It must be some kind of *special* woman that's got you having second thoughts though."

I laughed. "You know… that description sounds about accurate."

Morgan grinned. "Is this her?" he asked, pointing up to Jemma's portraits on my wall, and I nodded.

"Yep. That's her."

"She's beautiful," he complimented as he examined the picture. "And that's some nice ass brushwork. Good composition and layering, excellent tonal choices."

"Yeah," I agreed. "This is the level of excellence she pulls out of me."

"Okay…," Morgan turned back to face me. "That definitely makes it more understandable why you would want to lock her down. So what's the issue?"

"Uncertainty," I answered, and Morgan pulled his head back in disbelief.

"Uncertainty? I don't buy that at all. You are definitely the most certain motherfucker I know."

I laughed. "What does that even mean?" I asked.

"Man, we've known each other for how many years? You've been telling folks for years about what the type of artist you were going to be – how you were going to *be* somebody, even when nobody was trying to believe you. You were just another dude out here making corny ass art for Grandma's living room." He motioned around us. "But look at you now. Look at the clients who've commissioned you, your resume. This center. Look at what you've done. All because you were certain of your talent even when all those… notable art critics on social media were saying the exact opposite. So, I'm saying. If you stayed solid through that, then it doesn't make sense to me why you'd believe you're not fully capable of making a decision and sticking to it about this woman. Give me a different excuse, bro. What is the hold-up?"

"Okay, I see what this is," I said, shaking my head. "You finally stop playing games about Elaine, make that happen... and now you're the *hoe days are over* expert."

Morgan shrugged. "If the shoe fits, I got no problems wearing it," he laughed. "Seriously though - if you know you're feeling her, what's the problem with giving it a shot? Because it might not last? Shit, the same could be said for democracy, but you still vote, don't you?"

Again I laughed at his silly ass analogies. "Did I lie though?" he asked, and I couldn't do anything except shake my head in response. Because... no, he had not.

"I just don't want to pull her out of her comfort zone if I'm not even really sure I can be about that life."

Morgan nodded. "Okay, that I can respect. But tell me more about her not being about that life. You stressing over a woman that's not even checking for you?"

That was definitely a way to put it.

A *correct* way to put it.

"That's fairly accurate," I admitted. "This woman is... not exactly jumping up and down to be linked to me, or *anyone* for that matter. But we have this connection that's undeniable. So distinct that I'm afraid to pass it up."

"Oh so you're on some soulmate shit?" Morgan asked.

I shook my head. "No, I wouldn't exactly say that. But I *do* know that she motivates and inspires me in a way that no one else does."

Morgan blew out a breath. "That is pretty intense."

"Yeah," I agreed. "It's pretty intense. But that's just what our chemistry is like."

"Okay," Morgan said. "I get you. I see where you're coming from. But my thing is, if you're feeling her like this, and she's feeling you like this... even if there's some uncertainty on both parts..."

"Relax."

"Nah, this is like the type of shit where you get to be 85 years old, telling your biographer about this after your third divorce, cause you were searching for something you never could find again cause you let her go."

"That is wildly specific," I said. "Being in love really got your ass turning philosophical."

"You have to admit I'm right, though."

I shook my head. "You *might* have a point. But again, I'm not trying to push her into anything she doesn't want to do. It's really just not my vibe."

"Of course. I'm not saying you should knock her over the head and drag her off caveman style, but I *am* saying you have to at least make your position clear. If she's not with it, cool. But at least you won't have that regret on your mind. At least you tried. Right?"

Morgan *was* right.

Even as the conversation moved on to something else - to plenty of other things, as I took him on a full tour of the center to show him how everything was coming together - Jemma stayed at the back of my mind.

It wasn't *new* for Jemma to be at the back of my mind, but this...

This was different.

My mother had never been one to try to push me towards a marriage just so that she could get her grandkids - that really wasn't what she was about. That's not to say she didn't *want* them, just that she wasn't trying to pressure me into something that didn't fit with my lifestyle.

Her biggest concern was that she didn't want me to end up alone.

She had her own accomplishments, her own goals she'd met, dreams she'd reached, outside of her marriage to my father. But that didn't change the fact that she considered their relationship an enhancement to her life – one of the things she treasured most.

And of course I did too, considering the fact that their relationship had produced me.

The real point though, was that she found a high value in having someone standing alongside her, someone to spend her life with. And she wanted the same thing for me.

She had a point.

I could absolutely see the value of it, and could even see it for my own life.

I just wasn't sure I was ready to make the trade-off in freedom.

Honestly though... if Jemma were standing in front of me right now, and said *"Yes, let's do this. Let's make it happen."*

I would take her up on it in a heartbeat.

What did that shit even mean?

That I would throw away all my convictions, everything I thought I knew and understood about my personal desires for an intimate relationship... for this is one woman.

"Damn bro," Morgan said clapping me on the shoulder when I hadn't said anything for a while. "You've really got it bad."

Yeah.

I really fucking did.

Once Morgan had left, I went back to my studio to retrieve my clipboard again, intending to get back to work. But, before I could regain my focus, the latest addition to my wall caught my attention.

The masterpiece I'd co-created with Jemma.

I'd sealed and finished the canvas, mounting it on a frame. Obviously, I had no idea if something *so* intimate, so intensely private, would ever be made visible to the world. But for now, I could certainly admire our work of art.

One that could be the last.

Shit.

The idea of that... almost made me sick to my damn stomach.

And... it wasn't just about the sex, it was... the thought of being around her, engaging in conversation, seeing that pretty ass smile... and, yes, putting a look of pleasure on her face.

Morgan was right.

I put my clipboard down, and took my cell phone out, navigating to Joseph Wright's number. Then, I thought better of it, going to

Devyn's instead, since she was the one who'd been not-so-subtly trying to hook me and her cousin up.

She had the information I needed to... do *something*, at least.

If Jemma wasn't interested, fine, that was a possibility I could handle.

But not even *trying*?

Nah... that wasn't an option.

NINE

JEMMA

I really tried not to be *that* girl.
I wasn't really into the whole "ghosting" people thing, or ignoring them, which is why I tried to simply not give contact information to people I didn't want to have it. If I willingly gave it to someone, and I decided I didn't want to be in contact anymore, I was good for simply saying so.

If they kept it up after that, my block button was always available.

But, when someone was respectful, weren't getting out of line or anything like that, I tried to be decent and not leave them hanging.

Which is why *not* responding to Levi's text really made me feel like shit.

It wasn't even anything that serious, just a simple request for us to get together and talk. Still, it may as well have been a request for me to solve all the unanswered questions of the universe.

Hell...

That might actually be easier.

"Earth to Jemma," Toni said, snapping me out of my daydreaming. "That was a pretty intense ten-mile stare you had going on there."

"Sorry," I said. "What were we talking about?" I asked, sticking my cell phone back into my pocket, and returning to my task of signing books. These were for general stock, not just at Tones&Tomes, but ones that would be shipped out to bookstores across the world.

"We were talking about a new book - about when to travel to certain places, travel deals, suggestions for international girls' trips, solo sabbaticals, etc. An actual guide this time, instead of your memoirs, like the first book."

I lifted my eyebrows. "You *barely* got the first book out of me," I laughed. "You're trusting me with a second one?"

"Well, your *audience* trusts you with a second one," Toni countered. "They've been asking for it. I know you won't let *them* down."

She was right.

Probably.

Before the book had even really been a possibility, my brand had been built on people following me to see pictures and commentary from where I was going. There were plenty of women who voyaged indirectly through me. While my travel was for my own gratification, I had to admit, I did often make sure that I did certain things while I was in certain places simply for the cool factor. So that people could – even just vicariously - see places they might normally not.

I was definitely in this for me, but I was in it for *them* too.

"Well, if you think it's a good idea, I'm all for it. I *need* something to occupy my brain."

Yes, I was sticking around because Joia had the baby, but a week had passed since then, and baby TJ was still in the NICU. Which meant Joia and Teddy were spending all their time at the hospital.

I showed my face every day, bringing them hot meals, fresh clothes, and doing my best to provide general entertainment. But mostly, they were really wrapped up in their own little family unit right now, which I wasn't offended by at all. It was a stressful time while they waited on the doctors to do everything baby TJ needed.

There really wasn't space for me to be around.

Which, again, was fine.

But Joia having her baby was really the reason I had stuck around Blakewood. I wasn't ready to leave yet, with that situation still not being in the clear. But in the meantime, I was definitely going to need something to do.

Someone to do wasn't an option.

"Why do I feel like there's a story there?" Toni asked. "Spill the beans, girly," she said, leaning across the bookstore counter.

"Just the usual *"do I really want to settle down and give up my freedom"* existential crisis."

"*Ahhh*," Toni grinned. "I know *plenty* about that one."

I scoffed. "Right, and here you are about to freaking get *married*. And adopting a child!"

"What can I say," Toni shrugged. "Life comes at you fast."

"*Real fast*," I agreed. "I just... I wish I knew what to do."

"Okay," Toni said. "So you're struggling with this. What is it, *exactly*, that appeals to you about settling down? What are the things that even really make it a consideration for you? What are the pros?"

"The pros? A hot body in my bed. Somebody I can count on. Good, consistent dick. Someone I can hold a conversation with, who makes me laugh. Consistently."

"Those are definitely some pretty strong pros," Toni laughed. "But okay, now what about the cons?"

I sighed. "I think... not being able to come and go as I please. Having to consider someone else's needs. The possibility of someone coming along and wanting to clip my wings."

"Again, understandable," Toni agreed. "But what if there was somebody who would give you the consistency you're looking for, without trying to stifle you?" After she said that, Toni tipped her head to the side. "Wait though," she said. "I guess that might be kind of a unicorn, right?"

I pushed out another, deeper sigh. "Maybe so," I said. "But then also maybe not. There *is* someone who kind of makes me wonder. Well... more than *kind of*, actually. He makes me wonder a *lot*."

"Wow," Toni exclaimed. "Are you serious right now? Jemma Love, captivated by someone."

"Yeah," I breathed. "Crazy, right?"

"Tell me about him," she demanded. "Tell me everything."

"There's really not a lot to tell that you don't already know. If you need a refresher, you could... just turn back to chapter five in my book."

Toni's eyes went big. "You're *seeing* Mister Chapter Five?!"

"Well, *seeing* is not quite what I'd call what I've done a couple of times with Mister Chapter Five since the book released. I'm having a hard time *not* letting it become that though."

"Why wouldn't you — oh shit, never mind. you already told me that, Toni said. Okay so... what are you going to do? Are you going to let it become something, or are you going to keep running scared?"

"*Wow*. You too, Toni? Is *everybody* really just going to give me the business like this?"

"What *should* we do?" Toni asked. "Do you want me to lie to you?"

"No, of course not. It's just that...honestly, I really don't know what I'm going to do. I feel like I know what I *should* do, but I'm scared," I admitted. "There it is, no denying it anymore. Jemma Love is scared to be serious with anyone, in case she falls in love and that nigga ruins her amazing life. *Boom*, there it is."

Toni grinned. "Well, I'm certainly proud of you for putting it all out there, and being honest with yourself. And, might I say, that as someone who has definitely had her heart broken before, please know that I understand exactly how you feel. Honestly, it was part of why I started traveling too. To avoid settling in."

"But you *are* settled in," I reminded her. "*Engaged and a mother* settled in."

"Yeah, when the right person happened along. Remember, I was engaged before Justin."

I nodded. "Yeah I know, and that motherfucker was *fine* too."

Toni laugh. "Yes, he was. But I had reservations. I *knew* he wasn't right for me. That wedding was never going to actually happen. But with Justin, once I got over our unfortunate pause in friendship, that is. It just feels right with him. But I was scared, and he *did* fuck up a bit at first. Yes, I did have some fear. But once I opened my mind to the possibility and decided to just let it be what it *so clearly* already was... I knew for sure. Justin was it."

"So... what are you saying I should do?" I asked, completely enthralled by what she was telling me.

"I'm suggesting that you stop overthinking it. Give it a chance. If it doesn't work, it just doesn't work, and you move on. You let the chapter end."

Hm.

I guess that didn't sound so bad.

I finished signing my stack of books and said my goodbyes to Toni in the back stockroom. I had a million things going through my mind as I headed back up to the front of the store, so many that I barely realized Levi was in the bookstore until I almost walked into him.

He was, unsurprisingly, browsing the art history section.

"So, she lives," he quipped, looking *good as hell* in a simple tee and cargo shorts.

An obvious jab at my lack of response to the text message he'd sent me.

"I'm sorry," I told him. "I swear, I wasn't ignoring your text. I just didn't know what to say to it."

"You say *yes,* Jemma," he prompted with a smile.

As if it was so easy.

"Right," I nodded. "I say yes, we end up in bed, and you've gotten all you needed from me. A little ass and your next inspiration for your art."

"That's what you think?" he asked, eyebrows raised.

"Is that *not* what this is? You were the one who set this precedent between us."

"Am I?" He scoffed. "Or was that simply all you would agree to? I've maintained, since we reconnected, that I wanted to get to know you, Jemma. The possibility of being my muse was the only thing you responded to."

"So why don't you tell me what this is then, Levi? Tell me what you're looking for from me. Tell me what *this* is about."

"It's about me being willing to step outside of a self-imposed box to explore what could be between us, instead of letting it skirt past."

"And *what*, exactly do you think this could be?" I asked

"Whatever we'd like it to be. Nothing we don't want it to be. Everything we *do*."

I pushed my hair back over my shoulder, suddenly feeling a little bit overheated. "Here you go again," I said. "Saying exactly what I want to hear."

"Okay, now the question is, are you going to see it as game, or are you going to see it how *I* see it. As the intensity of our connection continuing to draw us together."

I smiled and shook my head. "I don't know how I'm going to see it Levi. And I don't know what I'm going to do."

"Would you like me to tell you?" He asked.

I was tired.

Not physically, but mentally and emotionally I was downright *exhausted* from trying to figure this out. I didn't want to consider things, or explore the possibilities, or weigh my options.

I wanted it to just be *plain*.

"Yes," I told him. "I want you to tell me what to do."

"Come to the Center opening next week," he said.

"And what about right now?" I asked.

"Right now... you come home with me. And you stay until morning."

I THINK I MIGHT WANT YOU

Can you stop overthinking this for just two seconds?

I posed that question to myself as I stood on the other side of Levi's kitchen counter, watching him prepare a meal for the two of us. It was simple, supposedly, just a salad that would be topped with shrimp he was grilling at his stovetop right now. He claimed it was the only thing he knew how to make, but somehow, I felt like that wasn't true.

"I'm not sure if this is going to be up to standard for a palette as refined as yours," he teased turning to me with a smile. "I don't know if I can compete with your worldwide experience, as important as food seemed in your book."

I smiled over the fact that he'd *actually* read more than just the sexy parts, then replied, "Contrary to popular belief, I'm really not a picky eater. I enjoy good food, period. But it doesn't have to be fancy to be good."

"Well that makes me feel a lot better, because *this* is definitely not fancy," he said, taking the shrimp off the fire and washing his hands before moving back to the handmade remoulade dressing he'd been working on.

"I really think that your *not fancy* would defy a lot of people's definition of that," I said. "Whatever you're doing over there, it smells really amazing."

"Thank you. And thank you for giving me this time. I asked you over here on a whim, so I'm glad I had something in the fridge at all. Figured if I was interrupting your day, at least I could fix you lunch."

"I must say... you sure do know how to make a girl feel welcome."

"Do I?" he asked, turning to me with a raised eyebrow. "Cause I was starting to think you really didn't want anything to do with me. Starting to think I smelled bad or something."

I shook my head, laughing. "No, not that at all. Like I said... I'm just trying to figure myself out. The only reason I didn't answer that text was because I didn't know what to say."

"Yes, you said that," he reminded me. "And I thought I made it clear there was only one thing to say."

"We talked about this, Levi. I know you like to be on your Floetry, *all you gotta do is say yes*, but... just because you want something to be a certain way, doesn't make it so."

"But I don't believe that applies to this situation," he said. "To *our* situation. I understand that you're concerned about commitment, and I'm not trying to be the one who forces you into a situation where you're not going to be happy. But what I *would* like is for you to at least give it some consideration. With the understanding that I'm a very flexible man, Jemma. I'm not asking for you to stay *here*," he said, waving a hand to motion at his beautiful big house like it was a prison - showing me that he understood that's exactly what it would be for *me*. "I'm not trying to have you in this kitchen, barefoot and pregnant, none of that. That's just not where I am right now, and I know it's not where you are either. Maybe neither of us will *ever* want that."

"You are absolutely right," I nodded. "I don't want to feel smothered. I don't want to feel stifled. I don't want to feel handcuffed to any place, or to anyone."

He smirked. "Why do I feel like that sentence has a "but" that goes with it?"

"Because it does," I confirmed, grinning. "*But*, I don't quite know how to articulate it."

"So how about for now, we don't even try? Right now, it's not even important. We can talk about something else, while we eat. How about that?"

"Well, it depends on what you want to talk about."

"Anything," he answered. "Everything. Whatever your heart desires."

I thought about it for a second, then looked him in the face.

"What if I don't want to talk at all?" I asked. "What if I want to eat this salad and then have you take me up to your bedroom and make love to me until we pass out?"

Levi smiled. "Well, love... All you gotta do..."

TEN

JEMMA

"If I die from this cuteness, promise you'll make sure I'm remembered well," I told Joia as I held up my cellphone, pointing through the window of the NICU with my camera app. Teddy's big fine ass was in there, bare-chested, cradling a tiny, curly-haired baby TJ in his arms, getting in that ultra-important skin-to-skin time.

I was pretty sure it was *the* most adorable thing I'd ever seen, and I'd seen a lot of cute shit in my life.

"He is *so* insanely sweet with that baby," Joia said, shaking her head as I put the camera down and shoved my cell back into my pocket. "I mean, I knew how he was going to be as a father, I could tell really easily. But seeing it in action? That is this whole other panty-wetting thing that inexplicably makes me want to give him three or four more. It's a fucking setup, is what it is."

I chuckled. "It is *absolutely* a setup."

"Okay so anyway though," Joia said, grabbing me by the arm and pulling me away from the waiting room. "As much as I love these two,

I really need you to talk to me about anything *except* the NICU. What happened to you yesterday? I thought you were coming back up here."

I pushed out a sigh, and shook my head. "Well, yeah I intended to. Right after I finished signing those books up at Tones&Tomes. But then... I ran into Levi again."

"*Again?*" Joia asked. "Girl, will you finally just admit that this shit is fate?"

I groaned. "Oh my *God*, I am sick to death of that." I huffed. "Yes, I realize it's fate. And it doesn't make the shit any less scary."

Joia's face dropped into a sympathetic grimace. "I'm sorry, for adding to the noise. But just give me a second here, okay?"

Honestly?

I'd give Joia a lot more than a second.

I loved the hell out of both of my sisters, but when it really came down to it, Joia was easily the most level-headed of the three of us - the one who wasn't really swayed by outside pressures to do something she didn't want to do.

Aspirational.

"I don't think you should do *shit* that you're scared of," she started. "Well, let me rephrase that - I don't think that you should make any rushed decisions based on fear. My thing is, if it's meant to be, it's going to be. And his ass can wait for you to be ready to make a move. If it's really supposed to be, once you have time to mull and think over your decision, his ass will be right there," she insisted. "It's really easy for me, for Jac, for mom, to have a whole lot to say about what you should do. "*Stop playing girl, you know you want that man. Why don't you just do this? Why don't you do that?*" Uh, because you're fucking scared! Nobody's trying to talk them into a room full of killer clowns or some shit like that, so guess what? You don't have to *this shit* either. My vote - even though, for the record, I *do* think Levi would be a good look for you - is for you to take every little bit of time you need to make a decision that works for you."

"That's really how you feel?" I asked.

I THINK I MIGHT WANT YOU

Joia nodded. "Girl, hell yes. We're both in the public eye, right? This social media thing has everybody who follows us - *or not* - feeling like they have some real input over our lives. But nobody but us has to actually *live* these lives, Jem. If it's supposed to be with Levi, it'll be. You know what I *really* think you should do?" She asked.

"*Of course* I want to know what you *really* think I should do," I said.

"Instead of catching these feelings, you should catch a *flight*. Get away from all of this, and just go be Jemma. If Levi *isn't* waiting for you when you get back, oh well. The world has never had a shortage of niggas, and it's not about to have one now. *His loss.*"

Hm.

I followed my little sister's advice.

And by following her advice, I found myself on what was intended to be a week-long, mostly self-guided tour of Barcelona. Filled with delicious indulgence in Spanish food, loads of flirting with fine ass Spanish men, and plenty of time to think and reflect.

The conclusion I ended up coming to?

That I'd rather be back in Blakewood with my family.

And Levi.

My wistfulness wasn't a sign that I needed to be back in Blackwood permanently by any means. But it definitely felt like *this* wasn't where I wanted to be right now.

That was supposed to be the beauty of this nomadic lifestyle, not feeling tied to any certain place for any certain time. But the other side of that was always having at least *somewhere* that felt like home.

Home was calling me.

And so was that nagging ass tether to Levi.

Even in all my flirting and exploring, in one of my favorite cities in the world, I still found my thoughts drawn back to him.

Which was maybe the point of Joia's advice.

If nothing else, I felt like I'd made a good decision by coming on this trip, to give myself the reset I'd been trying to employ for a while.

Still, I found myself on social media late in my room one night, scrolling for an inkling of what was happening in Levi's life.

He hadn't called. Which was fine – neither had I.

He'd said he was going to let me make the decision for myself, and I appreciated the lack of pressure he tried to employ when I wasn't around him.

Levi wasn't super active on his social accounts, but there was one image that he'd posted just yesterday that immediately made me smile.

"*Just a few more days...*", the caption read, under a picture of the nearly completed *Marie Anders Art Center*. I remembered him asking me to come to the opening, but my trip wasn't supposed to be over for several more days – past the date of the opening. Still... I navigated to my internet browser to purchase a flight.

If nothing else, I was a woman of my word.

In the meantime, I'd promised my Barcelona guide that I would accompany her to her friend's birthday party. Usually, I was the kind of girl that was *always* up for a party, but my energy was a little half-hearted as I did my hair and makeup, and put on a dress to go out.

But I did it, I'd promised, and Valencia was a wonderful guide. She'd shown me lots of little-known treasures about the city, and had helped cement my love for it.

Whoever her friend was, they must have had *money* because the party was taking place in a gorgeous Spanish hacienda style home. The stucco walls were covered in ivy and patina, decorated with tiny white string lights that made the whole thing really romantic and beautiful.

High-end liquor flowing, great music, and a whole lot of beautiful people showing a lot of glowing brown skin – this was *exactly* my vibe.

But tonight...I was just *there*.

That is, until the tiny hairs on my arms stood up with a sudden prickle of recognition.

My body was reacting to a familiar energy.

I THINK I MIGHT WANT YOU

When I turned around... there was Levi.

It took my breath away.

He had to have noticed me before I noticed him, because when I turned, he was already staring in my direction. He looked good as usual, dressed in white linen that could have very, very easily have been really corny on anybody else.

On him, it was downright decadent.

He had a drink in his hand, and he raised it in my direction, a move that made me feel like he was tugging on some imaginary string that drew me closer to him.

"You know what this is, right?" he asked, as soon as I approached him.

"I do," I nodded. "But don't say it."

"I won't," he agreed, giving me that sexy grin. "You look amazing."

"You don't look so bad yourself. What are you doing here?"

He gestured around us. "The homeowner is an art collector, and a good friend of mine. It's his birthday, and I needed a little bit of a getaway to take a little bit of a breather before the center opens."

"Ah," I nodded. "That's probably wise. Well, I'll let you get back to the party. I just couldn't see you and not say hello."

Levi grabbed my hand before I could move even an inch away, pulling me into his body. His eyes raked my face with animalistic intensity before his mouth broke into a smile. "Don't play with me, Jemma." he said. "I was ready to get out of here, but something was holding me back. For some reason, I couldn't make myself leave. Now I see why."

"So what exactly are you proposing?" I asked, breathless from the way he'd snatched me against him.

With his other hand, he took a sip of whatever was in his glass. "I'm proposing that we... recreate our time in Havana," he said.

There was no need for a verbal response.

I just nodded, because I couldn't think of *anything* I wanted more.

Levi.

I wasn't remotely surprised when I woke up back in Blakewood without Jemma in my bed. I would have been more surprised if she *had* been there. I was, however, shocked to wake up in my little bungalow in Barcelona to find her still there.

Happily.

So I made the most of it.

And for the next two days, she and I did exactly what we'd done in Havana, and then we parted ways because I had to get back to Blakewood for the final preparations at the center. I didn't ask Jemma when she was coming back to Blakewood, didn't ask if she was planning to attend the opening, because in the grand scheme of things neither of those things mattered. Jemma was going to be where Jemma wanted to be, and I didn't want anything more than that from her.

But... I'd be lying if I said it didn't make me happy as hell when, at the center's opening, I turned a corner to find Jemma standing there. In a dress seemingly designed to induce heart attacks, staring up at one of the pieces in the gallery.

I tried my best not to get distracted from the people I was talking to - the mayor of the city and a couple of other people from his entourage. I forced myself to stay engaged with the conversation, to graciously accept their congratulations and thanks about opening the center, and their pledge of city resources to keep it going. Those things were amazing, and I was grateful. This building was packed with people who were all interested in what was happening here, people who were interested in supporting the vision, and supporting *me*.

But all I wanted to do was get to Jemma.

When I managed to get away, Jemma was still in the same place, fascinated by the particular piece she was looking at. I walked up to her, placing a hand at the small of her back, and it was so, *so* gratifying that rather than move away or look surprised, she melted into my touch.

"*Unfathomable Connections*," she said, reading the name of the piece - one of the largest here in the gallery. "*Artists, Levi Anders... and Jemma Love.*" She looked at me with this mischievous glint in her eyes. "This is a rather bold move, Mr. Anders. You have a little naughty streak in you."

"I didn't make this by myself, Jemma," I told her, turning my gaze up to observe the canvas too. "I seem to recall having some very eager assistance."

Indeed, I had not made this by myself, and to the casual observer it had to just look like an abstract piece.

But she and I knew what it was about.

"So you made it," I continued. "To the opening, I mean."

She turned to me, looking up to meet my eyes. "I told you I would."

"Yes, but I also haven't heard from you since Barcelona... so I'm sure you can understand it if I wasn't quite sure what my place was with you."

"Well, that would make two of us," she admitted. "All I know is, I like being around you."

"Okay. So let me propose this: Whenever in Blakewood, you consider my home open to you. Whether I'm there or not. I have that big empty house, plenty of room. We wouldn't even have to see each other if we didn't want to."

At first, her face was relatively expressionless, but it quickly became clear that she was trying to suppress a smile. Eventually it became impossible, and she had to let it break free, but quickly tempered it into a close-mouthed grin.

"Okay. That is a *very* attractive offer... And I think I'll accept that."

"Terrific," I told her, happily.

Was it a little intense?

Yeah, it was.

But it also felt right, and there was no downplaying how much her acceptance pleased me.

"Can I make a counter-offer?" She asked, tipping her head to the side. "Well, not really a counter-offer, I guess. More like... something that would sweeten the pot."

"Absolutely." I pushed my hands into the pockets of my slacks, giving her my full attention. Not that she didn't already have it, but I was even more interested now.

"Well, it was quite nice to see you in Barcelona. And... I was thinking... maybe... what if I shared my travel schedule with you? And if you happened to be in the same place I was, we could spend a few days getting reacquainted. I... wouldn't hate that. I'd actually like it very much. I mean, when our schedules aligned of course. If you wanted to. I wouldn't expect you to—"

Before she could finish overthinking something I thought would be a perfect compromise and alignment of our values, I pulled my hands from my pockets to grab either side of her face and pulled her in for a kiss, something I'd wanted to do since I walked up to her.

She melted right into *that* too.

A few seconds later, I heard an unsurprising chorus of wolf whistles and other encouragement of our public display of affection.

Shit.

I've gotten a little too wrapped up in the moment, and hadn't considered the fact that we were in an extremely public place, with all kinds of press and other people there, including members of both of our families. This moment was probably being uploaded to social media right as we stood there.

Jemma didn't seem to care though.

She laughed, then pressed herself up to plant another soft kiss against my lips. "This is your night," she reminded me. "You have interviews and stuff to give."

I nodded, knowing she was right. "Will you be here?" I asked, not giving a single fuck if it sounded thirsty. Because... hell, it was. And

Jemma Love was my refreshingly sensual, limited edition drink of choice.

She gave me the kind of smile that heated me from the inside out and nodded. "Right now... I don't want to be anywhere else."

The end.

EPILOGUE

~ two years later ~

Jaclyn

"What exactly is the purpose of this again?" Kadan asked, from his shirtless position beside Kenzo. They were both holding today's main attractions - a kitten in one hand, a cup of ice cream in the other.

"Squint a little more," I demanded, ignoring his objections to my obvious objectification. I got their fine asses perfectly framed in the shot and then snapped it with my camera phone. "Perfect," I declared, then immediately navigated to the appropriate apps to upload the image to both the pet clinic and *Dreamery* social media pages.

Today was a big day.

The vet clinic parking lot was teeming with people, and I was confident that my impromptu marketing just now would attract even more. Visitors were here from all over the state for the pet adoption drive the clinic was co-hosting, featuring hopeful animals from nearly every shelter in a hundred-mile radius of Blakewood. While they looked at pets - and hopefully started the paperwork to take one home - they were treated to ice cream from one of the many mobile carts sponsored by *Dreamery*.

There were other sponsors from local businesses nearby, but mostly, this was a joint venture put on by Kadan and me.

Coochies & Cream.

It had taken a little convincing to get him on board with the name, but now it was on all the banners, flyers, and whatever else I'd been able to slap it on, because it was perfect.

"What are you going to tell people when they see that picture and come up here asking where the hoes at?" Kadan asked, pulling his *Blakewood Animal Clinic* tee shirt back over his head.

"I'm gonna point them in your direction, duh," I teased, smacking him on the ass. "How many adoptions were we at, at last count?"

"My last count before you turned this into Magic Mike was sixteen."

I grinned. "See? And you thought it wasn't going to work."

"I never thought the adoption drive wasn't going to work," he countered, following me into the cool, air-conditioned comfort of the clinic. "I thought the sexual innuendo would stop people from bringing their kids."

I sucked my teeth. "Fuck them kids," I laughed. "But you see they're out there anyway, don't you?"

"I do." He pulled the clipboard I was holding from my hands and put it on the counter, out of the way so he could draw me into his arms. "I shouldn't have doubted you, Ms. Love."

"Damn right." I puckered my lips for a kiss and he obliged, shamelessly pulling me into a full-bodied make out that was much deeper than the quick peck I expected.

When we pulled back, he met my gaze with full-blown lust that had me ready to forget we had a lot full of people outside. Instead of giving in to it though, I gave him a teasing grin as I pulled away, holding up my hand.

"How would you feel if I kept my last name?" I asked, wiggling my fingers so that the engagement ring he'd put there just last week could catch the light. "I don't know if *Mrs. Davenport* is going to have the same... *je ne sais quoi* as Love."

Kadan chuckled. "Woman, long as you *coucher avec moi ce soir* or whatever the fuck Patti said, I'll call you whatever you want."

My eyes went wide. "Don't tell me Judge Auntie was a disco fan?"

"Had Patti and her sisters in my ear every damn Saturday morning," Kadan confirmed, grabbing my hand to pull me back toward him. "As consistently as I'm trying to be in your guts, even after you're Mrs.... DickyMcStrangerballs."

I cackled laughing at that, but that was quickly stifled by his lips on mine again, and I melted into my future husband.

"We gotta get back out there," he said, even though his hands were gripping my ass in a way that didn't inspire me to go back outside.

Still, I knew he was right.

As if she knew too, Ms. Thing came from wherever she'd been hiding in the back, meowing and making the usual noise. She went straight to the window, putting her paw against the glass, and I followed the direction she was looking until I saw something that made me smile.

"Her friend is here," I told Kadan, grabbing his hand to pull him toward the door. "Come on."

Joia

"Look who it is, TJ! Look!"

I couldn't help the big smile on my face over TJs reaction to the sight of Ms. Thing in Jaclyn's arms. I didn't know what it was between my baby and that damn cat, but they had the most epic of friendships going on.

TJ - Theodore James, not junior - wiggled his way out of Teddy's arms, and Ms. Thing did the same with Jaclyn, allowing the two of them to run together like they were star-crossed lovers in some emo romance novel.

Teddy threw up his hands in defeat while we watched TJ - usually a wrecking ball of energy - interact ever-so-gently with the cat, using his budding vocabulary to tell her about... trains, I think.

I reached up, circling my hand against Teddy's back. "It's okay baby," I soothed him, teasingly. Whenever TJ got around animals - *especially* Ms. Thing - he tended to forget we existed.

Teddy shrugged it off, turning to me with a grin. "It's fine. The boy is just developing an early appreciation for pus—"

"Can you not?" I interrupted, and Teddy pursed his lips, nodding.

"I can, indeed, *not*," he agreed. "I knew it wasn't right when it was coming out of my mouth, but it's like I couldn't stop it, you know?"

"What are y'all whispering about over here?" Jaclyn asked, suddenly a lot closer than she'd been a few seconds ago. When I glanced around her, TJ was in Kadan's arms, and Ms. Thing was perched on his shoulder, something that seemed to greatly amuse my baby.

"Trying to peep this ice cream," Teddy told her, rubbing his hands together. "I heard you were the plug."

Jaclyn's head dropped, playing along. "Yeah nigga, I got that lemon verbena, brown sugar apricot, tiramisu, got it in scoops, pints, quarts. I *own* this block and listen - we got whatever you need."

We laughed at her antics, and then on a slightly more serious note she sent us off to explore, assuring us that she and Kadan could handle TJ.

I didn't have to be told twice - I grabbed Teddy's hand, and we went the other way, where the vendor stands were all set up.

"You know you should be out here with them, right?" Teddy asked in my ear, his hand perched at the small of my back as we walked down the line.

"Don't start...," I warned.

"I'm just saying, baby - Joia's Joyous Jambalayas should be out here represented."

Any annoyance I felt about him bringing up this topic was instantly erased by today's ridiculous name suggestion. I'd made the mistake of telling him I wanted to - with my brand-new nutrition certification - *officially* get into the meal planning and preparation business, based on the hundreds of people I'd helped with their diet. It was a good idea, especially in the face of so many people with any real credentials scamming people with harmful, unsustainable pipe dreams that left them worse off than they started.

Why was it a mistake?

Well, because mentioning it to Teddy meant he was going to hold me to it.

"You don't like that one?" he asked, pulling me into him with a grin. "I'm gonna stop suggesting shit to you. I should've stopped after you pretended "Don't Eat *THAT* Shit. Eat THIS Shit." Wasn't absolute *flames*."

"DETSETS was *easily* the worst," I giggled. "I was pretty partial to *Real Meal Plan Shit* myself."

"Okay so why aren't we out here with a booth, blasting some Stallion, some Vanity. Or y'all don't do Hot Girl Summers no more?"

Instantly, I scowled at him. "Don't even mention that to me - need I remind you this is the second summer body you'll have ruined for me, in the past three years? Not to mention *last* summer, when I was marrying your ass. I haven't had a *Hot Girl Summer* since I let you hit again."

My ugly expression didn't last long in the face of Teddy's grin - he was way too thrilled about the course of things between us.

TJ.

A summer wedding almost a year ago.

And now… another positive pregnancy test.

Not live streamed this time.

This time, I was well versed enough with the symptoms that I'd immediately known something was up. Sure enough, I'd presented a positive pregnancy test to my husband this morning.

"Sexy Spring Equinox?" Teddy suggested, grinning. "Cause I don't think you're gonna make winter solstice."

"You make me so damn sick, "I laughed, shaking my head as I pulled my ringing cell phone from the pocket of my jeans.

"My baby is doing that, actually, Teddy quipped, and I flipped him off as I answered the call from Jemma.

"Hey big head. What's going on?"

Jemma

"Hey big head. What's going on?"
I grinned at Levi as he stepped back into the room, right when Joia answered the phone. He was in nothing but boxer briefs, carrying a tray that held what I recognized as mimosas and omelets. I had to look away from him, so I could focus on call I'd made.

"Where are you?" I asked her. "You at Jac's thing yet?"

"We just got here, maybe ten minutes ago. You're still coming right?"

"Absolutely. I was about to get ready to head out now, but umm... Something just came up, so I might be a little while."

Joia giggled. "Mmmhm. Something came up. You and Levi don't make any babies."

"My IUD is locked and loaded, believe me," I quipped back, my gaze turning back to Levi as he sat the tray down and climbed into the bed with me.

"Clink clink!" Joia teased, and then we got off the phone so I could give my attention to Levi, who I hadn't seen in several weeks.

"I thought I was quiet when I came in," I told him, accepting his lips as he leaned in toward me.

345

He nipped my bottom lip with his teeth, then soothed it with his tongue. "You were. I didn't know you were here until this morning. Felt you when I woke up."

"And decided to bring breakfast in bed. Aren't you a gentleman," I mused, picking up my mimosa and taking a drink to cover the fact that his *"felt you this morning"* thing was... sexy as hell.

He didn't mean physically - he'd slept in the master bedroom, while I'd taken the guest room we'd, without needing to discuss it, designated as mine.

He meant *intuitively*.

"Well, you took great care of me in more ways than one in Lagos last month," he growled into my ear, then sat back to pick up his own glass. "This is a small way to return the favor."

I laughed. "I enjoyed Lagos *just* as much as you did, trust me." I picked up my plate. "What do you have going on today?"

"Nothing too heavy. I'm due at *Coochies and Cream* in about an hour. I donated two hours of quick portraits of people with their new pets."

I nodded. "So you're already going anyway. I was going to ask if you wanted to come with me."

Levi's eyebrows shot up, and he choked a bit on the forkful of omelet he'd just put in his mouth. "You were going to let me be seen with you?" he asked. "Is it already a new quarter?"

"Oh shut up," I laughed. "I'm not that bad, am I?"

Levi grinned. "You're not, I'm only teasing you, love. I did think you were going to throw blows in Curacao though, with that woman who wouldn't stop taking pictures of us."

Ugh.

My nose turned up at just the memory of it.

Even though sex with Levi was amazing, and we got in plenty of it, we did enjoy other things as well. There - for us, at least - had to be more to having a "traveling bae" than just sex in exotic locations.

I wanted to make out in public in exotic locations too.

Obviously, we weren't just making out - we were exploring the world together, finding each other at least once a month at this point. And the last thing I wanted, after not having seen him for weeks, was some nosy chick with her cell phone pointed at us long enough to shoot a feature fucking film.

Obviously, I was still annoyed about it.

But that didn't stop me from wanting to do things with Levi, embracing the evolution of our relationship as it happened.

I kept getting asked to write a book about it.

I wasn't sure about *that*, since I barely believed this arrangement was actually working for *me,* and couldn't dare recommend it for someone else, as if I were an expert. For now, I was just focused on enjoying the happiness I'd carved out of this life.

"You're gonna make me lose my appetite," I threatened.

He shook his head. "Well we definitely don't want that. I worked hard on these omelets."

"Exactly," I nodded. "So let's eat. And then you can paint me like one of your French girls."

Levi laughed. "Yes, let's eat. And then I'm definitely gonna do something to you. But painting wasn't what I had in mind."

ABOUT THE AUTHOR

Christina C. Jones is a modern romance novelist who has penned many love stories. She has earned a reputation as a storyteller who seamlessly weaves the complexities of modern life into captivating tales of black romance.

ALSO BY CHRISTINA C. JONES

THE CLARKE BROTHERS

Collision Course

Controlled Chaos

Close Contact

THE WRIGHT BROTHERS

Getting Schooled

Pulling Doubles

Bending the Rules

THE LOVE SISTERS

I Think I Might Love You

I Think I Might Need You

I Think I Might Want You

SUGAR VALLEY

The Culmination of Everything

The Point of It All

INEVITABLE SERIES

Inevitable Conclusions

Inevitable Seductions

Inevitable Addiction

THE TROUBLE SERIES

The Trouble With Love: a tale of two sisters

The Trouble With Us

The Right Kind of Trouble

IF YOU CAN SERIES

Catch Me If You Can

Release Me If You Can

Save Me If You Can

HIGH STAKES SERIES

Ante Up

King of Hearts: A Short Story Collection

Deuces Wild

EQUILIBRIUM SERIES

Love Notes

Grow Something: An Equilibrium Novelette

In Tandem

Frosted.Whipped.Buttered: An Equilibrium Short

Plus One: An Equilibrium Short

Bittersweet

Press Rewind: An Equilibrium Short

SWEET HEAT SERIES

Hints of Spice

A Dash of Heat

A Touch of Sugar

SERENDIPITOUS SERIES

A Crazy Little Thing Called Love

Didn't Mean To Love You

Fall in Love Again

The Way Love Goes

Love You Forever

Something Like Love

CONNECTICUT KING SERIES (Collaboration with Love Belvin)

Love on the Highlight Reel (Book 2)

Determining Possession (Book 3)

Pass Interference (Book 6)

STRICTLY PROFESSIONAL

Strictly Professional

Unfinished Business

TRUTH AND LIES

The Truth: His Side, Her Side, and The Truth About Falling in Love

The Lies: The Lies We Tell About Life, Love, and Everything in Between

FRIENDS & LOVERS

Finding Forever

Chasing Commitment

ETERNALLY TETHERED

Haunted

Coveted

STANDALONES

Mine Tonight

Wonder

Equivalent Exchange

Love & Other Things

A Mutually Beneficial Agreement

Relationship Goals: a novella

Anonymous Acts (Five Star Enterprises)

The Reinvention of the Rose

Me + Somebody's Son: A Heights Story

The Rose That Got Away

Made in the USA
Las Vegas, NV
31 March 2025